WHAT HAPPENS AT CHRISTMAS

Camille's eyes widened with a look one could only describe as horror. "What do you mean you've come for Christmas?"

"Now, now, Camille, you needn't look so shocked." Gray resisted the urge to chuckle.

He wasn't entirely sure why he had introduced himself as her cousin, as her *poor relation*, although it was apparent to him she had no idea of his financial state. His announcement that he would be staying for Christmas was as much a surprise to him as it was to her. Still, now that he had said it, he quite liked the idea. If Camille insisted on going through with this theatrical farce of hers, the least he could do, as her old friend, was provide his assistance. He owed her that much, really. And what better way to help than by residing in her family's home, where he could be close at hand?

Besides, while he hadn't realized it before she had walked into the room, there was unfinished business here. He and Camille were a play without a last act, and it was past time to see how it would end.

The moment he saw her again, he knew the final curtain hadn't fallen, not for him . . .

D0974333

Books by Victoria Alexander

THE PERFECT MISTRESS

HIS MISTRESS BY CHRISTMAS

MY WICKED LITTLE LIES

WHAT HAPPENS AT CHRISTMAS

THE IMPORTANCE OF BEING WICKED

Published by Kensington Publishing Corporation

What Happens At Christmas

VICTORIA ALEXANDER

ZEBRA BOOKS
KENSINGTON PUBLISHING CORP.
http://www.kensingtonbooks.com

ZEBRA BOOKS are published by

Kensington Publishing Corp.
119 West 40th Street
New York, NY 10018

Copyright © 2012 by Cheryl Griffin

All rights reserved. No part of this book may be reproduced in any form or by any means without the prior written consent of the Publisher, excepting brief quotes used in reviews.

If you purchased this book without a cover you should be aware that this book is stolen property. It was reported as "unsold and destroyed" to the Publisher and neither the Author nor the Publisher has received any payment for this "stripped book."

All Kensington titles, imprints and distributed lines are available at special quantity discounts for bulk purchases for sales promotion, premiums, fund-raising, educational or institutional use.

Special book excerpts or customized printings can also be created to fit specific needs. For details, write or phone the office of the Kensington Special Sales Manager. Attn.: Special Sales Department. Kensington Publishing Corp., 119 West 40th Street, New York, NY 10018. Phone: 1-800-221-2647.

Zebra and the Z logo Reg. U.S. Pat. & TM Off.

ISBN-13: 978-1-4201-1709-7
ISBN-10: 1-4201-1709-2
First Kensington Books Hardcover Printing: November 2012
First Zebra Books Mass-Market Paperback Printing: October 2013

eISBN-13: 978-1-4201-3268-7
eISBN-10: 1-4201-3268-7
First Zebra Books Electronic Edition: October 2013

10 9 8 7 6 5 4 3 2 1

Printed in the United States of America

One

"And you believe this is a good idea," Beryl, Lady Dunwell, said to her sister. Her expression failed to reveal whether her words were in the guise of a question or a comment, which was, as always, most annoying. More so, as her sister's face was the mirror image of her own, and one should never be in doubt as to what one's own twin was thinking.

"No, in truth I don't believe it's a good idea. Wearing the appropriate cloak for the weather is a good idea. Insisting on references before hiring a new servant is a good idea. Having an equal number of ladies and gentlemen at a dinner party is a good idea. This"—Camille, Lady Lydingham, leaned forward slightly and met her sister's gaze with a firmness that belied any niggling doubts in the back of her mind—"is a brilliant idea."

"I suspect the brilliance of it is dependent upon whether or not it goes awry." Beryl studied her sister over the rim of her teacup.

In recent months, the twins had made it a habit to meet

at least every other week at the Ladies Tearoom, at Fenwick and Sons, Booksellers. It had become quite the place for ladies of society to gather. Even now, there was scarcely an empty table to be had. Camille wasn't sure why it had become so popular; the room itself was not unlike the other rooms in the bookseller's establishment, lined with shelves and filled with books in what appeared to be a random order. The tea and cakes were excellent, but in society excellent did not always go hand in hand with fashionable. Regardless, the sisters were nothing if not fashionable; and if this was the place to be, this was indeed where they would be.

"And it does seem to me there are any number of things that could go awry," Beryl continued. "Horribly, horribly awry."

"Nonsense." Camille waved off her sister's warning. "I have given this a great deal of thought, and it is a practically perfect plan."

"It's the 'practically' that should give you pause," Beryl said in a wry tone.

"No plan can be completely perfect, although . . ." Camille thought for a moment. "I daresay, this is as close to perfect as possible. Mother and Delilah are spending Christmas in Paris with her friend, Countess Something-or-other, and will not return to England until well after the new year. Uncle Basil is on safari in Africa and, as you well know, when he goes off like this, he will not be back for months. Which serves me quite well, as I need a proper English family, having a proper English Christmas, in a proper English country house." Camille heaved a long-suffering sigh. "And while we might well appear proper from a safe distance, close at hand there is very little truly proper about our family."

"Millworth Manor is rather proper," Beryl murmured.

"Thank goodness for that." Camille nodded. "And

this year, that proper country house will be filled with a proper family for Christmas." She narrowed her eyes. "There shall be no dallying between Mother and whatever potential lover has thought the spirit of the season would ease his way into her bed. There shall be no lecherous uncle pursuing any unsuspecting females, who have caught his eye. There shall be none of Mother's usual stray foreign exiles bemoaning the olden days in whatever country they're from. Nor will there be aspiring poets, flamboyant artists and absolutely no creative sorts of any type hoping to curry favor and patronage from Mother or any of us."

"You make it sound like a circus."

"There's very little difference between Mother's house and a circus, especially at Christmas, although a circus is probably less chaotic." Camille heaved a heartfelt sigh. "If Father were still with us—"

"Well, he isn't," Beryl said sharply. "He's been gone for twenty years now, and even at Christmas, there is nothing to be gained by wishing for what one can't possibly have." She drew a deep breath. "However, I suppose, as you are going to a great deal of trouble and expense no doubt—"

"Good Lord, yes." Camille shook her head. "I had no idea the price of hiring a troupe of actors would be so dear."

"Well, you are replacing an entire household. Let's see." Beryl thought for a moment. "There's one to play the role of the well-meaning, ambitious, somewhat flighty mother, another for the aging rogue who doesn't quite understand he is neither as charming nor as dashing as he once was, one for the role of the always indignant, somewhat superior, younger sister. . . ." Beryl fixed her sister with a firm look. "Delilah would never go along with this, you know."

"Then it is fortunate she is in Paris with Mother." It never failed to amaze either Camille or Beryl that their younger sister had a distinct lack of imagination and an overdeveloped sense of propriety. Where did she get it? "And don't forget, aside from the primary players, there's the supporting cast." Camille ticked the roles off on her fingers. "I needed a butler, of course, as well as a housekeeper, a cook and an assortment of maids and footmen. I am bringing my lady's maid, however."

"What did you do with Mother's servants?" Beryl stared. "What have you done with Clement?"

"You needn't look at me as if I've done away with him and buried him in the garden." Camille rolled her gaze toward the ceiling. "As even Mother is rarely at the manor for Christmas, in recent years, Clement has spent Christmas with his niece in Wales, I believe. It's silly to have a butler on the premises if there is no one there. I sent the rest off on holiday—paid, of course."

"Of course," Beryl murmured.

"Yet, another expense. However, I have been assured most of the troupe is better at keeping a house than they are on stage, which is fortunate, as I do expect them to do so." Camille lowered her voice in a confidential manner. "From what I understand, most of the players have been in service fairly recently. So that part of it should work out nicely."

"Oh, well, as long as they can tend to the house."

"They are not the least bit famous as actors, that is, which, on one hand, is convenient, and on the other, something of a concern." Camille drummed her fingers absently on the table. "I do need them to be believable, but I should hate to have any of them recognized, so their lack of theatrical success is a benefit."

Beryl stared as if she couldn't quite believe her ears. "It is so hard to get good help."

"Indeed, it is. However, as they are not in particular demand, they are more than willing to take on this . . . production as it were. And as costly as they are, they would have charged so much more if they were well known." Camille smiled smugly.

"It's fortunate you can afford them."

"Thank goodness Harold left me with a tidy fortune."

Harold, Viscount Lydingham, had been substantially older than Camille when they had wed. But then, older men with wealth and position were precisely the type of gentlemen their mother had trained her three daughters to wed. And Beryl, Camille and Delilah had obediently done so. Their reward was to be widowed and financially independent at an age young enough to enjoy life and pursue love, should they be so inclined.

Still, Harold had been a very nice man. Camille considered herself fortunate to have found him, and they had been, for the most part, happy or at least content. His demands on her had been minimal through the eight years of their marriage. She had proven herself an excellent wife and, indeed, she had been quite fond of him. Why, she hadn't even considered dallying with another man for a full two years after his death, out of respect. Even now, four years after his passing, she still rather missed Harold.

"And you're doing it all to impress a man—"

"Not merely a man. A prince," Camille said in a lofty manner. Yes, both of her sisters had married well, and Beryl's second husband might well be prime minister someday, but neither of her sisters had ever come close to genuine royalty. "Prince Nikolai Pruzinsky, of the ruling family of the Kingdom of . . . of . . . Oh, I can't remember where, but it's one of those tiny countries that litter Central Europe."

"But you barely know this man."

"Marriage will solve that."

"Still, this scheme of yours seems rather excessive."

"Perhaps it is, but it's well worth the trouble and the expense. He has an immense fortune and his own castle—besides which, he is quite handsome and dashing, and, well, he's a prince. Which means I shall be a princess. He is everything I have ever wanted and he is this close"—Camille held up her hand and pinched her forefinger and thumb to within an inch of each other—"to proposing. He hasn't actually said the words yet, but he has dropped more than a few hints. I'm confident all he needs now is to be assured that our family is worthy of being elevated to royalty."

"Which you shall prove by presenting him with a proper English family and a proper English Christmas?"

"Exactly." Camille nodded.

Beryl refilled her cup from the pot on their table and Camille knew—the way one twin nearly always knew what the other was thinking—her sister was choosing her words with care. "It seems to me that, should you indeed marry him, at some point in time he shall have to meet Mother and Delilah and Uncle Basil. The real ones, that is. Perhaps at the wedding. Have you considered that?"

"Admittedly, I have not worked it all out, but I will." She waved off her sister's comment. "First and foremost is Christmas, which involves a great deal of planning. You may not have noticed, but Christmas is bearing down upon us with the inevitability of a . . . a . . ."

"A boulder rolling downhill ready to obliterate all in its path?" Beryl asked with an overly sweet smile.

"I wouldn't put it quite that way, but yes."

"And after Christmas? What then?"

"Admittedly, I don't really know yet. But I will. The rest will fall into place," Camille said with a confidence she didn't entirely feel. "I shall cross those awkward roads when they present themselves. I can't be expected to know every minor detail as of yet, but I am certain I shall come up with something brilliant."

"As brilliant as hiring actors to play the part of your family for Christmas?"

Camille clenched her teeth. Beryl had an annoying habit of being entirely too sensible on occasion. "Even more brilliant, I should think."

"You'll need it. Your current brilliant idea is the most ridiculous thing I have ever heard. It can't possibly succeed."

"Goodness, Beryl, at this time of year in particular, one should have a little faith."

Beryl stared in obvious disbelief. "Faith?"

"Yes, faith," Camille said firmly. "Before the wedding, I suspect, I will confess all. He is already smitten with me, and by then, I have every confidence he will forgive this tiny farce on my part—"

Beryl choked on her tea. "Tiny?"

"Relatively tiny." Camille nodded. "He will probably find it most amusing. He is easily amused. And it's not as if I am misrepresenting who I am or who we are. Not really. Our family lineage is exactly as I have said. It's just the individual personalities that can be a bit . . . unorthodox. Mother and Uncle Basil, that is. In truth, I am simply trying to protect the poor man and give him the traditional English Christmas that he expects and deserves. In many ways, it is my Christmas gift to him. And I am confident we shall have a good laugh about all this. Eventually."

"You do realize you're quite mad."

"Or quite clever." Camille tapped her temple with her forefinger. "Like a fox."

"An insane fox, perhaps. You haven't thought this

through, Camille. This is another one of your impulsive adventures."

"Nonsense. I gave up impulsive adventures at least a year ago."

"After the Brighton Incident?"

"Yes, well, probably. It's of no significance now."

She did so hate to be reminded of what her family referred to as "the Brighton Incident." It had not been her finest hour and embodied all the errors in judgment she'd ever made rolled into one, even if it had seemed so delightful when she had thought of it. The incident had skated on the sharp edge of full-fledged scandal involving an ill-conceived wager prompted by entirely too much champagne, two of her close friends who were even more inebriated than she, a masked out-of-doors ball and costumes that came perilously close to no clothing at all. They had only been saved from complete and utter ruin because their faces were hidden, they had relatively spotless reputations (who would have suspected them of all people?) and it was the off-season. Few knew the names of the ladies behind the masks.

"I have given this a great deal of thought." Indeed, she'd had so much to accomplish she hadn't thought of anything else.

"I can't believe you are going to all this trouble." Beryl narrowed her eyes and considered her sister. "It's not for his money. Harold left you with more than you can possibly spend in a lifetime, certainly more than enough to buy your own castle, should you wish to do so. Is it for his title?"

"I have always thought 'Princess Camille' has a lovely sound to it."

"Even so, I can't . . ." Beryl's eyes widened. "Are you in love with him?"

"There is nothing about the man *not* to love," Camille said in a cautious manner.

Still, she'd only been in love once, and that was when she was very young and quite foolish and hadn't quite realized she'd been in love until it was too late. She'd been extraordinarily fond of Harold and had loved him after a fashion, but she'd never been in love with him. She wasn't at all sure there was much use for true love in a practical world; although, admittedly, it would be nice.

"I suspect he may well be in love with me."

"That wasn't my question."

"We've never married for love in this family," Camille pointed out. It wasn't entirely true. She had long suspected Mother had married for love, which was no doubt why she had raised her daughters to marry for other reasons. In this respect alone, Mother was a very practical woman.

"But do you—"

"Not at the moment. But I fully expect to," she added quickly. "Indeed, I am quite confident in no time at all I shall love him with my whole heart and soul. There is nothing about him not to love."

"You said that."

"It bears repeating."

"Yes, well, an immense fortune and a royal title does make it easier to love." Beryl cast her sister a pleasant smile.

Camille wasn't fooled for a moment. The smile might well be pleasant, but the sarcasm was unmistakable.

"You're scarcely one to talk. You married your first husband, Charles, for precisely the same reasons I married Harold."

"I was quite fond of Charles."

"Yes, but you weren't in love with him. Nor were you in love with Lionel when you married him."

"No." Beryl drew the word out slowly. "But . . ."

Camille stared. "Good Lord, Beryl, don't tell me you're in love with your husband."

"I might be."

"Nonsense, no one is in love with their own husband." Camille scoffed. "It simply isn't done. You certainly didn't marry him for love."

"No, I married him because his ambitions matched my own. Now, however . . ." Beryl paused. "In recent months, since very nearly the start of the year, Lionel and I agreed to forgo our various amorous pursuits and restrict our attentions to one another."

Camille stared. Her sister's and brother-in-law's extramarital escapades were very nearly legendary. "And?"

"And it's turning out far better than I would have imagined." She shrugged. "As it happens, I might indeed be in love with my husband." A bemused smile curved her sister's lips, as if she couldn't quite believe her own words. She looked, well, content, even happy. Camille wasn't sure she had seen a look like that on her sister's face before. But then she was fairly certain Beryl had never been in love before. The oddest twinge of jealousy stabbed Camille. She ignored it. If her twin was happy, she was happy for her.

"That's . . . wonderful."

Beryl's eyes narrowed in suspicion. "Do you mean that?"

"Of course I do. You know I wouldn't say it otherwise." Camille nodded. "Lord and Lady Dunwell have always had a certain reputation for dalliances and lovers and that sort of thing. It's simply unexpected, that's all."

"No one expected it less than I," Beryl said under her breath.

"What will the gossips do without you?"

Beryl laughed. "They shall have to make do."

"I am happy for you."

"Then you should consider following in my footsteps."

"What? Marrying a man who might run the country one day?"

"No." Beryl's blue-eyed gaze met her sister's. It was, as always, like looking in a mirror. "Fall in love."

Camille drew her brows together. "It's not at all like you to go on and on about love. I always thought you considered it rather silly."

"That's before I was in love," Beryl said simply, then paused. "You were in love once, if I recall."

"That was a very long time ago," Camille said quickly. It was not something she wished to be reminded of. She had turned her back on love then, although she'd really had no choice. And if, through the years, there had been a moment or two of regret, a chance thought as to what might have been, it was pointless. She had put him completely out of her head and her heart. She had never asked after him, and her sister was wise enough never to bring up his name. Such was the way of life, after all. One did hate to be reminded of mistakes one might have made. There was nothing to be done about it, and it was best left in the past where it belonged.

"Don't you want to know that again?"

"I scarcely knew it at all, but I shall," Camille said firmly. "I fully intend to fall in love." She picked up the teapot and refilled her cup, taking the time to sort her words.

Why she wished to marry Nikolai wasn't at all easy to

explain without sounding quite mercenary and extremely shallow. And while she certainly had a few mercenary moments and was, on occasion, a bit shallow, she did not think herself to be mercenary and shallow, all in all. It wasn't the prince's fortune; she had more than enough money. It wasn't even his title, although "Princess Camille" did have a lovely ring to it. It was, perhaps, the adventure of it: the adventure of being swept away to a foreign land by a handsome prince and to live there happily the rest of her days; adventure that she scarcely knew existed; adventure that appealed to something deep inside her. Beryl was entirely too levelheaded to understand, but then she had always been the more sensible of the twins. It was the stuff fairy stories were made of, and what woman wouldn't want that? And want it, Camille did.

"It isn't as if I set out to catch a prince. I didn't even know he was a prince when we first met. He is traveling incognito, which he much prefers to do when he is in a foreign country. He says it's much easier to get to know the people of a country when he is not beleaguered by all the trappings of his royal position, when he is not treated as royalty but rather as an ordinary person."

"What an . . . enlightened philosophy for a prince."

"He is most enlightened and very modern. He takes his responsibilities quite seriously and says he wishes to be a prince for the people. It's quite admirable, even if I don't understand it entirely, but then he is foreign and therefore his minor eccentricities can be forgiven. Why, he even prefers that I don't address him by title, 'Your Highness,' and that sort of thing. He says, until he ascends to the throne, he prefers, when traveling abroad, simply to be known by one of his lesser titles, Count Pruzinsky. In most respects, though, he is extremely proper. Why, he hasn't even kissed me. Although he has requested, begged really, that I call him by his given name. Not proper, of course, but so wonderfully intimate."

"Not what one would expect in a prince."

"I find it most charming. There is nothing at all like being in the confidence of royalty, you know."

"I don't, but I shall take your word for it." Beryl considered her curiously. "And how did you meet this unusual prince?"

"We crossed paths quite by accident. I was leaving a ball and he was just arriving. I stumbled on a pebble and he caught me." She smiled at the memory. "It was quite romantic and, well, fate."

"I see."

"I like him a great deal."

Beryl nodded. "You wouldn't marry him otherwise."

"He might well be my last opportunity to marry and fall in love."

"You might consider falling in love first and then marrying the man in question."

"Odd advice coming from you. And how long shall I wait for that to happen, dear sister?" Camille wrinkled her nose. "We have, after all, passed our thirtieth year, and who knows how many more opportunities for . . ."

"Happiness?" Beryl offered.

"Exactly." Camille nodded. "This may be my last chance. I have no doubt he will make me very happy, and I intend to be an excellent wife."

"And princess."

"I shall make a very good princess." Camille grinned. "We shall have little princes and princesses and grow old together. And we shall be very, very happy."

Beryl smiled. "Then you should let nothing stand in your way."

"I don't intend to." She drew a deep breath. "But I will need your assistance."

"Oh?"

"I intend to go to Mother's house the day after tomorrow, and it certainly wouldn't be Christmas without my sister, my twin sister. . . ."

Beryl's eyes narrowed.

"So"—Camille's words came out in a rush—"I do hope you and Lionel will join us for Christmas in the country."

"Us?"

Camille nodded.

"As in you, the prince and a troupe of actors pretending to be family?"

Camille sighed. "It sounds rather absurd when you say it that way."

"There's no way to say it that it doesn't sound absurd."

"You must understand, it's not simply that we are not especially traditional, but Nikolai seems to have some sort of odd passion for an English Christmas. Yet another eccentricity, but then foreigners can be so very . . ."

"Foreign?" Beryl offered.

"Exactly." Camille nodded. "He has read all of Mr. Dickens's Christmas works. Oh, *The Cricket on the Hearth* and *The Chimes* and, of course, *A Christmas Carol.* And I want to give him a traditional English Christmas, with a proper sort of English family. It's what he longs for." She forced a wistful note to her voice. "It seems so very little, really."

"As well as convince him he would not be marrying into a family of questionable propriety."

"Oh, well, yes. That too." Camille waved off the comment.

Beryl thought for a moment. "This is not the sort of thing Lionel would favor."

"But surely for a man who wishes to be prime minister, it cannot but be helpful to know a foreign head of state."

"You do have a point there."

Camille stifled a satisfied smile. "And you can make him see how important it is to me. Besides, it's been years since either of us spent Christmas at the country house. It will be like it was when we were children. We shall decorate and have a Yule log and sing carols and it shall be quite, quite wonderful." A pleading note sounded in her voice. "Oh, please, Beryl, do this for me. I promise never to ask you to do anything involving actors for Christmas ever again."

"Oh, well, as long as you promise, how could I possibly say no? Besides, darling sister"—Beryl's eyes twinkled with amusement—"I wouldn't miss this Christmas for anything in the world."

December 21st

Two

"Good to have you home, Grayson." Lord Fairborough studied his nephew with an assessing gaze. "You've been away far too long."

"It hasn't been that long, sir." Grayson Elliott's smile belied the truth in his uncle's words.

Uncle Roland raised a skeptical brow. "I would say eleven years is a very long time."

"Perhaps." Gray sipped his brandy and considered the older man. He looked far better than Gray had feared. In truth, the years had been kind to his uncle. His hair was a bit grayer; his face was a bit more lined; but, all in all, Uncle Roland wore his age well. Still, he couldn't help but think a few of the lines in his uncle's face might be attributed to Gray himself. He knew his uncle, as well as his aunt, had worried about him through these past eleven years. The only one who hadn't worried was his cousin, Winfield. But then, on more than one occasion, Win had admitted his envy of Gray's freedom to do as he wished and Win's own enjoyment, if vicariously, of his cousin's exploits. Gray would be the first to admit the regularity of his correspondence to his aunt and uncle had been haphazard at best. He had gone as long as half a year without sending a letter. He ignored a stab of guilt. "But it has passed quickly."

"For you, perhaps, more than the rest of us." Uncle Roland chuckled. "I suspect you have had quite an adventurous time of it."

"It has certainly been that on occasion." Gray grinned. There had indeed been adventures in the course of building his fortune, but it had by no means been easy. His efforts and subsequent investments in shipping and railroads and imports in America had been grueling through the years and had left little time for frivolities or the enjoyment of his success. But his hard work had paid off. He had the fortune now he had set out to make. "And I have you to thank for it."

"Rubbish." His uncle scoffed. "It was insignificant and you paid me back, with interest, more than two years ago." He paused for a moment. "It wasn't necessary, you know. Your father was my only brother and I have always thought of you as a second son."

"And for that I have always been grateful."

Indeed, he had always known how lucky he was not to have been treated like an unwanted responsibility. He had been barely five years of age when his father and mother, an American, had died. His aunt and uncle had then taken him in to raise alongside their own six-year-old child. They had treated him no differently than they had their own son, but there was a difference. Win bore the honorary title of Viscount Stillwell and would one day be Earl of Fairborough. Gray would never be more than an untitled relation.

"It wasn't necessary, you know, to go out into the world as you have." A gruff note sounded in his uncle's voice. "I have always planned to leave you well off, to divide my fortune and property as evenly as possible between you and Winfield. Certainly, he will inherit my title and Fairborough Park, but—"

"It was necessary, Uncle," Gray said, his tone a bit sharper than he had intended. But then they'd had this same discussion when he had left Fairborough Hall and England to make his fortune. His tone softened. "There are some things one must do on one's own."

"You always have been obstinate and independent. Some of which can certainly be blamed on that American blood of yours." His uncle stared at him for a long moment; a wistful smile played on his lips. "But there is so much of my brother in you. More so now than when you left." He raised his glass. "Welcome home, boy."

"Thank you, Uncle." Gray smiled. "It's good to be back."

It was indeed good to be home at last. He hadn't realized until now how much he had missed England and his family—although in some ways, it was as if he had never left.

Everything in the country house was exactly as he remembered. He glanced around his uncle's library. The floor-to-ceiling shelves with their precisely arranged volumes were unchanged. If he looked closer, he would no doubt see not a single volume was out of place, exactly as his uncle preferred it. The comfortable leather chairs and sofa stood in the same places they always had and looked scarcely any worse for the wear of years. The massive mahogany desk, which had been Gray's grandfather's and his grandfather's before him, still occupied the same spot between two leaded-glass windows. The same family portraits hung in precisely the same arrangement as they had always hung, with the notable exception of the one over the fireplace.

When he had last been in this room, that place of honor had boasted a portrait of his grandfather. Now, in its place, two portraits hung side by side. Both were remarkably similar and yet not at all the same. Both were portraits of young boys and all four faces shared a similarity of features that bespoke of family. Aside from the difference in the artists' styles, the two portraits could have been of the same two boys. But the one on his left was of his father and his uncle when they were perhaps ten and twelve years of age. The one on the right was of Gray and Win, painted when they were ten or eleven. While the style of the older painting was a bit more formal, the artist had managed to capture the affection of the older brother for the younger. As for the other portrait, Gray distinctly remembered sitting for the artist and putting him through their own version of a ten-year-old's hell. Finally the beleaguered artist had threatened them with dire consequences if they did not behave. "Dire," as Gray recalled, meant their behavior being brought not to the attention of Uncle Roland but of Aunt Margaret. It was Aunt Margaret who had wanted the boys' portrait painted, even if a photograph would have been easier and less painful for all concerned, and woe be it to anyone who thwarted her desires.

"Are you back for good, then? Or is it too soon to ask?"

"It is something to consider." Gray didn't mean to be elusive, he simply wasn't sure how long he would stay in England. He wasn't certain if this was merely a visit or if his return was permanent. At the very least, he would stay as long as his uncle needed him, although he had taken the precaution of booking passage on a ship back to America the day after Christmas. The passage, however, could always be canceled.

"We shall discuss it later, then," Uncle Roland said. "Your aunt will be delighted to see you as well."

"Where is she? I expected to see her fly down the

stairs the moment the servants brought news of my arrival."

"If you had written of your intention to at last return home, she would have been here." A chastising note sounded in his uncle's voice. "But as she had no idea, she has been in London for the last few days visiting with her sister's family, shopping for Christmas gifts and whatever else she deems necessary to ensure the merriment and festivities of the season. She is expected back the day before Christmas." He smiled. "You, however, are the best gift she could have asked for. She has missed you. As have we all."

"As I have missed you." He studied his uncle closely. "Uncle, how are you?"

"Well enough for a man of my age, I suppose." Uncle Roland shrugged. "I take regular exercise. I am not able to eat everything I used to, which is to be expected but is nonetheless annoying. My bones creak a bit, but, all in all, I think I am holding up rather well against the vestiges of time."

"You haven't been . . . ill?"

"Oh, I had a nasty bout with a head cold a few months ago."

"That's all?"

"It was a very unpleasant cold," Uncle Roland said firmly.

Gray chose his words with care. "Then you're not . . . dying?"

"Dying?" Uncle's Roland's eyes widened. "Do I look like I'm dying?"

"You do look in good health, but—"

"We're all dying, Cousin. Some of us sooner than others." Win strode into the library, dressed in riding clothes, a broad grin on his face.

Gray rose to his feet and stared at his cousin. Irritation at Win's obvious lie mixed with delight at seeing once more the man he considered his brother. "You wrote he was dying."

"He is." Win shrugged. "We all die eventually. Can't escape it."

Uncle Roland's forehead furrowed. "Winfield, what have you done?"

"What I have done, Father, is given you and Mother what you want most for Christmas, second only to my marrying and providing an heir, that is. And that shall have to wait for another Christmas." Win cast his father the infectious smile that had been the downfall of more than one reluctant lady, the irresistible smile that very nearly always got him exactly what he wanted.

"Well." He stepped to his cousin and met Gray's gaze straight on. The two were both tall, with no more than half an inch difference in their respective heights. They were of similar builds as well, both physically fit. "Do you want to admit that you were wrong? Confess that you should have come home years ago, and you are secretly pleased that I have at last forced you to do so? Or shall I take you out into the garden and thrash you thoroughly, as I used to do when we were young." His grin widened. "You uncivilized American."

"You couldn't then, and you can't now." Gray's grin matched his cousin's. "You pompous English prig."

Uncle Roland groaned.

Win clasped his cousin's shoulders. "Forgiven, then?"

Relief battled with annoyance, and affection won. Gray shrugged. "Well, after all, as it is Christmas. . . ."

Win laughed and embraced him. "Good to have you back."

"Good to be back." Even as he said the words, he knew the truth of them. He had been away far too long.

Uncle Roland cleared his throat and the cousins turned toward him. For a moment, the older man's eyes fogged and Gray knew Uncle Roland was thinking of himself and his beloved younger brother. There was no denying how much Win looked like a younger version of Uncle Roland, with his dark hair and blue eyes, and how Gray was a distinct replica of his father, with hair a shade darker than Win's and eyes a deep brown.

Uncle Roland fixed a firm eye on his son. "I cannot approve of deceit under normal circumstances. However, as it is Christmas, and your intentions were apparently noble . . ." He tried and failed to hide a pleased grin. "I suppose the occasional deception can be forgiven, in the spirit of Christmas and all." His eyes narrowed slightly. "Now, about that second matter . . ."

"Never fear, Father," Win said, a confident smile on his face. "I have a plan in the works even as we speak. Why, I would be willing to wager I am wed by Christmas next."

Uncle Roland studied him suspiciously; then snorted with disbelief and moved away to refill his glass.

Gray spoke low into his cousin's ear. "Do you have a plan?"

Win's smile flickered. "Not so much as an inkling."

Gray bit back a grin. The room wasn't the only thing that hadn't changed.

"My lord." Prescott, who had been the family's butler for as long as Gray could remember, appeared at the door. "You wished me to remind you when it was nearly one."

"Yes, thank you, Prescott." Uncle Roland cast a last look at his son and nephew. "Not approving, mind you, but it was not your worst idea."

Win chuckled. "Thank you, Father."

Uncle Roland started toward the door. "I do hope your plan regarding that other matter is as successful."

"As do I, Father."

Uncle Roland's doubtful response drifted into the library behind him. Gray thought it best that the words were undecipherable, even if the tone was unmistakable.

Gray chuckled. "I see the campaign to see you wed continues."

"As it shall until the moment I chain myself to some poor, unsuspecting creature for the rest of my days." Win strode across the room to the brandy decanter on Uncle Roland's desk and poured a glass. "It's your fault, you know."

Gray laughed. "How is it my fault?"

"If you were here, Mother and Father would divide their efforts between the two of us instead of concentrating on me alone. While Father wants an heir, all Mother really wants is another female in the family." Win aimed his glass at his cousin. "You can provide that, as well as I."

"I suppose I can."

"Therefore you owe me an apology."

"Do I?" Gray raised a brow. "It seems to me, I am the one owed an apology."

"Because I wrote you that Father was dying?"

Gray stared. "Don't you think that calls for an apology?"

"I don't know," Win said thoughtfully, and propped his hip on a corner of the desk. "As I said before—we are all dying. The fact that Father isn't dying anytime soon is really insignificant."

"I wouldn't call it 'insignificant.' "

"Regardless, it did what it was intended to do." Win

sipped his brandy and considered his cousin. "I should have thought of it years ago."

"You could have simply requested my return," Gray said and then winced.

"And haven't I?" Win's eyes narrowed. "Let me think, when you had been gone for three years, I requested your return."

"I couldn't—"

"The next year, when my first engagement was broken and my heart was shattered, I asked you to come home and help me drown my sorrows."

"I wasn't able—"

"And two years later, I asked you to come to my wedding and you couldn't be bothered."

"But that was yet another wedding that didn't take place."

"It didn't take place at the last possible moment. I was very nearly left standing at the altar." He shook his head in a mournful manner. "I was devastated, you know. I could have used the support or, at the very least, the comforting shoulder of the man I consider my brother—the man who is my dearest friend. But, no, you couldn't be bothered."

"Circumstances were such—"

"And two years after that, when you had at last amassed the fortune you had worked so hard for, when you were no longer penniless with no prospects—"

"Win." A warning sounded in Gray's voice.

His cousin continued mercilessly. "When she was widowed and the opportunity came to throw it in her face—"

"Win!"

"You didn't come home then either." Win heaved a resigned sigh. "If that couldn't lure you home, I had no idea what would." He sipped his brandy. "I'm quite displeased with myself that I didn't think of this years ago. Father dying." He chuckled. "He's entirely too obstinate to die and leave everything in my hands, capable though they may be."

"I had every intention of returning to England sometime soon."

"I know."

Gray's brow furrowed. "What do you mean?"

"There's been a tone in your letters these last two years and a vague hint in the year before that. You might not even be aware of it. But I know you as well—no, better than you know yourself."

"I still have no idea what you are trying to say."

"You know exactly what I am trying to say, but as this talk is eleven years in coming . . . eleven years, Gray." Win shook his head, accusation shaded his eyes.

Gray stared. "I . . . apologize?"

"As well you should." Win got to his feet and circled his cousin. "You left, letting Mother and Father believe you needed to make your fortune on your own because of some sort of obligation to your parents or yourself, that never was entirely clear, although it did sound good."

"That's exactly why I left," Gray said staunchly.

"Is it? You knew full well Father's plan was to put you in charge of the family's business interests, whereas I would handle the estates and properties. I suspect he thought together, as a family, we could, I don't know, rule the world or something a step below that."

"Yes, well—"

"It wasn't a misplaced sense of obligation on his part, and it certainly wasn't charity, and you know that as well."

"I suppose, but—"

"But, instead, you turned your back on your family and allowed a woman who had discarded you for someone with a fortune and title to influence how you lived your life."

Gray bristled. "It wasn't—"

"Wasn't it?" Win's eyes narrowed. "If I recall correctly, Camille Channing, now Lady Lydingham, the woman you loved, threw you over to marry a much older man with wealth and position. A man who had what you did not. Am I accurate thus far?"

"In a manner of speaking—"

"At very nearly the same time, you, who had always seemed a most sensible sort, got it into your head to flee the country and go off and seek your fortune, armed with little more than a modest loan from Father. Again, am I correct?"

Gray nodded. "Go on."

"And then, when she was widowed and you had made a great deal of money, indeed, at that point, you could have been considered almost unseemly wealthy—"

"I don't know that—"

"Nonetheless . . ." Win continued to circle Gray, like a beast of prey moving in for the kill. It was most annoying. "You still refused to come home. Because . . ."

Gray clenched his teeth. "Because?"

"Because it wasn't enough." Triumph sounded in Win's voice. "You needed to prove to her not only were you as good as the man she chose, you were better. No title, perhaps, but more money. And as she and her sisters have always been rather mercenary in that regard, returning once your fortune was greater would be a lovely triumph over the woman who broke your heart."

Gray could scarcely deny it. "I admit, that might have been a factor of motivation—"

"Aha! I knew it." Win raised his glass. "Now you can throw your success in her face."

"Once perhaps, but now . . ." Gray shook his head. "It's simply not worth the effort."

" 'Not worth the effort'? Good Lord." Win stared. "When did you become so noble?"

"I'm not noble." He sipped his brandy thoughtfully. "It—she—is of no consequence anymore. The past is the past, over and done with. It cannot be changed and I see no need to dwell on it. I put Camille—Lady Lydingham—behind me longer ago than I can remember. As I said, proving something to her now is simply not worth my time."

"Oh, bravo, Gray. Excellent speech." Win raised his glass in a salute. "Most impressive. I don't believe a word of it, of course, but still, it is impressive."

"It scarcely matters whether you believe it or not." Gray shrugged. "I have no interest in anything regarding Lady Lydingham—aside, perhaps, from the friendship we once shared."

"I see." Win sipped his brandy and considered his cousin thoughtfully. "You do realize she remains a widow and has not remarried, as I might have mentioned in my letters?"

"Indeed, you have." Gray sipped his drink. "With remarkable frequency."

"And you don't care?"

"Not a bit."

"Then were I to add, she is residing at her mother's house for Christmas this year, no more than a thirty-minute ride from here, it would make no difference to you?"

"None whatsoever."

"And if you were to come across her unexpectedly

on the road, your heart would not beat faster like a trapped bird fluttering in your chest?"

"A trapped bird?" Gray laughed. "Good God, man, what has come over you?"

"I was trying to be poetical," Win said in a lofty manner. "I have the heart of a poet, you know."

"You do not."

"Perhaps not." Win shrugged. "It's of no consequence at the moment, as it is not my heart we are discussing but yours."

"Win." Gray leaned forward and met his cousin's gaze directly. "Admittedly, I once offered my heart to Camille Channing. And, yes, that did indeed contribute to my desire to make my way in the world, which I have done in a most successful manner. In that respect, she was the means to an end. Perhaps once, she was indeed the end, but no longer. I have no lingering feelings for her whatsoever, save those that one old friend has for another."

"Then you would make no effort to avoid her?"

"I don't see why I would."

"And were you to meet her again—"

" 'Unexpectedly on the road'?" Gray grinned.

"Or wherever," Win continued, "you would treat her as—"

"As one does any neighbor one has known for much of one's life, as the friends we once were," Gray said firmly. "With polite cordiality."

"You would feel no need to sweep her into your arms, shower her with kisses and pledge your undying love?"

Gray laughed. "Good Lord, no."

"If you are sure—"

"I am."

"Excellent." Win nodded. "Mother left for London three days ago with instructions that when Lady Lydingham or the rest of her family arrived, Cook should prepare a basket of her best scones and cakes and biscuits to be sent to Millworth Manor as a gesture of neighborly goodwill. They are still the best in the county. Mother was a bit confused as to whether or not Lady Lydingham's mother and sisters would be in residence for Christmas as well, as she had heard Lady Briston and her youngest daughter were in Paris."

Gray cast his cousin a suspicious look. "And?"

"And, according to my information, Lady Lydingham arrived yesterday. Cook has prepared the basket and it needs to be delivered."

"And?"

"And, while I can certainly send a footman, Mother would have my head if it wasn't delivered by a family member."

"I suspect she intended that family member to be you."

"Only because she didn't know you would be here. But I have a great deal to do." Win aimed the younger man a hard look. "While you have been off making your fortune, I have been learning everything Father intended the two of us to share—business, finance and management of all the family's properties and investments. Which means I am an extremely busy man. It is an immense burden, you know—"

"I can only imagine," Gray murmured.

"And leaves me little time for social niceties."

"Probably why you keep losing fiancées."

"I wouldn't be at all surprised. Why, I had to practically steal the time for a ride today before you arrived. And I need you to deliver this gesture of neighborly Christmas cheer to Lady Lydingham."

Gray stared. "No."

"Why not?"

"I'd prefer not to, that's all."

"Why?" Win studied him closely. "You said you weren't avoiding her."

"I'm not."

"And the two of you were friends long before you fell in love with her."

"True enough."

"You said you have no lingering feelings. You have put her behind you. And should you meet, you would treat her with nothing more than polite cordiality, as one old friend encountering another."

"I did say that, but—"

"But?" Win's brow rose. "Unless, of course, you didn't mean it. Unless, you still harbor feelings of affection. Unless you fear seeing her again will bring back—"

"Bloody hell, Win," Gray snapped. "I'll take the blasted basket."

"It is, after all, the very least you can do after abandoning me for all those years to—"

"I said I'd do it!"

"Yes, I know, but I was having so much fun." Win cast him a triumphant grin and started for the door. "I'll tell Cook to ready the basket and you can be on your way in, oh, a quarter of an hour, I would say." He reached the door, paused and turned back to his cousin. "Regardless of what you say, I know this will be a bit awkward for you. You haven't seen her for eleven years, and until you do, you can't truly say with any certainty that your feelings for her are completely dead."

"Rubbish," Gray said. "There isn't a doubt in my mind, even if there is in yours."

Win considered him for a moment, then nodded.

"Excellent. And when you return, you can help me with my plan to at last be wed by next Christmas."

"I suspect you need all the help you can get, as you have no one in mind at the moment." A wry note sounded in Gray's voice.

"It just makes it more of a challenge, old boy. And I have always loved a challenge." Win grinned in the wickedly confident manner he had had since boyhood and took his leave.

Gray's smile faded with the closing of the library door. Damnation, why did Win have to force this visit on him today? Tomorrow, perhaps, or the day after, or maybe even on Christmas Day. . . . Yes, that would be perfect. A chance encounter at Christmas services surrounded by any number of people, that would be the civilized way to see again, after so long, the woman who had, however unintentionally, broken his heart.

Gray swirled the brandy in his glass and paced the room. He hadn't lied to Win, not really. He had long ago put Camille in the past. Just as he had long ago come to the realization that what happened between them was as much his fault as it had been hers, more perhaps.

He had known Camille for years, but he hadn't realized he loved her until she was about to wed Lord Lydingham. No, that wasn't true. He had realized it long before, when one day he abruptly saw the girl who lived on the neighboring estate had become a woman. The woman who owned his heart. He simply hadn't done anything about it. He had been young and uncertain; and when he looked back, something of an idiot as well. It wasn't until the day before she was to marry that he had at last declared his feelings.

He had been a fool to expect she would abandon all she'd been taught her entire life, but he had hoped. He knew she understood her responsibility in life was to marry well, as one never knew what might befall one's family. They had discussed it, now and again through the years, and it had seemed an eminently practical way of looking at a woman's lot in life. Poverty, she had once told him quite earnestly, was always just around the corner. Not that, to his knowledge, Lady Briston had ever been close to impoverished. Still, one never knew what went on in another household. Lord Briston had been gone for many years, and Lady Briston had never remarried. Lord Briston's twin brother still preferred to use his military rank of colonel, instead of the title he had inherited from his brother, in homage to the deceased, no doubt. So, perhaps, neither Colonel Channing nor Lady Briston had ever completely come to terms with Lord Briston's demise. Camille's sister Beryl had already married well, and now it was Camille's turn.

She had been shocked by his declaration of love and had told him, in as kind a manner as one could hope, that it simply wasn't possible. And, indeed, she had thanked him for trying to stop her from marrying without the true love she had always longed for. But there had been something in her eyes that had belied her words.

That's when he had kissed her. For the first time, and for the last. And she had kissed him back. And for one incredible moment, he knew, deep in his heart, that anything was possible. That regardless of what she said, she did indeed love him.

Then she had pushed him away and suggested it would be best if he left at once. He'd made the stupid charge that she would marry him if he had money; and she had said, as he didn't, it scarcely mattered. He knew the moment he said the words that he was wrong; he knew her better than that. He had started to argue with her but realized it would do no good. She was determined to go through with her wedding. With the life she had planned. Perhaps if he hadn't waited so long to tell her of his feelings. Perhaps if he had been stronger or they had not been so young. She had been nineteen, he was just twenty. Perhaps . . .

So he had left her. She had become Lady Lydingham and he had gone off to make something of himself. Now he had returned home and she was free. Still, it scarcely mattered. Too much time had passed for them both. He was a different man than he had been all those years ago. And she was, no doubt, an entirely different woman. A widow of independent means with her own plans for her own life. Whatever might have been between them once was lost with the passage of years.

But once they had been friends, and it was as a friend that he would make his aunt's delivery. They would exchange pleasantries. She would inquire as to his uncle's health. He would ask about her sisters. He would linger for the correct amount of time required for a call of this nature; then he would bid her felicitations of the season and take his leave. And that would, at long last, be that.

He ignored the voice in the back of his mind that whispered, *What if it wasn't?*

Three

"Now then, Mr. Fortesque." Camille studied the actor standing before her in the parlor. "Are your players ready?"

"We are always prepared for a performance, my lady," Frederick Wenceslas Fortesque said in a lofty manner. Fortesque was the manager and lead player of the troupe of actors she had hired. He had taken the part of the family butler because, as he had said, regardless of the play, the butler was the pivotal role. Camille bowed to his expertise in this particular matter, even if she wasn't entirely convinced. "The prince noticed nothing out of the ordinary when he arrived this morning."

Indeed, Nikolai had arrived an hour or so ago in a most discreet manner, in an elegant hired coach. He was now freshening up from his travels and would shortly join her for tea. He had arrived unaccompanied, which had struck Camille as odd. She had always assumed royalty, even royalty traveling incognito, would travel, nonetheless, in a manner befitting, well, royalty. Or, at least, nobility. Still, the prince was adamant about not attracting undue attention. Not merely because of his desire to see the true nature of a country he was visiting, but because he had hinted darkly to her that one never knew what sort of brigands might be lurking about. Kidnapping and assassination were a constant threat for a royal. She had never quite considered that, but it did tend to dampen a bit of her enthusiasm for becoming a princess.

"That's something at any rate," Beryl said sotto voce. She sat on a nearby sofa to lend her sister what she called moral support, although Camille suspected Beryl simply hated to miss the opening act.

"It was an excellent beginning," Camille said with more confidence than she felt. She twisted her hands together absently. She would never admit it to Beryl, but she was far more apprehensive about this farce than she had expected. In spite of her assurances to her sister before their arrival, she was well aware of exactly how many things could go wrong. What had she been thinking, anyway? Still, it was too late to turn back now.

"Perhaps it would ease your mind somewhat if I were to reiterate, again, who is playing which of the primary roles," Mr. Fortesque said with a helpful smile.

Camille couldn't help but like the man; he was a most likable sort. Older, somewhere in his forties, she thought, quite tall, with a head of hair that had seen fuller days, he had thrown himself and his players into this production with enthusiasm. Naturally, she'd had no other choice but to take him into her confidence, at least to some extent, to explain why she thought it was necessary to conceal her family's eccentric nature from Prince Nikolai. Mr. Fortesque appeared to understand and had vowed he and his troupe would do all in their power to ensure a successful performance. But then she was paying them a significant amount to do so. Mr.

Fortesque understood as well that if their farce did not end happily, payment for services rendered might be far less than expected.

"Oh, please do," Beryl said brightly.

Camille cast her a quelling glance. "That would be most appreciated, Mr. Fortesque."

"Very well." He cleared his throat. "The role of your mother, Lady Briston, is being played by Mrs. Angela Montgomery-Wells. She has vast experience, has spent years touring the provinces and has played mothers of every ilk and fashion. A fine actress in her day." He winced slightly, as if he had said more than he had intended.

"Do go on, Mr. Fortesque," Beryl said.

He chose his words with care. "On occasion she might be somewhat absentminded. Rarely she has been known to forget her lines. But I have rehearsed her quite thoroughly," he said in what was obviously meant to be a reassuring tone. "She could play this part in her sleep. This role was made for her."

Beryl bit back a grin. Camille did wish her sister would desist being quite so amused.

"The part of your younger sister, Lady Hargate, is being played by our ingénue, Edwina Murdock. Not overly experienced before she came to us, but most enthusiastic and extremely friendly, with a natural gift one does not see often." He lowered his voice in a confidential manner. "With her looks and her talent, that young woman will make her mark in the theater one day."

"Talent will tell," Beryl said.

"She is quite pretty." Camille wasn't entirely sure of the girl's acting ability, however. Upon meeting Miss Murdock, one wasn't struck so much by the young actress's intelligence as by her appearance. Still, no man in her presence would question what she was saying, as they would, no doubt, be too busy staring at her red curls or her pouting lips or voluptuous bosom. Camille suspected the young woman's primary success on the stage would be in catching a wealthy husband.

"And the role of your uncle, Colonel Channing, will be ably managed by Mr. Wilfred Henderson. A fine Shakespearean actor with extensive credits and, even now, a considerable presence on stage."

"Really?" Beryl's brow rose. "I've never heard of him."

"He never quite gained the acclaim he should have." Mr. Fortesque paused. "Mr. Henderson had the unfortunate habit of imbibing more than was wise before a performance." He hesitated. "Afterward as well. But he has given up overindulgence," he added quickly.

Beryl snorted.

He ignored her. "The rest of the troupe will be playing the parts of maids and footmen. And while they may be actors now, very nearly all of them left a life of service to seek their fortune among the footlights."

He met her gaze with confidence. "You may rest assured, Lady Lydingham, this shall be our greatest performance ever."

Camille cast him a grateful smile. "Thank you, Mr. Fortesque."

"It is I who should thank you." He hesitated. "I should confess that we are not, as yet, a very accomplished troupe. We have only recently formed, in fact, and, indeed, some of us are as yet lacking in . . . *extensive* experience on stage. We are most grateful for the opportunity you have provided us to hone our skills, as well as spend Christmas in as magnificent a house as Millworth Manor."

Camille stared. "How recent?"

"Specifically?" Concern flashed across the actor's face.

"No, no." She thrust out her hand to stop him. "I don't think I want to know, after all. It's far better to maintain hope than have it shattered."

"That's what I always say," Beryl added.

"Not that I've noticed," Camille snapped. Perhaps she should have been somewhat more selective in hiring the troupe, but she'd never hired actors before and considered herself fortunate to have found these. Besides, nothing could be done about it now, but hope for the best. She adopted a pleasant smile. "I'm certain you will all do an excellent job."

"The theater is in our blood, my lady. We have all thrown off the shackles of ordinary lives to pursue the dream that is *the theater*." His voice rose, and he stared off into the distance. Camille exchanged glances with her sister. "The dream of speaking the words of Shakespeare as they were meant to be spoken or performing the works of Mr. Gilbert and Mr. Sullivan as they intend them to be performed." He reached his hand out, palm up, as if to catch something just out of reach. "The dream of taking an audience away from their dull existence and bringing them, however briefly, to another place, another time, to a story they will long remember. And that"—he closed his hand and pulled it back to rest over his heart—"is the dream and, yes, the magic of the theater." He bowed his head.

Beryl choked back a laugh. Camille wasn't sure if she wished to laugh or cry.

"Quite," she said in a weak voice, then cleared her throat. "Well, then, Mr. Fortesque—"

"Simply Fortesque, my lady," the actor said. "If I am to play the role of your butler, you should address me as such."

"Yes, of course." Camille nodded. "Thank you, Fortesque."

"Now, then, if there is nothing else at the moment, I shall make certain your mother, sister and uncle are preparing themselves for their first appearance, as well as oversee the preparation of tea." He nodded at the sisters and took his leave.

"That went well." Camille forced a cheery note to her voice.

" 'Well'?" Beryl stared in disbelief. " 'Well'?"

"Yes," Camille said firmly. "Well."

"It doesn't concern you that you have a house filled with actors who need to *hone their skills* because they are lacking in *extensive* experience?"

"But what they lack in acting experience, they hopefully make up for in the positions of servants."

"Thank God for that," Beryl said sharply. "Have you also considered that you have a drunkard playing your uncle—"

"Former drunkard, if you please." Camille sniffed. "He has given up overindulgence and we should give him the benefit of the doubt."

"What we should do is inventory the brandy. And probably the silverware as well," Beryl added darkly. "Add to that, a tart for a sister—"

"With a natural gift—"

"No doubt." Beryl sniffed. "One suspects that gift is not for acting."

"You haven't mentioned Mrs. Montgomery-Wells," Camille said. "She apparently has a great deal of experience at playing the role of a mother."

"She forgets her lines!"

"So does Mother." Camille shrugged. "Yet another way in which this role was made for her."

"Good Lord, Camille—"

"We just have to get through Christmas, Beryl." Camille paced the room. "Just Christmas. A traditional,

Mr. Dickens's Christmas, with a proper English family. That's all. Certainly, I had planned to stay here through Twelfth Night, but I can see now that might be a mistake. Of course one never knows." She cast her sister an optimistic look. "This might go much better than anticipated."

"It would have to."

Camille paused in midstep and glared. "Thank you for your support."

"I'm here, aren't I?"

"Yes, and I am indeed grateful for that. And Lionel is still coming as well?"

Beryl nodded. "Yes, but probably not until Christmas Eve. He is a very busy man, you know. And he does hate to be away from London for any length of time. But once I explained the circumstances . . ." She chuckled. "He has a better sense of the absurd than I give him credit for. He said he wouldn't miss it."

"Wonderful. Very well, then." Camille resumed pacing. "I shall come up with some reason why we must return to London at once. You can help me with that. You can be quite devious when you wish."

"Thank you."

"Perhaps we could arrange . . ." Camille thought for a moment. "I know! A telegram from his country calling him home."

"How on earth would we do that?"

"Oh, it wouldn't really be from . . . from . . . oh, wherever it is."

"Do try to remember the name of his country, Camille." Beryl shook her head. "It's rude to become the princess of a country whose name you can't recall."

"As I cannot recall it, it's difficult now to fit asking what it is into the conversation."

"Even so—"

"Regardless." Camille pinned her sister with a firm look. "I think sending a telegram insisting he return home is a brilliant idea. A crisis of some sort, I would think. Now, what sort of crisis . . ." Her mind raced. "I suppose a declaration of war on the Kingdom of Whatever would be extreme?"

Beryl grimaced. "Probably."

"Then perhaps—"

"Monetary," Beryl said abruptly.

" 'Monetary'?"

Beryl nodded sagely. "Tiny countries are always having monetary crises of one sort or another."

"It sounds rather dull."

"It can be, which is what makes it perfect for your purposes. A monetary crisis is at once vague and threatening."

"Excellent." Camille beamed. "Then we shall lure him back to his country with the report of a monetary crisis. Although . . ." She frowned. "I should hate to worry him unduly."

"That's the lovely thing about monetary crises. If his country's economy is stable, it's a momentary problem. If not, well . . ." Beryl shrugged. "If not, he shouldn't be traipsing across England in the first place."

"Then he should have nothing to cause undue concern. Although, when he's worried or is concentrating, he gets the faintest little furrow between his brows. It's quite delightful and makes him look rather serious and . . ." Of course, she should have seen it before now. She cast her sister a smug smile. "I know what is going to make this all much easier."

"Oh, do tell."

"I should have realized it before. English is not Nikolai's native language. Aside from that charming accent, one would never know it, as he seems quite proficient.

But he has confessed to me that, on occasion, there are things he doesn't understand. Any odd occurrences in conversation or behavior from Mrs. Montgomery-Wells or Mr. Henderson or Miss Murdock, he will attribute to his failure to completely comprehend." Delight washed through her. "He won't question a thing. I've noticed this before. When he doesn't quite comprehend, that tiny furrow appears and he smiles and nods and pretends to understand. It's most endearing."

"You don't think he'll notice if he's smiling and nodding all the time?"

"I doubt it. I know all sorts of people who smile and nod continuously as they have no idea what is going on around them." Camille shrugged. "They seem quite happy."

"This is getting worse and worse," Beryl warned.

"Nonsense. I think it's getting better and better." Camille ticked the points off on her fingers. "The actors are in place. They all know their roles. Nikolai will attribute anything odd to his own misunderstanding. We have a plan as to what happens immediately after Christmas. One can't ask for more than that."

Camille breathed a deep sigh of relief. Certainly, she still had no definitive idea on how to eventually reveal all to Nikolai, but she would. At the moment, she was oddly confident of it. "Indeed, I can't imagine what could possibly go wrong."

Gray couldn't quite put his finger on it, but something here struck him as wrong.

The butler had shown him into the front parlor at Millworth Manor and taken the basket from him, saying he would fetch Lady Briston. That meant he would not have to see Camille yet. Not that he cared. Still, it was a relief, and he wasn't entirely certain why. Surely, after eleven years, he was prepared to see her again.

He absently circled the parlor. The room itself was precisely as it was in his memory of the last time he'd been here, the day before Camille's wedding. The furnishings were placed as they had always been, the furniture itself appeared none the worse for the passage of time. Even the clock on the mantel and the paintings on the wall remained in the positions he remembered. But then, according to Win's letters, Lady Briston and her daughters were rarely here, much preferring to spend their days in London. Of course, Lady Briston's children all had lives of their own. Beryl was apparently on her second husband, a political type Win had written. Delilah was a wealthy widow, but then she would be. A wry smile curved his lips. Lady Briston's daughters had married exactly as she had trained them. Upon reflection, he realized it was odd the mother had not remarried in the manner of her offspring.

Perhaps his vague unease was due to the presence of a new butler at Millworth Manor. For as long as he could remember, the butler was a man named Clement, stiff and stodgy and eminently proper, but usually with a vague air of long-suffering about him and often a hint of amusement in his eye. And at Gray's last visit, a touch of sympathy as well. He was particularly suited to the eccentric household of Lady Briston's family. Gray didn't recall Clement as being especially old, but it had been eleven years. He had no doubt retired from service. Gray would have to ask Camille. At least that would give him something not fraught with hidden meaning to talk about.

That's it. He pulled up short. This new butler—he had said his name was Fortesque—was entirely too perfect for this household. Gray wondered how long he'd had his position. And how soon, if indeed Lady Briston and her daughters were in residence, it would be before he left.

"I heard we had a visitor." An elderly lady swept into the room in a dramatic manner. "And such a dashing visitor at that."

"Good afternoon," he said cautiously, wondering who this might be. Although, as he recalled, there were always a few unique sorts staying at Millworth Manor. Camille had referred to them as lost tribes—the wandering, displaced nobility of Europe—but he had never quite been certain if she was amused by them or merely tolerant.

The lady was a good half a foot shorter than he, of matronly figure, with nearly white hair and a face that must have been beautiful once and was still quite lovely. Her blue eyes sparkled and she held out her hand. Gray wasn't sure if she expected him to shake it or kiss it.

She cleared her throat, glanced pointedly at her hand and raised it an inch. Kiss it, then. He smiled and obediently did so.

"What a handsome young man you are." She cast him a flirtatious smile, and it was all he could do to keep from snatching his hand back. "And who, exactly, are you?"

"My apologies, I have not introduced myself," he said slowly. "I am Mr. Elliott. Grayson Elliott."

"Grayson? I knew a Grayson once. Oh, he was quite mad, in a very good way, of course. One never knew what he might do next. I remember once, at a gathering at Lord . . . what was his name?" She paused as if searching her memory; then apparently thought better of what she was about to say, much to Gray's relief. "It scarcely matters at the moment, I suppose. I shall tell you my stories later, after we have come to know each other much, much better."

Gray smiled weakly.

"Welcome to my home, Mr. Elliott, Mr. Grayson Elliott," she said in a grand manner. "I am Lady Briston, Millicent to my close friends, and I do think we are going to be close, close friends."

"Bernadette," he said without thinking.

Her eyes widened. "I beg your pardon?"

"Lady Briston's given name is Bernadette."

Her brows drew together. "Are you certain?"

"Fairly certain."

"I could have sworn it was Millicent," she murmured.

A thought struck him, but surely his cousin would have mentioned this. "Unless, of course, you've married Lord Briston. Colonel Channing, that is."

"Dear Lord, no. Absolutely not. Such an idea." She shook her head. "I am definitely not married. As far as I can recall, although I was once." She heaved a heartfelt sigh. "It did not go well."

Gray stared. "Then I'm afraid I don't understand."

"That's quite all right." She patted his arm and cast him a sympathetic smile. "It happens to everyone on occasion. I myself don't understand, rather more often than not. Let me see if I can explain." She thought for a moment. "I am Lady Briston. I have a brother-in-law, Colonel Channing. Right, thus far?"

Gray nodded mutely.

"I knew I was right." She beamed. "And I have three daughters. Two of them look exactly alike, you know." She shook her head. "It's most confusing."

"Lady, er, Briston." Gray chose his words carefully.

"I have been gone for a number of years. Still, there are things—"

"I beg your pardon." Fortesque stepped briskly into the parlor. Gray wouldn't have thought it possible from their initial meeting, but the man looked a bit harried. "Lady Briston, I was sent to find you."

"And so you have, my dear Fortesque."

The butler slanted a quick glance at Gray. "I was to find you before you greeted any visitors."

"Then you do need to be on your toes, Fortesque," she said in a chastising manner. "Why, I have already met Mr. Elliott. Mr. Grayson Elliott. Delightful name, don't you agree?"

"Yes, my lady." Fortesque's jaw tightened, but his tone was eminently proper. "Your presence is required elsewhere."

"Is it, indeed?" She cast the butler what could only be described as a saucy look. Who was this woman?

"Yes, my lady," he said in an overly stern manner. "Elsewhere. At once."

"To meet the prince, no doubt." She leaned toward Gray confidentially. "I haven't met him yet, but I understand he's very handsome and quite taken with one of the blond daughters. I'm not sure which."

Gray drew his brows together. "What prince?"

"At once, Lady Briston," the butler said again.

"Oh, well, then." Her eyes twinkled with amusement. "I shall make my exit with the grace and dignity befitting my position." With that, she raised her chin and fairly floated out of the room, Fortesque a step behind.

Gray stared after them. Perhaps that was one of the odd guests who were so often to be found residing at Millworth Manor. Still, he was certain few of them believed themselves to be Lady Briston.

A young woman passed by the doorway, casting an absent glance in his direction. Less than a moment later, she reappeared and favored him with an interested smile.

"Good day."

Her hair was a vivid shade of dark red and she was extremely pretty, with large doelike brown eyes and an exceptional figure.

He smiled. "Good day."

She studied him curiously. "Are you another one of the players?"

"The players?"

"Mr. Fortesque said he might have to hire additional players, as this house is so very large and requires a fair number of servants." Her gaze wandered over him in an assessing manner. "I must say, you're handsome enough, even if you are entirely too well dressed for an actor, especially one who might take this role. It's not as if this was Covent Garden, after all. You certainly don't look as if you are here for the money." She considered him closely. "No, you look as if you have money."

He chuckled. "I shall have to do something about that."

"Oh no," she said quickly. "It's always better to look as if you don't need money than you do."

"I shall keep that in mind."

"The pay is better than usual here, probably because we are all sworn to secrecy under threat of legal action. Indeed, I should hate to cross Lady Lydingham." She shuddered. "I think the woman would track us to the ends of the earth if we were to cross her, and God knows she has the money to do so. Nonetheless, one can always use more performing experience, so keeping one's mouth shut is a small price to pay. Besides, this is a pleasant enough place to spend Christmas, and—" She sucked in a sharp breath and her eyes widened. "Oh, dear Lord, you're not the prince, are you? Please say you're not the prince."

What prince? "No," he said slowly. "I'm not the prince."

"Thank goodness." She breathed a sigh of relief. "I should hate to have let on to the prince that Lady Lydingham had hired . . ." The young woman's eyes narrowed. "If you're not the prince, and you're not an actor, then who are you?"

It had been Gray's experience that complete honesty was not always as effective as partial honesty. "I never said I wasn't an actor."

"Oh, how lovely." Her expression brightened. "I'm Miss Murdock, Edwina. Perhaps you've heard of me?"

"I'm afraid not."

"Don't be." She raised a shoulder in a casual shrug. "I'm not famous yet, but I will be. I intend to be as famous as Ellen Terry one day."

"She's a very good actress, you know."

"As am I." She tossed him an impudent smile. "And at the moment, I am Lady Hargate, the younger sister of Lady Lydingham." She paused thoughtfully. "She's supposed to be quite proper and was described to me as something of a stick in the mud, but I'm not sure I see the part that way."

"And how do you see it?" What was going on here?

"Well, goodness, how proper can she be? She married a much older man and now she's a wealthy widow. A very wealthy widow, apparently. And her name is *Delilah,*" she added pointedly. "I don't see her as being the least bit proper, but rather"—she deepened her voice slightly—"*provocative,* I would think. The kind of woman who knows what she wants and does what she must to get it." She met his gaze directly, and he wasn't sure if she was acting or simply very dangerous.

"Well . . . um . . ."—he swallowed hard—"it's been my observation that nothing makes a performance more realistic than when an actor plays the role the way he—or she—feels it should be performed."

She gasped. "That's exactly how I feel. Then you think I'm right, to play the part as I see it, that is?"

"Without question. If you think Lady Hargate is, well, something of a tart—"

"And I do. Really, how could she be anything else?"

"Then you owe it to your audience to play the role as you feel it—" He laid a hand over his heart. "Here."

"You're quite right. I don't know why I hesitated. And I have always been very good at playing the tart." She raised a shapely shoulder in an offhand shrug. "It just seems to come naturally for me."

"I can see where it would."

She cast him a brilliant smile. "You're obviously very good as well, but I didn't realize there were any more roles for men other than servants, of course, and you don't seem suited to play a footman."

He shrugged.

"The butler is being played by Mr. Fortesque, and Mr. Henderson is cast as Colonel Channing. Do you know what role you have?"

"I'm afraid not." He shook his head. "I have only just arrived."

"There's probably another part I am unaware of." She heaved an overly dramatic sigh. "I don't know how they expect me to be prepared when the script is constantly changing. Although, I suppose, as there is only an audience of one, one can allow for changes."

"Audience of one?"

"The prince, of course." She raised a brow. "You didn't know?"

"As I said, I have only just arrived."

"Of course. And, as no doubt Lady Lydingham would prefer the entire world not know she has hired a troupe of actors to play her family to impress a prince at Christmas, it makes perfect sense that you would not know all until you arrived."

"It does indeed make sense." And more so with every word from the actress's mouth.

"I believe I shall rehearse a bit more before I meet the prince. Now that I know I was right about my portrayal of Lady Hargate." She tilted her head and considered him. "Wouldn't it be great fun if you are here to play the role of Lady Hargate's secret lover?"

"That would indeed be interesting." He grinned.

"I shall hope for the best, then." She smiled in a flirtatious manner and left the room.

Surely, he misunderstood, although Miss Murdock was quite clear as to why she was here. Why on earth would Camille hire actors to play her family? And who was this prince everyone kept waiting to meet? None of this made any sense to him; it all seemed entirely farfetched. Beryl was probably behind it. She had always been more devious than Camille, although the two of them together had made a dangerous pair. Apparently, in that respect too, nothing had changed.

"Miss Murdock," a harried feminine voice sounded from the hall. "Have you seen Fortesque?" The voice grew closer. "Apparently, Mrs. Montgomery-Wells is wandering about freely—" His heart skipped a beat. Regardless of the passage of years, he would know that voice anywhere. "And who knows what kind of mischief she might get into." Camille passed by the door, glanced his way, then pulled up short and stared.

Her hair was as blond, her eyes as blue, her face as lovely as the last time he had seen her. Nothing had changed. The moment her gaze met his, the clock turned back eleven years. To the day before her wedding when she had gazed into his eyes and he had known without question that she loved him. A myriad of emotions flashed through her eyes—disbelief, delight, annoyance, even anger. But there was more. So subtle that he doubted she was aware of it. No more than a hint or a vague promise perhaps of something deeper and richer and forever shone in her eyes.

And Gray suspected he had lied to his cousin; and worse, he had lied to himself.

Four

Surely, her eyes were deceiving her. Or she'd gone mad. She stared at the figure standing in the parlor, in very much the same place where she'd last seen him. Yes, that was it. She was mad—quite, quite mad. Her scheme had completely destroyed her mind. They would be hauling her off to Bedlam at any—

"Camille?" the imaginary creature that looked suspiciously like Grayson Elliott said in a cautious manner. Of course he would be cautious, as she was so obviously mad.

She shook her head to clear it. Damnation, he was still there. "Grayson?"

"None other."

A broad smile broke across his face, and the most absurd desire to dash across the room and into his arms gripped her. She ignored it.

"How very good to see you, Camille."

"Is it?" She stepped into the room slowly, as if she were moving in a dream. A dream she had had before. There was indeed something not quite real about all this. He was the last person she expected, or wanted, to see now or ever again. He was a road not taken. Over and done with, and not to be considered again. Nonetheless, it—he— apparently was real. Grayson was here, looking every bit as wonderful as she remembered, with his dark eyes and dark hair and devastating smile, the smile which had once touched her heart. Not that it mattered at the moment. She drew a deep breath. Time enough later to examine the unexpected emotions coursing through her. "What are you doing here?"

He chuckled. "My aunt sent a basket of Cook's baked goods to welcome your family back to Millworth Manor."

"How very kind of her." She glanced around the room. "Where is it?"

"I gave it to your"—his eyes narrowed slightly— "butler."

"Ah, well, then . . ." She wasn't sure why he was still here. She wasn't sure how she felt about him being here at all. All she was certain of was that she wanted him to leave. At once, if not sooner. "Do give my thanks to Lady Fairborough. If that's all—"

"What happened to Clement?" he asked abruptly.

"Gone." She said the first thing that came into her head.

"My condolences." Sympathy showed in his eyes. "Hard to imagine he's gone. He was such a fixture here."

"He's not dead. He's gone to Wales. To be with his family." It was true, as far as it went, although it made no sense for the butler to be gone when the house was full. "He retired," she added as an afterthought. Oh yes, that made it plausible.

"I see," he said slowly. "You must miss him."

"We do," she said with a firm nod. "He was a part of the family. And an excellent butler."

"It must be difficult, with a new butler, that is. And the entire family here for Christmas."

"You have no idea." And getting more difficult every minute. "But Fortesque is very well trained." She smiled in what she hoped was a pleasant manner. He had delivered his aunt's basket—what was he still doing here? "Again, do thank your aunt for me."

"Oh, I will." He studied her coolly. The man obviously had no intention of leaving.

"As you said, it is a bit awkward to have a new butler at this time of year. There does seem to be an endless list of things that need to be attended to, with the entire family in residence and all. I'm sure that you are busy as well, so I won't keep you—"

"Ah yes, the whole family you say?"

She nodded.

"Your mother and Colonel Channing, your sisters and Beryl's husband?"

"Yes, yes, that's everyone." Impatience edged her voice. The last thing she needed at this moment was to deal with the distant past in the guise of Grayson Elliott. The present was entirely too complicated already. "Although Lionel, Lord Dunwell, is engaged in town and won't be arriving until Christmas Eve."

"I see. But your mother and uncle and sisters—"

"Yes, yes, all of them," she snapped. "Now, if there is nothing—"

"It's been a long time, Camille."

She deliberately misunderstood him. Now was not the time. "Indeed, it's been entirely too long since we have all been at Millworth Manor for Christmas, and we are quite looking forward to it. However, I have a great deal to—"

"I met your mother." His gaze bored into hers.

Her breath caught. "Did you?"

"A few minutes ago." He smiled. "She's changed."

There was no way to explain Mrs. Montgomery-Wells.

Best to simply pretend complete and utter ignorance. She usually did that very well. "As have we all." She shrugged. "It's been eleven years since you were last in this house, after all. People change, but life goes on. I daresay, nothing is as it used to be."

He laughed.

She narrowed her gaze. "What do you find so amusing?"

"I met your sister as well."

"Beryl?" she said hopefully.

"No, Delilah."

She winced. "Oh."

"What is going on here, Camille?"

"Christmas?"

His brow rose.

"It's complicated, Grayson, and it's none of your concern." She huffed. "Now, if you would be so good as to take your leave." She gestured at the door. "I would be most appreciative."

"Oh, I think not." He sauntered, *sauntered*, over to the fireplace, crossed his arms over his chest and leaned against the mantel in a most arrogant manner. "I'm not going anywhere."

She widened her eyes. "Why not?"

"Not until you tell me what's afoot here."

"Why do you want to know?" She mimicked his stance, folding her arms over her chest. "This has nothing to do with you. This is none of your concern whatsoever. Indeed, nothing having to do with this household or its respective members has been your concern for, oh, more than eleven years now."

For a long moment, he stared at her in silence.

"If you have something to say, do be so good as to simply say it. Then"—she jerked her head toward the door—"get out. Or better yet, get out now!"

His tone was cool, calm and entirely too reasonable. It was most infuriating. "The last time I was here—"

"No, no! I don't want to hear it!" She clapped her hands over her ears and squeezed her eyes closed tight. "I didn't want to hear it then. I don't want to hear it now!"

"Camille—"

Damnation, she could still hear him. "I'm not listening! Go away!"

He didn't respond. With her hands over her ears and her eyes shut, she couldn't tell if he was still here or if he'd left the room. With any luck at all, he was gone. She counted to ten slowly, then opened her eyes and groaned.

"You're still here."

"I said I wasn't leaving."

"Why not?"

"Because I am fairly certain you need my help," he said simply.

She stared in disbelief. "I need what?"

"My help."

"My God." She nearly choked on the words. "You are as stubborn and arrogant as you always were."

"Come now, I was never arrogant."

"No?" It was her turn to raise a brow.

"Admittedly, there might have been a moment now and then—"

"A moment? Hah!"

"I don't remember—"

"I can name any number of examples of your arrogance in the past, if I were so inclined, but I'm not." Her voice rose. "Because that would take a great deal of time and I want you to leave!"

He ignored her. "What have you gotten yourself into, Camille?"

"You can't simply appear in my life after all these years without a word and insist on . . . on . . . rescuing me!"

"Is it that bad?" His brow furrowed. "Do you need rescue?"

"No, no, everything is going quite well." The lie flowed easily from her lips. "Better even than I had expected."

"Not to my observation," he said wryly.

"You're not leaving, are you?"

He shook his head.

She studied him closely. "If I tell you, will you leave?"

"If you tell me, I will consider leaving."

"That's something, at any rate. Very well, then." She threw her hands up in resignation. She had been completely confident when she had first revealed her plan to Beryl. Now, however, it was only the first day and she was already beginning to note a flaw or two. Perhaps, before she said anything, it would be best to find out what he already knew. Or thought he knew.

"First, let me ask you this." She adopted a casual tone. "What do you think I've gotten myself into?"

He laughed. "Camille, I had nearly forgotten how thoroughly delightful you can be."

"I have no intention of being delightful to you," she said in a lofty manner. "Thoroughly or otherwise."

"Nor would I expect you to." He grinned, straightened and started toward her. The last time he had crossed this room toward her, she had ended up in his arms; his lips had claimed hers for the first—and last—time. The memory of that single, unforgettable kiss swept through her, and it was all she could do to keep her knees from buckling. Blasted man!

Without thinking, she took a step back. "What are you doing?"

He frowned. "What are *you* doing?"

She raised her chin. "Nothing, not a thing, nothing at all."

He stared and then sucked in a sharp breath. "You thought I was going to kiss you, didn't you?"

"No, of course not. Not for an instant."

His eyes narrowed. "Because when we were last in this very room—"

"What utter nonsense, Grayson. You are entirely too full of yourself." She waved off his comment. "Your kissing me was the last thing on my mind. Indeed, it wasn't on my mind at all. Not that I would allow you to do so, anyway."

"Excellent, as I have no intention of kissing you." He shook his head. "I made that mistake once and I'll not do it again."

"Mistake?" she said without thinking.

He nodded. "It was presump—"

"No!" She shook her head and glared. "I have no desire to speak of that now. It's been eleven years, Grayson. It's in the past, and it does neither of us any good to dwell on what happened between us." And what didn't.

"Still"—he chose his words carefully—"as we were always friends, I have long thought I owed you an apology. My behav—"

"Accepted!" She drew a calming breath. "If that's all, then—"

"It's not."

"I was afraid not." She sank onto the sofa. "Very well. What do you think you know?"

"I know the woman who introduced herself as Lady Briston, Millicent—"

"Bernadette," she said. "My mother's name is Bernadette."

"She didn't seem to know that—this particular Lady Briston, that is. She appeared more than a little confused."

"She has a problem remembering her lines," she said under her breath.

"Then there was the young woman who claimed to be your sister Delilah."

Camille shifted uncomfortably on the sofa.

"We had quite an interesting conversation."

"She has always been good at small talk." Camille forced an offhand note to her voice.

"Oh, I wouldn't describe this as 'small talk' or idle chatter," he said coolly. "Indeed, she was most informative."

Camille's heart sank. "Oh?"

"Yes, you see, she thought I was here to audition for a role she was unaware of."

"Really?" She widened her eyes in feigned surprise. "How very odd."

"I thought so, at first." He studied her intently. "Until, of course, she explained that Lady Lydingham had hired actors to play her family for Christmas."

"She said all that, did she?" Camille said weakly.

He nodded. "Apparently, to impress a prince."

She stared at him for a moment, then stood. "Well, that's it, then. You know it all. Now you can leave."

"Who is this prince?" he said in a stern manner.

"That, too, is none of your concern."

"Camille." His tone eased. "I'm not leaving until you tell me everything."

"You know everything."

He studied her, determination in the very lines of his body. It had been a long time, but she recognized his resolute manner.

"If that's the only way to get rid of you . . ." She blew

a resigned breath. "He is Prince Nikolai Pruzinsky, of the Kingdom of . . . Oh, I can't recall—"

"Ah yes, lovely place," he murmured.

She cast him a scathing glance and continued. "He longs for a traditional English Christmas. I still don't see why, but he is foreign and he's read any number of English Christmas stories, and, well, you understand."

Grayson's forehead furrowed. "Not entirely."

"He expects, as well, a proper English family, and I intend to give it to him. As my family has never been what one might call proper, in the strict definition of the word—"

He snorted.

"It seemed to me, as Mother, Delilah and Uncle Basil are out of the country, anyway, hiring actors to play my family for Christmas was a rather brilliant idea."

His brow arched upward.

"I intend to make this Christmas with my family—"

"Your bought-and-paid-for family?"

She ignored him. "All he has ever thought it would be." She hesitated. She might as well tell him everything. The damnable man wouldn't be satisfied until she did. And they had never lied to each other, not really. "And, while he is here, I fully expect him to propose."

"You love him, then." His resigned gaze met hers.

"I don't . . . not love him."

"Do you love him or don't you?"

She huffed. "Once again, Grayson, this is none of—"

"None of my concern. Yes, yes, I know." His tone hardened. "Tell me, Camille. Do you love him or not?"

"I fully plan to love him," she said in a sharper tone than she intended, but then Grayson was so annoyingly persistent. "There is nothing about him not to love. Why, he's every woman's dream."

"So you are going to do it again. Marry someone you don't love."

"Stop it at once, Grayson." She drew her brows together. "This is not the same. Not at all. I am not a nineteen-year-old girl. I am a woman who knows her own mind. He is what I want, and I intend to have him."

"Why? You don't need his money." He paused. "I assume he has money."

"Of course. He's a prince." Camille scoffed. "And how do you know I don't need his money?"

"You're a very wealthy widow." He shrugged. "Win has kept me apprised of your life these past eleven years."

"Yes, of course, he would, wouldn't he?" He and his cousin had always been as thick as thieves. Precisely why she had kept her distance from Winfield Elliott for all these years.

"As I assume you are aware of the twists and turns of my own life."

"Not at all. I have made it a point not to be." In truth, she had avoided any talk of him whatsoever, going so far as to forbid Beryl to so much as mention his name. Beryl must have said something to Mother, who never spoke of Grayson either. Given that Camille's social circle rarely crossed his cousin's, or that of most of his friends, it had been remarkably easy to go for years without hearing a word about him. She knew he had gone off to America shortly after her marriage and had been involved in some sort of business enterprise. She had heard as well that he had never married; but beyond that, she had no idea how he had lived his life or what had become of him. She hadn't wanted to know, hadn't wanted to think of him, hadn't wanted to regret. "Indeed, I know nothing about your life from the moment you left this house until today. Nor do I wish to."

"I see."

"If you have heard enough now, perhaps you would be so good as to take your leave." Again she gestured at the door. "Finally."

"What happens after Christmas?"

"You refuse to let this be, don't you?"

"You said I was stubborn."

"And I was right, wasn't I?" She sighed. "The day after Christmas, Nikolai shall have to return to his country because of a monetary crisis—"

"A what?"

"A monetary crisis. Beryl assures me it happens all the time." She waved her hand absently and continued. "I shall accompany him, of course. And then, at some point before the wedding—"

"Dependent, of course, on whether or not he proposes."

"That is not in doubt," she said with a confident smile. "As I was saying, before the wedding, I shall confess my little Christmas ruse and explain to him, as most of my family was out of the country, I simply wanted him to have the kind of English Christmas he has longed for. It is, well, my gift to him."

"Are you mad?"

"Admittedly, there might be a flaw or two—"

"Or two?"

"I merely need to smooth out some of the rougher edges."

He stared in disbelief. "So this is another one of your schemes that you have not thoroughly thought out?"

"I have given it a great deal of thought." She glared. "I am thinking about it every waking moment. I am dreaming about it as well. Indeed, there is little else on my mind!" She clenched her teeth. "And for your information, Beryl is the schemer. I haven't schemed for years!"

"Camille." Concern sounded in his voice. "Aside from the fact that this is complete and utter madness—"

"So I've been told," she snapped.

"It can't possibly succeed."

"I've been told that as well."

He shook his head. "You've gotten yourself into this and you have no way now to escape."

"There is no need to escape. Yes, there are a few unanticipated problems, but it shall all work out beautifully in the end." She adopted a note of complete confidence. "I have no doubt of it."

"Camille, this is not the—"

"Good afternoon," a voice sounded from the doorway and Camille's stomach twisted.

She threw Grayson a warning look, then turned toward the door and her prince. "Your—Nikolai." She adopted her most welcoming smile and held out her hand. "I trust your rooms are suitable."

"Quite." He stepped to her, took her hand and raised it to his lips. His gaze never left hers in a manner so polished as to be perfect. But then, he was a prince. "I must tell you again how grateful I am that you have welcomed me into your home for Christmas."

"It's our very great honor to have you here." She gazed into his blue eyes, simmering with promises and just the right hint of desire. She shivered with anticipation.

"I cannot find the words to tell you how much I am looking forward to the time spent here with you." He smiled an altogether perfect smile. He was every bit as tall as Grayson; and with his blond hair and blue eyes, square jaw and broad shoulders, he was a handsome devil. The perfect picture of a perfect prince; and, if all went well, her perfect prince. "And your family, of course."

"Of course," she murmured.

Grayson cleared his throat, breaking the spell. She withdrew her hand with a reluctant sigh.

"Forgive me." Nikolai directed his attention to Grayson. "I do hope I was not interrupting."

"Not at all," Camille said.

"I was not aware that we were not alone. But then when I am in a room with Lady Lydingham, I can see nothing else, save this enchanting creature," Nikolai said smoothly.

She cast Grayson a satisfied smirk.

"In my experience, Lady Lydingham is nothing if not an enchanting creature," Grayson said pleasantly. "But then, even as a young girl, she was enchanting. Why I can recall—"

"Recollections that are best left for another time," Camille said quickly. The only thing worse than Grayson being here in the present was his reminiscing about the past.

"Oh, but I should like to hear it." Nikolai favored her with an affectionate smile. "I wish to know everything there is to know about you, my dear."

"How . . . perfect of you." She sighed up at him.

Grayson choked.

"Again my apologies." Nikolai shook his head. "I fear in Lady Lydingham's presence, I quite forget all else. Allow me to introduce myself. I am Count Pruzinsky, of the Kingdom of Greater Avalonia." He clicked his heels together. "And I am at your service."

Grayson frowned. "I do beg your pardon, but I was under the impression you were a prince."

"He is a prince." Camille huffed. "He just prefers not to be addressed as such when traveling in a foreign country." She lowered her voice. "There are dangers, you know."

"Really?" Surprise or perhaps skepticism sounded in Grayson's voice. She could cheerfully strangle him right here and now. And, as everyone already thought she was mad . . . "I never would have imagined."

"I would prefer not to discuss such dire possibilities," Nikolai said in an offhand manner. "Christmas and all."

Grayson nodded. "To be expected, of course."

"Forgive me." Nikolai glanced from Grayson to Camille. "We still have not been introduced."

"I am sorry. What was I thinking?" Camille smiled in as pleasant a manner as she could muster. "This is Mr. Grayson Elliott. He is—"

"Her cousin. Camille's cousin." Grayson grinned an altogether wicked and, perhaps once, devastating, grin.

"My what?" She stared. What was he up to now?

Nikolai's brow rose in confusion. No doubt he'd smile and nod at any minute.

"Distant, you know," Grayson said. "Our connection is tenuous at best. Scarcely worth mentioning, but nonetheless we are family. In truth, I am little more than a poor relation, but I am exceptionally fond of Camille and her sisters. And it is Christmas."

"Yes, this is my cousin," she said reluctantly. "My very distant cousin. It's been years since we've seen him. Why, we have practically forgotten what he looks like."

"A family reunion! How delightful," Nikolai said with a genuine smile. "You are the first of Lady Lydingham's relations I have met and I am quite looking forward to meeting the rest. You have my everlasting gratitude for welcoming me into the bosom of your family for Christmas."

Grayson chuckled. "We are an interesting lot."

"We are not." Camille forced a laugh. "We are no more interesting than anyone else's family. Quite proper and really, on occasion, even somewhat dull."

"Nonsense, Camille." Grayson shook his head. "There is nothing the least bit dull about this family."

"And what is it you English say?" Nikolai thought for a moment. "Ah yes. The more, the merrier."

Camille shook her head in confusion. "The more . . ."

"I assume, as a member of your family, Mr. Elliott has come—"

"For Christmas." Grayson's wicked grin widened, if possible.

Camille stared in disbelief.

"Yes, indeed." Laughter flashed in Grayson's eyes. "I am Camille's cousin and I've come for Christmas."

Five

Camille's eyes widened with a look one could only describe as horror. "What do you mean you've come for Christmas?"

"Now, now, Camille, you needn't look so shocked." Gray resisted the urge to chuckle.

He wasn't entirely sure why he had introduced himself as her cousin, as her *poor relation*, although it was apparent to him she had no idea of his financial state. His announcement that he would be staying for Christmas was as much a surprise to him as it was to her. Still, now that he had said it, he quite liked the idea. If Camille insisted on going through with this theatrical farce of hers, the least he could do, as her old friend, was provide his assistance. He owed her that much really. And what better way to help than by residing in her family's home, where he could be close at hand? Besides, while he hadn't realized it before she had walked into the room, there was unfinished business here. He and Camille were a play without a last act, and it was past time to see how it would end. The moment he saw her again, he knew the final curtain hadn't fallen, not for him.

"It's simply a surprise, that's all." She could barely choke out the words.

"A delightful surprise, no doubt," the prince said in an accent Gray couldn't quite place. Hungarian, perhaps? Or Russian? Regardless, as he'd never met anyone from the Kingdom of Greater Avalonia, it sounded very much as one would think it would sound. Rather perfect, really. Still, there was something about the accent that struck him as odd. Too perfect, perhaps?

" 'Delightful' is not exactly the word I had in mind." A feigned smile graced Camille's lips, but her livid gaze fixed on Gray. "Stunned is perhaps more accurate."

"I know my presence is the last thing you expected—" Camille choked.

"But when I heard the rest of the family was to be here, how could I fail to join them?" Gray addressed the prince. "You see, I have been abroad for a number of years and have only recently returned to England."

The prince nodded. "There is nothing better than being surrounded by one's family for Christmas."

"Nothing at all." Gray paused. "Might I ask, Your Highness—"

"No, please." Pruzinsky shook his head. "As I am traveling merely as Count Pruzinsky, I much prefer not to be addressed as 'Your Highness' but simply as 'Count.' "

"Do you?" Gray's brow rose. "How very unusual."

"No, it's not," Camille said firmly. "It's enlightened."

"In truth, it's not at all unusual for my family." Pruzinsky chuckled. "We have long had a tradition of traveling the world without the accoutrements of our royal stations. Sort of a surreptitious grand tour, as it were. It enables us to see the true nature of the world and other lands. Quite beneficial when the time comes to rule. Diplomacy is an art, you know. And people treat you differently if they know your true position in life. Don't you agree?"

"Yes, I suppose," Gray said. Would Camille treat him differently if she knew he now had the wealth and power he hadn't had eleven years ago? He slanted a quick glance at her. While she had adopted a calm air, her gaze when she met his blazed with fury. At this moment, probably not.

"But you had a question for me, Mr. Elliott."

"I was just wondering why, given your comment about being with family at Christmas, you choose to spend Christmas here in England."

"I have to confess, Christmas caught me unaware," Pruzinsky said wryly. "I have been away from home, traveling the continent and, most recently, the British Isles for nearly a year. I simply lost track of the days. No doubt the direct result of meeting your cousin. I daresay, she could make anyone forget their own name." He directed a warm smile toward Camille and she beamed back at him. "By the time I realized how close Christmas was, it was too late to make the journey home."

"I see," Gray said. "Forgive my ignorance, Count, but where exactly is your country?"

"No apology is necessary, Mr. Elliott." Pruzinsky smiled in a benevolent manner. "We are a very small country and quite secluded, wedged between the Russian, Austrian and Germanic empires."

"But from what you have said, it sounds quite lovely," Camille said. "I should very much like to see it someday."

"And I would very much enjoy showing it to you. There is nothing as beautiful as the view from the castle of

the snow-covered mountains of Avalonia in December."
Pruzinsky sighed wistfully. "Unless, of course, it's the
green hills and valleys in the spring."

"Of course," Gray murmured. He was not well versed
in the geography—or climate—of that part of Europe.
Indeed, the map of that particular region seemed to
change nearly every year. Still, like the prince's accent,
his explanation struck an odd chord as well. Although,
admittedly, Gray might well be suspicious of anyone
with whom Camille was this enamored. That realization
was as surprising as his impulsive decision to stay and
help her with this farce.

"But while I will not be joining my own family, I now
have the pleasure of joining Lady Lydingham's family
for Christmas," the prince said with a yet another fond
look at Camille. No, there was more than fondness in
that look. Gray's stomach tightened. "The first of many
such gatherings, perhaps."

"Perhaps." Camille fluttered her lashes at him.

Good God! Why didn't the woman fling herself into
his bed right now? Gray ignored the thought that perhaps she already had and absolutely refused to consider
why he found that idea annoying.

"Now then." Pruzinsky smiled pleasantly. "It appears
my bags have been misplaced. I was hoping your butler
might know of their whereabouts."

"Oh, dear, that is a problem." Camille shook her
head. "I am sorry, I'm afraid the staff here in the country is not quite as efficient as it should be. I shall find
Fortesque immediately." She stepped toward the door,
paused, then extended her hand to the prince.

Pruzinsky took it at once, and brought it to his lips.
Gray resisted the urge to groan. Camille sighed and
slanted a pointed look at Gray. "I shall be no more than
a moment."

"Even a moment without your presence is too long," Pruzinsky said gallantly. A bit overdone to Gray's thinking, but then the man was a foreign prince and perhaps allowances should be made.

"I shall do my best to be as entertaining as possible until you return," Gray said with a smirk.

"As only you know how." She paused. "On second thought—"

"No, my dear, we shall be fine." Pruzinsky met Gray's gaze directly. "It's obvious to me your cousin has some reservations about my presence in your home. He is your male relation, so it is, no doubt, to be expected."

"Nonsense," Camille said in a firm tone. "It's just his manner. Think nothing of it. Everyone in the family has long said Grayson is entirely too suspicious." Her jaw tightened. "It's one of his more charming attributes."

"Not at all," the prince said smoothly. "I would feel entirely the same, were our positions reversed."

"Grayson simply doesn't understand I am no longer the girl he left behind." Camille glared.

Pruzinsky's considering gaze slipped from Camille to Gray and back.

Camille's hands clenched at her side. "It has been eleven years since he left England, after all."

Gray shrugged. "It seems like yesterday."

"It wasn't," she said sharply; then obviously remembered she was trying to impress a prince and smiled. "Indeed, it feels like another lifetime altogether."

"Eleven years." The prince's eyes widened with surprise. "Then I did interrupt a reunion. I do apologize."

"Not necessary." Camille blithely waved off the comment. "Grayson had said hello and was about to leave—"

"To fetch my bags." He leaned toward the prince

and lowered his voice in a confidential manner. "I, too, have encountered a few baggage difficulties, especially at the train station."

"I quite understand." Pruzinsky nodded. "It is at once the benefit and misfortune of not traveling as a prince. No one treats you as a prince." He flashed an amused grin. "And, as I am more than capable of finding a servant myself, I shall leave you to reminisce." He nodded. "Mr. Elliott, Camille." He looked as if he were about to grab her hand once again; then apparently thought better of it and took his leave.

"That's the man you want to marry?" He turned toward her.

"What do you mean—my cousin come for Christmas?" she said at precisely the same time.

"I thought you could use some help in this convoluted plot of yours."

"I don't need your help, and, yes, that is the *prince* I intend to marry." She glared.

"He's not like any prince I've ever known."

"Oh, really?" She raised a brow. "How many princes have you known?"

"That's not what I mean, and you know it," he said sharply. "Doesn't his manner strike you as odd? All that traveling without the trappings of his position? Capable of finding the butler himself? He doesn't act the least bit royal."

"He's traveling incognito," she said in a lofty manner. "It's quite progressive of him."

"It's odd, extremely odd."

"I think it's perfect."

"Do you?" He narrowed his gaze. "You've never been one to forgo the accoutrements of wealth and position."

"And, I daresay, in his own country, neither does

Nikolai." She paused. "Nor will we as a royal couple, of course."

"I think it's suspicious."

"It doesn't matter what you think."

"I don't trust him," Gray said flatly.

"You scarcely met him."

Gray shook his head. "He's entirely too polished. He's exactly what one would think a prince would be, aside from that nonsense about not traveling as a prince."

"It's a family tradition." Camille's jaw clenched.

"He's entirely too"—Gray shrugged—"perfect. No man is that perfect."

"He's a prince and he is perfect." She raised her chin. "And charming and dashing and handsome. He is everything any woman would ever want. Everything I have ever wanted."

"I see." He studied her closely. It had been a long time, but once he had known her as well as he knew himself. And right now, she was not being completely honest with him or perhaps with herself. Or, more than likely, both. "Well, then, Camille, if he is what you want—"

"He is," she said staunchly.

"Then I shall do everything I can to assure your success."

Suspicion sounded in her voice. "Why?"

"Because . . ." He blew a long breath. "All I have ever wanted was your happiness."

She stared at him for a moment. "Come now, Grayson, if you truly meant that, you would leave."

"Oh, I can't possibly leave now." He shook his head. "Your long-lost cousin leaving before Christmas? What would your prince think?"

"I shall tell him you were called away. Some sort of emergency."

"A monetary crisis, no doubt." A wry note sounded in his voice.

She ignored it. "Perhaps not, but something equally plausible." Speculation flashed in her eyes. "Will you? Leave, that is?"

"Oh, I wish I could, but . . ." He shook his head in a mournful manner. "I wouldn't miss Christmas at Millworth Manor for anything in the world."

"Imagine my surprise." She studied him closely. "Do I have your word you won't muck this up? That you will indeed help and not hinder my efforts? That you will act as a member of the family and behave accordingly?"

"Given the family members I have met thus far—"

"Grayson!"

"You have my word." He nodded in a solemn manner.

"Regardless, I don't trust you."

He gasped. "I am nothing if not trustworthy."

"Hah!" She heaved a resigned sigh. "I really have no choice in this, do I?"

He grinned. "None whatsoever."

"Very well, then." She smiled although the look in her eye was anything but welcoming. "Welcome home, *Cousin*."

"Excellent." He started toward the door. "I will fetch my bags and explain this interesting turn of events to Win and my uncle—"

"No!"

He turned back. "I have to say something to explain my absence."

"But you can't tell them the truth. Say anything but

the truth." Her gaze met his. "If you truly want to help me, start here. I cannot have the entire world knowing about this."

"You're right, of course." He nodded. "I shall try to think of something believable." He paused. "Perhaps a monetary crisis . . ."

"Get out!"

He laughed. "I shall return in time for tea."

"Oh, good, I was worried," she muttered.

He opened the door, then turned back to her. "Camille?"

"What now?" she snapped.

"Why are you so angry with me?" he asked quietly.

"Why? Aside from the fact that you have claimed to be a relation and are preparing to move into my mother's house and make my life difficult? For Christmas?" She huffed. "I can't imagine why that would anger me."

"No." He shook his head. "You were angry with me before that."

"Don't be absurd. I haven't seen you for . . ." She stared at him for a long moment; her gaze locked with his. "In truth, Grayson, I have been angry with you for a very long time."

He started to say something, anything, then thought better of it. He nodded and left the parlor. What was there to say, anyway? Not that he hadn't given some thought through the years as to exactly what he would say when at last they met again.

He had planned to point out his wealth, how far he had risen in the world, but he hadn't so much as mentioned it. And while, in many ways, proving himself to her had been a driving force in his life, he was old enough now—and hopefully wise enough, and most certainly confident enough—to see that it was no longer of primary concern. Then, of course, he had been distracted by the Christmas charade Camille was orchestrating. How on earth did she ever think she could manage to pull it off?

He had said he would help her, and he would, but he couldn't ignore the nagging suspicion that there was something not quite right about her prince. Her *perfect* prince. Although, if there were something amiss, you would think Camille of all people would recognize it. After all, in her childhood, there was more often than not a minor disposed monarch or an exiled member of an obscure royal family or an overthrown foreign duke in residence at Millworth Manor. Lady Briston collected homeless foreign nobility like his uncle collected rare manuscripts.

What if the prince was exactly like those lost tribes of Lady Briston's? What if his travels through Europe were not accompanied by any vestige of royal trappings because he could no longer afford it? What if her prince was perfect because he knew perfection was exactly what might appeal to a wealthy widow? Camille was so taken with him she had no doubt scarcely looked behind his entirely too perfect smile and his entirely too perfect hair and the entirely too perfect sparkle in his entirely too perfect eyes. Bloody hell. What woman wouldn't be taken with him? Camille had her own fortune, but perhaps what she wanted was the title. Or, possibly, the man. He was handsome enough and charming. Gray blew a frustrated breath.

He was being absurd and he well knew it. Aside from the eccentricity of traveling incognito—unusual, perhaps, but he had heard of much stranger behavior from royals—there was no real reason to be suspicious of the prince. Even if Camille wasn't in love with the royal, she was definitely smitten, and the prince was obviously taken with her. Gray wouldn't trust any man who looked at Camille the way Pruzinsky did.

And therein lay the problem.

Gray had honestly thought he had put Camille in the past. It was obvious now he had merely put her out of his head. And even then, hadn't she always been there, somewhere in the back of his mind? Wasn't she there when he danced with another woman, or shared a kiss in the moonlight with someone who might be the start of something new? Or when he had stared at the stars on a lonely night, wasn't she there, even if he hadn't acknowledged it? A whisper, a hint, a barely discernible lingering presence that surfaced when he least expected and made him long for something always just out of reach. Unnamed and undefined until now. He was a fool not to have recognized it before. But then, he had always been a fool when it came to her.

He should have realized he loved her, long before it had been too late. He should have returned when she was widowed. He should have . . . So many things he should have done. What he shouldn't have done was agree to help her carry off her farce. A farce designed to impress the man she wished to marry.

Still, residing in her house opened up all sorts of possibilities, as well as opportunities. He simply had to decide where he wanted them to lead. If, of course, he hadn't already.

He was more than halfway back to Fairborough Hall when the thought struck him that Camille's anger might not be a problem to overcome. Indeed, the very fact that she was angry at all might well be an indication of feelings she was not ready to admit. A woman didn't stay angry for eleven years at a man she didn't care about for eleven years.

Ah yes, there were all sorts of possibilities and opportunities ahead. If he'd learned nothing else in the past eleven years, he'd learned one did not ignore opportunity when it presented itself.

And Camille's Christmas farce was a once-in-a-lifetime opportunity.

Blasted, bloody beast of a man! Camille sank into the sofa and buried her face in her hands. How dare he insinuate himself back into her life after all these years?

Of course she was angry with him. Why wouldn't she be? She rose to her feet and paced the floor. Eleven years ago in this very room, he had declared that he loved her and then he had kissed her. It was a kiss that, in spite of her determination, had lingered in her mind, in her heart, ever since that moment. A kiss that had changed everything.

Next to Beryl, Grayson had been her dearest friend, and she had once thought he always would be. But then he had said he loved her. It was absurd, of course, and she had told him so. She'd told him the love he felt for her was that of one friend for another. He had argued that it was entirely different. That he hadn't realized the difference until he was about to lose her. Nonsense, she'd said. Why, she was about to be wed and he was being silly. He was simply trying to save her from marrying without the kind of love she'd always said she wanted. He'd then made an absurd charge that she would marry him if he were wealthy and titled. She'd snapped at that comment and said, as he wasn't, it was a moot point. She'd regretted it the moment the words were out of her mouth, but it was too late. It was as if she had slapped him, hard. She'd ignored the look in his eyes because she couldn't bear that she had hurt him and said she was quite fond of Harold and they would have a lovely life together. She still recalled how Grayson had stared at her for an endless moment and then nodded, wished her well and took his leave.

Camille had collapsed onto this very sofa then and noted the odd tremble in her hands and the lump in her throat and the shock that held her in its grip. And she admitted to herself for the first time that, of course, she loved him. She had always loved him. But he had never behaved toward her as anything other than a friend, treated her as a sister really. She had long before recognized and accepted that there could never be anything between them but friendship; even if she did, on occasion, wish it could be otherwise. And until he had put his feelings into words, she had not really recognized her own. But it was too late. She was to marry Harold. He was the type of man she'd been raised to marry and she had given her word, after all. Besides, he was a very nice man and she would not have hurt him for anything in the world.

But if a man truly loved a woman, would he give up so easily? Wouldn't he fight for her? Wouldn't he appear at the last possible moment and sweep her away? Like a prince in a fairy tale? And wouldn't another very nice man see the truth of it all and graciously step aside?

But Harold had done no such thing, because her prince had never appeared. And so she and Harold were wed, and she had put Grayson out of her head and her heart with a ruthless determination. And if, through the years, she would catch a glimpse of a man on a London street who resembled Grayson and her heart would leap, she would ignore it. And if, on occasion, late in the night, just before sleep, his smile would appear in her mind's eye and his laughter would ring in her ears, she ruthlessly pushed it aside. And if, now and again, she would dream of a single kiss, it had no place in the light of day.

Of course she was angry. He had claimed to love her, but then he had disappeared so completely from her life, it was as if he had never been there at all. When Harold had died and she was free, she had thought that perhaps . . . No, she had every right to be angry. Or maybe she had no right at all. She hadn't fought for him either. Nonetheless, the anger remained.

"If you continue to pace like that, you shall certainly create a trough in the floor."

Camille stopped short. Beryl stood inside the door of the parlor, studying her sister.

"You didn't even hear me come in. Whatever is the matter?" She winced. "Not that I can't think of any number of things that might be wrong, given the nonsense we are all embroiled in. And have you spent more than a few minutes with Mr. Henderson? Although a few minutes was all that was necessary. My God, Camille, he's worse than Uncle Basil. The man tried to pinch my—"

"Grayson's back."

Beryl's eyes widened. "Grayson Elliott?"

"Do you know another Grayson?"

Shock colored Beryl's face. She was the only person Camille had ever told about Grayson's ill-timed declaration; she was the only one who knew how it had crushed Camille's heart. "What do you mean Grayson's back?"

"Exactly what I said." Camille drew a deep breath. "He's back from wherever it is he has been—"

"America," Beryl murmured.

"He was here. He met the prince and he introduced himself as . . ." Camille could barely say the words aloud. "As our cousin."

Beryl gasped. "Our what?"

"You heard me." Camille groaned. "He said he was our cousin, come to join us for Christmas."

"Good Lord." Beryl stared. "Where is he now?"

"He left to fetch his bags." Camille rubbed her forehead. When had her head started to ache? No doubt the same moment she had looked into the parlor and seen Grayson. It would have been so much easier had she simply been mad.

"He wouldn't want to miss tea." The corners of Beryl's lips twitched.

"Go on, then," Camille said sharply. "Say whatever it is you're thinking. I know you want to. You can barely restrain yourself."

"I . . ." Beryl shook her head, then burst into laughter. Long, hard and totally inappropriate hilarity.

Camille folded her arms over her chest and glared at her twin.

"I am sorry." Beryl could barely choke out the words through her laughter. Camille's jaw clenched. "But you must admit, the addition of your long-lost love—"

"He most certainly is not!"

Beryl ignored her. "Grayson's involvement completes the cast in a manner that, well . . ." Again she shook with uncontrollable mirth.

"This is not amusing!"

"No." Beryl sniffed and wiped her eyes. "Of course not." She inhaled a steadying breath and made an obvious attempt to control herself. "So what do you intend to do about our cousin?"

"Nothing." Camille shook her head. "There's nothing I can do, really. He has already introduced himself as our cousin."

"How did this happen?"

"I'm not entirely sure. He met Mrs. Montgomery-Wells, who apparently does not know her first name.

And then Miss Murdock thought he was another actor and confided everything. And one thing led to another. . . ." She heaved a heartfelt sigh. "But he has promised to behave accordingly and to lend me his assistance as well."

"Has he?"

"He seems quite sincere."

"No doubt."

Camille narrowed her eyes. "What are you thinking now?"

"Nothing, darling, nothing at all. Except . . . perhaps . . ."

"Yes?"

Beryl grinned. "I'm just dying to see what the next act in your little Christmas pageant will reveal."

"As am I, Beryl." A grim note sounded in Camille's voice. "As am I."

Six

"Prescott," Grayson called the moment he strode through the doors of Fairborough Hall.

"Yes, sir?" The butler appeared at once, seemingly from nowhere. Gray bit back a grin. Fortesque could take lessons from Prescott. "Have my bags been unpacked?"

"I believe so, sir."

"In that case, please have one repacked."

"Very well." Prescott paused. "Are you leaving again so soon, sir?"

"Just for a few days. I'll be staying at Millworth Manor."

"Ah yes, of course, sir," the older man said in a sage manner. Odd, but then Prescott's comportment often implied vast wisdom, as if he knew everything. Admittedly, he usually did, at least when it pertained to the Elliott household.

"My cousin?"

"The library, sir."

"Excellent." Gray nodded and turned toward the library.

Win stood in the open doorway, leaning against the doorjamb, arms folded over his chest. "What do you mean, you're staying at Millworth Manor?"

"I mean"—he waved his cousin into the library, joined him, then closed the door behind them—"that I am spending Christmas at Millworth Manor."

"Well, well, are you now?" Win studied him for a moment. "I suspect I'll need something stronger than brandy for this."

"Pour two."

Win pulled a bottle of fine Scottish whisky from the bottom drawer of the desk where Uncle Roland had long kept it as Aunt Margaret, while known to indulge in wine and the occasional glass of brandy, did not approve of harder spirits. Nonetheless, she knew exactly where Uncle Roland kept his whisky, and he knew she knew.

"So"—Win filled two glasses—"I gather the baked goods were appreciated."

Gray accepted a glass and sank down into one of the leather wing chairs facing the fireplace. "You might say that."

"While Cook does make excellent scones, they have never elicited responses like this before. Which does indicate a welcoming Christmas basket has nothing to do with the matter at hand." Win settled in the chair matching Gray's and considered his cousin. "Well?"

"Well, what?" Gray grinned.

"You know 'well, what?' Are you going to tell me everything, or are you going to make me guess?" Win raised his glass to the other man. "Surely, you remember that I have a very fertile imagination."

"Not this fertile. Even you could not conceive of this."

"My, my, now I am intrigued."

"Can you keep a secret?"

"Depends on the secret, I would think. My third fiancée used to say I was very good at keeping the best secrets and not good at all at keeping everyday sort of secrets."

"Third fiancée?" Gray raised a brow. "You never wrote to me of a third fiancée."

"But I do believe I mentioned in one of my letters that I had begun to think telling you I was to wed was somehow bad luck." He sipped his whisky. "As it turns out, apparently not."

Gray stared. "How many fiancées have you had?"

"Officially?" Win grinned.

"Whatever you prefer."

"Just three." He thought for a moment. "As far as I can recall, although you should not hold me to that."

"I suspect you and I need to have a long talk about all those things that were omitted from your letters."

"No doubt. But as you have returned for the foreseeable future, there will be time. Long evenings sitting by the fire with Father's good whisky and nothing to do but rehash the last eleven years." Win shuddered. "Sounds entirely too domestic for my way of thinking. Still, I imagine your adventures are much more stimulating than mine have been."

"I wouldn't wager on that." Gray laughed. Lord, he had missed this man.

"And speaking of returning home . . ." Win eyed him curiously. "Why are you staying at Millworth Manor?"

Gray considered the question. On his return ride, he had tried to think of something believable to explain his stay at the manor. Unfortunately, nothing came to mind. Nothing that made sense, that is. Still, if he trusted no one else in the world, he trusted Win. "I need your word that you will not repeat to anyone what I am about to tell you."

"That good, is it?"

"Better."

"Very well, then." Curiosity sparked in Win's eyes. "I shall carry your secret to my grave."

"It's not really my secret."

"Even better."

"Your word, then."

"Such as it is." Win shrugged. "You have it."

"Well . . ." Gray sipped his whisky and thought for a moment. He wasn't sure where to begin. The whole thing was so preposterous. "Camille has set her cap for a prince."

"That comes as no surprise."

"She's not quite as shallow as you think."

"She couldn't possibly be." Win's opinion of Camille and her sisters was nothing new. Nor was Gray's defense of her.

"Beryl was always much shallower than her sister."

"As they look exactly alike and, to my observation, behave in exactly the same manner, explain to me, yet again, why she isn't as shallow as her twin."

"You don't know her the way I do."

"Correct me if I'm wrong, but isn't this the woman who broke your heart to marry someone with a title and fortune?"

"In hindsight . . ." Gray chose his words with care. "What should she have done? She was about to be married."

"Even so—"

"She's still angry with me," Gray said.

"*She* is angry with *you*?" Win said slowly.

Gray nodded. "Still."

"After eleven years, *she* is still angry with *you.*" Win's brow rose. "How very interesting. I didn't know she had any right to be angry with you at all." He studied his cousin for a long, thoughtful moment. "I thought you were the wounded party."

"I was," Gray said staunchly.

"I thought you and she were in love." Win studied his cousin closely. "And that she chose someone else over you because he had money and you did not."

"She did."

Skepticism glittered in Win's eyes.

"I was in love with her."

"And was she in love with you?"

"I thought so. No, I knew so." Gray blew a long breath. "Admittedly, we had never spoken of love and she had no idea of my feelings until that very day."

"She never said she loved you as well?"

"No, but—"

Astonishment widened Win's eyes. "You told this woman, who had long considered you her friend, that you loved her on the day before her wedding?"

"I told you all that at the time."

"Not exactly." Win shook his head. "You only told me that you loved her and she refused to marry you because you had no prospects."

"That's what happened." Perhaps he had not fully explained everything all those years ago.

"I thought there was more between you. The way you talked about her and your behavior, you led me to believe you and she had some sort of understanding."

"I never said—"

"No wonder she's angry." Win shook his head. *"Still."*

"I think it's a good sign," Gray said.

"A sign of what?"

"Of her feelings."

"It seems to me her feelings are those of anger." He sipped his whisky. "Justifiable, I might add."

Gray choked. "Justifiable? How can you say that?"

"Oh, let me see." Sarcasm colored Win's words. "You sprang this on her without warning just as she was about to marry someone else. And then you left."

"I thought it best." Although at this moment, it did sound rather stupid.

"To leave her and your family and your country?"

"Well, yes, but—"

"After declaring your love, you made no effort to speak to her again that day or the next. Correct?"

"It seemed pointless." A defensive note sounded in Gray's voice. He had recognized his foolishness years ago. It wasn't at all pleasant to have his cousin now point it out.

"Furthermore, you have made no effort to contact her for eleven years. Is that correct as well?"

"Yes." Gray forced a cool note to his voice. "As I said, it seemed pointless."

Win took another swallow and studied his cousin. "Has it never occurred to you that this abrupt declaration of yours might have been so unexpected as to leave her stunned? Speechless?"

"She did manage to get a few words out," he snapped. "She did admit she would marry me if I had money."

"Did she?"

"Not in those exact words, perhaps . . ." Indeed, as Gray thought back, he had been the one to say she would marry him if he had prospects. She had simply said, as he didn't, what was the point?

"So you asked her to marry you instead of Lord Lydingham?"

"No." Gray resisted the urge to squirm in his seat. "But I intended to."

"My dear cousin. It appears you have a great deal to make up for."

"I am well aware of that."

"So"—Win swirled the whisky in his glass—"now that you have seen her again, do you still say you have put her in the past?"

"I don't know."

Win cast him a skeptical glance.

Gray shrugged. "Perhaps not."

"I see."

Gray frowned. "What do you see?"

"Why are you staying at Millworth Manor, and what does Camille wanting a prince have to do with it?"

Gray started to point out Win had changed the subject; then thought better of it. The subject of his feelings for Camille was best left alone for now. Still, he had known the moment he looked into Camille's blue eyes again that something still lingered between them. She could deny it as much now as she had then . . . but then she never really had, had she? She'd never told him she didn't love him. At once his mood lightened.

"Camille's prince is eager to experience an English Christmas the way it is portrayed in literature. He's quite a fan of Mr. Dickens. So she is determined to provide him with that proper English Christmas, as well as a proper English family to go along with it."

"Where is she going to get one?"

Gray leaned forward in his chair and met his cousin's gaze. "She's hired one."

Win stared. "She's what?"

"You were right, Lady Briston and Delilah are in Paris. So Camille has hired a group of actors to play the parts of her family, as well as all the other servants."

Win gasped. "My God."

Gray nodded. "That was my—"

"That's brilliant!"

"Brilliant?" Gray drew his brows together. "It's mad is what it is."

"That too." Win waved off the comment. "But no less brilliant for the insanity of it."

"I suppose one could look at it that way," Gray said wryly.

"And you will have a front-row seat at what will surely be the best farce of the season." Win paused. "Which brings us back to how you have that seat."

"It's quite simple, really." Gray settled back in his chair and raised his glass. "I am to play the role of her cousin, visiting for Christmas."

"Camille wants you to be a part of this?"

"Absolutely not. She's furious about it, but I convinced her I could be of help."

"I still don't understand—"

"I'm not sure exactly, but somehow, when I was introduced to her prince, the words just came out of my mouth as if of their own accord." Gray grinned. "It's the spirit of the theater, you know. When one forgets one's lines or has no lines to start with, one finds it necessary to improvise." His grin widened. "I improvised and did a damn fine job of it, if I do say so myself."

"Good Lord." Laughter danced in Win's eyes. "May I be a cousin too?"

"No," Gray said firmly. "One unexpected cousin is enough."

"Then I could be her brother." He set down his glass and jumped to his feet. "Her long-lost brother returning home at last for Christmas. Oh, the drama, the pathos. I would be excellent in the part." He swept a bow to an imaginary audience. "I can hear the applause now."

"No." Gray laughed.

"I would have been magnificent on the stage, you know." Win sank back into his chair. "And I would like to offer my assistance in this endeavor. Whether to Camille or to you, I'm not sure."

Gray narrowed his eyes. "Why?"

"Because you're my cousin, my dearest friend, even if you have treated me abominably—"

Gray snorted.

"And I only wish to see you happy. If you have now decided, after all this time, to truly pursue this woman—as you failed, again abominably, once before—then you have my full support and all the assistance I can render."

"You have my thanks, but should I decide to do so, I am confident I can manage without—"

"Furthermore," Win continued, "I have not been as cordial to Camille these past eleven years as I should have been because I was under the mistaken impression that she had toyed with your affections. Not that I have had many opportunities, mind you. Camille and I have only seen one another in passing at one social event or another. I have long thought she was actively avoiding me." He shook his head. "Now I understand why."

"I was an idiot, I admit it."

"As long as you admit it." Win studied him closely. "Given your accomplishments, I suspect you are no longer an idiot, although that may not be the case when it comes to Camille. At least there is hope. You have insinuated yourself into her household under the guise of lending your assistance. That's rather clever."

Gray smiled modestly.

"Now what can I do to help?"

"Nothing, really, I . . ." Gray paused. "There is something . . ."

"Oh, I do hope I get to wear a costume." Win grinned.

"Nothing like that, but this prince of Camille's . . ."

"Yes?"

"I don't trust him."

"Because he has interest of a prurient nature in the fair Lady Lydingham?"

"Not entirely, although I admit I would be distrustful of any man who looks at her the way he does." Gray paused to pull his thoughts together. He was probably being absurd about Pruzinsky. Still, there was something about the man that did not sit well with Gray. His instincts had served him in the past, and instinct now told him something was not right. "He travels alone, without retainers or accompaniment of any sort, claims it's a tradition in his family."

"And this is a genuine royal?"

"Apparently." Gray nodded. "Prince Nikolai Pruzinsky, of the Kingdom of Greater Avalonia."

" 'The Kingdom of Greater Avalonia'?" Win frowned. "Are you sure?"

"That's what he said."

"That is interesting." Win got to his feet, crossed the room and studied a shelf of books.

"What are you looking for?"

"Give me a moment." Win ran his finger along a row of books. "This is it." He pulled a book from the shelf and leafed through it.

"What are you looking for?"

"Patience, Cousin," Win murmured. "Aha! Here it is."

"What?"

"I thought so."

"Thought what?" Impatience drew Gray's brows together.

"The Kingdom of Greater Avalonia was annexed by Russia nearly seventy years ago after the death of the last king." Win scanned the page. "It says here his son, Crown Prince Alexei, renounced all claims to the throne after Russia annexed the country. A wise move, no doubt, as Russia would certainly crush a small kingdom without any hesitation."

"So there is no Kingdom of Greater Avalonia?" Gray stared. "No castle overlooking snow-covered mountains in December or green valleys in the spring?"

"I imagine the mountains and valleys are still there," Win said absently. "Apparently, the crown prince had a younger brother." Win raised his gaze from the book in his hand and looked pointedly at his cousin. "Prince Nikolai."

"Then he is legitimate," Gray said slowly.

"Not unless he's a descendant." Win snapped the book closed. "This Prince Nikolai would be well into his eighties."

"But there is no Kingdom of Greater Avalonia?"

"So it would seem."

"Camille thinks she's going to marry him and live in his castle in Avalonia." Gray tossed back the last of his drink and stood. "She needs to know the truth."

"Perhaps, but you don't really know the truth as of yet, do you?"

"Of course I do. You just said—"

"I said his country no longer exists, whether or not he is really a prince is another matter altogether." Win slipped the book back into its spot on the shelf. "And, as Camille's mother, through the years, has long welcomed homeless royals, you have no idea what Camille does and does not know about this particular prince. Even though his country is gone, it doesn't mean he's penniless. He might well have a royal fortune. Many deposed monarchs do, you know. Family money spirited out of a country as a precaution against revolution. For that matter, he may well have a castle somewhere in Europe as well." He shook his head. "If I have learned nothing else from four fiancées—"

"Four?" Gray stared. "I thought it was three."

"Three, four, one loses count." Win shrugged. "As I was saying, I know women. They do not like to have their mistakes pointed out to them, nor do they like to be proved wrong. However, as you will be staying in Millworth Manor, it should be easy for you to discern the truth."

"And if he is a fraud"—Gray narrowed his eyes—"I shall make her aware of it."

"And she'll be so grateful, she'll throw herself into your arms?"

"That had occurred to me."

"You weren't listening, were you?" Win cast him a pitying look. "Do you wish to win her affections?"

"I really hadn't considered it. I simply wish to . . . to protect her. As one friend would look out for the best interests of another. As her friend, I feel it's, oh, a duty on my part."

Win's brow rose in disbelief. "A duty?"

"You may rest assured that is my only desire." Gray hesitated. "Admittedly, there is something as yet unfinished between us, but there's nothing more to it than that."

Win stared. "I don't believe you."

"Believe this, then." He leaned closer and met his cousin's gaze directly. "The possibility of winning Camille's heart is the furthest thing from my mind. Indeed, until I saw her again, I thought anything between the two of us was all over and done with and in the past."

"You don't lie well, you know."

Gray sighed. "Certainly, there might be some affection, but no more than that of, oh, a brother."

"Are you sure?"

Gray paused, then nodded. "Quite."

"Don't muck with her life until you are." A warning sounded in his cousin's voice. "You did it once, don't do it again."

And she was still angry.

"Does she know you are now quite wealthy?"

He shook his head. "I don't think so. Nor do I wish her to know."

"Why?"

"I'd rather money didn't play a part in this." He shrugged. "That's all."

"I see. And isn't that interesting?"

"Why?"

"It just is." Win paused. "Well, regardless of whether you wish to be her friend or something more, the last thing that will improve your standing in Camille's eyes is for you to tell her she's been deceived by another man. You need to make her aware of the truth without making her feel like a fool. You were her friend once, you need to be her friend now. At least until you decide whether or not friendship is enough."

"That makes a certain amount of sense, I suppose." In spite of his words, was friendship really all he wanted? Still, Win was right. For now, Gray would be her friend.

"Well, then." Win crossed the room, picked up his glass and drained the last of his whisky. "Your bag should be packed by now. And we should be off."

" 'We'?" Gray said slowly. "What do you mean *we?*"

"Why, I am coming with you, of course."

"Camille does not need another cousin or a brother."

"While I heartily disagree, and I hate to pass up an opportunity to be part of this theatrical enterprise, I have no intention of adding to the cast." Win smiled an altogether too mischievous smile. It did not bode well. "I am simply paying a call on Lady Lydingham and her family to wish them felicitations of the season. As any good neighbor would do."

"You could have delivered the basket," Gray pointed out.

"And then where would you be?" Win started for the door. "Besides, I should like to meet this prince. I am an excellent judge of character, you know."

"As evidenced by the growing number of fiancées," Gray said mildly.

"Exactly." Win nodded. "But I am most astute when it comes to men."

"You would have to be."

Upon reflection, it wasn't a bad idea to get Win's observations of the prince. Besides, the theatrical machinations at Millworth Manor were just too delicious not to share.

"Perhaps on our way, you could tell me just how many betrothals you have had and why none of them led to matrimony."

Win laughed. Gray grinned. It was indeed good to be home. Especially now that, at long last, he had realized what he wanted. Camille's little Christmas play was exactly what he needed. While she was busy trying to control her cast and impress the prince, he would be busy gaining her forgiveness. As for what happened after that, well, that remained to be seen.

And the curtain was about to go up.

Seven

"I think it's all going surprisingly well, don't you?" Beryl said in an aside to her sister.

"It's only the first day," Camille said more to herself than her sister. Still, Beryl was right, at least thus far.

The tableau in front of them did look rather perfect. Nikolai sat on the sofa between Mrs. Montgomery-Wells and Miss Murdock. Both women gave him their utmost attention; even if, at any given moment, the attention of one or both of them was a bit more flirtatious than Camille would have preferred. Why, she might as well have had Mother here if impropriety was what she wanted, although Nikolai certainly didn't seem to mind. Mr. Henderson sat in a nearby chair and was—all things considered—rather more charming than she had expected. He played the part of Uncle Basil with enthusiasm, even if the stories of his military exploits were vaguely Shakespearean in tone, as was the actor's manner. Nikolai didn't seem to notice. He was, however, smiling and nodding quite a bit, which struck Camille as beneficial. After all, he couldn't question what he didn't understand.

"I don't think it's wise to leave them by themselves."

"Nonsense," Beryl scoffed. "We're scarcely ten feet away." The sisters stood near the tea cart, which had been placed, at Beryl's direction, closer to the door than to the guests. It was, no doubt, an effort to provide a discreet method of escape. One could simply fill one's cup and slip out of the room without any undue effort. Why, one would think Beryl had absolutely no confidence in Camille's plan at all. "And I, for one, needed a momentary respite from inane conversation. I find it surprisingly wearing to watch every word I say, as well as every word everyone else says."

"I remember the winter of '78," Mr. Henderson began. "Damnably snowy that year. Why, I recall . . ."

"As long as the conversation is confined to the weather," Camille murmured.

" 'Blow, blow, thou winter wind,' " Mr. Henderson continued. " 'Thou art not so unkind as man's ingratitude.' "

"Shakespeare," Mrs. Montgomery-Wells said cheerfully. "From *As You Like It*, I believe." The woman had no trouble remembering obscure quotes written hundreds of years ago, but her name was an entirely different matter.

"And perhaps Shakespeare," Beryl said. "That seems safe enough. Besides, we can't be with them every minute. Like any good director of plays, you must step aside at some point and trust in your cast. They are professionals, after all."

"One can only hope."

"Even the food is better than expected." Beryl filled her cup from the pot on the tea cart.

"The food is excellent," Camille said with relief.

She had considered at least hiring a real cook, but Mr. Fortesque had assured her that his wife was a far better cook than she was an actress. While Mr. Fortesque's troupe might not be the most accomplished actors in England, it was a relief to know he had been fairly accurate as to their abilities as servants. Although the very idea of former servants turned actors now in the role of servants made her head swim.

"All in all, I think it's going quite smoothly." A confident note sounded in Camille's voice. She wondered where it came from.

"That alone should be cause for concern. As you noted, it is only the first day," Beryl said wryly. "Still, no need to borrow trouble."

"No, of course not." Camille blew a long breath.

There would be trouble enough when their *cousin* returned. Why on earth Grayson had decided to become a part of all this was beyond her. No doubt he was just trying to be annoying, which then begged the question of why.

Her gaze settled on Nikolai. He was everything she'd ever wanted. Handsome and charming and perfect and, well, everything a prince should be. It was as if he had stepped directly from the pages of one of the fairy stories she'd devoured as a girl, tales of dashing princes rescuing fair maidens from fire-breathing dragons. But he was a real prince with a real kingdom and she was a grown woman now, a widow of independent means. Certainly not a fragile, delicate creature that needed to be rescued. Not by Grayson and not even by a prince, real or fictional.

Then why on earth was she so determined to have a prince at all? The thought popped into her head without warning.

"I met a grand duke once, you know," Mrs. Montgomery-Wells's words drifted across the room. "Charming man. Do you know him, Your Highness?"

"I cannot say," Nikolai said with a smile. "There are any number of grand dukes, I should think. Which one are you speaking of?"

"Let me see." Mrs. Montgomery-Wells frowned; then her expression brightened. "The tall one! That's right, he was the tall one. Quite dashing, I must say."

"Come now, Millicent," Mr. Henderson chided.

"Bernadette," Beryl said under her breath.

"Florence," the older actress said.

"Are you sure?" Miss Murdock asked.

"Absolutely." Mrs. Montgomery-Wells nodded. Camille winced.

"As I was about to point out," Mr. Henderson continued, "just because one is a prince does not mean one knows every other prince or, in this case, grand duke who is floating about the continent. Isn't that so, Your Highness?"

"Well, I—" Nikolai began.

"I knew a grand duke once," Miss Murdock said thoughtfully. "Or at least he said he was a grand duke."

Mrs. Montgomery-Wells shook her head. "You can't always be certain, my dear. One should always ask for credentials of some sort. They very often carry, oh, medals and the like. Great, gaudy things worn on sashes. Most impressive." She turned toward Nikolai. "Isn't that right, Your Highness?"

"Please, Lady Briston," Nikolai began. "As we are among friends, I would much prefer not to be addressed by royal titles, 'Your Highness' and such."

Mrs. Montgomery-Wells sucked in a sharp breath. "My word, Your Highness, we couldn't possibly. You are a prince, after all. It wouldn't be the least bit proper."

"Surely, Lady Briston," Nikolai said in a kind manner. "As I am traveling as Count Pruzinsky, and it is Christmas, we can relax formality."

"But, Your Highness"—Mrs. Montgomery-Wells leaned forward and patted Nikolai's hand—"we all have roles to play and yours is the prince. If we do not play our roles as scripted, why, they'll be nothing but confusion and . . . and anarchy."

"Can't have anarchy," Mr. Henderson said darkly, as if hordes of anarchists would stream through the doors of the parlor at any minute, should formality lapse and the prince be addressed as anything less than royal.

Nikolai stared. Obviously, the poor man was too confused even to smile and nod.

Beryl sighed. "We'd best—"

"So much for everything going smoothly," Camille muttered. She and Beryl quickly crossed the room and returned to their chairs.

"Mother," she began in a firm tone, "we do want Nikolai to feel at home here. As he cannot be with his own family in his own country this year at Christmas, it would be lovely if we made him feel as much a part of ours as possible. You don't call *Delilah* Lady Hargate or *Beryl* Lady Dunwell." Camille emphasized her sisters' names in the hope that the actress might remember somebody's name. "And you certainly don't call me Lady Lydingham."

Mrs. Montgomery-Wells's gaze slid from Camille to Beryl. She lowered her voice and spoke in an aside to the prince. "They look so much alike, don't you agree? Why, I can scarcely tell them apart. It's most confusing."

Nikolai smiled weakly and nodded.

"Although that one"—the older woman nodded at Beryl—"has a look in her eye as if she is keeping a most amusing secret, whereas the other one"—Mrs. Montgomery-Wells's eyes narrowed—"she looks as if she is about to explode in some sort of nervous fit."

Beryl coughed in an obvious attempt to keep from laughing.

Camille's teeth clenched. Mrs. Montgomery-Wells was very close to the truth.

Mr. Henderson sighed. "Now, now, Millicent—"

"Florence," Miss Murdock said.

"Eloise," Beryl offered.

Camille cast her a scathing look. Beryl smiled innocently.

"Constance," Mrs. Montgomery-Wells said firmly.

Camille bit back a groan. Her comment to her sister pounded in her head like a bad refrain. Or a curse: *"It's only the first day."*

"As I was about to say," Mr. Henderson began again, "as he is our guest, and we are among friends—"

"Family," Camille said.

"Family, then." Mr. Henderson nodded. "If the prince does not wish to be addressed as 'Your Highness,' then we should honor his wishes. Even if 'yet looks he like a king.' "

"Richard the Second," Miss Murdock noted.

Mr. Henderson favored her with an approving look. For her knowledge of Shakespeare, no doubt, and not for her ample bosom, which threatened to escape from the altogether too low cut of her bodice. Still, didn't his gaze seem directed somewhat lower than her face? Camille shuddered at the thought that she had traded one lascivious uncle for another. Although, admittedly, the man was playing his part accurately.

"But I digress," Mr. Henderson continued. "I once met a prince in India, son of the ruling raj of the province, who felt exactly the same way about traveling sans retainers or . . ."

Camille breathed a sigh of relief. If nothing else,

the actor could be counted on to fill the conversation with relatively interesting anecdotes about whatever happened to cross his mind. Whether they were real or imagined, Camille didn't particularly care. In that respect too, he was much like the genuine Uncle Basil.

"Admittedly, on occasion the prince's penchant for . . ."

And just like with the genuine Uncle Basil's stories, Camille allowed her mind to drift. As much as she hated to admit it, even to herself, Grayson was right. This scheme of hers was not at all well thought out. Once again she had jumped into something without giving it due consideration. Of course this was on a scale rather larger than usual. Typically, her ill-advised impulses leaned toward rash purchases of things she couldn't possibly use but seemed exciting at the time. There was the life-size mechanical monkey, which had struck her as charming when she had purchased it, but sitting in her parlor was really rather unsettling. The eyes did tend to follow one. There was the ill-fated expedition she had invested in to recover the lost gold of South America. It was most exciting, even if, as it turned out, not entirely legitimate. Then, of course, there were all those llamas . . . and the incident at Brighton, which she refused to think about. In each and every instance, it had seemed like such a good idea at the time.

And now she wanted a prince, even if she was no longer sure why. Damn Grayson, anyway. He was the one who had put doubts into her head. Nikolai was not at all like the monkey or the lost treasure or the llamas. This was not an impulse on her part. She had always wanted a prince; and when a prince unexpectedly walks into one's life, and one seized that opportunity, it's not impulse. No, it's fate. Certainly, she hadn't known Nikolai for long, but they would have the rest of their lives to better know each other. Wasn't that what marriage was for? Besides, knowing someone well—as well as one person could know another, really, or thought one did—did not ensure there would be no startling revelations—revelations that one was not prepared for. Did not expect. Had never dared to dream of . . .

Nonsense. Grayson's abrupt appearance had simply muddled her mind. Confused her as to what she wanted in life. There was nothing more significant to the odd thoughts that kept popping up in her mind than that. And if he was determined to become part of her effort to give Nikolai the perfect Christmas with the perfect family, well, it was the least he could do to make amends.

For saying he loved her or for not doing anything about loving her? She ignored the unwanted question.

"Psst."

A soft hissing sound caught her attention and she glanced toward the doorway. Fortesque stood just outside the open parlor doors, beckoning to her. She mumbled an excuse and rose to her feet. A moment later, she closed the parlor doors behind her and glared at her alleged butler.

She kept her voice low. "You do realize real butlers are not supposed to go *'psst'*?"

"Forgive me, Lady Lydingham, but I didn't know how else to attract your attention." He leaned closer in a confidential manner. "The gentleman who was here earlier, Mr. Elliott, has returned. And he has"—Fortesque closed his eyes for a moment as if praying for strength—"luggage."

"Blast it all, I was hoping he'd change his mind." She huffed. "There's nothing to be done about it, I suppose."

"Who is he?"

"He is a bloody nuisance, that's who he is. However, for the moment"—she struggled for calm—"he is to play the role of my cousin."

"Lady Lydingham." Fortesque squared his shoulders and raised his chin, making him seem substantially taller, if possible. "If you had need of yet another player, I would certainly have been able to provide you with someone well suited to the role."

"Like Mrs. Montgomery-Wells?"

"She is a well-seasoned actress."

"She may be well seasoned, but her goose overcooked years ago!"

He frowned down at her. "I did tell you she was a fine actress in her day."

"When exactly was her day?" Camille snapped.

"Do keep in mind, Lady Lydingham, that expertise on the stage takes years to develop. And furthermore, you gave us very little time to rehearse."

"Even so, Mr. Fortesque—"

"Just Fortesque, my lady, I am in character," he said in a lofty manner.

"You are insane is what you are!"

He gasped. "I daresay—"

"No, *Fortesque*, my apologies." She heaved a frustrated sigh. "I am the one who is obviously quite mad to think for a moment that we could pull off this farce."

"Lady Lydingham." He drew himself up and stared down his nose at her. "I have never abandoned a performance before the final act. However, if you are unhappy, you may pay us what we agreed upon and we shall take our leave."

"Oh no, you won't." She shook her head. "We are indeed in this *together* until the final curtain falls, if, of course, you do wish to be paid."

He hesitated, then nodded. "Very well."

"But after dinner, when the rest of us have retired, you will take your principal players and rehearse them again. Especially Mrs. Montgomery-Wells."

"I shall see what can be done to improve her performance. And that of the others," he added.

"Thank you."

"And what of your *cousin?*"

"Have a room prepared for him. As far away from my rooms as possible." She thought for a moment. "Put him in the west wing. It's the oldest part of the house, lovely in the summer but quite drafty in the winter, and the heating has always been insufficient. That should serve him well."

"Now, now," a familiar voice sounded behind her. "That certainly isn't in the spirit of Christmas."

She spun around to find Grayson grinning with amusement, accompanied by his equally smug cousin. She narrowed her gaze. "What are you doing here?"

"I have come to offer my assistance," Lord Stillwell said in a gracious manner, which nonetheless set her teeth on edge.

"Why?" she snapped.

Stillwell paused. "Let us just say it is in the manner of a debt long overdue."

"I have no idea what you're talking about." Indeed, on those rare occasions in the last eleven years when she and Stillwell had crossed paths, he had treated her with as much disdain as she had treated him.

"Nor do you need to." Stillwell cast her the engaging smile she remembered from years ago. It struck her that he was a casualty of the rift between her and Grayson. A pity, really; he had always been most amusing and she had always liked him. "The past is over and done with, and I am here to lend whatever help you may need. In the spirit of friendship and, of course, Christmas."

She studied him suspiciously. "I don't trust you, my lord."

Grayson chuckled.

Stillwell gasped in feigned dismay. "That's not at all fair, Lady Lydingham." He grinned. "Wise perhaps, but not fair."

"I can assure you, Win has only your best interests at heart," Grayson said.

"I find that difficult to believe." She sniffed. "As for you . . . you promised not to tell anyone about this."

"Not exactly. I said I would try to think of something plausible to explain my stay here, and, well, I couldn't." Grayson shrugged apologetically.

"You, no doubt, did not try very hard."

"On the contrary," Stillwell said. "He didn't say a word for, oh"—he glanced at Grayson—"a good ten minutes, would you say?"

Grayson nodded. "Perhaps even fifteen."

"There you are, Camille, he held his tongue for fifteen minutes. Perhaps more."

"And I think it was more," Grayson said.

"You really can't ask for more than that, especially given the magnitude of your venture here." Stillwell flashed that smile of his again. Fortunately, she had long been immune to it.

"I can and I did," she said sharply. "And it's 'Lady Lydingham.' "

"Come now, Camille," Stillwell said smoothly. "I've known you since you were a child. I've always called you Camille, just as you have always called me Winfield. You can't expect me to change now." He glanced at Grayson. "Can she?"

Grayson shook his head in a somber manner. "I would think not."

Stillwell glanced at Fortesque. "Can she?"

The actor stared. Good Lord, he'd probably smile and nod at any minute. "I couldn't say, my lord, but probably not, no."

Camille shot him a scathing glance and he cringed.

"There you have it." Stillwell grinned. "Camille."

Fortesque lowered his voice and inclined his head toward Camille. "About the room—"

"Ah yes, Fortesque," Grayson began. "I'm afraid the west wing won't do at all. I hate drafts."

Camille glared.

"And I was informed by one of your"—Grayson cleared his throat—"footmen that the room across the hall from Lady Lydingham's is vacant. I instructed him to put my bags there."

Camille choked. "I scarcely think—"

"Now, now, what would the prince think if your dear cousin was exiled to a room where he would likely catch his death of cold?" Grayson shook his head forlornly. "Besides, I can't sleep if the room is too cold. And if I don't get enough sleep, well, there is always the possibility I might reveal something I shouldn't in the course of idle conversation with the—"

"Fine! Sleep wherever you want!"

Stillwell grinned. She ignored him.

"I do hope we are in time for tea." Grayson glanced at his cousin. "Weren't you just saying how parched you were?"

"Oh, I am definitely parched," Stillwell said, amusement glittering in his eyes. "And hungry as well."

Camille hesitated, then met Grayson's gaze. "There's no way to prevent this, is there?"

He shook his head. "None whatsoever."

"Very well, then, *Cousin*." She nodded at Fortesque to open the parlor doors. "But please, both of you, if you truly mean to assist me, be on your best behavior."

"I am always on my best behavior." Stillwell took her arm to escort her into the parlor. "It's what makes me so delightful."

"That's not the word I would use," she said under her breath, and the trio stepped into the parlor.

"Oh, look, Cousin Grayson has returned," Beryl said in an overly merry manner, and rose to her feet, Nikolai a beat behind her.

"And he's not alone." Camille's tone matched her twin's. "Why, look who he met on the way here."

"Lord Stillwell." Beryl stood and stepped closer, offering her hand to Grayson's cousin. "It has been entirely too long."

"Too long, indeed." Stillwell kissed her hand. "To my utter regret."

"I was between husbands for a while, you know." Beryl tossed him a flirtatious look and Camille's jaw tightened. She trusted Stillwell no more than she did Grayson. There was no need for her sister to be overly pleasant to them.

"An opportunity lost." He heaved a dramatic sigh. "Unfortunately, I was betrothed."

Beryl grinned. "You always are."

Stillwell chuckled. "So it would appear." He studied Beryl curiously. "There is something different about you, Beryl. You seem, I don't know, serene?"

She laughed. "Do I?"

"Perhaps the next time you are between husbands—"

"The next time I fully intend to be a very old woman," she said. "Besides, you and I have never suited, Winfield. I am entirely too clever for you."

"Are you?" He arched a brow. "And I thought I was too clever for you."

"And once again you are wrong." Her eyes twinkled with laughter.

"If the two of you are quite finished," Camille said. "Lord Stillwell, allow me to present our guest, Count Pruzinsky. Nikolai, this is our nearest neighbor, Viscount Stillwell."

"Welcome to England, Count," Stillwell said smoothly.

"Thank you, Lord Stillwell." Nikolai smiled in the pleasant yet reserved manner one expected of royalty. Camille smiled to herself. Oh, he was perfect. "But I have already been here for several months, traveling about the countryside."

"Ah yes." Stillwell nodded. "Mr. Elliott said you have been traveling throughout Europe for some time." He paused and studied Nikolai. "Forgive me for being forward, but have we met?"

"Not that I recall." Nikolai shook his head.

Stillwell's eyes narrowed. "Perhaps at a gathering of some sort? Possibly in London?"

"It's entirely possible, I suppose," Nikolai said with a pleasant smile. "I have been to a great number of balls and soirées and dinners since my arrival in England. Obligatory sorts of things, you know. Representing my country and all." He shrugged. "Not that they aren't enjoyable, if somewhat overwhelming. My apologies, but surely you understand. One meets so many people."

"Yes, of course," Stillwell said politely.

"I was just about to encourage him to relate some of his adventures. You should join us, my lord." Miss Murdock gazed up at Stillwell with a look that invited more than his attendance at a chat about travel. Camille would have to speak to Fortesque about curbing the actress's natural tendencies toward flirtation.

"I should like nothing better," Stillwell said cautiously, staring at Miss Murdock.

"If you recall," Beryl began, "my sister *Delilah* has always been fascinated by travel. Haven't you, dear?"

"Oh, my . . . yes." Miss Murdock fluttered her lashes at Stillwell. "There are all sorts of places I long to visit. Why, there is nothing more stimulating than travel." She turned her attention toward Nikolai. "Don't you agree, Your—my lord?"

The prince smiled. "I am constantly learning and encountering something new and unexpected."

"I confess, save for a grand tour in my youth," Stillwell began, "I have traveled very little."

"That, my boy, is what's wrong with this generation," Mr. Henderson began. "Why, in my day . . ."

"Do tell us about your day." Stillwell grinned with delight. *"Colonel."*

Mr. Henderson frowned at the interruption. "Yes, yes, now, where was I?" He paused, then continued. "Ah yes, when I was in the service of Her . . ."

Camille breathed a sigh of relief. At least her uninvited guests were more capable of carrying off this ruse than her professional actors. Perhaps Grayson would be of help, after all. She caught his eye and nodded discreetly in the direction of the tea cart; then slipped away to the other side of the room. She poured Grayson a cup of tea and handed it to him when he joined her.

"I would be most appreciative if you were to encourage Stillwell to be on his way." She addressed him in a low voice, but kept her gaze on the group across the room. "I don't trust him."

"Under normal circumstances, I would commend you for your caution." Grayson sipped his tea and studied the gathering. "But Win is determined to be of assistance in your endeavor."

She huffed in exasperation. "Why?"

"He feels he has done you a disservice," Grayson said coolly. "My fault entirely, I'm afraid. However inadvertently, I led him to believe, all those years ago, when you broke my heart—"

"When I did what?" Her voice rose.

"Shh." He nodded at the others. "Unless you want your prince to wonder why you are being sharp with your beloved cousin."

"You're not my beloved cousin," she snapped, but lowered her voice, nonetheless, and glanced at the group. Indeed, Nikolai looked in her direction, speculation on his face. She smiled in a reassuring manner and he returned his attention to whatever Mr. Henderson was going on about. "What do you mean—when I broke your heart?"

"It scarcely matters now. Besides, you said you didn't want to speak about the past." He paused thoughtfully. "Which is probably for the best, all things considered."

"What things?"

"Your prince, for one, and your Christmas production, for another. You have a lot to contend with at the moment, Camille. You needn't concern yourself with the past." He nodded at the others. "And it appears all is going quite well."

"Thank you, but it is only the first day," she said absently. How on earth did she break his heart? That wasn't at all how she remembered it. He was right about one thing though: She had neither the time nor the inclination to dwell on his charge at the moment, ridiculous as it was. She pushed it from her mind and blew a resigned breath. "Who knows what might happen tonight or tomorrow or on Christmas? It is far too soon to be anything but vigilant."

"You may rest assured that I will do all within my power to assist you."

"You've said that before," she said in a sharper tone than she had intended. "Why, Grayson? Why do you wish to help me?"

"I'm not entirely sure yet," he said so softly that she surely misunderstood.

"What?"

"We were friends once—"

"A very long time ago."

"And it's in the interest of that friendship that I am lending you my assistance." He bent closer and spoke softly, his breath warm against her ear. "I meant it when I said I want only your happiness. As your friend, no matter how long ago, it is my . . . my duty to help you."

She stared at him, then snorted. "Hardly."

"Admit it. With none of your family, your real family, here—"

"Beryl is here and her husband will be here in a few days as well."

"A political type, isn't he?"

She nodded.

Grayson sipped his tea thoughtfully. "And from what I have heard, he's rather stiff and stodgy."

"Not in the least," she lied.

"Not really the sort to fling himself into this production with the wholehearted abandon it deserves."

"Nonetheless—"

"And it seems to me, given the magnitude of this farce, that you need all the help you can get." He shook his head in a mournful manner. "You need me, Camille."

"I most certainly do not."

He cast her a skeptical look.

"I do not!"

He smiled in an annoyingly smug way, as if he knew something she did not, and sipped his tea.

Blasted man. She trusted him no more than she trusted his cousin. Still, they had been friends once, before . . . Broken his heart, indeed. How could she possibly have broken his heart? He had made a declaration of love out of the clear blue sky on the day of her marriage to another man, and then he vanished like a frightened rabbit gone to ground, never to be heard from again until today. No, if anyone's heart had been broken, it had been hers.

Not that it mattered now. Not that it had mattered for a very long time. Not that it had ever mattered.

Still, a voice in the back of her head whispered, *But it did.*

Eight

Observing the group at the dinner table, an uninformed spectator would think there was little out of the ordinary in the gathering. Certainly, the older lady had a tendency to make comments that made no sense whatsoever. The older gentleman monopolized much of the conversation with endless tales of travel and military service in Africa and India, peppered generously with quotes from Shakespeare. Whether his stories were true or not, Gray had no idea, but they were entertaining enough. The youngest lady, with the fiery red hair, said far more with her eyes and the inclination of her body than she actually put into words, but there was no doubt as to the flirtatious message she delivered. As for those members of the family who were not pretending to be someone they weren't, it was all Beryl could do to hide her amusement while Camille adopted a pleasant manner, although tension lingered in the set of her shoulders and the look in her eye. Still, Camille might well be the best actress in the room.

". . . and I should love to hear more about your travels in the Alps," Mrs. Montgomery-Wells said to the prince. "I have never seen an Alp, but I understand they are quite scenic."

Camille had provided the real names of the actors, as Gray claimed it was awkward for him otherwise. After all, if one knew the real Lady Briston, calling the actress "Lady Briston" simply did not ring true if one was not a professional actor. And if Gray was to be part of the cast, he did want to play his role as well as possible.

"If you would be so kind, Your Highness," the older woman continued.

Henderson cleared his throat. "Among family, remember, Constance?"

"Regina," Beryl said sotto voce.

"Yes, of course." Mrs. Montgomery-Wells heaved an exasperated sigh and returned her attention to the prince. "If you would be so kind, Your Highness, dear."

Camille winced. Gray bit back a grin. The prince, however, with his overly perfect face and his overly perfect manner—Camille's *perfect* prince—did exactly what a charming, perfect prince would do and acted as if it was not at all uncommon for him to be addressed as "Your Highness, dear."

One might have attributed his response to a lack of understanding of the English language; and, indeed, he did spend much of the meal smiling and nodding, as if he were perpetually confused. Yet, there was a gleam of intelligence in his eyes; and Gray wagered he understood far more than he let on. Which did lead one to wonder why he would act otherwise. One more reason to mistrust the royal.

Add that to the fact that Pruzinsky watched Camille with a look that was part speculation and part possession. Studied her, really, as if he was trying to determine . . . what? How best to seduce her? If he hadn't already. Gray pushed the thought from his head. It was none of his concern, really. And why wouldn't the prince wish to seduce her? Why wouldn't any man?

Camille was as lovely now as she had been when he had last seen her. Certainly, the twins had always been pretty in that blond-haired, blue-eyed, classic-English-beauty way. But Camille had been a girl when they'd parted; now she was very much a woman. One could see that in the set of her chin and the look in her eye. There was a strength about her now; there was a confidence and grace that had come with the passage of years. This was not a woman who would marry a man because she was expected to do so. This was a woman who knew her own mind.

How could she not know she had broken his heart?

"The Alps meander through several countries, Lady Briston," the prince said. "Are you speaking of the Italian Alps or the Swiss Alps or the German Alps?"

"A mountain's a mountain, I say." Henderson nodded. "Unless you're speaking of the Himalayas. Why, I recall an expedition when I was . . ."

The actor was well worth whatever Camille was paying him. Once he launched into one of his tales, no one else could get a word in. Which meant no one could make a mistake. It was entirely possible Camille might be able to pull off her charade. Of course, as she herself had pointed out: it was only the first day.

When the final course was cleared, Mrs. Montgomery-Wells rose to her feet; the gentlemen following suit. "Now then," she announced in what was obviously her best lady-of-the-manor voice. "The ladies shall retire to the parlor and leave the gentlemen to their brandy and cigars."

"Excellent idea, Aunt *Bernadette*," Gray said. If he could keep Henderson from monopolizing the conversation, he could use this opportunity to find out more about Pruzinsky. "We shall join you shortly."

"Nonsense, Cousin," Camille said quickly. "There's no need to be so formal. We are at home, after all. Why don't we all adjourn to the parlor? Besides, *Mother,* you haven't allowed cigars in the dining room since Father was alive."

Confusion furrowed Mrs. Montgomery-Wells's forehead. "I haven't?"

"No, Mother." Camille fixed her with a firm look. "The smell makes you sneeze."

"I had no idea," the older woman murmured.

"But brandy is permitted," Henderson said in a hopeful tone.

"It always is, Uncle. My goodness, we are all so forgetful tonight." Beryl took his arm and started to lead him away from the table. "Why don't we all gather around the piano and sing Christmas carols?"

"A delightful idea, Lady Dunwell. Lady Briston," the prince said in a gallant manner and presented his arm. "Might I escort you into the parlor?"

Mrs. Montgomery-Wells giggled. "I should be delighted, Your Highness, dear."

"Cousin?" Miss Murdock fluttered her lashes at Gray.

As much as he knew Miss Murdock was the type of woman who made every man feel as if she were interested in him, and him alone, Gray would have to be dead not to respond to her inviting manner. He grinned and offered his arm. "Shall we?"

"Indeed, we shall." Camille took his other arm. "Delilah plays beautifully."

Miss Murdock peered around Gray at Camille. "No, I don't."

"You're supposed to," Camille said through clenched teeth.

"I do," Beryl said quickly, and the group moved into the parlor.

Beside him, he felt Camille huff in annoyance.

Beryl's suggestion was nothing short of inspired. In spite of her continued amusement, she was obviously sincerely trying to help her sister. The carols left little time for idle conversation as they slid from one traditional Christmas song to another: from "The Wassail Song" to "The First Noel," from "The Cherry Tree Carol" to "The Holly and the Ivy," from "Silent Night" to "God Rest Ye Merry Gentlemen." Mrs. Montgomery-Wells and Henderson took seats while the others stood around the piano. Camille's false family proved to be far better singers than they were actors. The prince, too, had an excellent voice and joined in the singing with enthusiasm. This was one area in which he seemed to have no trouble with the language. Odd, but perhaps not surprising given his fascination with a traditional English Christmas. Even Camille's tension seemed to ease. It was a convivial group and a surprisingly pleasant evening.

"If you will forgive me," the prince said after an hour or so. "I find I am somewhat weary after today's travel and should like to retire for the night." He moved to the doorway, then turned. "Camille? If you have a moment."

"Of course." She smiled and joined him.

"Ladies, Colonel, Mr. Elliott. I bid you all a good night." Pruzinsky nodded and stepped into the corridor, Camille at his side.

Gray excused himself, leaving the others to chat by the piano, and casually stepped to the table bearing the brandy decanter to refill his glass and get a better view of the couple outside the open doors. He couldn't hear the conversation, but at least he could be close at hand if Camille needed him. To do what? Protect her honor? She'd likely smack him if he dared to try. Regardless of whether Pruzinsky was legitimate or not, interference was one thing Camille would never tolerate.

Still, one could tell a great deal about a couple by simple observation. The way they might lean toward each other, or the casual touch of a hand, or the manner in which their eyes met. He didn't trust Pruzinsky one bit. But Camille was an intelligent woman and one couldn't help but wonder exactly what it would take to make certain she didn't trust the prince as well.

"What a lovely evening, Camille." Nikolai gazed down at her. "Your family is delightful."

"They can, as well, be a bit . . ." She searched for the right word. "Eccentric, perhaps."

He chuckled. "No more so than mine. Your mother reminds me very much of an aunt of mine." His blue eyes twinkled with amusement. "She, too, has a tendency to forget her own name."

"Oh, dear." Camille winced. "You noticed that, did you?"

"Even with my inability to completely grasp the nuances of the English language, it was hard to miss. Although such things are to be expected in the elderly."

Good Lord. If her mother knew she was being thought of as *elderly*, there would be hell to pay. With any luck, she would never know.

"I find those little quirks to be quite charming."

"My mother is nothing if not charming." Which was entirely true, regardless of whether she was speaking of the real Lady Briston or the actress playing her.

"Camille." He gazed into her eyes, took her hand and raised it to his lips. "We have much to discuss, you and I."

"Do we," she said lightly.

"Indeed, we do." He turned her hand over and kissed her palm in a manner that should have sent shivers up her spine. Yet, it did nothing more than tickle. Not at all what she expected. Surely, the last time he had kissed her hand, she had shivered. Hadn't she? "I must confess, I have given the question of the two of us much consideration."

"Oh?"

"I have thought of little else since the moment we met." He chuckled, then sobered. "I have long believed in fate. That our futures lie in the hands of forces more powerful than ourselves. And fate cannot be denied." His gaze searched hers. "A beautiful woman fell into my arms and it seemed no less than fate. No less than what I had been waiting for all my life."

For once, words failed her. She stared up at him.

"It is not often one meets one's dreams come true."

"Goodness, Nikolai." She laughed softly. "You shall quite turn my head with talk like that."

"Excellent." He lowered her hand but continued to keep it firmly clasped in his. "As it is such a lovely head." He paused. "The addition of a crown would only make it lovelier."

"And yet"—she raised a shoulder in a casual shrug—"I have no crown."

"Perhaps that can be remedied."

"Can it?" Surely, he wasn't going to propose? Now? It was what she'd wanted. What she had planned. The sole purpose of this entire Christmas charade. Why, this was going to be easier than she had thought.

"It would be difficult, you know. There are all sorts of

matters to be resolved. Details to be sorted out, arrangements to be made, permissions to be sought." He shook his head. "Yet, I think well worth it. You would make an exquisite princess. My exquisite princess."

Still, now that a proposal seemed imminent, it seemed, as well, not quite . . . right. "Given your position, it is not a decision to be made lightly."

"Nor would I make it lightly." He squeezed her hand. "Dare I tell you how much I long to take you in my arms, to make you truly mine."

"Oh, my."

"Camille"—he bent closer and spoke softly into her ear—"I wish to feel the heat of your body next to mine, the beat of your heart in tandem with my own, your breath mingling with mine." He straightened and his gaze bored into hers. "You feel the same. There is passion in you, Camille, simmering beneath the surface. Waiting only for the spark that will burst it into flames. I can see it in your eyes."

"Can you?" she murmured.

This perfect man, her perfect prince, was gazing down at her with desire flaring in his eyes. She should be falling into his arms, into his bed, and all she could think about was that Grayson was in the bedroom across the hall from hers. Why, even now he was standing near the parlor door pouring himself a brandy. Annoying creature. This was his fault.

"As I said, we have a great deal to talk about." His gaze locked with hers. "Let me come to you tonight."

"Oh, but my family, Nikolai. They are all in the rooms next to mine. Should we be discovered . . ." She shook her head, in part to hide her relief. She wasn't her sister. They were entirely different when it came to this sort of thing. Beryl was much more adventurous. Camille had always considered herself rather discriminating. She had never fallen into bed with a man just because it might be, well, fun. "It would be most . . . improper."

"Yes, of course." He released her hand and stepped back. "Forgive me. I lost my head for a moment." He smiled. "Not an uncommon occurrence when I am with you, I fear."

"You are a most charming devil, Nikolai." She adopted a teasing smile.

"I cannot help myself, it seems, with you. I am allowing my heart to lead my head. Too quickly, perhaps." He sighed. "But then I am a man who knows what he wants when he sees it. And I always get what I want."

"One of the privileges of being a prince, no doubt."

"I should warn you, Camille, I am a most impatient man."

"Ah, but patience is a virtue, Nikolai."

"Alas, one I have never cultivated." He shook his head in a mournful manner. "You will, no doubt, be a good influence on me in that respect."

"One can only hope."

"I daresay, my nature is not easily changed." He laughed. "But who knows what changes might be wrought with the right woman by my side."

"Who knows, indeed?"

"Do you realize I have not yet kissed you?" His gaze drifted from her eyes to her lips and back. "Were I to pull you into my arms and kiss you quite thoroughly here and now, would your family object?"

"My family would be thoroughly shocked." She smiled weakly. "As would I."

"Ah, well. Then that, too, shall have to wait." He considered her for a moment. "Not forever, I hope."

"One never knows." She laughed and he joined her.

"Now, then, tell me," he said. "What manner of Christmas frivolity do you have in store for us tomorrow?"

"Oh, I thought perhaps tomorrow you would enjoy a walk around the grounds. The estate is quite extensive, and, of course, there's the pond, and if the . . ."

Camille rattled off the plans she'd made to occupy Nikolai and the others, but her mind was anywhere but on the next day's activities.

Whatever had come over her? She had exactly what she wanted within her grasp, and it no longer seemed to be what she wanted at all. And the blame could be laid squarely at Grayson's feet. Perhaps not entirely, but most of it. Had he not appeared, she would have dashed aside any minor doubts she might have had and at this very moment, no doubt, be betrothed to her prince. She'd been certain that she wished to marry Nikolai—and certain, as well, that it was the hand of fate throwing them together. Grayson's presence had managed to take those minor, little doubts—scarcely worth mentioning, really—and magnify them out of all proportion.

Still, if one believed in fate, how did one explain Grayson's untimely reappearance after eleven years? Unless that, too, was fate.

Blast it all. She needed to give this entire matter further consideration as—it was now apparent—she had failed to do before plunging into her Christmas deception.

Certainly, Nikolai didn't make her shiver when he kissed her hand, but it was only her hand, after all. When they shared a proper kiss, it would be an entirely different matter. Nikolai was exactly what she had always wanted, exactly what she wanted now.

Wasn't he?

Nine

"You don't trust him, do you?" Beryl said in a quiet voice by Gray's side.

"No." He glanced at her. "Do you?"

"I want to. He is extremely charming." She watched the couple outside the doorway. "But although I have heard of royals traveling incognito, I have never yet to meet one who doesn't have so much as a valet. At least not one who allegedly has a castle and kingdom and fortune."

"So you don't think he is who he says he is?" Gray held his breath. He and Beryl had never been especially friendly, but she might well prove to be an unexpected ally.

"I have no reason to believe otherwise. I simply find his behavior odd." She shrugged. "But then, nobility is often odd."

Gray's gaze returned to Camille and her prince. "What do you think she sees in him?"

"My God, Grayson, have you looked at the man?" Beryl studied the prince. "He might well be the most attractive creature I have ever met. Why, I swear, when he smiles, the sun flashes off his teeth."

"His perfect teeth," Gray said under his breath.

Beryl laughed. "Besides that, he is a prince, and Camille has always wanted a prince." She paused. "You probably don't remember, but Camille read far more than I did as a girl. Usually, it was stories involving handsome princes who rescued maidens from wicked trolls or evil stepmothers. Stories of true love and all that."

"I remember," he said quietly.

"She married who she was expected to marry and, don't mistake my words, she cared a great deal for her husband, but he was not the love of her life. Now, even though she denies it, I suspect she is looking for that fairy-story true love."

"She says she's not in love with him."

"But she intends to be. She's quite adamant about it." Beryl sighed. "She doesn't understand that it doesn't really happen that way. You don't fall in love because you wish it or you should."

Gray's throat tightened. "No, of course not."

Beryl studied the couple for a moment. "I gather your cousin has kept you well informed through the years?"

Gray nodded. In the corridor, Pruzinsky drew Camille's hand to his lips.

"Then I imagine you know I was not especially, oh, celibate during my widowhood."

He chuckled. "And from the gossip Win related, not especially faithful once you remarried."

"That's all water under the bridge." Beryl waved off the comment. "I have reformed, mended my wicked ways, as it were, as has Lionel. We are both more than happy with each other now. It's quite lovely, really."

He drew his brows together. "Why are you telling me this?"

"Because I think you might wish to know, while Camille and I may look exactly alike, in many ways that's where the resemblance ends." She hesitated, as if determining how much she wished to confide. "While Camille has certainly seen gentlemen since Harold died, to my knowledge, and she would certainly tell me something of that nature, she has not had any, well, affairs. She's not opposed to them," she added quickly, "I just think she's never found someone worth the, oh, effort. And I think she wants more."

"Then she and the prince?"

"Goodness, Grayson." She huffed. "Don't make me say it."

"I see." And wasn't that interesting?

"I don't want to see her hurt." She returned her attention to her sister and Pruzinsky. "She's much more romantic than I am. Although one would think that after growing up in this household with Mother's constant procession of usurped dukes and overthrown monarchs, she would be a better judge of character. Still, Nikolai might be exactly who and what Camille thinks he is, but I wish to be certain. To that end, I initiated an inquiry before I left London."

He turned toward her. "Have you learned anything?"

"Not yet." She shook her head. "But the moment I do, when I have proof, I will inform Camille. I truly hope he is what she thinks he is. And yet . . ."

"You don't trust him."

"No, I don't. But then"—she met his gaze directly—"I don't trust you either."

He stared. "Why don't you trust me?"

Beryl's eyes narrowed. "Because you broke her heart."

He gasped. "I did what?"

"You heard me. You know full well—"

"What are you two talking about?" Camille joined them. "You both appear entirely too intense, as though you are discussing something of great consequence."

"It's been an intense sort of evening." Beryl raised the back of her hand to her forehead in a dramatic manner. "The stress and strain of a performance is quite exhausting, you know."

"Actually, we were saying how well the evening went," Grayson said quickly. "Singing carols was a brilliant idea, Beryl."

"Oh, I am full of brilliant ideas." Beryl smirked.

"No doubt," he murmured.

"Any more brilliance shall have to wait. There's a great deal to accomplish and time is fleeting." Camille ticked the points off on her fingers. "There's the decorating to oversee." She glanced at her sister. "We shall have to foray into the attic and find the ornaments for the tree. There are any number of other Christmas details to attend to as well. I must speak to Mrs. Fortesque about Christmas dinner. I have already ordered a turkey."

"Turkey?" Beryl frowned. "But Mother always has goose for Christmas."

"Mother is not here," Camille pointed out. "And since Mr. Scrooge procured a prize turkey for the Cratchit family, turkey is what Nikolai expects, and turkey is what he shall have."

"I like turkey," Gray said in a helpful manner.

"No one cares what you like. You were not invited." Camille pinned Gray with a firm look. "However, I do expect you to make yourself useful tomorrow. And you may do so by engaging Nikolai in some sort of manly, out-of-doors pursuit."

"I could take him out and shoot him," Gray said under his breath.

Beryl choked back a laugh.

"I was not going to suggest shooting, as you will more than likely have Mr. Henderson with you and I'm not at all sure you wish to give him a gun." Camille glared. "Do you?"

He chuckled. "Perhaps not."

"I thought not. But you once knew this estate as well as your own family's property. Perhaps you can take exercise together. A lengthy walk should do nicely and occupy most of the morning."

"It's rather cold for a long walk."

"Then you shall have to walk briskly. It will do you good."

"We could look for a tree," Gray offered.

"Not necessary." Camille waved off his suggestion. "Before I sent the gardener off on holiday, he selected a tree and arranged for a boy from the village to cut it and deliver it on the day before Christmas. Decorating it should take much of the day and then we shall gracefully slide into Christmas Eve. After that is Christmas Day, which shall take care of itself, followed by Boxing Day, which will be interrupted by news of a monetary crisis."

"You've thought of everything, haven't you?" Admiration sounded in Gray's voice. He was right; she was not the same girl he once knew.

"Nearly everything." Camille raised a brow. "Surprised?"

He grinned. "Shocked."

She ignored him. "I suggest your walk tomorrow takes you down to the pond. If it's frozen, we could skate in the afternoon. I'm sure Nikolai would adore that and it would nicely fill the rest of the day." She nodded. "And tomorrow night after dinner, we shall play games. Cards perhaps or charades, something along those lines."

"I do so love organized activities," Beryl said wryly.

Camille scoffed. "You always have."

"Is that it, then?" Miss Murdock called from across the room. "Are we done for tonight?" Her gaze flicked to Gray. "I know I am ready to retire."

"Not yet." Camille crossed the room and tugged at the bellpull. Fortesque appeared almost at once. The man had probably been listening at the door. Camille directed him a firm look. "Your troupe, Fortesque, needs further rehearsal."

"I thought we did quite well," Mrs. Montgomery-Wells said in an aside to Gray. "She's very fussy, isn't she?"

"You have no idea," Beryl said.

"You." Camille pinned the older woman with a hard look. "Need to remember your name."

"I know my name." Mrs. Montgomery-Wells picked at invisible threads on the arm of her chair.

Camille's eyes narrowed. "Then what is it?"

The actress considered the question thoughtfully. "Let me think."

"Regina," Henderson prompted in a less than effective stage whisper.

Miss Murdock glanced at the others. "I thought it was Florence."

Camille looked at her sister. "And do you have any suggestions to offer?"

"Absolutely not." Beryl shook her head. "I know my name."

"As well you should." Camille turned her gaze toward Fortesque. "You will resolve this?"

He nodded. "Without fail, my lady."

"Excellent." Camille addressed Miss Murdock. "You need to restrain what is obviously a natural desire to flirt. I gave you all dossiers on my family, and nowhere do I recall saying my youngest sister was a tart."

The actress again glanced at Gray. He couldn't resist a slight nod of the head. Miss Murdock raised her chin. "I am playing this part as I see it. And doing a fine job of it as well. Don't you think so, Mr. Elliott?"

"I've never seen Delilah in better form," he said.

"Thank you." Miss Murdock smiled smugly. "The prince seemed to like me."

"What man wouldn't?" Beryl said with a pleasant smile.

"And Mr. Henderson." Camille turned to the older man. He smiled pleasantly, but it was obvious he had had one brandy too many. Or perhaps four. "While, all in all, I think you did a splendid job of it, perhaps you need to make your anecdotes a touch more realistic."

"I am an actor, my lady," he said gruffly. "I make them sound real."

"Come now, Mr. Henderson," Camille said gently. "Some of your stories were distinctly Shakespearean in tone. Honestly, being shipwrecked—"

"Entirely possible." He huffed.

"And misplacing your twin sister?" she continued.

"I understood Uncle Basil is a twin," Henderson said staunchly. "I studied my role quite thoroughly, my lady, and I am certain he has a twin."

"A twin *brother*, Mr. Henderson." Camille sighed. "My father."

"Oh." Henderson winced. "Must have missed that."

"I assure you, Lady Lydingham," Fortesque said quickly, "we shall thoroughly go over our roles before we retire for the night."

"See that you do." Camille nodded in a weary manner, started toward the door, then stopped. "Oh, and do tell Mrs. Fortesque that dinner was excellent. I couldn't be more pleased."

"Thank you, my lady."

"Good evening, then." Camille smiled shortly and took her leave.

Now that Camille was gone, Gray could continue his conversation with Beryl, but she, too, bid the others a good night and left the parlor. He had no intentions of letting her get away that easily. What did she mean: He had broken Camille's heart? What utter absurdity. He started after her.

"You're leaving as well, Mr. . . . ." Mrs. Montgomery-Wells frowned in confusion and glanced at Fortesque. "Who is he playing?"

"He is Cousin Grayson. A very distant cousin." Miss Murdock's gaze caught Gray's. "Isn't that right, Mr. Elliott?"

He nodded. "It is, indeed. And as Lady Lydingham had no criticism of my performance, I believe I, too, shall make my exit and retire for the evening."

"But it's not at all late." Miss Murdock pouted. "And now that Lady Lydingham is gone—she's rather a nervous sort, isn't she?"

Mrs. Montgomery-Wells snorted.

"She can be," Gray said.

"As I was saying, now that she has retired for the night, I thought we might get to know one another better. I was hoping to convince you to show me the library and perhaps help me select a good book. You can learn so much about a person by the type of books they read."

"We shall have to save the library for another night, then, perhaps," Gray said smoothly.

"I had no idea she read," Mrs. Montgomery-Wells said in an aside to Henderson. "She doesn't seem the sort, does she?"

Miss Murdock flashed the older woman a sharp look. "I like nothing better than going to bed with a good book." She returned her attention to Gray. "Don't you?" The look Miss Murdock directed toward him belied her words. It was obvious that there were other things she liked even better than a good book in her bed.

Fortesque cleared his throat. "We still have work to do, Edwina."

"Yes, indeed, one can never be too prepared and we don't wish to incur Lady Lydingham's wrath. Good evening." Gray nodded and hurried out of the parlor. He was grateful for the older man's reminder of the need to practice their parts, and grateful, as well, for Camille's insistence they do so. Edwina Murdock was a dangerous creature and he vowed to keep his distance.

He started for his room, then paused and changed direction. Miss Murdock's suggestion about the library had more merit than she intended. If he recalled correctly, the Millworth Manor library was stocked not only with classic literature and current offerings but with all manner of referential material as well. Camille's father had been something of an amateur scholar. Perhaps there was a book in the library that could help him discover more about Pruzinsky and whether or not he was legitimate.

He pushed open the door, surprised to find a lamp already lit. And surprised as well to find Pruzinsky standing in the shadows near the desk, replacing a book on the shelf.

"I beg your pardon. I didn't realize anyone was in here."

Pruzinsky studied the shelves in front of him. "I found I was entirely too restless to sleep and thought perhaps a book might help."

"Miss Murdock suggested the very same thing a few minutes ago." Gray nodded at the shelves. "It's been some time since I've been in the manor's library, but it doesn't look as though much of anything has changed. Perhaps I could help you find something suitable."

He glanced around the shadow-filled room. Even in the dim light from the single lamp on the desk, the room looked exactly as he remembered. Shelves flanked either side of a massive fireplace, reaching from the floor to a wide plaster frieze beneath ornate carved molding and a coffered ceiling. The room was longer than it was wide, with one end dominated by a bowed window, covered at night with heavy drapes. What walls didn't host shelves had portraits of ancestors dating back generations. To the right of the door hung a portrait of Camille as a girl, together with her sisters and mother, exactly where it had always hung.

"That would be most kind of you," Pruzinsky said in a polite manner.

Gray moved to his side and perused the shelves. This section primarily held books of history, records of ancient civilizations, discourses in philosophy, treatises on economics. There was, as well, a large set of encyclopedias and several rows of nothing but various years of Debrett's and Burke's guides to the aristocracy.

"Are you looking for anything in particular? I know there's quite a bit of Shakespeare on the other wall, as well as Dickens, Thackeray, Trollope, Ruskin. What are you in the mood for?"

"Something that isn't the least bit interesting, I should think. As the purpose is to put me to sleep." He smiled coolly. "Something quite dull should do nicely."

"I suppose dull is as much in the eye of the beholder as beauty. Personally, I have always found works of a philosophical nature to be most efficient at inducing sleep."

Pruzinsky nodded. "Philosophy it is, then."

They studied the shelves for a few moments in silence.

"You don't like me, do you?" Pruzinsky said at last.

"I wouldn't say that."

"You don't trust me with your cousin."

"I would not trust anyone with my cousin." Gray shrugged. "She has a significant fortune and a tendency toward impulse. Which is not to say she is not intelligent. She has simply always allowed her emotions to rule her head."

"Then we have much in common." He paused. "You do realize I intend to marry her."

And I intend to stop you. "I suspect that depends on whether she wishes to marry you."

"Oh, she does." He smiled in an overly smug manner.

"But you have not yet proposed?" Gray held his breath.

"A minor detail." Pruzinsky waved off the question.

"Well, then, allow me to be the first to congratulate you."

"As her soon-to-be fiancé, I must say I do not like the way you look at her."

Grayson started. "How do I look at her?"

"Not like a cousin, no matter how distant."

"Camille and I have always been close," he said slowly.

"And yet you didn't see her for"—Pruzinsky glanced at him—"eleven years, was it?"

"I was abroad and engaged in enterprises that fully

occupied my time and thought." Even to himself, he sounded somewhat defensive. "Surely, you understand how the demands of business supersede all else?"

Pruzinsky cast him a condescending smile. "I know nothing about business, nor do I imagine I will ever be engaged in such."

Gray clenched his jaw, but kept his tone level. "Nonetheless, I would think there are any number of demands put upon you by the very nature of your position. Being the heir to the throne and all."

"It is a position I was born to," he said in a lofty manner. "But admittedly, the responsibilities of state can indeed be most demanding. However, at the moment, as I am far from home and traveling on my own, my time is free to do with as I please."

"Ah yes, you disdain the accoutrements of royalty when you travel."

"I find travel without accompaniment to be both exhilarating and enlightening."

"Still, you can't travel forever. You must return to your country eventually. To assume the throne, if for no other reason."

"My father is in excellent health, and, God willing, it will be many years before I take his place as ruler. However, I intend to return to my country soon in the new year." He met Gray's gaze. "With my new wife."

"I see."

"I am a man used to getting precisely what he wants, Mr. Elliott. I want Camille. I am fairly certain she wants me as well." His eyes narrowed. "You would do well to remember that."

Gray forced a light note to his voice. "I could scarcely forget it."

"See that you don't." Pruzinsky nodded. "Good evening." He started for the door.

"Count Pruzinsky, I believe you have forgotten something."

Pruzinsky turned toward him. "Oh?"

"Your book." Gray pulled a book off the shelves and offered it to him. "Samuel Bailey's *Letters on the Philosophy of the Human Mind* should induce sleep rather quickly, I would think."

"Ah yes, this will do." Pruzinsky accepted the book. "Once again, I bid you a good evening, Mr. Elliott."

"Count." Gray watched him take his leave. Even if he didn't have all the facts yet, regardless of Win and Beryl's caution in the matter, there wasn't a doubt in his mind that Pruzinsky was a fraud. Why, the man talked about assuming the throne of a country that no longer existed. Still, Beryl was right. Solid proof was needed.

He turned toward the shelves, then thought better of it. If Miss Murdock noticed he had gone to the library, after all, she might well follow him. No, he could return to the library in the morning for this.

A few minutes later, he was in his room—a room with a distinct lack of frills and fripperies obviously designed for a male inhabitant. A spacious four-poster bed dominated the space, accompanied by a large wardrobe, matching dresser and comfortable chairs positioned before the fireplace. It was directly across the hall from Camille's room and well worth the money he had paid to a footman. After all, if he was going to help Camille, it would be wise to stay as close to her as possible.

His bag was sitting untouched on the bed. In a fully staffed household, it would have been unpacked and his clothing attended to, although someone had seen to the fire and he was grateful for that. He smiled and opened his bag. Fending for himself was a small price to pay for being at Millworth Manor. In truth, he hadn't had a valet since he had left Fairborough Hall. But if he was to remain in England, a valet would be expected for a man in his position. As would an appropriate house in the country and a respectable place in town and . . .

When had he decided to stay in England? The thought pulled him up short. He had told his uncle he wasn't sure if he had returned home for good. Indeed, he even had passage back to America. Now he had apparently decided. He unpacked his bag, including a copy of *The Innocents Abroad*, so appropriate for travel, and considered the matter. Why not stay? England was home and today he had realized how much he had missed it. Still, he was not a man used to making impulsive decisions.

But hadn't Win said that his letters in recent years indicated he would at last be returning home? Perhaps this was a decision he had been coming to for some time. The more he thought about it, the more it seemed right.

He put his clothes away in the wardrobe and dresser and removed his jacket. For a man who prided himself on not acting on impulse, he had introduced himself as Camille's cousin without a second thought. That, too, now seemed right.

He may not be a prince, but as her friend, he had her best interests at heart. And the best way to protect her was to spend Christmas, and every night until then, in her house.

Try as he might, he couldn't get Beryl's charge out of his head. How had he broken Camille's heart? She had been the one to reject him. He was the one whose hopes and dreams had been crushed. He was the one with a broken heart. How could anyone think otherwise? How could she?

Camille refused to talk about the past. However,

Beryl's charge, coupled with Win's reassessment of what had passed between him and Camille years ago, as well as the discovery that she was still angry at him—well, there was definitely much unfinished between them. There were things he needed to know, and no doubt things she needed to know as well, although she was probably too stubborn to admit it. It was past time they cleared the air between them. And perhaps when they did, he could finally put her out of his head once and for all. If indeed that was what he still wanted.

He stepped to his door, yanked it open and froze.

"Good evening, *Cousin.*"

Ten

"Finished so soon?" he said in a casual manner.

"Oh, I know my part, Cousin." Miss Murdock smiled up at him in a wicked manner. "And I know yours."

He stepped into the hall and closed the door behind him. Even if he was mistaken as to her intentions, it was far wiser to deal with her in the relative safety of the still-lit public corridor rather than his private bedroom. He didn't know if the actors/servants had forgotten to extinguish the sconces or had not yet gotten around to it. Regardless, he was grateful. "I am nothing more than a distant cousin come for Christmas."

"Very distant."

There was no mistaking the look in her eyes. He was right: She was dangerous. Not that under other circumstances, he wouldn't be tempted. There was much to be said for dangerous women.

"And yet . . ." She reached out a finger and ran it down the middle of his shirt. "Such an important role and you play it so well. I thought perhaps we could rehearse. Together. I'm certain we could both benefit."

"Be that as it may." He caught her hand against his chest and grinned down at her. She scarcely came up to his chin. "I don't need rehearsal, remember?"

"Then perhaps you have a good book I might borrow." She pressed closer against him, trapping their hands between them. "I do so love a good book before bed."

"Yes, you mentioned that earlier. I am sorry." He shook his head regretfully. "I doubt that I have a book that would interest you."

"Certainly, you have something of interest in there. We needn't read, you know. We could, oh, talk."

"Miss Murdock—"

"Edwina." She raised up on her toes and brushed her lips across his. "You should call me Edwina."

"Ah, Miss Murdock, as flattered as I am, that wouldn't be at all proper, now would it?"

"But we are family, aren't we, Cousin Grayson?"

He chuckled. "Very well, then, Edwina."

"I knew it when I first saw you. Even as handsome as you are, you're not an actor, are you?"

"I am through Christmas."

"And then?"

"Then I go back to being Mr. Grayson Elliott, who is not an actor."

"What are you, then?"

"Nothing more than a man of business."

Her eyes widened. "You're one of those captains of industry, aren't you?"

He chuckled. "I wouldn't say that."

"You're obviously a gentleman of quality."

"Yes, well, I suppose one could say that." He gazed down at her. "While it is most delightful to have you pressed against me like this, it might be best if we didn't stand quite so close together."

"Why?"

"Yes, Grayson, do tell, why?"

He raised his head. Camille stood in her doorway, arms folded over her chest, leaning against the door-jamb. She was obviously ready for bed, wearing a robe that, while eminently practical, was, nonetheless, sur-prisingly tantalizing. Beneath it, her nightwear but-toned nearly to her chin. In the back of his mind, he noted how the glorious redhead pressed against him triggered little more than amusement, but the sight of Camille in sensible nightwear sped up his heart.

Edwina heaved a frustrated sigh and stepped back. "Well, that's that, then."

On one hand, he would prefer not to be caught by Camille in what appeared to be a compromising posi-tion; on the other hand, it wouldn't hurt to have her re-alize not every woman found him annoying. He smiled down at Edwina. "I'm afraid so."

"Oh, don't let me stop you," Camille said dryly.

"Frankly, Camille, if there was something to stop, we would be in my room rather than here. As we aren't"— he smiled—"there's nothing to stop."

"Pity," Edwina said under her breath.

"It's none of my concern, really." Camille shrugged. "I simply thought I heard something in the corridor, that's all."

"The prince, perhaps?"

Camille's eyes narrowed. "That would be none of *your* concern."

Edwina's gaze slid from Gray to Camille and back. Even the young actress could no doubt sense the tension, which now hung in the air. "Well, if you don't have a book to loan me, after all, Mr. Elliott, I believe I shall go to my room. Good evening." She nodded a bow to Camille and hurried off down the hall.

"I do hope I didn't ruin your evening." Camille's gaze followed Edwina.

"As I said, there was nothing to ruin."

"Am I to assume that was by your choice? It's obvious that was not what Miss Murdock had in mind."

"You may assume whatever you wish. You will, anyway." He chuckled. "But I have no interest in Miss Murdock."

She stared for a moment, then laughed. "Oh, come now, Grayson. Miss Murdock is not only attractive, but she is extraordinarily willing as well. Why, she practically exudes willingness around her like a fog of cheap perfume. That is not a combination most men can easily resist."

"I didn't say it was easy."

"No doubt." She paused. "She's very pretty, isn't she?"

"If you like red-haired vixens with the figures of goddesses, flawless skin and long lashes."

"And do you?"

"A man would have to be dead not to."

"I see. Not that it's any of my business," she added quickly. "Not really."

He studied her curiously. She was not nearly as unconcerned as she would like him to think. "I believe you mentioned that."

"I simply want to make certain you understand. You may certainly do as you wish regarding Miss Murdock. Or any woman, for that matter."

"Thank you for granting me permission."

She drew her brows together. "You are being deliberately annoying now, aren't you?"

"Not deliberately."

"Then it's a natural gift of yours?"

He chuckled. "Apparently."

"I know you find this all so amusing."

"It's hard not to." He grinned. "Surely, even you can admit some of it has been most amusing."

"Not in the least," she said in a lofty manner.

"Come now, Camille." He stepped closer. "You can't tell me Mrs. Montgomery-Wells not being able to remember your mother's given name isn't amusing."

"Not at all."

"Or that Henderson's unending and, for the most part, fabricated stories aren't cause for at least a bit of a smile?"

"No. In fact, I find Mr. Henderson's ability to completely dominate the conversation to be of great benefit," she said firmly, but the corners of her lips twitched as if she were indeed holding back a smile.

"And certainly Miss Murdock's unrelenting charm—"

"There is nothing about Miss Murdock I find the tiniest bit amusing."

"Not even wondering how appalled the real and eminently proper Delilah would be at the actress's version of her? At least according to the comments Win has written about her. Unless, of course, your younger sister has changed in that respect."

"No, if anything, she is even more stuffy than she used to be. And, yes, admittedly, that thought is cause for a modicum of amusement." Camille bit her lip, but laughter danced in her eyes. "Good God, Grayson, she would be apoplectic if she knew of Miss Murdock's portrayal. I gave all the actors detailed information on the parts they were to play, you know. I can't imagine how she came to the conclusion that Delilah is something of a tart."

The tiniest twinge of guilt stabbed him. He ignored it and shook his head. "You know actors. They are a mysterious lot."

"Yes, I suppose." She paused. "In spite of the fact that you and Miss Murdock—"

"There is no me and Miss Murdock."

"Regardless." She waved off his comment. "While it is none of my concern, I would be most appreciative if you would refrain from any dalliances with her while you are here. It's very important to me to have this family look as proper and respectable as possible."

"Because you wish to marry the prince?"

She hesitated for no more than a fraction of a second, but it was enough. She nodded. "Yes, of course, that's exactly what I want."

"Then I shall do everything I can to assist you," he said in as gallant a manner as he could muster.

She studied him for a moment. "You do realize that I still don't trust you?"

"It's completely understandable." He nodded. "But I shall endeavor to earn your trust."

"Thank you." She paused. "I fear I owe you something of an apology as well."

"Oh?"

"I have, perhaps, not been as gracious to you as I should have been. Your arrival took me by surprise. Well, it was a shock really." She twisted her hands together in a nervous fashion. "I must confess you were the last person I expected. . . ."

"To be in your parlor?"

"To ever see again. There were things I had planned

to say, and, well, I had thought . . . It scarcely matters now what I had thought." She shrugged. "But we were friends once and I should have at least been polite."

"No apology is necessary." He smiled and took her hand. "I hope we still are . . . friends, that is."

She met his gaze directly, but didn't pull her hand from his. "Shall I be perfectly honest?"

"Aren't you always?"

She grimaced. "Apparently not, as I am trying to pass off a house filled with less than accomplished actors as my family." She drew a deep breath. "I don't know if we can be friends again, but perhaps we could try. I have, on rare occasions, missed being your friend."

"Excellent." It was a beginning and he couldn't ask for more than that. Could he? "I have a confession to make as well."

"Go on, then."

"This afternoon, when you asked if I intended to kiss you . . ."

She started to pull her hand away, but he held firm.

"And I said no, it was the truth."

"That's scarcely much of a confession."

"Now, however"—he stared into her blue eyes—"I do."

"You do what?" Caution rang in her voice.

"Intend to kiss you."

Her eyes narrowed. "Now?"

He nodded. "Now would be a good time, yes."

"Why?"

"Because everyone is abed and we are alone."

"No." She huffed. "Why do you intend to kiss me?"

"Do I need a reason?"

"Yes."

"What man wouldn't want to kiss you? You are more

desirable and lovelier now than you were eleven years ago."

"Flattery, Grayson, will not get you what you want."

He smiled slowly. "What will?"

"Honesty, perhaps." She studied him. "If I recall, we always had honesty between us. Or almost always."

"Very well, then." He pulled her into his arms and gazed down at her. "I kissed you once, and I should like to kiss you again, because I wish to know if a second kiss can live up to the memory of the first. I remember a great deal about that kiss."

Her brows drew together. "And you wish to see if it's the same?"

"Something like that."

"That's absurd." She shrugged as best she could in his arms.

"You kissed me back."

"Not that I recall," she said coolly.

"Oh, but I remember. Quite clearly. I remember the softness of your lips beneath mine." He brushed his lips across hers.

"I don't recall that either."

"Then perhaps you remember how your body melted against mine." He pulled her tighter against him.

"No." A vague breathlessness in her voice belied her words. "Not at all."

"What a pity. Well, I know you won't remember what else I can recall, because it is my memory and mine alone." He shifted his head and kissed a spot on her neck right below her ear. She shivered and he smiled against her skin.

"I do remember you didn't do that," she said with a slight gasp.

"Unfortunately not," he murmured against her skin.

"I remember you tasted faintly of cinnamon and you smelled of violets. Did you know you taste of cinnamon?"

"Utter nonsense," she said weakly.

"And I remember, when my lips pressed to yours, I wanted it to go on forever."

"I don't. . . ."

"Oh, but I do." Before she could protest, he pressed his lips to hers. For a moment, there was no response; then her mouth opened to his. He angled his mouth over hers and deepened the kiss. The lightest scent of violets surrounded him and the past engulfed him. She tasted as he remembered, the faintest hint of cinnamon, warm with a touch of brandy. And more, of chances lost and promises never made. Her arms slipped around him and she clung to him. And she tasted, as well, perhaps of hope and beginning anew. His heart beat faster and he knew everything he had denied was true.

And now, as then, she kissed him back.

At last he raised his head and smiled down at her. "Pity you don't remember."

For a long moment, she stared up at him, desire and uncertainty in her eyes. Finally she smiled apologetically. "I am sorry, but I don't remember."

Surprise and disbelief coursed through him. Surely, even she wasn't as good an actress as that. "Are you certain?"

She nodded reluctantly. "My apologies, but I'm quite certain."

He released her and took a step back. "I don't believe you."

"It was just a kiss, Grayson, nothing more than that."

"Nothing?"

"Not that I can recall, which would seem to be an indication that it was not"—she winced—"significant."

He studied her closely. "Not earth-shattering, then?"

"Apparently not."

"Or life altering."

"Don't be silly." She shrugged. "It was just a kiss, not unlike any other kiss."

"Not something you will remember for the rest of your days?"

"Not the first or the second."

He studied her for a long moment; then he blew a relieved breath. She wasn't the only good actor here. "That is a relief."

" 'A relief'?" She narrowed her eyes. "What do you mean?"

"Well, I would feel dreadful if you had been pining for me all these years because of a mere kiss."

" 'Pining'?" Camille scoffed. "I have certainly not pined. I haven't given your kiss or you a second thought."

"You did pale a bit when you first saw me."

"Only because, as I had not heard from you for eleven years—*eleven years*—I thought surely you were dead. Understandably, I thought I was seeing a ghost." Her eyes narrowed. "After all, when a man kisses you and makes the kind of declaration you made, then vanishes from your life without another word, one assumes he must be dead. Or perhaps"—her jaw tightened—"one simply hopes he is."

He stared. "You wished me dead?"

"Oh, if you had been standing before me and I had a pistol in my hand, I probably wouldn't have shot you." She thought for a moment. "Although there were moments when I would not have guaranteed your safety."

"I left because I didn't think there was anything more to say."

She stared in disbelief. "There was a great deal more to say."

"Well, I am here now. Perhaps we can talk—"

"*Now* is entirely too late." She glared at him. "Eleven years too late."

"You said you didn't want to talk about the past."

"I don't," she snapped. "It's over and done with, and as it was not significant enough to discuss then, it's certainly not the least bit important now." She turned on her heel, stepped back into her room, and then turned back. "I assume, now that you have kissed me again, not that this kiss was any more memorable than the last—"

"Certainly not for me."

She ignored him. "Your curiosity has been satisfied."

"Completely."

"Then there shall not be a repeat of it."

"You needn't worry on that score. I have no intention of kissing you ever again."

"See that you don't." She nodded, moved into her room and snapped the door sharply behind her.

Who did he think he was fooling? He had every intention of kissing her again. Over and over again, until she melted into a puddle at his feet. Or he melted into a puddle at hers.

It was past time to admit the truth, if only to himself. Gray had known from the moment he looked once more into her blue eyes that he wanted her as much now as he had eleven years ago. Nothing had changed.

Nothing had changed . . . but him. He was no longer that uncertain boy who had taken his broken heart and wounded pride and vanished from her life, determined to make something of himself. Eleven years of making his own way in the world and building his fortune had taught him much. He no longer took "no" for an answer. He had learned anything worth having in this world was worth fighting for. And he had learned to fight for what he wanted. And what he wanted now, what he'd always wanted was Camille. And she wanted him as well. She could deny all she wished, but she had kissed him back then and she had kissed him back tonight. And that told him all he needed to know.

He smiled and returned to his room. Win was right. He would have to win her friendship again before he could win her heart. Certainly, it would not be easy. Along with her friendship, he would have to earn her forgiveness. He had made a start of it, in the corridor, before he had kissed her. Afterward, well, she was an excellent actress. Regardless of what she had said, she had been as affected by that kiss as he had. And he had no doubt that she remembered their first kiss. Yes, indeed, it was a start.

The first thing he needed to do, as her friend, was save her from this prince, whom even her sister found suspicious. And save her from herself as well. He suspected she was already beginning to doubt her desire to marry Prince Perfect. Fanning that doubt would be tricky; he would have to be subtle, but surely it was not impossible. Especially if it became more and more difficult to carry off her farce. Oh, he wouldn't do anything overt. However, throwing a twist into the proceedings now and then, just to muck things up the tiniest bit, was not a bad idea. Admittedly, given the peculiarities of her actors, it was entirely possible they could manage to mess up this production without any help from him. Still, he would take advantage of any opportunity that came his way.

Besides, what play didn't benefit from a few unexpected twists?

Spice and heat and desire. Of course she remembered how he had tasted eleven years ago. She remembered everything.

Camille leaned back against her closed door and struggled to regain her composure. Struggled to breathe.

She remembered how his heart had beat against hers even through the layers of clothing between them. She remembered the heat of his body, the excitement of being enfolded in his arms. She remembered how her blood had pounded through her veins, how her knees had seemed too weak to support her. She remembered the yearning that filled her for more, for him. And she remembered how she had never wanted it to end.

But of course it had. Damnable man. She pushed away from the door and paced the floor.

Why did he have to dwell on that long-ago kiss? Why did he have to bring all that back up? Why did he have to go on and on about everything he remembered? Why did he have to make her feel again all that she had put behind her? Why did he have to come back into her life?

And why did he have to kiss her now?

He had taken her as much by surprise now as he had then. Certainly, that long-ago kiss hadn't been her first. But it was unlike anything she'd ever experienced. She had felt that kiss down to her toes and into her soul. No, she hadn't forgotten anything.

And tonight?

She blew a long breath. She was no longer an inexperienced nineteen-year-old girl. She was thirty years of age, a widow, a woman who managed her own life. A woman who made her own choices. A woman who knew what she wanted.

And yet, when he had kissed her tonight, it was every bit as wonderful as it had been that first time. Even more perhaps, because she'd waited to be kissed like that again for eleven years. Her husband, dear man that he was, had never made her toes curl or her knees weak. No man ever had. Blasted, blasted man!

Once again, Grayson had appeared right when she intended to marry another man. Of course he hadn't said he loved her, but any fool could see it was entirely possible. It was, well, bothersome. It brought back all sorts of feelings she much preferred not to have. And only added to her doubt.

She'd been entirely too busy organizing her Christmas farce to pay any attention to the doubt nagging at the back of her mind about Nikolai. But tonight, when he had been right on the verge of declaring himself, she wanted nothing more than to stop him.

For as long as she could remember, she'd wanted a prince with a kingdom and a castle. She'd wanted to be a princess. Nikolai was certainly handsome and dashing and charming and really, well, perfect. But while the girl she once was wanted a prince, the woman she was now was beginning to think perhaps one should look for more in the man one would spend the rest of one's life with than the dreams spun from fairy stories. Besides, did one really want to spend the rest of one's days with a man who smiled and nodded quite as much as he did?

As much as she hated to admit it, and would never tell her sister, but Beryl was right about . . . love. Not that she didn't intend to love Nikolai one day. It hadn't seemed at all important at the beginning, but now, well, she was thirty years of age and it might be wiser to marry a man she already loved as opposed to one she planned to love. As she was not getting younger, it seemed rather foolish to waste time waiting to fall in love. There was, as well, always the possibility she would never love him at all. And while she did like him, did she wish to spend the rest of her days merely in like? Aside from anything else, shouldn't one feel more than a mere tickling when a man kissed her palm in a most seductive manner? Shouldn't that make her ache and yearn for more?

Still, she should kiss him properly before making any decision, even if she suspected she already had. One never knew really. Why, a proper kiss could change everything.

Regardless, the very least she could do was give Nikolai the kind of Christmas he expected. There was surely no need to reveal the truth about her family to him. She wasn't entirely sure she could trust him to keep it secret. It was a most amusing story, after all. But she certainly couldn't marry a man she couldn't trust.

She sucked in a sharp breath. Good Lord, she would be a laughingstock if this got out. She would never be able to hold her head up in society again. While Nikolai was a charming man, honorable and a decent sort, who knew what might happen if she rejected his advances or, worse, his proposal? Men who had been spurned were not the least bit rational and sought vengeance in all sorts of unpleasant ways. While much more like Beryl than Delilah in terms of propriety, she had made a considerable effort to make certain her reputation wasn't nearly as colorful as her twin's. But once it got out that she had orchestrated this massive deception—and then hadn't married the prince, after all—why, no one would believe it was she who had turned him down. She would not only be a joke, but a pathetic joke at that. Even worse, escapades like this tended to become legendary. The Brighton Incident would pale in significance. She would be in her dotage and would still no doubt hear whispers behind her back about the extreme and futile measures poor Lady Lydingham took to snare a prince.

Not if she could help it. Determination surged through her. She had gotten herself into this and she would get herself out. Nikolai could never learn the truth. They would continue on precisely as originally planned. After Christmas a monetary crisis would call Nikolai home to the Kingdom of Whateveritwas. She would make some excuse as to why she couldn't accompany him and then eventually write and gently tell him they would not suit. Of course, if he proposed, things would be a little more awkward. And he had very nearly done so tonight. Still, as much as she had started out with the express purpose of extracting a proposal, it surely wouldn't be all that difficult to keep him from proposing.

Dear Lord, she was an idiot. She did hope this Christmas served to remind her to think through her schemes thoroughly before setting them into motion. Perhaps now she might be able to see the amusement in the proceedings that Beryl and Grayson so obviously saw, but she doubted it.

As for Grayson, there was no need for him to know she was reconsidering her desire to marry Nikolai. No need to take him into her confidence in any manner whatsoever, since it was so clearly his fault. Perhaps someday she would feel more charitable toward him; but at this moment, if he wanted to be her friend, well, these were the boundaries of friendship.

And if his kiss made her long for something just out of reach, it was nothing more than memories of what might have been. She would not allow herself to be swept away by the kiss of the man who once broke her heart.

And she would never allow him to break it again.

December 22nd

Eleven

Camille surveyed the breakfast offerings arrayed on the sideboard in the dining room and wondered what it would take to entice Mrs. Fortesque to stay on with her. Camille's cook was ready to retire from service; and while Mrs. Williams had been excellent in her day, her standards had slipped considerably in the last year or so. Not that Camille had the heart to tell her. She had been with Camille's late husband's family for most of her life.

Mrs. Fortesque's cooking skills were nothing short of amazing. The woman obviously had a natural talent in the kitchen, as did the young woman who had been assisting her. Perhaps Camille should have a chat with them both—although Mr. Fortesque would certainly be part of any arrangement. And he did so love being an actor.

Grayson strolled into the room, looking annoyingly well rested. He approached the sideboard and studied the offerings. "Mrs. Fortesque does an excellent job of acting like a cook."

"Thank God." Mrs. Fortesque's cooking was the only thing she needn't worry about.

"Oh, you might be interested to know"—Grayson picked up a plate and continued to consider the breakfast offerings—"your footmen are in the upstairs gallery practicing sword fighting for the theater. From a book."

"How delightful." She grimaced. "I shall summon Fortesque to take care of it."

"Fortesque was reading the book to the others." He selected a few slices of bacon and put them on his plate.

She glared. "Why didn't you do anything?"

Grayson glanced at her in surprise. "I offered them advice."

"What? On how not to kill one another?"

He chuckled. "Exactly."

"Grayson!"

"I was trying to be helpful. I thought it might be awkward to have dead actors, or dead footmen, for that matter, lying about the house."

"That's not what I meant." She huffed. "I meant you should have stopped them."

"It's really not my place to do so. I am merely the distant cousin, a very minor role. Why, if this were a play of murder and treachery, I would no doubt be the first one done away with."

"That can yet be arranged."

He considered her for a moment. "It's rather early in the day to be quite so cranky, isn't it?"

"I am not cranky." Indignation rang in her voice. "If anything, I am tired."

"I see." He nodded in a sage manner. "You didn't sleep well."

"I slept exceptionally well," she lied.

"All that pining, no doubt."

"Pining?" She stared at him, then uttered a short laugh. "You were right, Grayson, there is much about this situation that is amusing." She moved to the table and sat down.

"I didn't mean me," he said wryly, and took the seat across the table from her. "But I am surprised to see you up and about so early. I didn't expect to see anyone down yet."

"I have a great deal to accomplish today," she said in a prim manner. "As soon as Beryl makes an appearance, I intend to go up to the attic and find the ornaments for the tree."

"If she doesn't come down before you're finished with breakfast, I could assist you with that," he said casually.

"Would you?"

"I would be happy to."

"Really?"

"You needn't look so suspicious. I said last night that I intended to help you, and I meant it." He stabbed a piece of bacon much more viciously than the bacon deserved. Apparently, he found her as annoying as she found him. Good.

"Very well, then." Camille wasn't at all sure if she wanted his help or not, but she did want to get as much as possible finished before Nikolai and her "family" made an appearance. She had no desire to leave them all to their own devices. God only knew what might happen without constant supervision. "I accept your offer. And I appreciate it," she added reluctantly.

"Do try not to sound so gracious."

"I am doing my best, Grayson." She stared at him. "Even you must admit your presence is something I neither expected nor desired."

"Because you hoped I was dead." He selected a piece of toast from the rack and slathered it with marmalade.

"I didn't hope." She shrugged. "I simply assumed."

"Disappointed?"

"Yes," she snapped, then blew a long breath. "No, of course not. In spite of what I said last night, I wouldn't have you dead."

"That's comforting to know."

"But I wouldn't have you here either."

"And yet"—he grinned in a smug fashion—"here I am."

"Indeed," she said under her breath. "Here you are."

They ate in silence for a few minutes. One might have thought Grayson hadn't eaten in years the way he devoured his food with the enthusiasm of one long deprived and the enjoyment of a connoisseur. He'd had a bit of everything offered on the sideboard: broiled kippers, deviled kidneys, stewed fruit, bacon, sausages and eggs. She couldn't blame him, however. Mrs. Fortesque was a treasure.

"That was excellent." He sighed with the satisfaction of a man well fed. "Do you think Mrs. Fortesque would be interested in forgoing a life on the stage for one in the kitchen?"

"I was thinking the same thing myself," Camille said. "My cook will soon be leaving me and going to live with relatives somewhere in the country." She glanced at him. "Why do you need a cook?"

"I believe I am going to stay in England."

Although she'd never confirmed it, she'd long ago assumed he was out of the country. "I see."

"And, as I will be needing a staff, a small one, I thought I would start with the cook." He paused. "Admittedly, I didn't come to that conclusion until I tasted Mrs. Fortesque's food."

"Well." She moved her plate to one side, folded her hands together on the tablecloth and smiled. "I do hate to disappoint you, as much as you liked Mrs. Fortesque's cooking. But if anyone hires the woman, it shall be me."

He slowly moved his plate out of the way, then folded his hands and rested them on the table, his position a mirror image of hers. A tiny trickle of apprehension slid down her spine.

"If I wish to hire Mrs. Fortesque," he said in a measured tone, "I shall do so."

"Not if I hire her first."

"Then I shall have to hire her last." He smiled pleasantly. It was most unsettling.

Her smile matched his. "Don't be absurd, you can't pay her the salary I can." His clothes were nice enough, but he couldn't possibly be of more than modest income. If he had done well, in spite of her avoiding all talk of him, she surely would have heard something about it. That sort of information did not stay quiet for long, let alone years. "Whatever you offer her, I shall simply offer her more."

"Because you have a great deal of money and I obviously have none?"

"It's so impolite to talk about money," she said in a lofty manner. "But yes."

He studied her for a long moment. "Salary aside, I would be willing to wager I can get the woman to come work for me."

At once, she was swept back to the days of their youth and silly wagers over insignificant contests: how many times in a row who could beat whom at chess, or who would spot the first clouded yellow butterfly in June, or who could identify the most constellations. She hadn't thought about their wagering in years. He had won more often than not. In hindsight she wasn't sure if that was attributable to his luck and skill or her own reluctance to best him. Resolve swept through her. Those days were over.

"What an interesting idea." She smiled. "I shall take that wager, Grayson."

"I thought you would. And I know that as you are a fair woman, and as I don't appear to have the same resources you do, you will agree that we do not use salary as a weapon. We both offer her precisely the same amount."

"I certainly wouldn't wager on my being fair, if I were you. You have no idea if I am a fair woman or not. Indeed, I rather prefer victory to being fair. However, I can agree to that." *For now.* She raised a questioning brow. "The usual stakes?"

"Absolutely." He nodded. "Shall we set a deadline?"

She thought for a moment. This would all be over the day after Christmas. "Let us say Christmas, shall we?"

"Christmas it is then." He stood, leaned forward and extended his hand across the table.

She leaned toward him, accepted his hand and nodded. "Christmas it is."

"I don't intend to lose, you know."

She laughed. "Goodness, Grayson, neither do I."

"Excellent." He grinned and his gaze caught hers. For a long moment, neither said a word. His hand still held hers across the table. Something nearly palpable wrapped around them. Something intense and unrelenting, pulling them closer. For one wild instant, an image flashed through her mind of his dragging her onto the table and ravishing her amidst the breakfast dishes and beneath the hundred-year-old chandelier commissioned for Millworth Manor by a long-forgotten ancestor. The two of them mad with passion and lost in desire. The chandelier above them quivered, and the table rocked and creaked, and—

"Camille?"

Camille started and yanked her hand from his. "What?"

Concern shadowed his brown eyes. "Are you all right?"

"Yes. Quite. Of course." She nodded vigorously. "Never better."

"Did you hear me?"

"Every word."

"Then after you." He gestured toward the door.

"To . . ."

"The attic?" He studied her closely. "Are you sure you're all right? You had the oddest look on your face a minute ago."

"Did I?" Without thinking she glanced at the chandelier. "It was the . . . something I ate, I think."

"You do look a bit flushed. Perhaps you should rest—"

"Don't be silly, I'm fine." She turned and started toward the stairs. He followed a half step behind.

Goodness, what was wrong with her? All that nonsense about ravishment and desire and passion. Whatever would have made her think such things? Why, she didn't even like the man. No doubt it was simply that last night he had brought back all sorts of memories and then he had kissed her. And kissed her quite thoroughly too. A kiss that worked its way into her dreams in those few moments last night when she'd managed to sleep at all. But she'd vanquished all dreams of his kiss years ago and she was not about to let one unguarded moment put it back in her head.

Nor was she about to let him snatch Mrs. Fortesque out from under her nose. She hadn't the least doubt she could win Mrs. Fortesque. But first, she had to win Mr. Fortesque. She had no worries about that either.

She led Grayson to the back stairway in the center section of the house. The manor was divided into three separate areas. The upper floors of the west wing, the oldest part of the house, were devoted mostly to bed-chambers and was little used in the colder months, un-less there were a great number of guests visiting. The top floors of the east wing housed the servants' quarters and the old nursery. The attic at the top of the main portion of the house was reserved for storage. They ran into no one on the stairs—not surprising, as the num-ber of actors/servants she had hired was less than half the usual staff.

"I was wondering," Grayson said on the stairs be-hind her as they approached the attic door, "why have Christmas here?"

She pushed open the door. "You mean at Millworth Manor?"

"Yes. Wouldn't it have been much easier to have staged this Christmas farce of yours at your own house? From what Win has written through the years, I under-stand you have a country estate, as well as a house in town."

She sighed. "Has Winfield told you everything about my life these past years?"

"Not everything." Grayson shrugged. "I can't imag-ine he knows everything."

"And men say women like to gossip." She moved into the attic. It was at once annoying and gratifying to know Grayson had followed the twists and turns of her life—especially as she had gone to great pains *not* to fol-low his.

"In answer to your question, the manor is where we always spend Christmas. When we have spent it together," she amended. "Which has been rare in recent years. But there is nowhere else I would rather be for Christmas. Certainly, after Father died, when Mother began filling the house with her odd assortment of lost souls, it grew a bit unusual—"

He snorted.

"But in many ways, all those people who had lost their homes, sharing our home at Christmas . . . Well"—she shrugged—"I may make disparaging comments about Mother's guests, and, indeed, there were any number of times when they could be quite bothersome to have around. Lord knows, little of it was especially proper, but, for the most part, they were usually very nice. And grateful to be here. They didn't always say it aloud, but one could tell. And no more so than at Christmas." She thought for a moment. "When I think of Christmas, I can't imagine marking it anywhere but here. I realize it's overly sentimental of me, but there you have it."

"It was never what one might call traditional."

"But always interesting," she said absently, surveying the attic. Even on a winter's day, there was enough light from the windows in the porticos to be able to see. Neatly stacked boxes, labeled and marked with their contents, crates and assorted trunks lined the short walls under the eaves. Miscellaneous, discarded furniture hidden under dust-covered cloths like ghostly guardians of the past clustered around the cut-stone columns, which supported the roof. The organized manner of the attic, thanks to industrious housekeepers, left a large empty space in the center of the room. She headed toward the far corner, where the Christmas

ornaments had been kept for as long as she could remember.

"Funny to think of all your memories packed away
up here," he said behind her.

"Now who is being sentimental?"

"Blame it on the season."

"Not just my memories, you know, or Beryl's and
Delilah's and Mother's, but those generations that
came before us. And not our family alone, mind you.
Millworth Manor has changed hands any number of
times since it was built. Everyone who has ever lived in
this house has made his or her mark upon it. And judging from the endless boxes up here, each previous oc-
cupant left something behind as well." She glanced
over her shoulder at him. "Should you ever need a costume from another age, I daresay, you could find one
here."

He chuckled. "I shall keep that in mind."

"Here they are." She stopped before a stack of four
boxes labeled *Christmas Tree* and picked one up. "They're
not very heavy, but they are a little awkward. We shall
have to make more than one trip."

"You have changed, Camille. I never imagined you,
of all people, carrying boxes for yourself."

"Neither did I." She sighed. "But one does what
one must."

"Don't be absurd. You pull the boxes out and I will
ferry them down the stairs," he said. "We can have your
footmen bring them down to the first floor later."

"I should hate to interrupt their swordplay." She
handed him the box.

He started for the stairs. "Sacrifices must be made.
It is Christmas, after all."

They made short work of getting the boxes out of

the attic. Grayson carried the final box to the floor below them, then returned.

"Is that it?"

Camille nodded; her gaze circled the room. "I haven't been up here in years. I always fancied it was filled with hidden treasures."

He grinned. "Pirate booty and the like."

"I shall have to come up and have a good look around one day. I can't imagine what might be hidden in some of these boxes and crates." She cast him a wry look. "It's entirely your fault, you know."

He gasped. "Mine?"

"All that sentimental nonsense about memories packed away."

"Perhaps," he said casually, "it's time to unpack some of them."

"Some memories are best left undisturbed," she said firmly.

"And some memories should be cherished." He fell silent for a long moment; then blew a resigned breath. "And we are here now."

"It's tempting." She looked around the vast space. "But I have a great deal to accomplish today."

"Nonsense." He scoffed. "It's been my observation that there hasn't been a moment since I arrived when you haven't been thinking about what to do next or worried about who might say what. Indeed, you can see the strain of all this on your face. Right here." He reached out and placed his finger between her brows. "There is a small furrow here that appears when you are concerned or thoughtful or annoyed. If you do not take care, it will form a permanent wrinkle."

"Don't be absurd." She brushed his hand away, then rubbed the spot he had just touched. "It is still there? Still wrinkled?"

He laughed.

"I don't mean to be vain." She frowned, then realized it would only make the furrow worse and composed her expression into something less likely to produce wrinkles. "But when one is getting older, one becomes more and more concerned about this sort of thing."

"You have nothing to worry about." He grabbed her shoulders, pulled her closer and planted a quick kiss on the spot between her brows. "The first moment I saw you again, I thought you were even lovelier than you were as a girl."

She stared up at him. Perhaps she did like him a little, after all. Perhaps she'd never stopped liking him, which scarcely mattered at any rate. "Why did you do that?"

"I couldn't resist." He kissed her forehead again, then released her.

"I shall slap you if you kiss me again," she warned. "Hard!"

"No, you won't." He sauntered away. "Besides, it's a risk I am willing to take. Where shall we start?"

"We shan't start anywhere. I don't have time for such nonsense."

"Make time."

"Grayson." She hesitated. What could it hurt, really? It was more than likely that no one else was up yet, anyway. She sighed. "Very well, but only for a few minutes." She glanced around, then nodded at a stack of trunks. "Why don't you see what's in one of those?"

"Even better, I'll open one and you open another." He flashed a wicked grin. "I'd be willing to bet I find one that is more interesting than yours."

"Honestly, Grayson." She rolled her gaze toward the rafters. "You haven't grown up the least little bit."

"I know," he said mournfully. "It's a burden I fear I must bear." He dropped to his knees before one of the trunks. "And yet, my trunk will still be much more interesting than yours."

In spite of herself, she laughed. "Not if I can help it." She scanned the attic, spotted a large trunk and started toward it. "That one's mine."

"Are there any real stories of long-lost treasure in your family?" He raised the lid of his trunk, the hinges squeaking in protest.

"No, more's the pity." She reached her trunk, knelt down in front of it and blew at the lid in a futile effort to clear away some of the dust. "One could always make use of long-lost treasure."

She raised the lid and studied the contents, ignoring a twinge of disappointment. Not that she truly expected treasure but it would have been nice. Inside the trunk lay old silks and satins, ball gowns from another age. She pulled one free and held it out in front of her to examine. The colors, varying shades of blue, were still bright, but the style was one that hadn't been in fashion for a good sixty years or more. It was charming, but it was not worthy of winning a wager.

"Very nice," Grayson said behind her.

She glanced at him. "What was in yours?"

"Mostly papers, letters, that sort of thing. Nothing of any real interest." He shrugged in an offhand fashion.

She brightened. "Well, my trunk is more interesting than yours. And I win."

"This time." He smiled. "Chocolates, then?"

"Swiss, if you please." It struck her that it was sweet of him to remember that her winnings were always chocolate. But then, if she had lost, she would have owed him Turkish delight. She hadn't thought about their penchant for silly wagers in years; yet she remembered the Turkish delight. And he remembered the chocolate.

"Who do you suppose might have worn that?" He gestured at the dress in her hands.

"Elizabeth Bennet," she said without thinking.

"Correct me if I'm wrong, but wasn't Elizabeth Bennet a literary figure? A figment from the imagination of Jane Austen?"

"Yes, but this dress is from that time." She turned it this way and that. "It might have been worn to a grand ball once, possibly hosted by the Prince Regent."

"At a royal palace, perhaps?"

She bit back a smile. "Where else?"

"Where else, indeed. The lady who wore that, no doubt, attended any number of grand balls at royal palaces, where she would dance every dance with a handsome prince. Much like those in the fairy stories you used to read. I can see it now." He waved in a grand gesture. "She, and we, are in a massive ballroom lit with a thousand candles glittering in a hundred chandeliers of crystal and gold."

"Or she, *we,* could be in a dim, dusty attic." She folded the gown and put it back in the trunk.

"Not anymore. Over there"—he waved at a cluster of several pieces of tall, cloth-covered furniture—"is the orchestra. They're quite good, don't you think?" He winced. "Oh, dear. One of the violinists just hit a sour note."

"I think you're quite mad." But, admittedly, amusing.

He ignored her. "There are urns filled to overflowing with hothouse blooms. The ladies are wearing their finest jewels and their gowns are as colorful as the rubies and emeralds and sapphires around their necks."

"And the gentlemen?"

"Handsome and dashing."

She arched a brow. "All of them?"

"Well"—he glanced from side to side as though concerned he might be overheard—"all of them think they are." He held out his hand to her.

She accepted it and rose to her feet. She studied him for a moment, then surrendered. Regardless of anything else, she preferred he not think of her as stiff and stodgy. She used to be great fun and still was, when she wasn't busy orchestrating a perfect Christmas with a hired family for the prince whom she probably no longer intended to marry.

"Even those like"—she nodded discreetly toward a corner of the attic—"Lord SuchandSuch. He passed portly some time ago and has only a few teeth."

"He thinks it makes him look like a pasha."

"And Mr. Whoeverheis?"

"The one who is so short that his nose practically rests in your bosom when you dance?"

She choked back a laugh. "Grayson!"

"Oh, he most certainly thinks he's dashing." He peered around her as if looking past her through a crowd of guests. "And then, of course, there's the foreign prince."

"There usually are at these things." She shrugged.

"Handsome devil, though."

"Always at balls of this sort."

He nodded somberly. "Grand."

"Imaginary."

"So . . . the handsome prince, very blond, no taller than I." He glanced at her for confirmation.

She nodded.

"Charming as well. Everything one could want in a prince. One might even say 'perfect.' "

Nikolai really was perfect, all in all. Such a pity. She sighed. "Indeed he is."

"Well, then," Grayson said after a long pause. He swept a theatrical bow. "May I have the honor of this dance, Miss Channing?"

"Grayson, I—"

"Perhaps you've forgotten, but it was at your first ball, very much like this one, that I had the honor of being your very first dance partner."

"Of course I remember. I also remember it was only because your aunt made you."

"Not at all," he said indignantly. "My aunt made me attend dance lessons here with you and Beryl because your mother had hired a dance master. I'm not sure how Win ever learned to dance, as he was unfailingly absent." He opened his arms. "Now, will you dance with me or not?"

She hesitated. Why not? "I should be delighted." She took his hand and rested her free hand on his shoulder. "I do hope you are better at it now."

"I would have to be." He started to waltz her around the open center area of the attic. "Aside from that one note, they do play well, don't they?"

"I have always loved this waltz."

"I remember."

"You can't possibly know what waltz is in my head."

"The 'Vienna Blood Waltz,' of course. It was always your favorite."

"You do seem to remember a great deal."

"Ah yes, a blessing and a curse."

"A curse?"

He smiled and started to hum the music.

"This is ridiculous," she murmured but hummed along with him, nonetheless. Within moments they were flying over the rough wood floor of the attic. She wasn't sure if she hummed as much as she laughed, and wondered how long it had been since she'd been quite this silly. They danced well together, but then they had learned together. They whirled around the attic until they reached the music's crescendo, humming it in a manner no one the least bit familiar with the "Vienna Blood Waltz" would have recognized.

Grayson finished the waltz with a musical flourish, which was as theatrical as anything Fortesque might have come up with.

He grinned down at her. "Thank you for the dance, Miss Channing."

She could scarcely catch her breath. "My pleasure, Mr. Elliott."

He stared into her eyes for a long moment. Surely, he didn't intend to kiss her again? She had been quite serious when she'd threatened to slap him. Still, that didn't mean that she wouldn't kiss him back. She raised her head and leaned forward slightly.

"Well." He released her without warning and stepped back. "I don't want to keep you any longer. I know how busy you are today. We should be getting back downstairs."

Shock washed through her, as if she had indeed been slapped. Apparently, he had no intention of kissing her. Not that she wanted him to. Still, there were, well, procedures for this sort of thing. Steps that led logically from one point to another. Gazing into her eyes, not releasing her from his embrace and then . . . nothing?

Well, what could she expect from a man who declared his love, then abandoned her? Grayson never did know how to do things properly.

"Extremely busy." She marched toward the stairs, a brusque note in her voice. "I haven't time for this sort of nonsense." She turned on her heel and aimed a pointed finger at him. "Or for foolish memories." She nodded, turned and continued for the stairs.

"My apologies," he said softly.

"For what?" she snapped.

"Everything?"

"It's not that easy, Grayson."

"I didn't think it would be." He sighed.

No, it wasn't that easy to waltz back into her life. She would not allow it. Not allow him to pick up where he had left off. It wasn't easy at all.

For either of them.

Twelve

Of all the things he remembered about Camille, Gray didn't remember her being quite so confusing. Certainly, she'd been obstinate as a girl, and she had all too often leapt headfirst long before she looked. She was, as well, unbecomingly competitive on occasion—although she rarely bested him—but she was never especially confusing. No, if memory served him right, she had been as easy to read as an open book in those days.

Gray paced the entry hall by the front door. He was to take the prince on a long walk, as per Camille's instructions. At least she trusted him to do that much, but that was the extent of it. It was obvious that he had lost the trust that once went hand in hand with their friendship.

Still, she could deny it as much as she wished, but there remained something between them. Some spark, minimal perhaps, but there nonetheless. When he had told her he loved her, all those years ago, he had been certain she loved him as well. He had known it as he had never known anything before or since. Perhaps if he hadn't let pride and pain drive him away . . . Perhaps if he hadn't been so young and foolish . . .

Regardless, nothing could be done about the past now, save overcome it. For that, he would need time, and time was short. Christmas was a mere three days away, and Camille planned to leave with her prince the day after.

Determination narrowed his eyes. Not if he could help it. If he was to reclaim Camille's heart, he would first have to do something about Pruzinsky. With any luck at all, Beryl's investigator would uncover useful information about the man before it was too late. However, it had been his experience that waiting was not the best way to achieve one's goals. He hadn't made his fortune by waiting.

He organized the points in his head. Number one: Earn Camille's forgiveness. From what Win had surmised, her anger probably stemmed from Gray's declaring his love on the day before her wedding and then never speaking with her again. In hindsight that was a mistake. A mistake of epic proportions. He had been her friend. He had stunned her with his revelation and then given her no real chance to respond. If she had shared his feelings, as he knew in his heart she had, how must she have felt when he didn't come back that day? When he didn't stop her wedding? When years passed and her husband died and he still did not return?

He had never before put himself in her shoes. Now that he had—he winced—damnation. He would be angry in her place. Furious and unrelenting. And it would take a great deal to earn his forgiveness, if indeed it could be earned at all.

Number two: He had to regain the friendship they had once shared. Helping her in her Christmas farce was a start, even if he didn't want it to be successful. At least not to the point where she won the hand of her perfect prince. Of course, if it blew up in her face, there would be no way to keep the debacle quiet. Her reputation would be shattered. He couldn't have that either. What he had to do was make this Christmas plot even more difficult to manage than it already was, in hopes of bringing her to her senses. Make her realize that a man, even a prince, whom she needed to put on an act for, wasn't a man worth having. And certainly wasn't worthy of having her.

And therein lay his confusion. Last night there had been a moment when she was speaking of marrying the prince, when he thought she had surely changed her mind. But today in the attic, when they spoke of the imaginary prince at the ball—and it was obvious they were describing Pruzinsky—she had sighed in a most heartfelt manner, as if the prince was all she wanted in the world. Last night she had kissed him back. There was no doubt of that. Then today she had threatened bodily harm if he kissed her again; yet, only a few minutes later, she obviously wanted him to do just that. It was most confusing. He didn't know what she wanted.

Although, perhaps, neither did she. He smiled slowly. The Camille he remembered always knew her own mind, what she wanted and what she didn't. This was a very good sign.

So he would gain her forgiveness, earn back her friendship; then number three: He would win her heart. It was an excellent plan, lacking only the minor details. An idea flashed through his mind as to what else might make this a perfect Mr. Dickens's Christmas and complicate the proceedings as well. He grinned. She had everything else. How could she have forgotten this? He would arrange for it at once. He headed to the library and penned a quick note to Win. On his return to the entry, he gave it to a footman with instructions to deliver it at once.

For now, he would take Pruzinsky on a long walk to the pond to determine if it was frozen enough for skating. And in the process, he would see what he might be able to learn about Camille's prince.

Gray started back down the stairs to the front entry and his heart sank. Pruzinsky waited for him with Camille. Blast it all. He wanted to get the prince alone. His step slowed.

She glanced up at him. "We were beginning to think you had changed your mind."

No, not Camille—it was Beryl. Relief washed through him. He usually had been able to tell one twin from the other, if only because Camille's eyes lit with affection when she saw him—or at least they had once. Beryl's gaze, however, tended to be cool and assessing. There was a slight difference in the timbre of their voices as well. Of course, that was a long time ago.

He plastered a smile on his face. "Are you joining us?"

"There is nothing I like better than a brisk late-morning walk on a cold winter's day," Beryl said with an enthusiasm that didn't fool him for a moment. Beryl had never been the kind of woman who took well to the out-of-doors under less than ideal conditions. She was obviously here at the insistence of her sister. Still, this might give him the opportunity to pull her aside and find out exactly what she had meant when she'd said he had broken Camille's heart. He never went into a business negotiation without knowing all the facts and he wanted to know them now. Gray joined the couple and nodded a good day to the prince.

"Your Highness." What was it about foreign royalty

that gave one the oddest desire to click one's heels together? He resisted it.

Pruzinsky raised a chastising brow.

"My apologies, *Count*," Gray said.

"I know it is difficult for you English, dispensing with the formality of titles. I find it most amusing." The prince chuckled. "You may consider it a royal command, if it eases your British sensibilities."

"How very gracious of you," Beryl said with a smile.

The prince returned her smile; then stepped aside to allow the lone footman present to help him with his cloak.

Beryl stepped closer to Gray and lowered her voice. "Camille thought it would be better not to leave you alone with the prince."

"I said I wouldn't shoot him," Gray said quietly. "What more can she ask for?"

"Apparently, she thinks there is a great deal more. Besides, you know what they say about keeping your enemies closer than even your friends."

"I am not her enemy."

"It remains to be seen exactly what you are. Friend or enemy, it scarcely matters at the moment." Beryl shrugged. "Neither of us trusts you." Her gaze strayed to Pruzinsky. "Of course neither you nor I trust him." She closed her eyes for a moment as if saying a silent prayer. "Oh, it's going to be a jolly Christmas."

Gray choked back a laugh.

Pruzinsky glanced at them. "Are we ready?"

"As ready as we shall ever be." Beryl adjusted her fur-trimmed bonnet. A fetching thing, really, although he doubted that it would keep her warm. He wouldn't be at all surprised if Beryl abandoned them within moments of leaving the house. She took the prince's arm. "Shall we?"

Pruzinsky stared down at her. "This is something I shall have to get accustomed to, you know."

"What?" She smiled up at him. "A long walk on a winter's day?"

"No." He smiled. "Enjoying the company of two beautiful women who look exactly the same. I am a most fortunate man."

Gray coughed.

"Indeed, you are. And so clever to appreciate it." Beryl shot Gray a sharp look, then returned her attention to the prince. "Not all men are so intelligent."

The footman opened the door and they stepped outside, but not before Gray noticed the servant/actor in question now sported a long, drooping mustache, white hair and comically bushy eyebrows. Gray did wonder what part this particular footman was rehearsing. He caught the footman/actor's eye and winked. The young man's eyes widened in surprise. Gray stifled a grin. Excellent.

They strolled briskly down the road leading to the pond; Gray a step behind Beryl and the prince. Beryl hung on Pruzinsky's arm. Under other circumstances, Gray would have suspected her of flirting. Today he was fairly sure she was just trying to keep warm. He tried not to smirk. No, Beryl would not be with them for long. The prince, on the other hand, appeared invigorated by the cold winter day. Gray, too, found the crisp air refreshing.

Pruzinsky inhaled deeply. "I must confess, I enjoy days like this."

"Cold, gray and bleak," Beryl muttered.

"Not at all," Pruzinsky said. "I find serenity in the starkness of a winter's day. And there is nothing like sharp, cold air to get the blood moving. To reinvigorate one's senses."

"My thoughts exactly," Beryl said under her breath, then forced a smile. "Tell me, Count, is your country at all like England?"

"I haven't seen all of England, but I would say we are much more mountainous. You see, we are nestled between Russia, Prussia and Austria."

"Quite a strategic spot," Gray said, although that geography didn't seem quite right to him. Still, that part of the world was constantly shifting, and where boundaries were drawn today might not be where they were yesterday or would be tomorrow.

He had spent a few minutes in the manor's library after his foray in the attic with Camille, wanting to see if he could discover anything more about the prince's kingdom. And, indeed, he had found everything as Win had said. Avalonia hadn't existed as a sovereign country for more than sixty years. That meant there was no castle, certainly no crown prince and, more than likely, no fortune. Still, if he said anything to Camille before he knew exactly who this man was and what he wanted—and if he was wrong—she would never forgive him. There was, as well, the distinct possibility she would never forgive him if he was right either.

"Our location has proven our salvation more than once through the centuries," Pruzinsky said. "We have either been too small or too well protected or too inconvenient to be bothered with."

"How fascinating." Gray resisted the urge to point his finger and shout "Aha!" He had read the same thing, nearly word for word, in the encyclopedia where he'd found his information. Information anyone could find with minimal effort. Now that he thought about it, hadn't the book Pruzinsky replaced on the shelves last night been a volume of the encyclopedia?

"You must miss it," Beryl said.

"One always misses one's home." Just the right touch of longing sounded in Pruzinsky's voice. Oh, he was good, whoever he was. "Especially at this time of year."

"Do tell us about Christmas in your country, Count." Beryl glanced at Gray with a look that said she was as skeptical of what he was saying as Gray was.

"Oh, I daresay, you don't want to hear me reminisce about Christmases long past."

"Oh, but we do." Beryl fluttered her lashes at him. "I can't imagine anything more fascinating than hearing about Christmas in another land."

"Very well." Pruzinsky thought for a minute. "We are quite a merry people. The weeks leading up to Christmas . . ."

Pruzinsky proceeded to spin a tale every bit as elaborate as those told by Mr. Henderson and, no doubt, with just as little substance. His story of Christmas festivals and jolly villagers and gifts distributed by Father Christmas sounded more to Gray like a fairy story spun from sugar plums and gingerbread than anything that might conceivably be legitimate. Beryl was obviously thinking the same thing. She smoothly turned back the subject from Christmas to the country itself. Again his details were straight from the encyclopedia. By the time they reached the pond, Gray had no doubt the man had never seen the verdant valley and snowcapped mountains of the country that no longer existed.

Beryl surveyed the frozen expanse. Benches placed along the perimeter of the pond provided restful spots to sit and enjoy the peaceful setting in the summer and places to perch to attach skates in the winter. She nodded. "It looks solid enough for skating."

"We should do more than look if we are to allow anyone on it." Gray took a tentative step on the ice and bounced slightly. He had skated on this pond as a boy and knew how it looked when it was frozen solid and when it wasn't. It had the right appearance and he heard no telltale sounds of cracking. Regardless, it was best to be sure. "I'll go out a bit farther." He glanced at Pruzinsky. "I say, would you be a good chap and walk around to the other side and check the ice." He pointed to a bench on the opposite side of the pond.

"Are you certain?" Doubt shaded the prince's handsome face. "Perhaps I should stay here so that I might be of assistance, should the ice not be as sound as it appears."

"Oh, but until you get to the very middle," Beryl said quickly, "the water scarcely comes up to your waist. Even if Grayson fell through, he would barely be more than inconvenienced."

Gray raised a brow. " 'Inconvenienced'?"

"No more than that." Beryl shrugged. "It's entirely too shallow to drown. Certainly, you would be wet and cold. It would be most uncomfortable, but not fatal. Besides, I am here to assist you."

Gray eyed her skeptically. "You'll pull me out of the water?"

"No, Cousin, dear." Beryl grinned. "I shall fetch help."

"That is a relief," he said wryly.

"Then I shall leave you in capable hands and check the ice elsewhere." Pruzinsky nodded and started around the pond.

Gray took a few more cautious steps forward.

"Goodness, Grayson," Beryl called, "you can tell just by the color of it that the pond is suitable for skating." She joined him on the ice.

"I'm trying to make certain," he said in a lofty manner.

"You're trying to make a good show of it." She sniffed. "I know your main purpose in taking this endless walk in this dreadful weather was to find out what you could about Pruzinsky."

"And I thought I was simply being helpful by occupying his time and keeping him away from the 'family.' "

"You can do both." She glanced at Pruzinsky. "He can't hear us now." Nonetheless, she lowered her voice. "He's not who he says he is, is he?"

He studied her. "Have you heard from your investigators?"

"Not yet, but I did some investigating of my own. In the library." A hard note sounded in her voice. "There is no Kingdom of Avalonia, Greater or otherwise."

"I know."

She frowned in suspicion. "How do you know?"

He thought it wise not to mention how long he had known and that he had not shared that information with her. "Apparently, I had the same thought. I was in the library this morning."

"I wish Camille had shared our thoughts. She is not a stupid woman yet this . . . *him* . . ." Beryl blew a frustrated breath. "She was obviously swept away by charm and his dashing good looks and her own desires."

"What do you think he wants?"

"Money, of course. Camille's husband left her a considerable fortune. The nerve of the man." She huffed. "Admittedly, I have never been opposed to those who wish to better themselves by marriage. And Lord knows I have no difficulty with marrying for money."

"Not that I've heard."

"Nor am I the most, oh, aboveboard person—"

He snorted.

She ignored him. "When it comes to getting something that I want, I have never had a particular problem with a bit of deception. And if Camille and this man had fallen in love, even if he is penniless, I would not oppose such a marriage. However"—she studied Pruzinsky—"I do not wish to see my sister shackled for the rest of her life to a man who has led her to believe he is something he is not. A man who has deceived and tricked her."

He chose his words with care. "And yet she is deceiving him about her family."

"That's an entirely different thing." She waved off his comment. "It's an innocent deception, really. Intended to provide that bounder with the kind of Christmas he has told her he desires. Why, the man is using Christmas to get what he wants. Is there anything more despicable than employing Christmas to perpetrate a fraud?"

He resisted the urge to point out the irony. "Not to my knowledge."

"I know what you're thinking, Grayson, that Camille was doing much the same thing. But her deception was in the nature of . . . of . . . a good deed. Yes, that's what it was." She nodded. "Why, in many ways, it's not merely thoughtful, but it's rather noble of her."

" 'Noble' is not the word I'd use."

"No one cares about the word you would use," Beryl said sharply. "My sister has a good heart. And she never would have married him without telling him the truth about her masquerade."

"No doubt." He blew a long breath. Telling Camille the truth would not be easy, but it had to be done. "When do we tell her about Pruzinsky?"

"We don't," she said simply.

"She should be told, as soon as possible."

She cast him a pitying look. "You're really rather a stupid man, after all. I can't imagine how you managed to make all that money."

He clenched his jaw. "Why aren't we telling her about Pruzinsky?"

She stared at him in disbelief. "No one wants to be told they've been made a fool of. And in such a grand manner. She would hate us. You more than me, but she wouldn't be pleased with me either. And we really don't have any real evidence yet, do we?"

"He talks about becoming king of a country that doesn't exist."

"Yes, but he's obviously a clever devil, and such talk can be explained away. Even if we told her what we know, there is every possibility she wouldn't believe us at first and might do something rash. She has yet to conquer her own nature when it comes to surrendering to impulse. No, she must come to this realization on her own. And we have to let this drama play out."

" 'Play out'?" He stared. "She could marry him."

"Nonsense." She scoffed. "The plan was for him to be called away the day after Christmas."

"The monetary crisis." He grimaced.

She nodded. "And she was to go with him."

"We can't allow that."

"And we won't, if it gets that far, and I'm hoping it doesn't."

"Mr. Elliott," Pruzinsky called from the opposite shore, "it looks safe. Shall I try to walk across?"

"Excellent idea!" Grayson yelled back.

"Oh, do be careful, Count," Beryl called, then lowered her voice. "I should hate to get my skirts wet fishing you out, although an unfortunate accident—"

"Beryl!"

"I was just thinking aloud. I would never . . ." She paused. "Well, probably never resort to unfortunate accidents."

"Imagine my relief."

She ignored him. "Before we came up with the idea of calling him home, Camille had already planned to accompany him back to his country. I would be willing to wager, the count—and I am fairly certain he is neither a count nor is his name Pruzinsky—"

"It was the family name of the last rulers of Avalonia."

"I know that. Apparently, I read the same book you did." She rolled her gaze heavenward. "As I was saying, I suspect he never had any intention of allowing that to happen."

"As he has no country to take her to."

"Exactly." Beryl nodded. "So, as Camille was giving him the perfect Christmas and expecting him to propose, I would imagine his plan was similar. A quick marriage and some reason as to why they couldn't return to his country."

"Perhaps because it's been annexed by Russia and his family thrown out?"

"Very good, Grayson. A half-truth is always more believable than an outright lie."

"And who would know better than you?"

"Exactly." It was a measure of her concern for Camille that Beryl didn't bite off his head. Her gaze strayed back to Pruzinsky. "Whoever he is, he is clearly intelligent enough to have come up with this scheme, employing a country that no longer exists and the proper name to go along with it. I wouldn't have been the least bit suspicious if not for his lack of royal demeanor. No accoutrements, indeed." She huffed in disdain. "No, he is clever and we cannot underestimate him. If he knows we are the least bit suspicious, he might well seek to elope with her."

Gray crossed his arms over his chest and glared. "If we're not going to tell her, then what do you propose we do?"

"I don't know," she snapped. "But I do know my sis-

ter. Soon I suspect—and this is a point I have already
made to her, I might add—she will begin to wonder why
she is going to all this trouble for any man. Even a
prince. Then she will realize she can't possibly spend
the rest of her life with a man she cannot be honest
with. If nothing else, we have always been honest with
the men we married." She nodded slowly. "In the mean-
time, we must keep a close watch on Camille."

"And what about Pruzinsky? Shouldn't we be watching him as well?"

"It doesn't matter what he does, as long as he doesn't
do it with my sister." Her eyes narrowed in thought.
"She's been somewhat frantic trying to manage the actors and put together her perfect Mr. Dickens's Christmas. The busier she is, the more likely she is to come to
her senses about why she is doing it. Perhaps . . ."

"What?"

"Well, all in all, aside from a few conversational faux
pas, things ran smoothly yesterday and—as Camille has
every minute of today planned—today might be uneventful as well."

"And?"

"And while this farce of hers is fraught with the possibility of disaster, we cannot count on that."

"I'm afraid I don't see—"

"Goodness, Grayson, aren't you listening?" She
sighed the way one might when dealing with a very
young child. Or an idiot. "If things run smoothly, she
won't be as busy. If she isn't busy juggling this enterprise every moment, she won't think in terms of why
she is doing something so absurd and so difficult and
instead spend more time with whoever-he-is. And even
you must admit the man is practically irresistible."

"Aside from all that smiling and nodding."

"In truth, that was a nice touch." She watched Pruzinsky inching his way across the pond. "We need to make certain the Christmas pageant at Millworth Manor does not go well. Chaos, Grayson, would be most helpful." She glanced at Gray. "Why are you staring at me like that?"

"In horror, you mean?"

"Yes."

"It seems you and I think in much the same way."

She shuddered. "That is horrible."

"For us both. However, if you want chaos . . ." He smiled slowly. "I have just the thing."

"I like the wicked tone in your voice. You might well be smarter than I thought." She watched Pruzinsky approach. "He hasn't seduced her yet, or she hasn't seduced him. Regardless, it hasn't happened. That would make his betrayal so much worse." She shook her head. "Trust me on this point."

"Oh?"

"It's a long and sordid story, Grayson. One you shall never hear."

"What a shame." He chuckled. "It sounds so interesting."

"Oh, it's definitely interesting." She tried and failed to hide a wry smile. "Don't think because we are now allies to save Camille that we are friends as well."

"I would never think that."

"Good, because we aren't. I still don't trust you. But I am confident that you don't wish to see her hurt or seduced or, God forbid, married to this charlatan."

"I will not allow that to happen." His jaw tightened. "You may trust in that."

"Because you still love her?"

"Because I . . ." His gaze jerked to hers. "Why do you say that?"

"Oh, I don't know, Grayson." Sarcasm dripped from

her words. "Let me think. You're home for the first time in eleven years, and instead of being with your family, you're pretending to be a member of ours. There are other signs as well, which I don't think she has noticed, but are obvious to me. I would list them for you, but as the 'count' will be with us in another minute or so, that shall have to wait." She adopted a brilliant smile and waved gaily at Pruzinsky.

"That's not all you and I need to talk about," he said in a hard tone. "I want to know what you meant when you said I had broken her heart."

Beryl's eyes widened with disbelief. "You mean that, don't you? You really don't know?"

"Know what?" he ground out through clenched teeth.

"I take back anything I said about you being smarter than you look. Apparently, you are not." She moved away to greet Pruzinsky.

It struck him that winning Camille's heart meant Beryl would be his sister. For the rest of his life. He thrust the thought aside. Camille was worth it.

Beryl kept the count busy on the walk back expounding on life in Avalonia. Every now and then, he noticed the muscles of her jaw twitch, as if she was grinding her teeth, or fighting the urge to say something or maybe smack him. Still, of all the actors in her sister's Christmas farce, he had to admit Beryl might well be the best. It would have been most amusing if not for the stakes involved: Camille's fortune, Camille's heart and the rest of her life.

He had no need or desire for Camille's fortune, but her heart and the rest of her life would belong to him.

Now he just had to convince her.

Thirteen

For a moment, Camille was tempted to close her eyes and savor the serenity of gliding across the frozen pond. The stillness of the late winter afternoon surrounded her, crept into her soul, soothed her. She had nearly forgotten how peaceful it could be. How the tranquility she had once found here made her feel as if she could accomplish anything she set her mind on. Surrounded by the frozen fields and bare trees starkly outlined against the gray sky, it had always reminded her of a magical place to be found only in fairy stories. She'd skated often as a girl, but it had been a very long time since she last stepped foot upon the ice. Her hands were deep in her fur muff; her head was kept warm by her fur-lined hat. She reveled in the bracing feel of the cold breeze upon her face.

Grayson skated up beside her. "You're to be congratulated. All seems to be going smoothly."

The moment vanished and she cast him a skeptical look. "I am not as silly as that. The very instant I start thinking things are going well will be precisely when disaster strikes." She glanced at the bench by the side of the pond where Nikolai and Miss Murdock chatted and laughed together. Nikolai had begged off skating, claiming that a long-ago ankle injury limited his ability on skates, but he had gallantly insisted the others enjoy themselves. "And I don't like that one bit."

"Jealous?"

"Don't be absurd." She settled her hands deeper into her muff and raised her chin. "In spite of Miss Murdock's proclivity for flirtation, I have no doubts as to Nikolai's affections."

"I see," Grayson said slowly. "He has declared himself then?"

"Not yet." Nor did she intend to allow him to do so. While a kiss might well change everything, she was fairly certain that marriage to Nikolai was no longer her ambition. Her only goal now was to achieve her perfect Christmas, stay clear of a proposal, get rid of the man and avoid scandal. "I'm just not sure leaving him alone with Miss Murdock is a good idea. I do wish Beryl had come with us."

Beryl had refused to accompany them, saying she had spent more than enough time in the out-of-doors this morning, thank you very much, and had some reading she wished to catch up on in the library. Odd, as Beryl had never been especially inclined toward reading, but then she had never been overly fond of out-of-doors activities either.

"Camille," Grayson began, "about Pruzinsky—"

"Grayson, I know you neither like nor trust him, so I would much prefer not to discuss him with you."

"Very well." His gaze slid to the other couple on the ice. "Then shall we discuss how Mrs. Montgomery-Wells and Mr. Henderson are remarkably proficient on skates?"

She turned her attention to the older pair. "I'm not

sure 'proficient' is the right word. 'Adequate' might be better. Neither has fallen, at any rate." Mrs. Montgomery-Wells could be heard giggling like a schoolgirl and Mr. Henderson looked to be having a jolly time as well. Camille smiled reluctantly. "They do seem to be having an enjoyable time of it."

"No doubt reliving more youthful days." He chuckled. "Which I can well understand. I haven't skated in years."

"And yet you haven't fallen either."

"Nor have you."

"You should congratulate me for that as well. I can't remember the last time I was on skates." She shook her head. "Odd how things you haven't given a second thought to come back to you when you need them."

"This does bring back fond memories, you know." He made a fast rotation on the flat of his blade to skate backward, facing her.

She stifled a smile. "Now you're just trying to show off."

"And doing a fine job of it, I'd say." He grinned. The cold had reddened his cheeks and his dark eyes sparkled. Without warning, the years vanished and she was back to those long-ago days when she had ignored how much she had adored him because they were never meant to be anything more than friends. For a moment, she saw the fun-loving, adventurous boy he'd once been. Now, with the passage of years, he'd grown into the handsome promise of his youth, with a fine veneer of intelligence and experience that made him dashing and interesting and . . . seductive. Blasted man. "But if I really wanted to show off, I would challenge you to a race."

"Nonsense, Grayson." She sniffed. "We are not children now."

"Even so, I daresay, I could still beat you."

"You only beat me then because I allowed you to do so."

"That's not exactly as I remember it."

"Age is no doubt addling your mind."

He laughed. "I beat you then because I was stronger and faster. And you were a mere girl."

"As I am no longer a mere girl," she said, "should I wish to engage in such a childish pursuit, I have no doubt I could best you handily."

"I would be willing to take the chance." His eyes shimmered with laughter. "And I would win."

"Not if I threw a stone in your path to trip you up." She smiled sweetly.

He gasped. "That wouldn't be fair."

"Fair would be if you had to skate in skirts. As you would not, I would feel no qualms whatsoever about taking any advantage that came my way. Fair or not, I would still enjoy triumphing over you." She shrugged. "All is fair in love and war, you know."

"And what is this?" His smile remained, but his tone was abruptly sober. "Love or war?"

"Both," she said without thinking; then realized what she had said, turned and skated off. Whatever possessed her to say that? Perhaps it had been love once, but now . . . now it was . . . what?

"You're not getting away that easily!" he called after her.

She skated faster, but he was ahead of her in a flash. He turned and stopped abruptly, his blades shaving the ice in what might have been an impressive display under other circumstances. He was too close; and before she could veer away, she slid into him. He caught her in his arms and stared down at her.

"It's not war, Camille."

Her heartbeat quickened. "It's not love."

"It could be." His gaze bored into hers. "It was once."

She started to deny it, but what was the point? Even if she'd never told him. Even if he'd never given her the chance. " 'Once' was a very long time ago."

He studied her closely. "Your sister said I broke your heart."

"And you said I broke yours." She stared into his dark eyes.

"You did," he said simply.

"Oh, come now." She pulled out of his arms. "One would think a man with a broken heart would do something, anything, to—"

"Lady Lydingham!" One of her footmen ran toward the pond waving frantically. Odd, she didn't remember any of them having bright red hair.

"Excellent timing," Gray said under his breath.

"Indeed, it is," she snapped. "But you are right about one thing. We do need to talk about the past." She nodded and skated toward the footman waiting at the edge of the pond.

"Lady Lydingham." The poor man struggled to catch his breath. He must have run all the way. And was he wearing a wig? "Lady Dunwell says you must return immediately. She said it's of dire importance."

"Of course she does." Camille knew the moment she relaxed her guard, disaster would strike. She stepped off the ice.

"What is it?" Grayson said behind her.

"I don't know," she said sharply, grabbing his arm to steady herself while she removed her blades. It struck her how natural and familiar it seemed to lean on him for balance. She shoved the thought aside. There were far more pressing matters to concern herself with at the moment. She glanced at the footman. What could possibly be of dire importance? Nikolai and everyone else in the "family" were here. "I can't leave now. Are you sure it's important?"

"She said she would have my head if you did not return at once." The young man's eyes widened. "Pardon my saying, my lady, but I think she meant it."

"No doubt," Grayson muttered.

"You can make yourself useful by staying with the others. Here, take these." She handed Grayson her skates. "They'll only slow me down." She nodded at the servant. "Come along." They started back toward the house.

"I'm coming with you," Grayson called after her.

"No, you're not!" She didn't turn to see if he was doing as she asked; only picked up her pace. The footman was taller than she was, and she had to work to keep up with him. "And you, take that stupid thing off."

"Yes, my lady." He snatched the wig off his head. Obviously, she would need to have another chat with Fortesque.

They trimmed a good ten minutes off the half-hour walk. The house was almost in sight when Grayson joined them.

"I thought I asked you to remain at the pond?" She huffed.

"I thought you might need my help," he said. "If this is indeed of dire importance. And I have taken care of the others."

"Have you now?"

"I cut through the fields and went directly to the stables. I arranged for your carriage to pick up everyone at the pond. They should be no more than ten minutes behind us," he said. "Clever of you not to have actors take the places of your carriage driver and groom."

WHAT HAPPENS AT CHRISTMAS 203

"They're very loyal, they can be trusted and they don't gossip. Besides, I needed them. It appears servants who work primarily out-of-doors do not long to be on the stage the same way others might." She leveled a hard look at the footman. He winced and walked faster.

They turned onto the front drive and approached the manor. They were nearly there, when the door slammed open. Beryl fairly flew down the drive toward them.

"Good Lord, Beryl." Camille stared at her sister. "What is it?"

"Children!" Beryl could scarcely get the word out. Her always composed, completely self-possessed sister had the appearance of someone who had just escaped from Bedlam. "There are children here. Dozens and dozens of children! They were . . ." Her eyes grew wider if possible. "Delivered! And this"—she thrust an envelope at Gray—"came with them. For you!"

"Ah yes, of course. I was expecting this." He tore open the envelope. "Not so quickly, but I knew I could count on Win."

"Grayson." Camille stared at him in horror, a dreadful sense of apprehension twisting in her stomach. "What have you done?"

"A brilliant job, I would say." He pulled out a folded note, shook it open and read.

"Children!" Beryl sputtered and grabbed her sister's arm. "They're everywhere, Camille. Everywhere, I tell you."

"Grayson." Camille studied him closely. The damnable man didn't look the least bit concerned, but then perhaps children didn't affect him the way they did Beryl. "Why are there children in the house?"

"Well, as you are trying to have a Christmas based

on the works of Mr. Dickens, and most of his books have orphans in them . . ." He shrugged. "I thought a few orphans would only increase the authenticity."

" 'Orphans'?" Disbelief widened her eyes. *"Orphans?"*

He grinned in an all too satisfied manner. "Orphans."

"Grayson." Camille resisted the urge—no, the need—to scream. *"Oliver Twist* has orphans! *Great Expectations* has orphans! *The Old Curiosity Shop* has orphans! There are no orphans in *A Christmas Carol!"*

"Are you sure?" he asked with obvious suspicion.

"Yes," she hissed the word.

"My mistake." He shrugged. "But as it happens . . ." He glanced back at the note. "These are not orphans. They were simply going to *act* the part of orphans."

"I don't want orphans!"

"Not that we aren't concerned about orphans," Beryl said quickly. "Camille and I both raise funds and donate and do what we can to help the plight of—"

"Now is not the time," Camille snapped.

"I thought it was worth mentioning, as you're not being the least bit charitable at the moment," Beryl said, "toward orphans. At Christmas."

Camille clenched her teeth. "I do not want orphans for Christmas!"

"Excellent, as you do not have orphans but merely children. Although"—he leaned closer and lowered his voice in a confidential manner—"I suspect if they can play the role of orphans, they can certainly play the role of whatever else you might wish of them. Christmas elves, perhaps?"

"I don't want Christmas elves either!" She clenched her fists, closed her eyes and counted to ten. Considering ways to murder Grayson was not productive at the moment. Time enough for that later. Remaining calm and serene was the best way to handle this. She inhaled a calming breath and opened her eyes. "Let's start from the beginning, shall we? Where did these children come from?"

"I, well . . ." He considered the question, although it seemed fairly straightforward to her. "You might say I leased them."

"You did what?"

"In point of fact, I had Win lease them." He shrugged in a modest manner. "But it was at my direction."

"You leased children?" she said. "How many children?"

"Hundreds," Beryl whispered in horror. "There are hundreds."

"Nonsense." He cast Beryl a chastising look, as if she should know better than to think such a thing. "Where would Win find hundreds of children?" He glanced at the note. "There are only five."

"Five children?" Camille couldn't stop staring at him.

"Five *boys*," Beryl said pointedly.

He looked at the note again. "So it would appear."

"Send them back."

His brows drew together. "What?"

"You heard me." Camille waved in the direction of the road. "Send them back. All five of them. At once."

"If not sooner," Beryl added.

He frowned in confusion. "Why would we send them back?"

He couldn't possibly be this dull-witted not to see the problems a house full of children would cause. "First of all, Grayson, we have barely enough staff to provide for the people who are here now—let alone five children. Staff, I might point out, that while they were once servants, they are now actors acting as servants—"

"And doing a fine job, really," Beryl said. "Why, the cook is truly outstanding."

Grayson nodded. "Isn't she, though?"

"Have you tasted her—"

"Stop it, both of you!" Camille glared. "Regardless of how well they are working out, as far as I know, the staff we do have does not include anyone with any experience with children. And, I daresay, neither Mrs. Montgomery-Wells nor Miss Murdock has any more familiarity with the needs of children than Beryl and I do. In addition, how am I expected to explain an influx of children in the house?"

"Hmph." Grayson's brow furrowed. "I hadn't thought of that."

"No doubt." She gritted her teeth. "Now, send them back."

"Oh, dear." He shook his head in a mournful manner. "I'm afraid we can't do that."

Beryl stared in stunned fascination.

Camille braced herself. "And why can't we?"

"Well . . ." He shook the note at her. "It says right here that the family Win leased the children from—"

Beryl made a strangling sound.

"The butcher in the village," he continued.

Camille nodded. "Go on."

"It seems his wife hasn't been to London since she was a girl, so Win sent them on a bit of a holiday. In the manner of a Christmas gift, apparently. It was very kind of him." Gray smiled. Her hand itched to slap that smile away.

"A Christmas gift?" Camille could barely choke out the words. "When will they return?"

"Tomorrow. Unfortunately, we can only have them for one night."

"You leased the butcher's children?" Beryl's eyes widened. "The butcher—Mr. Carroll?"

He glanced at the note. "That's what it says here."

Beryl stared at him as if she wasn't sure if he was brilliant or insane. "We have Carrolls for Christmas?"

"Oh." He paused. "My God, that is brilliant."

" 'Brilliant' is not the word I would use," Camille said sharply. Surely, he was not this thick? To think that orphans would make this . . . She narrowed her eyes and studied him. He smiled in an overly innocent manner, but the vaguest hint of unease shone in his eyes.

Realization slammed into her. Of course he wasn't stupid. He knew exactly what he was doing. It hadn't been said aloud, but he was as much as wagering she couldn't create this perfect Christmas as he was that he could snatch Mrs. Fortesque from her. Well, two could play whatever game he was playing. And she would play it better.

"There is nothing to be done about it then, I suppose." Camille shrugged. "Save make the best of it."

"The best of it? How on earth do we make the best of it?" Beryl clutched her sister's arm. "You haven't seen them yet, Camille, but they're fast."

"Then we must be even faster." She gave her sister a firm look. "They are children and we are adults. And we outnumber them. However"—she turned her gaze on Grayson—"we shall all have to do our part."

"Oh?" Caution edged out innocence in his eyes.

Obviously, Grayson hadn't thought that far ahead. "As we can't send them back, and we can't turn them out in the cold, and as there is not enough staff to properly see to their needs, their care shall fall to all of us." She smiled. "Including you."

"Oh, but I like children." His smile matched hers. "I have always planned to have children of my own."

"As have I." She turned to Beryl. "You need to keep in mind, dear, they are only children. They are not savages from the wilds of Africa. They are, no doubt, quite civilized and probably well trained. Think of them as nothing more than short people."

Beryl stared at her for a long moment; then set her shoulders bravely as if preparing for battle. "Yes, of course." She patted a stray strand of hair back into place. "I don't know what came over me. Sheer numbers, I suppose. They swarmed in like rats and scattered." She cast an apprehensive look at the house behind her. "I don't know where they are now."

"Then we shall have to locate them and gather them all together." She hooked her elbow through her sister's arm and started for the door. "There haven't been children in this house at Christmas since Delilah was a child. It might be great fun to have them here. Why, we can play games and read stories, and they can help in the decorations. And, oh, Mrs. Fortesque does seem like the type that would enjoy nothing better than making Christmas sweets for little ones. Oh, my, yes. This will all work out beautifully." She glanced back at Grayson. "Thank you, Grayson, this was indeed an excellent idea."

"Just trying to help." His smile was less smug than it was a moment ago.

"Oh yes, excellent," Beryl muttered. "God bless us, everyone."

Fourteen

Even without Beryl's warning, Camille would have known there were children in the house the moment the door opened. The air was filled with the sound of children's voices and peals of laughter. On the staircase leading to the foyer, five little boys of varying ages slid down the banisters with squeals of delight. A maid at the top of the stairs tried, with no success, to grab the children. A footman at the bottom stared as if he wasn't sure if he should stop them, catch them or join them.

"Lady Lydingham." Fortesque appeared seemingly from nowhere. His clothes were disheveled; his few remaining strands of hair were out of order; there was a wild look in his eyes. "There has been a new development."

"I am well aware of that, Fortesque." She handed him her muff and pulled off her hat. "But it is nothing we can't handle."

"I don't . . . We can't . . ." The actor sputtered and couldn't seem to get a complete sentence out.

"Oh, he's going to be a great deal of help," Beryl said behind her.

Grayson snorted back a laugh.

"Come now, Fortesque, it is simply a change in the . . . in the script, nothing more than that." Camille stepped toward the stairway. "You there, boys," she said in a voice drawn from the governesses of her childhood. "Come down here this minute."

The children traded glances, then reluctantly came to line up at the foot of the stairway in a stair-step manner of their own, from tallest to shortest. Each and every head was topped with an unruly mass of curls in colors ranging from light brown to true blond, and each pair of eyes was very nearly the same shade of brown. The smallest two children looked exactly alike and held hands. The brothers would have looked like Christmas angels, had it not been for the mischievous glint in most of those eyes and an overall air of disarray.

"Now then," she said in a kind manner, "what are your names?"

The tallest and, no doubt, the oldest, who looked to be about nine or ten, glanced at the others and then stepped forward. "I'm Thomas." He nodded at the other boys. "These are my brothers. This is Simon." The next in line nodded in a far more somber manner than she would have expected, given their unruly activity a minute ago. "And Walter." Walter grinned a toothy grin. She bit back a smile of her own. "And George and Henry. They're twins." The two youngest boys, probably six years of age, smiled shyly.

"Well, my goodness." She adopted a look of surprise. "I have a twin as well." She glanced at Beryl. "You see, we look almost exactly the same."

Thomas peered around her at Beryl. "She doesn't look very friendly to me." He lowered his voice as if to share a great secret. "She's a bit skittish too, isn't she?"

Beryl's eyes narrowed.

Camille nodded. "Always has been, I'm afraid." She considered them for a moment. "Tell me, Thomas, do you know why you're here?"

"Lord Stillwell told Father that you didn't have any children," Thomas said.

"Of course he did." She would have to murder Stillwell the moment after she dispatched his cousin.

"And you wanted some for Christmas," Walter added, glancing around. "It's a big house if you don't have children."

"It is, indeed. And as I have only ever had sisters, there have never been any boys here."

Walter shook his head as if that was a great shame.

"And what did your parents tell you about your stay here?" she asked.

"We are to be on our best behavior." Simon glanced uneasily at the stairs.

"Or Father will tan our bottoms," Walter announced.

"Therefore, there shall be no more sliding down the banisters." She adopted a firm tone. "Agreed?"

Thomas looked at his brothers, then nodded.

"But"—Walter cast a longing look at the banisters—"they're very good banisters."

"Perhaps . . . ," Simon began, "if you were to try it, you would see why they are very good banisters." He shook his head mournfully. "And why it would be a shame to waste them."

She laughed in spite of herself. "I'll tell you a secret." She knelt down to be closer to eye level. "I did try it when I was a girl." She met Simon's gaze directly. "And I found myself in a great deal of trouble."

Simon nodded in a sympathetic manner.

"Now, as you are to stay for the night, I think perhaps you would like to help with the decorating tomorrow. And, oh, I'm sure Mrs. Fortesque is already making gingerbread and . . ." An idea struck her and she paused. It would certainly serve Grayson right. She gestured for the boys to come closer and they gathered around her. "Tell me, boys, do you know what a masquerade is?"

"Where people wear costumes and masks and the like?" Thomas asked.

"That's it exactly." She beamed. "Well, we are having something of a masquerade here and you are all going to have a part to play."

"Can I be a pirate?" Walter's eyes widened at the thought of piratical bliss. "With a cutlass and a patch over my eye?"

"I want to be a pirate," George, or maybe it was Henry, said.

"Me too," his twin echoed.

"I'm afraid it's not that kind of masquerade." She shook her head. "But we shall all be pretending to be someone we aren't."

"I don't know." Thomas shook his head slowly.

"We'd get in trouble if we lied." Concern creased Simon's forehead.

Walter elbowed him. "It's not lying. It's pretending. And if she tells us to do it, it would be disob . . . disbo . . ."

"Disobedient?" she asked.

Walter nodded. "That's it. Mum said to do what Lady Lydingham said."

"To start with, you may all call me 'Cousin Camille' and my sister 'Cousin Beryl.' And you see the gentleman standing beside Cousin Beryl?" She looked over her shoulder at Grayson, and the boys followed her gaze. "You may call him 'Uncle Grayson,' and we shall pretend that you are all orphans who have come to live with him."

The boys traded glances.

"Begging your pardon, Lady—Cousin Camille, but . . ."

Thomas grimaced. "We've read stories about orphans and orphanages and workhouses and—"

"Scary stories." Walter's eyes widened.

"We really don't want to be orphans, if it's all the same to you," Simon added quickly.

The boys held their collective breaths. Her gaze slid from one worried face to the next and her heart melted. No, Camille could see why they didn't wish to be orphans, given books like *Oliver Twist.* "Very well." She thought for a moment. "You are not orphans but his nephews, come for a visit before Christmas." Their expressions eased. "Will that do?"

They nodded.

"Now let me tell you a few things about your Uncle Grayson . . ." A few moments later, she sat back on her heels and studied the boys. "So you are clear on what you are to do?"

Once again they exchanged glances and nodded.

"And if you do it very, very well, when you leave, I shall give each of you a shilling."

There was a collective gasp.

"A whole shilling?" Simon asked, eyes wide at the thought of untold riches.

She nodded. "A whole shilling."

Suspicion narrowed Thomas's eyes. "For each of us?"

"Each and every one. Do we have an agreement?" She held out her hand. "Shall we shake on it?"

A wide grin spread across Thomas's face. "Agreed." He spit on his palm and held out his hand; his brothers followed suit.

Camille cringed, forced a smile, shook five damp hands and stood up. Beryl rushed forward and handed her a handkerchief.

"That was revolting." Beryl cast a disgusted look at the children.

"Initiations often are." She grimaced, and addressed the children. "Now, do give a proper greeting to your Uncle Grayson."

"Their what?" Confusion flashed in Grayson's eyes. At once, he was surrounded by little boys. The older boys made him the center of a barrage of suggestions and questions as to what kind of games he liked, and when should they play, and what should they do now; the twins simply clung to his pant legs.

Beryl glanced at her sister. "Camille, what have you done?"

"Well, I wouldn't call it 'revenge.' That would be beneath me. But 'retribution' has a nice ring to it. I believe I have solved the problem quite nicely," Camille said quietly, then raised her voice to be heard over the children. "They are playing the parts of your beloved nephews who adore you almost as much as you adore them."

"They do?" The look on his face was not quite as horrified as Beryl's had been but still apprehensive. Good! He tried gently to disengage himself. Her sister was right: It did seem as though there were hundreds or at least dozens of children. "I do?"

"That's why they have come to visit you." Camille turned to the footman and maid still watching the unfolding scene. "Surely, they came with hats, scarves, coats, mittens, that sort of thing. Have them dressed for the out-of-doors immediately, please." She caught Grayson's gaze. "You and your nephews can put some of that boundless energy to use and gather greenery for decorating the house tomorrow."

If anything, the level of noise from the boys increased at her words.

Grayson stared at her, then smiled. "Well played, Camille. Very good."

"Thank you." She smiled in a modest manner.

"That was inspired." Beryl studied her sister as if she had never seen her before. "By God, all those years of dealing with the results of impulse have certainly borne fruit."

"Now, then boys." A brisk note sounded in Grayson's voice. "Let me get a look at you." He crouched down in front of them. "You have me at a disadvantage, as you know my name, but I . . ."

"Lady Lydingham!" Urgency sounded in Fortesque's voice. "I must speak with you at once."

"Yes, of course," she said absently. There was something about seeing a man, a good man, surrounded by small children. . . .

"What are you thinking?" Suspicion sounded in Beryl's voice.

"I was just . . ." She couldn't seem to pull her gaze away from Grayson and the boys. He glanced up, met her gaze and smiled. The strangest feeling of what might have been, or perhaps of what could be, swept through her; and with it an odd sort of ache. Ridiculous really. She ignored it. "I was thinking we can put the children in the old nursery in the east wing."

"Yes, of course. I'll show one of the maids where it is. But first, you need to come with me." She grabbed her sister's hand and fairly pulled her up the stairs.

"What are you doing?" Camille huffed.

"I was just going to ask you the same thing." Beryl pushed Camille into the nearest parlor and shut the door behind them. "What are you doing?"

"I am trying to adjust to the addition of five children to the . . . the cast!" Irritation sounded in her voice. She really didn't have time for this.

"That's not what I mean, and you know it."

Camille crossed her arms over her chest. "I have no idea what you're talking about."

"I saw the way you looked at him."

"Oh." Camille shrugged. "That was . . . nothing."

"You've never been good at lying to me."

"I'm not lying."

"You're lying to someone, me or yourself. Probably both." Beryl's eyes narrowed. "Have you forgotten that he broke your heart? That your closest friend, next to me, declared his love—something you had longed for, for years—on the day before your wedding, then vanished from your life?"

"No, of course not."

"Have you forgiven him?"

Camille hesitated. Had she? "I may never forgive him, but . . ."

"But?"

"I may not be as angry with him as I once was." She paused. "He claims I broke *his* heart."

"He is an idiot."

"No, he's not," she snapped, then pulled a calming breath. "But it is something that had never occurred to me, that I might have hurt him."

"You were about to be married. What did he expect you to do?"

"I don't know," she said sharply; then pushed past her sister and paced the room. "We were both young and his declaration took me by surprise. It was the last thing I had expected from him. I didn't know how to respond, so, in hindsight, I didn't—I don't know—respond well, I suppose. I could have told him I loved him. That I had always loved him, but I didn't." She glanced at her sister. "I said he was being silly. And when he said I would marry him if he had money, I pointed out it scarcely mattered, as he didn't have any."

"Yes, yes." Beryl waved off the comment. "I know all that."

"Looking back on it, one might see where that sort of dismissal might well wound—"

"He left you!" Beryl stared. "He could have come back that day or the next or interrupted your wedding." Her eyes narrowed. "He certainly could have come back after Harold died, but he didn't!"

"No, he didn't! Nor did I expect him to!"

"But you wanted him to!"

"Yes, yes, I admit it." Camille huffed. "I wanted him to! There, are you happy now?"

"Not really." Beryl studied her closely. "What are you going to do about him?"

"Nothing. I don't know." Camille rubbed a weary hand over her forehead. "He is the least of my problems."

"Ah yes, that's right. You have a prince and a house filled with actors to attend to. Oh, and children as well."

"Sarcasm, Beryl"—she aimed a pointed look at her sister—"does not help matters."

"Has he proposed yet?"

"Nikolai?"

"Yes, Nikolai, your *prince*. Remember?"

"Of course I remember and no, he hasn't proposed." She drew a deep breath. "And I'm beginning to think I don't want him to."

Surprise mixed with relief in her sister's eyes. "I thought that was the whole purpose of this farce of yours?"

"Yes, well, once again I have leapt into something without thoroughly thinking it through," Camille said sharply.

"And?"

"And I've decided you might well be right."

"Aha!" Triumph rang in Beryl's voice, then her brow furrowed. "About what?"

"About marrying a man one loves rather than marrying a man with the hopes of love one day."

"I see," Beryl said slowly. "Then are we to end this deception of yours?"

"Good Lord, no!" She resumed pacing. "We need to continue precisely as planned."

Beryl shook her head. "I don't understand. If the purpose is no longer to prove the propriety of the family to Pruzinsky and give him a perfect Christmas—"

"For one thing, I could be wrong, and I do think I should kiss him—"

"You haven't kissed him?"

"The opportunity hasn't arisen."

Beryl stared in disbelief.

"As I was saying, just to make certain, I should do that before making any decision, although I doubt it would make much difference." Camille stopped in mid-step and met her sister's gaze directly. "If Nikolai proposes and I turn him down, and he knows this was all a massive deception, who knows who he might tell? Men who have been rejected are not especially trustworthy. No one would ever believe I turned him down. Gossips would be positively giddy over this. Being a rather impressive gossip yourself—"

"I do try," Beryl said modestly.

"You know full well the story of the measures Lady Lydingham went to in an effort to trap a prince, the *futile* measures, would be all over London—no, all over England in no time at all."

"It is rather juicy," Beryl said under her breath.

"The scandal would be enormous. I would be the subject of jokes for the rest of my life." She pinned her sister with a pointed look. "And you and Lionel would be tarnished with the same brush."

Beryl paled. "You're right. I hadn't thought of that."

"No, to save us all, we have to carry on exactly as planned," Camille said. "First the perfect Christmas. Then the day after, he shall be called back to his country—"

Beryl snorted.

"What?"

"Oh, nothing," Beryl said quickly. "Just thinking about the monetary crisis."

"Are we agreed, then?"

"Absolutely." Beryl nodded. "What can I do?"

"Nothing comes to mind." Camille thought for a minute. "Although you could distract the prince for me."

"Distract him how?" Suspicion sounded in Beryl's voice.

"I don't know. Keep him occupied. Flirt with him."

"I should say not! I have given up flirting with men who are not my husband," she said in a lofty manner. "Besides, I don't want to. And it wouldn't be at all proper, would it?"

"It wouldn't be especially improper if," Camille said slowly, "he thought you were me."

Beryl stared. "What?"

"I'm not suggesting you allow him to seduce you," she said quickly. "Just pretend to be me. You can wear some of my clothes—"

"You do have some lovely things."

"Why, you needn't even say anything specific. Goodness, Beryl, it's not as if the man will ask if you're you or you're me. Simply let him assume that you're me."

"And what if he proposes to me?"

"Then you'll smile and say while you're quite flattered, he has apparently confused one sister with the other." She cast her sister a pleading smile. "And then, at least, I shall be forewarned that a proposal is imminent and can take steps to avoid it."

"I could, as well, discourage him," Beryl said thoughtfully.

"Excellent."

"I won't fling myself at him," Beryl warned.

"Nor am I asking you to."

"Although . . . there is someone who would."

"Someone . . ." Camille shook her head, then gasped. "Miss Murdock?"

"I daresay, she can be quite distracting." Beryl smiled wickedly. "Nor do I suspect she will need much encouragement, no more than opportunity, really. Miss Murdock strikes me as the sort of young woman who is looking more for a wealthy husband than success on the stage. And what girl doesn't want a prince?"

"No doubt the thought has occurred to her as well. She was nicely occupying his attention at the pond." For a moment, the image of being a princess in a castle in the far-flung reaches of Whateverhiscountrywas shimmered in her mind; then faded with only the tiniest twinge of regret. Camille grinned. "That is brilliant, Beryl."

"I am often brilliant." She paused. "Now, about Grayson?"

"Grayson is of no consequence at the moment."

"Let us hope it stays that way," Beryl said.

A sharp knock sounded at the door and it opened an instant later. Fortesque poked his head in. "Lady Lydingham, I must insist we speak at once."

"I'll arrange for the nursery to be prepared." Beryl started for the door, then paused. "Oh, and I neither dislike children nor do they frighten me when taken in small doses. But a large number of them—and I do think five is a large number under these circumstances—acting much like a Russian invasion, well, even the most stalwart among us can be reduced to . . ."

"Fear? Panic?"

"Something like that. I am really quite fond of children on an individual basis." She yanked the door open and nodded at Fortesque. The actor hurried into the room and closed the door behind him.

Camille sighed. "What is it now?"

"The others have returned and have retired to their rooms, to rest before dinner."

"Very well." She studied him for a moment. He had straightened his appearance, but he still had the air of a man deeply inconvenienced. "Is there something else?"

"My apologies, Lady Lydingham, but I feel I must draw the line somewhere." Fortesque drew himself up. "When you engaged us, it was understood that the only additional guests would be His Highness and Lord and Lady Dunwell. Then your cousin joined the gathering, and one additional person was not a difficulty. But now, now there are *children*." He said the word as if it were an obscenity. "Not that I am opposed to children in limited quantities. One, or perhaps two, or possibly even three, but"—his eyes widened in horror—"there are five. Five! Five unruly, ill-behaved, disorderly little boys. And have you seen the look in their eyes?" He shuddered. "What shall we do with them?"

"Oh, I imagine we'll think of something."

"The theater, my lady, is no place for children!"

"This is not the theater, Fortesque." She huffed. "This is my family home. And this is my production. And if I say there are to be children, there are to be children!" She closed her eyes for an instant and prayed for strength.

"Lady Lydingham, you should be aware that I have never left a play in the middle of a performance. I have never walked off a stage in a huff. Even when I have been surrounded by others who have not studied their craft and learned their lines and have indeed made me look like a fool standing on the stage waiting for . . ." He shook his head, obviously clearing out the unwanted memories of a bad performance. "However"—he stared down his nose at her—"given the circumstances—"

"Mr. Fortesque." She met his gaze through narrowed eyes. "It seems we have come to a crossroads in which we have two choices. One, you may leave my employ at once—in which case, I shall consider our agreement nullified and you shall forfeit any and all wages due you and your troupe."

He gasped. "That would be most—"

"Unfair? I should warn you, this is the second time today I have been accused of being unfair, and I am not certain if I am annoyed or quite pleased with myself. Do you understand?"

He nodded but held his tongue.

"Excellent. Our second choice is to carry on bravely and rise to the occasion. And, Mr. Fortesque"—she leaned closer and lowered her voice—"is that not the tradition of the theater? Didn't Shakespeare say, 'The play's the thing'?"

He considered her for a moment, then squared his shoulders. "It's Fortesque, my lady. Do try to remember that."

She resisted the urge to laugh. "Yes, of course."

"Now, if you no longer require my services, I shall see to the arrangements"—he winced—"for the children."

"Actually, Fortesque, I was wondering. Isn't it difficult to make a decent living on the stage?"

"Oh, my. Yes." He shook his head forlornly. "Even if

one's heart is in the theater, one's stomach does require sustenance."

"I can imagine," she said thoughtfully. "And Mrs. Fortesque? Is she as taken with the theater as you are?"

He grimaced. "Unfortunately, I am of an artistic nature and she is made of far more practical stuff."

"I see. Then I would suspect, if she were offered a position with decent wages and living quarters, included for you both, of course," she added quickly, "thus leaving you to pursue your theatrical ambitions, would you and she be at all inclined toward an arrangement of that nature?"

"It would indeed be something to consider." Interest gleamed in his eyes.

"In which case, I have a proposal for you, Fortesque. . . ."

Camille smiled to herself. She could practically taste the chocolate now.

Fifteen

Gray wasn't sure when, if ever, he'd been quite so exhausted. But then again, he hadn't romped with little boys since he'd been one himself. Still, he had to admit, he'd had rather a good time of it.

The boys themselves had been remarkably well behaved when they returned to the house. He didn't know if that was due to whatever Camille had said to them or if he had worn them out nearly as much as they had tired him. They scarcely did more than mutter cryptic comments and mild objections when the housekeeper and the maids drew baths for them all, although it was clear none of them saw the need for it.

Their eyes had grown wide when they'd first stepped foot in the freshly dusted nursery. Camille's staff might not be the best actors in the world, but they did do a fine job as servants. And that reminded him: He did need to speak to Fortesque and his wife. The three beds Camille and her sisters had used as children were supplemented with two additional mattresses, which Camille or, perhaps, Beryl had arranged for. The boys, however, insisted on pushing the three beds together, saying they were used to sharing. Thomas, Simon and Walter confided to him that they had never slept in a bed by themselves before; and while they might well like it, the little ones would never be able to sleep by themselves. Gray was fairly certain it wasn't just the twins who did not want to sleep alone.

The children had explored the nursery and pronounced it to their liking, although the shelves had too many dolls and child-size tea sets and books—nothing that boys liked—which they agreed was a great pity. They were remarkably pragmatic about it for children, noting they would only be here for one night, after all, and it would do. The housekeeper had volunteered to sleep in the old governess's room, should the boys need something in the night.

They had eaten their supper in the nursery, insisting their beloved Uncle Grayson join them. Camille had certainly turned the tables on him, not that it didn't serve him right. He had to admire her cleverness, although the company of the boys was not an unpleasant way to pass the time. He hadn't thought it when he'd read Win's note, but having the children here for only one night was for the best. As Camille had put him in the role of beloved uncle, and had obviously instructed the children to occupy his every moment, he couldn't keep an eye on her, as he and Beryl had agreed. Nor could he continue to work his way past her defenses, and hopefully into her heart. And time was growing short.

In spite of his agreement with Beryl not to tell Camille of Pruzinsky's deception, he would indeed tell her the truth if he thought it necessary. Gray would not let her go off with the man, although he suspected Pruzinsky had no intention of leaving without at least a betrothal. Gray suspected as well, should Pruzinsky have Camille's promise to marry, that he would be more than willing to abandon his claim on her for a tidy payment.

Still, he couldn't concern himself with Pruzinsky at the moment. Right now, he had five eager children, tucked under the blankets, waiting expectantly. Although, given the way their eyes were barely open, he doubted he would have to read for long.

"Cousin Camille promised you would read to us," Thomas said, a frown of annoyance creasing his brow. "Will you?"

"I will indeed." He pulled a chair up close to the bed, sat down and held up a well-used book. "Fortunately, there was a copy of *A Visit from St. Nicholas* on the nursery shelves. As Christmas is just a few days away, I thought it would be perfect for tonight. What do you think? Will it do?"

Silence greeted him.

"No?" His gaze slid from one cautious face to the next.

"We have already heard it, you see," Simon said in as diplomatic a manner as possible.

"I imagine you hear it every year at Christmas."

"No, we heard it tonight." Walter sighed. "Cousin Beryl read it to us after our baths."

"The skittish one? Are you sure it wasn't her sister?"

"Uncle Grayson, we can tell one sister from another." Patience sounded in Thomas's voice, as if he were the adult. "We have twins of our own."

"Yes, of course," Gray murmured, rather nonplussed by being put in his place by a ten-year-old. "Very well, then. We'll find something else." He rose to his feet, strode across the room to the shelves and studied the offerings. "This will do, I think." He plunked the book from its spot, paged through it, then returned to his chair. "This is a story by Mr. Dickens called *The Magic Fishbone*. It's about a princess who gets one wish for anything she wants."

"I'd wish for a dog," Thomas said.

"Two dogs." Walter grinned.

"Three dogs," George or Henry added. The other twin giggled. "Four dogs!"

"And what would you wish for, Simon?" Gray asked.

"It's only one wish you say?"

Gray nodded.

"Then I should have to think about it." Simon considered the idea. "Can I wish for more wishes?"

"I am sorry." Gray shook his head regretfully. "I suspect that's against the rules."

"Not much of a wish if you can't wish for more wishes," Thomas muttered.

"No, if I only have one, I should have to think for a long time. About what I really, truly want." Simon's tone was solemn, as befit such an important decision. "Not that I don't want a dog," he added quickly.

Gray nodded. "That goes without saying."

Simon studied him for a moment. "What would you wish for?"

Camille's forgiveness. Her heart. Her hand. "Why, I agree with you. Something of this magnitude must be given a great deal of thought. One would hate to squander a lone wish on something of no importance."

"A dog is important." Walter pointed out, and snuggled deeper under the covers.

"A dog most certainly is. Now shall we see how the princess uses her wish?" The boys nodded their agreement and Gray began: " 'There was once a King, and he had a Queen; and he was the manliest of his sex, and she was the loveliest of hers. The King was, in his private profession, Under Government. The Queen's father had been a medical man out of town. . . .' "

No, he would not have to read long. He had scarcely gotten to the part where the king had arrived at his office, before the twins were asleep and the others were struggling against succumbing.

" 'There he wrote and wrote and wrote, till it was time to go home again. Then he politely invited the Princess Alicia, as the Fairy had directed him, to partake of the salmon. . . .' "

By the time the doll, which was really a duchess, was introduced in the story, all five children were fast asleep. They looked much like Christmas angels, although—he chuckled to himself—they were simply Christmas Carrolls. He would have to thank Win for that bit of whimsy. He stood, blew out the lamp and quietly moved to the door, closing it gently behind him.

"How long have you been listening?" he said without turning around.

"I heard them tell you they had already been read to once tonight." He could hear the smile in her voice.

He turned to face her. Camille stood far closer than expected, illuminated by the faint light of the gas sconces in the corridor. Close enough to kiss again, if he dared. "I thought Beryl didn't like children."

"So did Beryl." Camille laughed softly.

"And you? Do you like children?"

"I have always imagined I would like my children, although I suppose that isn't always true. And I like these children." She studied him curiously. "Are you surprised?"

"That you like children?"

She nodded.

"I've never really thought about it," he said. "I suppose, I thought, assumed as you don't have any—"

"Life does not always turn out as one expects, Grayson. I came to tell you, dinner is nearly ready. And I should hate to insult Mrs. Fortesque by any of us being late." She started down the hall. "I do hope to have children, you know."

He nodded. "Princes and princesses."

"Goodness, Grayson, that is what one has when one marries a prince."

A real prince. "Quite right."

She reached the stairs and glanced back at him. "You've been very kind to them—the children, that is."

"Well"—he shrugged—"I am their beloved uncle."

She smiled in an annoyingly satisfied manner. "And no one deserves that title more than you."

"I have to confess, I was not at all pleased when you aimed them in my direction. And apparently it is my lot to keep them away from the others."

"Who better than you?"

He chuckled. "But I must admit as well, I've quite enjoyed my day with them."

"Excellent, as you are the beloved uncle tomorrow too."

"I'm not sure I have the strength."

"Nonsense." Her gaze flicked over him. "You look to be in fine physical condition to me."

He grinned. "Is that a compliment?"

"It's an observation." She started down the stairs. "I saw how you skated and the speed with which you covered the ground from the pond to the stables and the house. I would say, you are well up to the herding of five little boys."

"I do hope so. I should hate for my epitaph to be: 'Small children were his undoing.'"

She laughed. He'd never forgotten how much he'd liked her laugh. But then, he now appreciated the passion of her anger as well. He couldn't recall her ever being angry with him in their youth. They reached the first floor and she turned in the direction of the public rooms. He stayed a step behind her for a moment, enjoying the way her hips swayed beneath her bustle. With very little effort, he could reach out and pull her hips back against his. How much more passionate would she be when she was in the throes of desire? When she was naked and writhing beneath him? When his hand caressed the curves of her—

"It's almost a shame they are only here for one night."

"What?" He stepped up beside her. "Who?"

"Pay attention, Grayson, we were talking about the boys." She slanted him a curious glance. "What were you thinking?"

"Me? Oh. Nothing, really." *Except picking you up in my arms, carrying you to the closest bed and making mad love to you until you begged for more and screamed my name and admitted that we belong together.* "Pity they fell asleep, though. I rather wanted to see how the story ended."

"Oh no, it's better that they don't hear it."

He drew his brows together. "Why not? Don't they live happily ever after?"

"The princess and her family do, but the magic fishbone, having lost its power, is swallowed by the nasty little pug dog that lived next door. How did Mr. Dickens put it?" She thought for a moment. "Ah yes, 'he expired in convulsions.' "

Grayson stared. "The dog dies?"

"He snapped at children."

"Dickens killed the dog?"

"He was a very unpleasant little dog," she said firmly.

"Nonetheless, with proper training . . ."

"It's nice to know you like dogs and children."

"Why?"

"If you didn't, I would think you had changed beyond all recognition."

"I haven't changed at all," he said staunchly, knowing that wasn't entirely true, although he had *grown* more than *changed*. "I am very much the same person I was eleven years ago."

"In some ways, perhaps." She paused and studied him. "But there is a strength in you now, a determination that you did not have as a youth. You have, as well, a look of responsibility about you, and the air of a man who refuses to give up, who fights for what he wants."

He grinned. "It's irresistible, isn't it?"

"For the most part, it's annoying." She raised her shoulder in a casual shrug. "Although, I suppose, if you and I were to meet as strangers, it might well be the tiniest bit—oh, I don't know—intriguing."

"Do I intrigue you?"

"No, Grayson. As I said, you annoy me." She turned and continued on. "The others have gathered in the parlor to await dinner."

"I would wager Miss Murdock finds me intriguing," he said casually.

"I daresay, there are few handsome, charming men Miss Murdock does not find intriguing."

"You think I'm handsome and charming?"

"Fishing for another compliment?"

"Always."

"Admittedly, you can be most charming, when it suits you, and most would consider you attractive, even handsome. You always were. Of course your arrogance does tend to overshadow your finer qualities."

"But don't forget, I like children and dogs. Surely, that overcomes my arrogance?"

"That's one wager I wouldn't take if I were you." They reached the parlor doors and she stopped and turned toward him. "I must confess, I am curious, though."

"Oh?"

"What would you wish for, if you had only one wish? What do you really, truly want?"

"You," he said without thinking, but it was the right answer.

She stared at him for a moment. "Do you?"

"I always have."

"Hmph." She turned away and stepped toward the parlor. "Now you are being ridiculous. In that, you haven't changed."

He grabbed her arm and pulled her back. "Today you said what lay between us was both love and war. You know, they say there's a fine line between love and war."

"No, they don't." She shook her head. "They say there's a fine line between love and hate."

"Do you hate me?"

"Of course not." She pulled out of his grasp. "I have been very, very angry with you, but I have never hated you."

"Do you love me?"

"Don't be absurd." She shook her head. "I don't know how I feel about you."

"Camille—"

"But for a man who says there's only one thing he wants, one thing he's always wanted, you have a poor way of showing it."

"What would you have me do?"

"It's eleven years too late, Grayson."

"It doesn't have to be." His gaze caught hers and he stared into the blue eyes that had haunted his dreams since the moment he'd left her. His tone softened. "What can I do, Camille?"

"I have no idea. I wish I did." She turned toward the parlor, took a step, then swiveled back. "Perhaps you should be the man you've become." She nodded and walked into the parlor, leaving him to trail behind.

What in the name of all that was holy did she mean by that? Be the man he'd become? He was the man he'd become; she just didn't realize it yet.

By God, Gray fully intended to fight for her. But the man he was now was smart enough to know he had best tread carefully and not leap headfirst without thought and due consideration. That was exactly how he'd ruined everything in the past.

If he hadn't been so young and stupid, he would have fought for her then. Fought for them.

He drew a deep breath and stepped into the parlor, just in time to hear Fortesque announce dinner was served. Good. He hadn't realized it, but he was famished. Obviously, that was the result of being with children all day.

They proceeded into dinner amidst a fair amount of chatting and laughter. Before he knew it, he found himself with Beryl on his arm, escorting her into the dining room.

She leaned close and spoke low into his ear. "I do not know what you are up to, Grayson Elliott, but if you muck it up or hurt my sister again, so help me, I will make it my sole purpose to make certain you are not long for this life."

He inclined his head toward her, his voice as low as hers. "Are you threatening me, Beryl?"

Her eyes widened in feigned innocence. "Does it sound like a threat?"

"Very much so."

"Excellent," she said through her smile, which wasn't the least bit legitimate. "Then you understand."

"I do, indeed." It was pointless to assure Beryl he had no intention of hurting Camille. Quite the opposite. He fully planned to spend the rest of his life making her happy.

Camille threw them a curious look and Beryl laughed as if he had just said something worth laughing at. "Goodness, Cousin." Her fingernails dug into his arm, hard. "You are so very amusing."

"I live to amuse you, Cousin." He placed his hand on hers and squeezed. She bit her lip to keep from wincing and he tried not to grin. She might never trust him or like him, for that matter. Once again he realized that, if he was successful in winning her sister, Beryl would be part of his life, part of his family, until the day one of them died. They would no doubt drive one another mad.

All in all, a small price to pay.

Camille was not at all a superstitious sort, under most circumstances. But the moment she looked around the dinner table—noting the prince occupied in animated conversation with her sister on one side and Miss Murdock on the other; Mr. Henderson and Mrs. Montgomery-Wells trading absurd tales; Grayson joining in, with obvious amusement—the thought struck her before she could banish it: Things were going well.

She knew better. It was like a curse destined to bring

disaster down around her head. And she would prefer to avoid disaster, thank you very much. Still, there were only two days left to survive until Christmas; and at the moment, while she refused to be completely confident, she couldn't vanquish an annoying ray of hope.

Nor could she get Grayson out of her head, where he seemed to have taken up permanent residence. He was perhaps the most confusing man she had ever met. One minute he was quite sweet and directing all that charm, which seemed to come as naturally to him as breathing, toward her; and the next he was trying to steal her cook and ruin everything by hiring orphans. Orphans, for goodness' sake! Whatever had possessed him?

And then there was all that nonsense about love and war and fine lines, and if he had one wish he'd wish for her—not to mention the way he had grabbed her and kissed her last night. She ignored the thought that he hadn't kissed her this morning, when she had rather hoped he would. But then she was never quite as strong in the morning as she was during the rest of the day. Yes, that was why she had, perhaps, a tiny bit, wanted him to kiss her.

If the man wanted her, he needed to do something about it. He needed to prove it, although she wasn't at all sure how she felt about that. Wasn't at all sure how she felt about him—at least not here and now. She'd been angry at him for so long; now that he was so abruptly back in her life, feelings she thought were long in the past seemed to simmer just below the surface.

She'd agreed they needed to talk about the past. Perhaps once they did, they could put it all behind them. But to what end? To resolve matters between them and finally lay the past to rest? Or to start anew?

"Psst." A faint voice sounded behind her.

She stifled a groan. She didn't need to look behind

her to know who was hissing. Obviously, something was amiss. Otherwise, wouldn't Fortesque simply have come into the room? Of course something was wrong. Hadn't she just been thinking how well things were going?

She quickly excused herself and left the dining room. Fortesque waited just outside the door.

She clenched her teeth. "Did I not tell you, butlers do not 'psst'!"

"I had no other way of attracting your attention, and I thought it best not to enter the dining room." He handed her a glass of brandy. "You might wish to drink this."

She accepted the glass and narrowed her gaze in suspicion. "Why?"

"Isn't it a butler's duty to anticipate the needs of his employer?"

"Yes, but—"

"You will need that."

"Very well." She took a sip. "Now, Fortesque, why did you think it best not to come into the dining room? And why do I need brandy?"

"Because if I entered the dining room, I would lose sight of the parlor doors." He lowered his voice and leaned closer. "And should there be pounding at those doors, I might not notice."

"Why would there be pounding?"

"Because I took the liberty of securing the doors to forestall anyone from wandering about freely. I assumed you would wish to prevent that."

She stared in confusion. "Who would wander about freely?"

"The new arrivals who are currently awaiting you in the parlor."

What had Grayson and his cousin come up with now? She bit back a groan. "It's not orphans, is it?"

"No, my lady." He shook his head. "These are most certainly not children."

"That's something, at any rate."

Fortesque cast her what could only be called a look of pity.

"Out with it, then, Fortesque. Who is it?" she demanded, trying and failing to ignore an impending sense of doom.

"They said they wished to surprise you and I was not to give you their names." His gaze slid from side to side as if concerned as to who might be listening. "They were quite confused when they arrived and I informed them that the family was at dinner. Then they were somewhat irate and, well, they threatened me with bodily harm if I spoiled their surprise. I don't mind telling you, Lady Lydingham, they look like the sort that would carry out their threat. Although, if you were to guess . . ."

"I would much prefer not to play games. I do not wish—" The most horrible thought occurred to her. She took a deep swallow of the brandy. "Tell me, these new arrivals . . ."

"Yes?"

"Male or female?"

Again, he gave her that look of pity. "Most certainly female."

"Good Lord." Of all the things that might go wrong, she had never expected this. "And you locked them in?"

"It seemed best, at the moment." He nodded. "I took great pains to turn the key quietly, so they may not, as yet, be aware I have locked the door. I suggest you speak to them before they discover that." He paused. "It might be upsetting to them."

" 'Upsetting'?" She snorted. "That's something of an understatement." At least she had a moment to compose herself, even if she had no idea how to handle this new turn of events. "All things considered, you handled this quite admirably, Fortesque."

"Thank you, my lady."

"And the brandy was an excellent idea as well."

"I thought so."

"There's nothing to be done about it, then, is there?"

"It does not appear so."

"Very well." She tossed back the rest of the brandy, handed him the glass and squared her shoulders. "You may unlock the door. As quietly as possible, if you will. No use adding fuel to the inevitable fire."

"As you wish." He turned the key with the quiet stealth of a master burglar, then stepped back. "And may I say, my lady, I wish you the very best of luck."

"Thank you, Fortesque, I shall need it." She summoned her strength, adopted her brightest smile, opened the doors and stepped into the parlor. "Good evening, Mother."

Sixteen

"**D**arling!" The smile on her mother's face belied the considering look in her eye. Delilah stood a few feet away, arms folded over her chest, tapping her foot. One would think she was the oldest daughter instead of the youngest. "Come and greet me properly."

Camille closed the door behind her and hurried to her mother, kissing her on both cheeks. "You are supposed to be in Paris. What are you doing here?"

"Don't you mean 'welcome home'? 'Happy Christmas'? 'Felicitations of the season'?" Mother said, a bright note in her voice. "Unless things have changed dramatically since I left—oh, I don't know, revolution, anarchy and the like—this is still my home. Isn't it?"

"Of course it is, Mother," Camille said. "Don't be absurd."

"What is going on here?" Delilah said. "Why did that butler say the family was at dinner? What family? And why is there a new butler? What have you done with Clement?"

Camille drew her brows together. "Why does everyone immediately think I have done away with Clement?"

Delilah sniffed. "I wouldn't put it past you."

"What utter nonsense," Camille said. Delilah was always so frightfully sanctimonious, at least when it came to her sisters. It was an entirely different story around people other than her family. Camille and Beryl had discussed this aberration of nature often through the years and they agreed. It wasn't something she did deliberately; it was simply her nature. Which made it no less annoying. She was the saint and the rest of them sinners. The fact that she was not nearly the saint she thought herself to be just added to the annoyance. "Clement is where he always is when Mother is not in residence for Christmas. He has gone to visit his family in Wales."

"And why are we not welcome in our own home?" Indignation rang in her sister's voice.

"First of all, this really isn't your home, is it?" Camille said in as sweet a manner as she could muster. "It's Mother's home."

Delilah gasped. "It's my childhood home! And why were we locked in the parlor?" Delilah narrowed her eyes. "Don't think we didn't notice."

"My, how observant you are, sister dear."

"Now, now, Camille," Mother said, taking off her hat. "I noticed as well, and I am not the least bit observant. I should point out, however, as this might be of use in the future, that no matter how stealthy the action, the click of a key in a lock does tend to be unmistakable. Now"— her mother met Camille's gaze directly—"do tell us exactly what manner of mischief is afoot here."

"It's rather a long story." Camille struggled to find just the right words. There didn't seem to be any. How did one tell one's mother that she was not proper enough to impress a prince?

"Fortunately . . . we have all the time in the world."

Delilah sank into the nearest chair and pulled off her gloves, a challenge gleaming in her eyes.

"Why are you here?" Camille asked her mother. "I thought you were spending Christmas in Paris."

"Sometimes things do not turn out as one expects." Mother shrugged off her cloak and draped it over the back of a chair. "Perhaps I am simply getting older and growing more sentimental, but I had the oddest longing to be in my own country and my own home at Christmas. Imagine my surprise when we stopped in London to insist that you and your sister and Lionel, of course, join us, only to discover you and Beryl were already here."

"You discovered that, did you?" Camille adopted a casual tone.

"Lionel told us, but he said very little else. Politicians." Delilah sniffed in disdain. "He was most evasive and even tried to discourage us from coming to the manor."

"Did he?" Camille would have to thank him for that—futile, though his effort had been.

"Why would he do that, dear?" A pleasant smile curved her mother's lips, but the look in her eyes was sharp.

"What are you up to?" Delilah glared.

Camille sighed. "I can tell you the entire story all at once, or I can allow you to drag it out of me, one question at a time."

"Let's drag it out of her," Delilah said with barely concealed delight. "I should quite enjoy that."

"Whereas I would prefer to hear it all at once." Mother perched on the edge of the sofa and looked at her older daughter expectantly. "Well, go on."

"It's rather hard to explain," Camille began.

Delilah snorted. "No doubt."

"You see, there was, well, a prince . . ."

Mother's brow rose. "A prince?"

"Who was quite taken with me, as I was with him," Camille added quickly. "Indeed, I was confident there would be a proposal by Christmas."

Delilah scoffed.

Mother cast her a quelling glance, then returned her attention to Camille. "Continue."

"He's really rather a proper sort, although somewhat unusual in terms of not traveling as royalty, incognito and all, and not being treated as royalty." She shrugged. "Things of that nature."

"Eccentric." Mother nodded in a knowing manner. "Not uncommon with royalty."

"He has, as well, ideas about a proper English Christmas and is quite enthusiastic about it, so, naturally, I wished to give that to him."

"To be expected, of course," Mother said.

"And, well, you and Uncle Basil weren't in the country, anyway, so it did seem rather harmless." Camille paced the room, trying to find the right words. "And I did think a proper English Christmas required a proper English family. . . ." She paused and met her mother's gaze directly. "And even you must admit, when you are here for Christmas, or any other time, for that matter, the house is filled with people and behavior that isn't the least bit proper."

"Not the sort of ambiance that would impress a prince deciding whether or not a family is the sort royalty would wish to be aligned with." Mother's voice was thoughtful. "Is that what you're trying to say?"

"I can understand that." Delilah nodded in that superior manner of hers.

"That's it exactly, Mother." This might not be as difficult as Camille had thought, after all. "So, as you weren't here . . ."

"We have established that, dear."

"Yes, of course. As you weren't here, and I needed a family . . ." Camille drew a deep breath. "I hired one."

Delilah stared in disbelief. "You did what?"

"You heard me, I hired a family."

"Where did you get a family?"

"And at Christmas," Mother murmured.

"I didn't actually hire a *real* family," Camille said as if the idea was absurd. "That would be impossible. I hired"—she braced herself—"actors."

Delilah's eyes widened with shock; her mouth dropped open; she couldn't seem to get a word out. Good.

"Actors?" Mother said. "Who are they to play, exactly?"

"Well, you and Uncle Basil and Delilah—"

Delilah emitted an odd sort of strangling sound.

"And then I had to replace all the servants because of the secrecy involved, of course—"

"Of course," Mother said.

"But the troupe was not large enough to replace everyone, so we have a much smaller staff than usual. But they're very well trained as servants, that is," she added quickly. "Unfortunately, they are not quite as skilled as actors."

"But they are good servants?" Mother asked.

Camille nodded. "Apparently, they were all in service until they decided they would rather be on the stage." She lowered her voice in a confidential manner. "Indeed, I'm not sure most of them didn't make the wrong decision. Why, Mrs. Fortesque is excellent in the role of cook. I am trying to keep her. Wait until you taste her scones."

"Oh, I do love a good scone."

"Mother!" Delilah glared.

"I suppose that is beside the point." Mother waved off her comment. "I'm assuming you did not fire my servants."

"I would never do such a thing!" Camille dismissed that suggestion. "I sent them on holiday, with an appropriate Christmas bonus."

"I see," Mother said thoughtfully.

"Get them back!" Delilah snapped. "Send for them all at once. And get rid of these . . . these *actors*!"

"That would be extremely difficult," Camille said sharply. "One doesn't stop a play at intermission."

Her mother glanced at Delilah. "It's not at all in the spirit of the theater, dear."

"But you can't let this go on!"

"I can do whatever I please." Mother met Camille's gaze. "And what part do you propose we play?"

Camille stared.

"Come now, darling, you needn't look at me like that." Mother smiled. "I think this is brilliant."

"You do?" Camille said.

"Dreadfully expensive, of course, but quite clever."

Delilah gasped. "Mother!"

"You needn't look so shocked, Delilah. Goodness, your sister is only doing what she felt she needed to do to marry this prince of hers. I should rather like to have a prince in the family. I commend her ingenuity."

"Then you're not angry?" Camille said slowly.

"My dear child, one does what one has to do. Indeed, I am delighted with your cleverness and quite look forward to lending you my assistance in whatever manner you need." Mother grinned. "Now, Camille, what parts shall we play? I acted a bit myself as a girl, you know, in plays at school. I don't mind telling you, I was quite good at it."

Delilah stared. "You're not seriously going to allow this charade to continue?"

"Oh, but I am." Mother directed a hard look at her youngest daughter. "As are you. And you shall do so graciously, if not with enthusiasm. If this is what your sister needs to extract a proposal from her prince, you shall do whatever is necessary to help her."

Delilah sputtered.

"Yes, well, about that." Camille grimaced. "It seems better to avoid a proposal than to turn one down. Therefore, I am trying to sidestep any proposal."

"Oh?"

"I have decided a man I need to lie to about my family is not a man worth having." The moment she said the words, she knew they were true. As much as she had ignored it, that thought had lingered in the back of her mind from the beginning. Despite the fact that few would consider her mother's, or her uncle Basil's, usual behavior to be completely proper—and Lord knows the characters her mother usually filled her house with were not at all the kind of people one would properly associate with, and there were any number of dalliances and liaisons that had gone on beneath this roof—her mother was a kind and generous soul. There was no need to apologize for her, or hide her, and Camille was abruptly ashamed of herself for having done so.

"Goodness, darling, when it comes to marriage, we all lie about something."

"I never did," Delilah said in a lofty manner.

"Your day will come, dear," Mother said; then studied Camille. "So if you no longer want him, why are you continuing with your farce?"

"Quite honestly—"

"A bit too late for that," Delilah said sharply.

Camille ignored her. "I'm not at all sure I can trust

him to keep his mouth shut, especially if I turn down his proposal. And if word leaked out about my deception—"

"Oh, dear." Mother winced. "The gossip—"

"Good Lord!" Delilah groaned. "We shall all be ruined! I will be ruined! I will not be able to hold my head up—"

"Which is why we will not let that happen," Mother said in her best no-nonsense manner. "You're absolutely right, Camille. We must play this out to the final curtain."

Camille wasn't sure when, if ever, she'd been so relieved. Not only was her mother not angry, but she was going to lend her assistance and make certain Delilah did so as well. She exhaled a long breath. "Thank you, Mother."

"No thanks are necessary, dear," Mother said. "There is nothing I would not do in this world to help you." She glanced at Delilah. "Or you. Or Beryl."

Delilah glared. "This is a dreadful mess you've gotten all of us into. Yet one more example of how you have never given due consideration to anything before plunging ahead willy-nilly." She gestured wildly. Obviously, the specter of social condemnation had her one step from hysteria. "One would have thought after Brighton—"

"That's quite enough," Mother said in a hard tone. "I'm sure your sister has learned more than her share of lessons along the way. Why, I suspect she will never again hire actors for Christmas. Will you, dear?"

"Absolutely not," Camille said staunchly, then paused. "There are perhaps a few more developments I should mention. Minor, really, in the scheme of things." She shook her head. "All has not progressed exactly according to plan."

"It would be a most boring production if all went according to . . . to the script." Mother beamed. "It is the unexpected twists and turns in a plot that make a performance memorable."

"Oh, do tell, sister dear. What could possibly have gone wrong?"

"Sarcasm, Delilah," Mother said, "does not help."

A knock sounded at the door an instant before it opened and Grayson entered the parlor. "Fortesque indicated you might need some assistance." His gaze skimmed the room, met hers, and he nodded slightly. At once, he moved to her mother and took her hand. "Lady Briston, you are as lovely as ever."

"And you are as . . ." Mother stared at him; then realization washed across her face. "Grayson Elliott? Is that really you?"

He chuckled. "I'm afraid so."

"My God, you have lived up to the promise of your younger days. Maturity sits well on you." She studied him in an admiring manner. "You're far more handsome than any man has a right to be."

He grinned. "And you are as delightful as ever."

Delilah cleared her throat and rose to her feet. "It's past time you came home."

"Delilah?" He stepped to her and took her hand. "Is this the same girl I remember?"

She tilted her head and favored him with a radiant smile. "The very same."

"You've grown." He brought her hand to his lips and gazed into her eyes. "And might I say, in a most enchanting way."

"Goodness, Grayson, you are as charming as I recall." Delilah gazed up at him through lowered lashes.

Good Lord, was she flirting with him? For a moment, Camille saw her sister as Grayson might. While all three sisters shared the same blue eyes, Delilah's hair was a deep sable instead of blond. She was several inches shorter than her sisters, as well, and, admittedly, quite lovely, even striking. That is, if one could get past her irritating nature, although Grayson didn't seem to have any problem with that. Camille ignored a stab of what, under other circumstances, might possibly be jealousy.

"Am I to assume this is one of the minor developments you mentioned?" Mother asked.

"One of them," Camille admitted.

"Camille, I couldn't keep them . . ." Beryl entered the parlor and pulled up short. "Mother!" Her eyes widened and almost immediately she recovered. "*Mother* is right behind me, as are *Uncle Basil, Delilah* and, um, Nikolai."

"Beryl," Mother said cautiously and stood. "How good to see you, my dear."

"And you. Always." The look on Beryl's face would have been priceless if Camille had not been busy trying to keep the same expression off her own face. She crossed the room to stand beside her mother, in case she had need of . . . prompting.

"New arrivals?" Nikolai strode into the room, the others right on his heel. If nothing else, given his looks alone, he certainly did make an excellent first impression.

"The prince," Camille whispered into her mother's ear. She nodded in response.

"I am Count Pruzinsky." He stepped to her mother, took her hand and raised it to his lips. "And I am at your service."

Camille wondered if he said that to everyone he met. Odd how it was most charming a few days ago and now it set her teeth on edge.

"*Count* Pruzinsky?" Mother cast her a quizzical glance. "Not 'Prince'?"

"He prefers to travel incognito," Grayson said quickly, and Camille threw him a grateful look.

Nikolai flashed his perfect smile. "I must reconsider my traveling indulgences. Although I consider them necessary, they are proving to be somewhat awkward." He turned his attention to her mother. "And you are?"

Mother's eyes widened. "I . . ."

"Allow me to introduce my mother," Grayson said smoothly. "Mrs. Elliott."

"Yes, of course, that's exactly who I am." Mother beamed. "And this is my daughter, Grayson's sister, Miss Elliott. Prudence."

Delilah choked. " 'Prudence'?"

"It's a virtue," Beryl said, sounding a bit sharper than necessary.

"And a beautiful name." Nikolai moved to Delilah and took her hand, his gaze never leaving hers. "For a beautiful woman."

"Oh." Delilah stared up at him as if mesmerized. Although, admittedly, it was hard not to be taken with all that blond hair and royal charm.

Beryl turned to the others. "Mother, Uncle Basil, Delilah, look who has come to join us."

Mr. Henderson's brow furrowed. "Who?"

"Cousin Grayson's mother and sister, of course." Beryl forced a smile. "Cousin Prudence and Cousin . . ." Panic flashed in her eyes.

"My dear Bernadette," Mother said, sweeping across the room to enfold Mrs. Montgomery-Wells in her arms. "How wonderful to see you again. And thank you so much for inviting us for Christmas."

"Why, it wouldn't be Christmas without you." The older woman gave Mother a warm smile. The actress seemed to be taking this new development in stride.

Perhaps her perpetual fog was at last lifting. "But it's not Bernadette, you know. It's Anastasia." Or not.

"Really?" Mother's eyes widened. "I could have sworn it was Bernadette."

"It's quite all right, my dear." The actress patted her mother's arm. "These things happen when one gets older. It happens to me all the time."

"Still," Mother said slowly, "I am fairly certain it's Bernadette."

Mrs. Montgomery-Wells frowned. "I daresay, I know my own name." She glanced at Mr. Henderson. "Goodness, Franklin, some people have no idea who they are. Lack of study, no doubt."

"No doubt." Mr. Henderson sighed. "And it's Basil."

Mrs. Montgomery-Wells threw Mother a pointed look. "What did I tell you?"

Mother smiled weakly.

"How delightful this is." Nikolai looked around the room. "To have so many members of your family here for Christmas. First Mr. Elliott and then the children—"

"Children?" Delilah said. "Whose children?"

Mother aimed Camille a pointed glance. "Another development?"

Camille shrugged in a helpless manner.

"I think we should all return to the dining room." Beryl herded the others toward the door. "I suspect Mrs. Fortesque has a wonderful dessert and we should hate to offend her."

"Damn fine cook," Mr. Henderson muttered. "And you should see her dance. . . ."

"And we should retire to our rooms to freshen up," Mother said as soon as the others had left the room. "Although I suspect our usual rooms are occupied."

Camille nodded. "It is rather a full house, but the red

bedroom, down the hall from yours, is still available," she added quickly. "However, we shall have to put Delilah in the west wing."

" 'The west wing'?" Delilah glared. "It's cold and drafty in *the west wing.*"

"Nonsense." Mother waved away her daughter's objection. "A few extra blankets should be more than sufficient to keep you quite comfortable."

Delilah stared. "But I don't want to sleep in the west wing. I don't want to be part of this at all. It's another one of your ill-conceived schemes and, no doubt, destined to ruin us all. I still think you should send them on their way right now."

Camille narrowed her eyes. "Or you could leave."

Delilah gasped. "You would throw your own sister out into the cold? And at Christmas?"

"With the tinkling of sleigh bells and a sprig of holly grasped between my teeth, if necessary," Camille snapped.

Grayson stepped forward. "You may have my room, if you wish."

Mother glanced at Camille. She shrugged. "He's in the room across from mine."

"I see," Mother said. Camille knew that tone. What exactly did she see?

Delilah cast him an entirely too flirtatious smile. Miss Murdock's portrayal of her might be close to the truth, after all. "That's so very thoughtful of you, Grayson."

"But she couldn't accept," Mother said firmly.

"Oh, but I could."

"Oh, but you won't." Mother directed her a quelling look. "Grayson can't be expected to move his things when he is helping Camille in her farce and there are no servants to spare to move him. So we shall leave things exactly as they are."

"Fortesque!" Camille yelled. It seemed pointless to use the bellpull, as he was no doubt listening at the door.

The actor appeared at once. "Yes, my lady."

"My mother and sister will be joining us as Mr. Elliott's mother and sister," Camille said with a sigh. "Please have rooms made up. They'll show you which ones."

The actor raised a brow. "Two more, then?"

She clenched her teeth. "Is that a problem?"

He heaved an overly dramatic sigh. "Of course not, my lady." He paused. "Will there be any others? Are there any additional family members unaccounted for?" His voice rose. "Shall there be more guests, perhaps wandering in off the roads?"

Delilah sucked in a sharp breath.

"As I did not expect these new arrivals, at this point, I really cannot say." Camille leveled him a threatening look. "However, I am certain you are more than capable of handling this new development as you have so ably handled everything else thus far!"

"Mr. Fortesque." Mother's eyes widened with feigned surprise. "You're not a real butler then? You are one of the actors?"

He drew a calming breath. "Yes, my lady."

"Why, I never would have known." Admiration sounded in her voice. "You're very good."

"Oh." He paused, then smiled modestly. "Thank you, my lady. I do work hard at my craft."

"And it's obvious." She studied him for a moment. "Have I seen you on stage before? In a London theater, perhaps?"

"Well, I have had a few roles—"

"How fascinating. I want to hear all about it." She favored him with a brilliant smile. "Why don't you arrange to have our bags brought up and we will show you what rooms we'll be staying in. And while we do, you shall tell me all about your theatrical credits. I have always been fascinated by the theater."

"As you wish." He glanced at Camille. "If there is nothing more?"

"Dear Lord, I hope not," Camille murmured.

"Now then, Mr. Fortesque . . ." Mother escorted him out the door, tossing a conspiratorial smile back at Camille. "Do tell me . . ."

"For whatever absurd reason, and God knows what goes on in her head, Mother has obviously decided to embrace this deception of yours fully. I shall do my part as well, as there seems to be no other way to save us all from scandal." Delilah's eyes narrowed. "But I am most distressed about it, Camille, most distressed."

Camille stared at her sister for a long moment; then adopted her brightest smile. "And Happy Christmas to you too, dear sister."

Fury blazed in Delilah's eyes. "I would not—"

"Prudence, dear, come along," Mother called from the hall.

Delilah sent a last, scathing look toward her sister, turned to Grayson and smiled apologetically. "Do forgive me, Grayson. I do not deal well with unexpected developments like, oh, discovering my family has been replaced by actors, and having to sleep in a cold, drafty room, and, oh yes, being called Prudence."

"To be expected, of course," Grayson said with a smile.

"Thank you." Delilah raised her chin and marched out of the room, like the brave little soldier she was.

"She doesn't seem to like you very much." Grayson studied Camille.

"She never has." Camille sighed. "She's not fond of Beryl either."

"That I can understand." He chuckled. "It must be difficult for her, though."

" 'Difficult'?" Camille drew her brows together. "What do you mean?"

"Well, being five years younger than twin sisters, who were lovely and sought after and did very nearly everything together. I would think one might feel left out, not important enough to include, that sort of thing. It might be difficult, that's all." He shrugged. "It's just an observation."

"Yes, I suppose." She had never thought of Delilah's position in that manner before.

"Although . . . this is a perfect example. This is your scheme, but Beryl is right by your side. You never considered Delilah might wish to be part of it."

Camille bristled. "She would *never* wish that. She is entirely too proper for something like this." Admittedly, she had never been asked. "Besides, she was out of the country with Mother, who, I might add, asked Delilah to accompany her, not Beryl or me."

"As I said, it was just an observation."

Still, she had never considered why Delilah might behave toward her sisters as she did. Why, it had never even crossed her mind that her younger sister might feel left out. And in Delilah's shoes, wouldn't Camille feel the same? She winced. "I haven't been very nice to her, have I?"

He shook his head. "I couldn't say."

"Well, I haven't. Or, rather, we haven't. We never considered that she might feel overlooked. We thought she didn't like us."

"I can't imagine she's overly fond of you."

"No, she's not. And it now appears, we deserve it." She sighed. "This is the second time today I've felt ashamed of my behavior." She wrinkled her nose. "I don't especially like it."

"It's most becoming," he said in a teasing manner.

"Only you would say such a thing." She wrapped her arms around herself. "Obviously, I—well, Beryl and I—should make amends in some manner. I would much prefer to spend the rest of my life with a younger sister who does not detest me—although I doubt it will be easy." She shook her head. "This rift has been years in the making."

"Making amends is never easy." He met her gaze directly. "Apologies for one's mistakes—those errors in judgment that we all make because of youth or selfishness or pride—are often difficult. Particularly when one realizes one's own behavior was unreasonable and even stupid."

Her heart skipped a beat. "Are we still talking about Delilah?"

"I don't know." He stepped closer; his gaze still locked with hers. "Are we?"

"I know I agreed that you and I should talk about what passed between us all those years ago, but not now, Grayson, please." The last thing she needed tonight was a discussion of the past—especially since she was not the least bit certain how she felt about anything, about him, now. It was all most confusing. "I simply cannot dredge up the past when the present is in such chaos."

"It can wait." He smiled. "I'm not going anywhere."

"This time," she said without thinking.

He nodded.

She stared at him for a long moment. "Thank you. For your assistance tonight," she added quickly. "I can't tell you how much I appreciate your help."

"It's the least I can do." He looked as though he

wanted to say something else, then thought better of it. Instead, he offered his arm. "Shall we join the others?"

"Before it's too late, you mean?"

He laughed and she took his arm, hard and solid beneath her touch. The arm of a man one could depend on. A man who could be relied upon when needed. Not that it mattered at the moment. Still, it was something to keep in mind. "Who knows what might be happening without us?"

"Who knows, indeed?" He glanced down at her. "In spite of the unexpected difficulties you've encountered thus far, I suspect you will somehow manage to triumph in the end."

"Goodness, Grayson, at this point I no longer care about victory." She cast him a rueful smile. "I am just hoping for survival."

Seventeen

Camille had planned games for this evening, but no one seemed interested at the moment in anything more than conversation and brandy. It struck her that everyone was somewhat subdued tonight, apparently worn out by the day's activities. Except perhaps for her mother.

Camille surveyed the gathering in the parlor. Mother flirted with Nikolai in a manner that might have been excessive—had she been anyone else's mother—but for her was simply her nature. Miss Murdock more than matched her in spirit and enthusiasm. Whereas the young actress's penchant for flirtation had been annoying at first, now Camille appreciated her steadfast determination. Nikolai certainly seemed to enjoy it. Grayson chatted with Mrs. Montgomery-Wells and Mr. Henderson while trying, as well, to charm, if not outright flirt with, Delilah. Indeed, her younger sister did appear to be reluctantly enjoying herself.

Beside her, Beryl, too, studied the group. "I must say, even with our surprise arrivals, it's all going—"

"Don't say it!" Camille grabbed her arm. "Whatever you do, do not say it."

Beryl stared in confusion. "Don't say what?"

Camille grimaced. "Obviously, I can't say, but you know what I mean."

"I haven't the faintest idea what you're talking about." Beryl's brows furrowed. "All I was going to say was—"

"Stop." Camille shook her head. "If you say it's going well, it won't. Such a declaration is like a curse. So I would be most appreciative if you kept any such observation to yourself."

"Very well." Beryl thought for a moment. "May I say it's going poorly then? That this house of cards you've built is likely to collapse at any moment, bringing it all down around your head? May I further add that I told you so?"

"No. But I do appreciate how difficult it is for you to restrain yourself."

"Oh, I'm certain the opportunity will yet be presented." Beryl studied her. "I have never known you to be superstitious before."

"I am clinging to any advantage that might avail itself at the moment, including superstition." Her gaze settled on her younger sister. "And you and I need to do something about Delilah."

"My thoughts exactly. What did you have in mind? Lock her in the attic? As we did when she was a child?"

"We're not proud of that; it was dreadful of us. And we will certainly not do it now or ever again." She glanced at her twin. "We need to be nicer to her."

"Why?"

"Because she is our sister, our only sister, and we have treated her abominably."

"No worse than she's treated us."

"Perhaps, but . . ." Camille searched for the right words. "It has been brought to my attention that it's entirely possible that Delilah might behave the way she does toward us because we have not included her in our lives."

"And?"

"And we should," Camille said firmly. "We should make more of an effort to see her."

"We went to her wedding. And her husband's funeral."

"We need to see her when it's not a wedding or a funeral or a family occasion that we are required to attend. We should invite her to join us at the Ladies Tearoom when we meet there, or when we attend gallery openings or lectures or museum exhibits."

Beryl stared. "Why?"

"Because we should, that's why. We have never made an effort to include her or really even get to know her better. Why, she's practically a stranger."

"No doubt because we were grown and had our own lives before she was of an age to be interesting. Not that she is now."

"Nonsense. I'm certain she is quite interesting. And, as I said, she is the only sister we have, and we should treat her as such."

"I still don't see. . . ." Beryl's eyes widened. "Oh, now I understand." She cast Camille an admiring look. "How very clever of you."

"What is very clever of me?"

"If we befriend our dear younger sister, she will be much more inclined to embrace your deception." Beryl's gaze shifted to Delilah. "As it is, she looks as if she has eaten something that has disagreed with her."

"I think she looks like she is enjoying herself, albeit

reluctantly." Delilah laughed at something Grayson said and Camille's stomach lurched. She ignored it. "Thankfully, Grayson is making an effort to entertain her."

Beryl raised a brow. "Jealous?"

"Don't be absurd," she said coolly. "He is simply trying to be helpful. And I am most grateful."

"Don't be too grateful," Beryl warned. "Don't forget what he—"

"I won't." Camille's tone was sharper than she had intended. "I have not forgotten anything, nor do I intend to. He is simply doing what he said he would do. He is being my friend."

"Well, I still don't trust him."

"Beryl, dear." She smiled. "You don't have to."

Beryl considered her for a moment, then sighed. "Good Lord."

"What?"

"Nothing. No indeed. Not a thing." She shook her head. "Well, I should rescue Mother, or perhaps Nikolai—not that they look like they need rescuing. But it is my turn to flirt with the prince." She squared her shoulders. "Not a bad way to spend the evening, really. He is most enjoyable to look at, and I do love his accent. All that smiling and nodding does tend to wear on one, however."

Camille laughed. "Your sacrifice is most appreciated. And I shall begin making amends with our sister."

"You're such a better person than I am."

"Someone has to be."

Beryl took a step, then turned back to her sister. "Where did you get this idea? About Delilah, that is?"

"Grayson mentioned it," she said in an offhand manner.

"Yes, he would, wouldn't he?" Beryl said under her

breath, smiled halfheartedly and crossed the room to join Nikolai and the ladies.

What on earth did she mean by that? Her gaze settled on Grayson and Delilah. One couldn't fault him for being observant. Or for being a genuinely nice person. And he was truly trying to provide his assistance. Oh, certainly he had arranged for the influx of *orphans*, and that did lead one to wonder if he was trying to help or hinder her efforts. Regardless, it could have been nothing more than a stupid mistake on his part. Thinking orphans would add to the farce—how utterly absurd. But he hadn't shirked responsibility when she had handed over the boys to him. In truth, he had behaved exactly as the doting uncle he was supposed to be. Indeed, if he hadn't seemed to be enjoying the children quite so much, Camille would have considered him the best actor in the cast.

Except for Camille herself, of course. All evening she had walked a fine line with Nikolai between friendly flirtation and obvious avoidance. It was not at all easy and now her head ached from the effort. Once again, she sent silent thanks in Miss Murdock's direction. The young actress did an excellent job of monopolizing Nikolai's attentions.

Still, while she refused to let herself believe all was going well, there was nothing at all dangerous about counting the days until Christmas. In that, she was like the children asleep in the nursery.

It did seem that Christmas would never come.

All in all, it was an interesting evening and relatively uneventful, if one discounted the arrival of the real Ladies Briston and Hargate. Gray resisted the urge to chuckle. That was one development Camille had not counted on. Still, she handled it well enough—with his help, of course. He wasn't about to let this farce of hers be her undoing.

He poured himself a brandy and watched Camille chat with her younger sister and her fraudulent family members. It looked as though she had taken his comments about Delilah to heart. In spite of his absence for all these years, the rift between the sisters was obvious. As well as a shame. His uncle had told him that he and Gray's father had once suffered an estrangement of sorts, and he was eternally grateful they'd settled their differences before his brother's death. It was a lesson that had stayed with Gray: One never knew how much time one had to make amends. His gaze lingered on Camille. Pity it had taken him so long to realize that lesson applied to him as well.

"There's something not quite right about him, isn't there?" Lady Briston said beside him. He wondered how long she'd been standing there.

"Who?"

"Camille's prince, of course."

Gray nodded. "You noticed that too?"

"My dear boy." She gave him a pitying look. "I have encountered far too many displaced royals in my life not to be able to tell when one is less than genuine. It is fortunate, then . . ." She paused, apparently having thought better of what she was about to say.

"Yes?"

"Just a random thought. Of no real significance." She sipped her brandy and studied Pruzinsky. "It is a pity, though."

"Why?"

"Dear Lord, Grayson, have you looked at the man?" She had the look in her eyes of a gourmand who had just spotted a delectable morsel. "I'm not sure I have ever met a living, breathing man who looks as tasty as that one does."

"I see."

She slanted him a sharp glance. "You thought I was going to say it was a shame because I wish to have a prince in the family."

He started to deny it, then thought better of it and nodded.

"I can't deny the idea of being connected to royalty has a particular appeal, but my daughters are no longer children. They each married well the first time." She slanted him a sharp glance. "As their mother, it was my duty to make certain they did so."

"Of course," he murmured.

"At this point in their lives, however, they are more than capable of making their own decisions. And I expect them to do so. I am not one of those mothers who interferes. My daughters are all intelligent, financially independent, and they are free to do exactly as they wish. Delilah is still trying to decide exactly what that is, of course, but she is still fairly young. Beryl's second marriage has turned out not at all as she expected and she appears quite happy. As for Camille, aside from not yet having conquered her tendency toward impulse, she, too, is searching, I think."

"Perhaps she has found what she is looking for."

"Goodness, Grayson, if you really believed that, you wouldn't be here." She glanced at him. "Why are you here?"

"I am simply trying to lend my assistance to a friend."

"Yes, that was my guess." She paused. "We can't allow her to marry him if he's not what he says he is."

"What happened to your daughters being more than capable of making their own decisions?"

" 'Capable' and 'correct' are two entirely different things. Can I trust you to stop this?"

"Why me?"

"For two reasons, I suppose. One, it keeps me from being an interfering mother."

He laughed. "Well, then, I have no choice."

"Why have you not declared yourself?" she said in an offhand manner.

"What?" He stared at her.

"You heard me." She sighed. "I am not a stupid woman, dear boy. Camille may not see it, but I do. I suspect Beryl does as well." She paused. "Although she is obviously not pleased about it."

"About what?" Caution edged his words.

"About reason number two. About the way you cannot take your eyes off Camille. About the look in your eyes when your gaze settles on her, or when her gaze meets yours. I doubt that anyone, besides Beryl and myself, has noticed. They do not forgive easily—my daughters, that is. Nor do I." She sipped her brandy thoughtfully. "I suspect it is one of those things that is passed from mother to daughter, from generation to generation. Nonetheless, we expect forgiveness to be earned."

"I am trying."

"Yes, of course, by being her friend. And is that going well?"

"I was able to explain your appearance."

"My, you are quick-witted. No doubt that explains how you made that lovely fortune of yours." She paused for a long moment. "I wouldn't have stopped you."

He shook his head. "I don't understand."

"No, I'm sure you don't." She heaved a resigned sigh. "I have encouraged my daughters, steered them in the proper direction, as it were, but I have never forced them to do anything. I daresay, I couldn't have, even if I tried. Perhaps you never noticed, but they are all annoyingly strong-willed." She smiled in a smug manner. "Yet something else apparently passed from mother to daughter."

"I still have no idea what you are trying to say."

"I am trying to say I did not force Camille to marry Harold. Had I known her affections were engaged elsewhere, I might, possibly, have tried to dissuade her."

He stared in stunned silence.

"Do not misunderstand my words, Grayson. I thought Harold was the right man for Camille at the time. Marrying for love has never seemed to me to be quite as sensible as marriage for more practical considerations. I lost any belief I might have had in true love and souls fated to be together, and all that sort of nonsense, longer ago than I can remember. However . . ." She heaved an exasperated sigh. "While you could not have provided for her the way he could, she would not have starved either. Your uncle, as I recall, had plans for your future. But it was not until long after she was wed that I had any idea about her feelings for you, as well as what passed between the two of you before her wedding."

"Camille told you about that?"

She shook her head. "Camille never said a word. Beryl told me."

"I'm not sure what to say," he said slowly.

"Some things never change, apparently." She cast him a pointed look. "One hopes you have changed in other ways. A better sense of timing, if nothing else. Still, as you have done well for yourself, one might expect that you would not be quite as willing to give up now, as you once were."

"Are you giving me your approval?" He forced a casual note to his voice. "To pursue your daughter?"

"Don't be absurd. You don't need my approval or my permission. Nor does she. I do try not to interfere."

"Of course not."

"However, I am more than willing to offer advice."

"And I am most willing to listen." He paused. "Do you have some? Advice, that is?"

"Nothing you don't already know. I would tell you not to be an idiot, to pursue what you want. But I cannot tell you how to win Camille's hand, or heart, if you prefer, because I don't really know how to do that. It is obviously something you must determine for yourself." She thought for a moment. "There is one other thing. Not advice, exactly, but something you should know."

"Yes?"

"If you are so lucky as to earn Camille's forgiveness or Beryl's or mine, for that matter, you should know one mistake might possibly be allowed. Another would be intolerable. Do keep that in mind, Grayson. And try not to muck up again."

"Yes, Lady Briston."

"Now, now, dear." She sipped her brandy. "At the moment, you may call me 'Mother.' "

Grayson smiled.

"It appears everyone is ready to retire." Camille joined them. "I know I am. It has been an exceptionally long day."

Lady Briston considered her daughter closely. "You look dreadfully tired, dear. A good night's sleep will do you a world of good."

"Yes, well . . ." Camille's gaze caught Gray's; then she quickly looked away. A firm note sounded in her voice. "That is my intention. A good night's sleep. In my own bed. Alone."

"I do hope that wasn't for my benefit," Lady Briston said.

Gray hoped it was for his. Nice to think that Camille wanted him to know she was not sharing a bed with Pruzinsky—even if Beryl had already told him as much. Still, Camille wanting him to know, as well, struck him as a very good sign. Was she coming to her senses about the man? And, more important, about Gray?

Camille ignored her. "Tomorrow shall be very nearly as busy as today. What with decorating the house, and the children, and all."

"Who are these children everyone is talking about?" Lady Briston frowned in annoyance.

"Lovely little boys from the village. Here just for the night. You shall meet them tomorrow." Camille smiled sweetly. "Their presence was Grayson's doing."

"But Winfield procured them," he said quickly. "They're the butcher's children."

"Goodness." Her gaze shifted between Camille and Gray. "The two of you sound like children again. The butcher's children, you say?"

Camille nodded, obviously aware of what was coming. Gray grinned.

"Mr. Carroll? Then we have Carrolls at Christmastime?" Lady Briston chuckled. "My, my, Grayson, how clever of you. And Winfield, of course."

"Thank you." He cleared his throat. "Mother."

Camille shot him a startled glance.

"Camille, darling, this just gets better and better."

Camille sighed. "Thank you, Mother."

"Oh, it wasn't a compliment, dear, simply an observation. Although . . ." She cast a considering glance at the rest of the gathering. "It does seem to be going well."

Camille winced.

"You should be pleased," Lady Briston continued. "Why, this is really quite a triumph, darling."

"It's not Christmas yet, Mother."

And the day after, Camille intended to leave with Pruzinsky. She'd challenged Gray to be the man he had become, and he intended to do just that. One way or another, he'd keep Camille from making the worst mistake of her life and convince her to forgive him for the worst mistake of his.

The man he had become would not lose the love of his life. Not this time.

Not this Christmas.

December 23rd

Eighteen

"You there, boy number two," Mother called to Simon, who was perched halfway up the main stairway. "Move that branch a bit to your right, if you please." She sighed. "No, dear, your other right."

Gray felt a tug on his pants and glanced down. Walter stared up at him. "Yes?"

"If she puts those branches and leaves and ribbons all over the banister, it wouldn't be any good to anyone, you know." Walter stared accusingly up at him.

The older boys were assisting in the decoration; the twins were in the kitchen being fed gingerbread and other Christmas treats. Fortesque had confided that his wife had been up much of the night making all sorts of Christmas delights. Gray had sampled the gingerbread, pronounced it excellent and had broached the subject of Mrs. Fortesque becoming his cook. With appropriate living quarters for the couple, of course, and the possibility of a small stipend for Mr. Fortesque, as well, so that he could continue to pursue his acting career. Something in the nature of artistic patronage, Gray had said, and Mr. Fortesque agreed to discuss it with his wife. After all, while Gray and Camille had agreed to offer Mrs. Fortesque the same salary, there was no prohibition against offering wages for her husband as well.

"I do so apologize, Walter, but the ladies apparently wish to decorate every spare surface." He shrugged. "There's nothing to be done about it, I'm afraid."

"Father says when a woman gets something into her head . . ." On Gray's other side, Thomas shook his head in a forlorn manner. "There's nothing a man can do but lend a hand or move out of the way."

"Your father is a very wise man," Gray said.

Walter snickered. "That's not what Mother says. Mother says—"

"Perhaps it would be best if you kept that to yourself." Gray chuckled.

"Boys number one and three," Lady Briston commanded. Apparently, she was no better at names than Mrs. Montgomery-Wells, although she did remember her own. "Do be so good as to fetch those swags in the corner and bring them to me."

Thomas let out a long-suffering sigh; then he and Walter scurried to do as she asked.

Lady Briston, the children and the maids were busy with the banister and stairway, while Beryl had Pruzinsky and the rest of the actors decorating the main parlor. Camille balanced on a ladder directing the footman hanging ribbon-bedecked garlands of holly from the gallery railing. Gray moved closer to steady the ladder.

Camille glanced down. "I do hope you are not looking at my ankles, Grayson Elliott."

"But they are such lovely ankles, Camille." As were, no doubt, the legs attached to them and all else beyond. His stomach tightened.

"Thank you," she said in a prim manner, and descended the ladder. She reached the floor and stood so close to him that she was nearly in his arms. A challenge gleamed in her eyes. "Are you going to move, or do I have to shove you out of the way?"

He smiled into her eyes. "But I quite like where I am standing."

Her breath caught. "Grayson, I don't know what you are thinking, but this is . . . It's most inappropriate, that's what it is."

He could smell the fresh scent of her hair, even over the scent of evergreen, which hung in the air. "I suspect you know exactly what I am thinking."

"Well, I am not thinking the same thing," she said in a firm tone, but made no effort to push past him.

He smiled. "I was simply wondering where you intend to put the mistletoe. We gathered quite a lot of it, you know."

"I did notice that. Rather an excessive amount, don't you think?"

"It is Christmas, after all." His gaze locked with hers. "Where will you hang it?"

"Where?" For a long moment, she stared at him, a hint of confusion and even—dare he hope—a touch of longing in her eyes. At last she shook her head, as if to clear it, then stepped away. "Somewhere safe."

" 'Safe'?"

"Yes, *safe*," she said sharply. "Somewhere discreet. I don't want it all over the house where the unsuspecting might encounter it every time they turn around and be compelled to kiss someone they would prefer not to kiss."

"That is, however, the purpose of mistletoe." He chuckled, "I must commend you, Camille. The house is beginning to look as it did at Christmas when we were young."

"It is, isn't it?" Her expression eased and she glanced

around. "I always loved this house at Christmas, with the ivy and holly and ribbons everywhere." She smiled. "I always thought it was very nearly perfect."

"That is what you want. A perfect Christmas."

She hesitated, then nodded. "Indeed, it is."

"Although I'm not sure 'perfect' can be achieved."

She frowned. "Why not?"

"Well . . ."

"What is it now?"

"Perhaps you're not aware, but this morning I found your mother rehearsing a scene from *Romeo and Juliet* with Mr. Henderson."

"Good Lord." She grimaced. "Was she . . ."

"Juliet." He nodded.

"And Mr. Henderson?"

"Romeo, of course." He grinned. "They were really quite good. It was rather impressive, all in all."

"I gather you did not find it necessary to stop them?"

He gasped in feigned dismay. "I would never dare to tell your mother what she may or may not do in her own home."

Camille bit back a smile. "It might be unwise, at that."

" 'Unwise'?" He scoffed. "It would be nothing short of fatal."

"And as you have only a minor role—"

"I could be done away with at any moment," he said in a somber manner. "Which would no doubt make your life easier," he added casually.

"Yes, it would." She nodded and studied him. "Although, at this point in our production, your role seems to have taken on greater significance. Why, the audience would be most annoyed were you to breathe your last."

"And would you?" He held his breath.

"I . . ." She caught sight of the footman struggling

with a garland and sighed. "No, no, that's not at all right. It should be higher. Here I'll show you." She started up the stairs, then turned back toward him. "Do be so good as to make yourself useful, Grayson. There is still a great deal to be done."

"Your wish is my command." He grinned. "Cousin."

"Hmph." She huffed and continued up the stairs.

He'd be more than happy to make himself useful, and the mistletoe was the perfect place to start. Somewhere safe and discreet, indeed. Safe and discreet were not in the spirit of the season. Besides, mistletoe provided opportunities he did not intend to pass up. He crossed to the pile of greenery. Someone had gathered the mistletoe into bunches tied with ribbons. He bent down and gathered the bunches together.

"I beg your pardon, Mr. Elliott," Fortesque said in a quiet voice behind him.

"Yes?" Gray stood up.

Fortesque glanced at Camille, then her mother, and leaned close in a confidential manner. "We have yet another new arrival. I put him in the library, and I thought perhaps it might be best if you were to handle this one, as I'm not sure Lady Lydingham is up to—"

"Yes, of course." He thrust the bunches of mistletoe at the actor. "See to it that these are hung throughout the house."

Fortesque took the greenery reluctantly. "But I was under the impression Lady Lydingham did not want—"

"Lady Lydingham wants everything to be perfect, and what is more perfect at Christmas than mistletoe?"

"Well, yes, I suppose, but—"

"Should she complain, you have my permission to place the blame entirely on me, although it might be wise to avoid her catching you in the act, as it were. So do try to be inconspicuous."

"Yes, sir, but—"

"And, Fortesque, there might be a little something extra in your Christmas stocking if you manage this."

"Yes, sir." Fortesque nodded. "I shall do my best, sir."

"I knew you would." Gray grinned and headed toward the library. Camille couldn't possibly complain about a kiss from him under the mistletoe. Of course, this also gave Pruzinsky increased opportunity; but as both Gray and Beryl would be watching, Pruzinsky's advantage would be minimal.

He stepped into the library and pulled up short. Colonel Channing stood there, gazing out the window. But the way the man held himself seemed different from the man he remembered. Certainly, it had been a long time, but there was a tension in the line of his body that didn't seem right. Perhaps it was what Gray had learned yesterday that still lingered in the back of his mind, or possibly it was instinct. And there was every chance he was wrong.

"Lord Briston?"

"Yes?" The gentleman turned toward him.

It had been years since he had seen Colonel Channing. Still . . .

"I'm certain you don't remember me, sir," Gray began. "I am Grayson Elliott."

"Ah yes, Lord Fairborough's nephew." The older man nodded. "I hear you have done quite well for yourself."

Gray nodded slowly and studied the other man, certainty growing within him. "You're not Colonel Channing, are you?"

The gentleman's eyes narrowed. "Why do you say that?"

"Because, for as long as I knew Colonel Channing, he never allowed himself to be called 'Lord Briston' out of deference to his brother." He paused. "His dead brother."

"Ah yes." The man waved off the comment. "Things change, you know, boy."

"Not this. Beyond that . . ." He drew a deep breath. "When Camille and I were looking for ornaments in the attic, I uncovered some letters. Letters from her dead father, dated long after his supposed death."

"I see." Lord Briston's eyes narrowed. "What do you intend to do about this discovery of yours?"

"Whatever you wish me to do, sir." He shook his head. "This is your home and your family. I would say the next step is yours. However, you should know"—he met the man's gaze directly—"I will do whatever I think best to keep Camille from being hurt."

"So that's how it is, is it?"

"Yes, sir."

"And does my daughter feel the same about you?"

"I hope so, but I'm not sure she has realized it yet."

"This sounds rather complicated."

"You have no idea," Gray muttered.

"Then I suspect explanations are in order." He blew a long breath. "From both of us." He glanced around. "Is the whisky still kept where it always was?"

"I believe so, sir."

"Pour us each a glass, a large glass, and come sit down." He moved to one of the chairs before the fireplace and settled into it. "This will take a while. It's a long story."

"It would have to be." Gray moved to the cabinet where the whisky and brandy and various spirits had long been kept, poured two glasses and joined Camille's father. He handed him a glass, then sat in the matching chair. "Might I ask, sir, why you are here? After all this time?"

"It's Christmas," Lord Briston said simply, and sipped his drink.

"Forgive me for saying, sir, but haven't nearly twenty Christmases passed since you . . ."

"Died?"

Gray nodded.

"That wasn't entirely by choice. Nonetheless, the fault is mine. But I have regretted every Christmas that I did not have the courage to return." He swirled the whisky in his glass. "I said it was a long story—one I've never really told before. However as I am here, and as you are determined to protect Camille . . ." He shrugged.

"Go on, then, sir."

"I should start from the beginning, I suppose." He paused, obviously to pull his thoughts together. "Bernadette and I married very young, Mr. Elliott. Too young, really. We were both filled with the passion of youth. Both of us had, as well, what one might call volatile temperaments. We were both quick to anger. When we fought, which was frequently . . ." He smiled a sort of private smile and then cleared his throat. "Let us just say, it could not be ignored by anyone within hearing.

"At any rate, I inherited my title and the responsibilities that went along with it. Before I knew it, I had not only a wife but three daughters as well. Through the years, I found myself resenting all that had fallen upon my shoulders because I happened to be born a few minutes before my brother."

He fell silent for a long moment. "He was free to wander the world and live a life filled with adventures and excitement, whereas I felt trapped. Can you understand that?"

"I can understand feeling that the circumstances of one's life are not especially fair," Gray said slowly, choosing his words with care. "I'm afraid I can't understand allowing your family to believe you were dead."

"That was not my decision, but I am getting ahead of myself." He stared into the fire, obviously gathering his memories. "Basil found himself in a bit of trouble in India, the details of which scarcely matter now. I felt I had no choice but to go to his aid. He was my twin, after all. Bernadette agreed with my decision and even encouraged me to go. It took some time to extricate Basil from his difficulties, but I had expected that and had made certain Bernadette had all the legal authority she needed to make decisions about property and finances and life here. We had been married, oh, a dozen years or so by then.

"One thing led to another, and . . . I was a very stupid man, Mr. Elliott, and selfish, thinking only of myself. I was consumed with what I was missing rather than grateful for all that I had. I wrote and told my wife that while I loved her and the children, I would not be coming home for the foreseeable future. She was, needless to say, furious and hurt as well, I suspect, although she never said that. Pride, no doubt."

"Understandable."

"Of course it was." He heaved a deep sigh. "She wrote and told me she would not allow her daughters to believe their father would abandon them. She'd rather they think he was dead."

"I see."

"A few years later, I wrote asking to come home. She refused to allow it. I wrote continuously after that, every few months, but she was adamant. And so the years passed." He tossed back the rest of his whisky and held out his glass. Gray fetched the decanter and returned to fill the other man's glass. "Can you understand how it feels to know you have made the biggest mistake of your life, and the one person you pray will forgive you refuses to so much as speak with you?"

Gray shifted uncomfortably in his chair. "I have an idea, sir."

"I have kept abreast of their lives, though. I see Basil frequently, in various parts of the world. In addition to my letters, he has acted as a courier of sorts. Spoken on my behalf and all. He thinks I am the worst sort of coward."

"Oh, I'm sure he doesn't—"

"He's right, you know." Lord Briston smiled ruefully. "I have been. Still am, I think. But you come to a point in your life when you realize the days in front of you are fewer than the days behind, and you realize, as well, how much of your life you have squandered. And somehow you find the courage you have lacked."

"So you're here now."

"That I am. Here to win my family back. God help me. Or them." He raised his glass. "And we shall see. It should be an interesting Christmas."

"In more ways than you can imagine." Gray paused. "There are a few things you should know about this particular Christmas before you see anyone else." Gray quickly explained about Camille's plan, which actor was playing which part, the addition of small children, the unexpected arrival of Ladies Briston and Hargate, as well as how he and Beryl were certain Pruzinsky was a fraud.

Lord Briston chuckled. "I'm not sure why, but none of this surprises me."

"Well, there is an element of amusement that—"

"There you are, Grayson." Beryl swept into the room. The two men jumped to their feet. "Camille needs your assistance and I—" She caught sight of her father and stopped short. "Uncle Basil, what are you doing here?

Not that I'm not pleased to see you. It is Christmas, after all. But your presence is not merely unexpected, but . . ." Her eyes widened and her face paled.

"Beryl." Lord Briston stepped forward.

She stared for a long moment. "You're looking remarkably good for a dead man."

"How did you know?" her father asked.

"I found some of your letters a few years ago." Her eyes narrowed. "What are you doing here?"

"I've come home," he said simply.

"For Christmas?"

"For good, I hope. One never knows how much time one has left and I have wasted entirely too much."

"That's all very well and good, but what about last Christmas? And the Christmas before." She folded her arms over her chest. "And all the Christmases that have passed?"

"There is nothing I can do to make up for the past. To make amends to you and your sisters and your mother." He shook his head. "But I am here now."

"Don't expect us to fall all over ourselves greeting you with open arms."

He smiled. "I never imagined that was a possibility."

"It isn't." She looked at Gray. "You understand Camille cannot be told. Not yet."

"You never told her?" Gray studied her.

"I didn't know how. To tell her now, before this Christmas farce of hers is over, would be a disaster of monumental proportions." There was the oddest tremble in her voice, as if she were drawing on all her strength and it was not quite enough. "I don't think Delilah should be told either. I have no idea how she might take the resurrection of her dead father, but as she was very young when he *died*—I daresay, she can't remember a time when she had a father." She looked at her father. "As for you . . ." She shook her head. "I don't know. . . ."

Gray had never imagined Beryl to be at a loss for words. She was right, though: Camille should not be told yet. If coming face-to-face with the father she knew wasn't dead did this to Beryl, he couldn't imagine the effect this revelation would have on Camille.

"I understand and you're quite right." Lord Briston nodded. "No need to complicate this Christmas any further. There will be plenty of time to set things right afterward."

"Or you could save us all the trouble and leave," Beryl said sharply. "Again."

"I could." His gaze met his daughter's. "Would you prefer that I do so?"

"Yes," she snapped. "But I doubt that my preference makes any difference whatsoever. Besides, you have two other daughters, and I shall not make this decision for them."

"Good, as I am here to stay." Determination sounded in the older man's voice.

"You shall have to allow Camille to think you're Uncle Basil until after Christmas. Dear Lord, we'll need to explain you somehow. Oh, and you'll have to play a part." She cast Gray a helpless look. It was as frightening as seeing her at a loss for words.

"He could play my father, I suppose," Gray said slowly. "I can't think of anything else. Although, as your mother is playing the part of my mother, I'm not sure if it's especially wise." He glanced at Lord Briston. "But then, I suppose, it's possible Lady Briston won't realize who you really are."

"Goodness, Grayson."

All eyes immediately turned to the doorway and Lady Briston.

"I should think I would recognize my own husband." Lady Briston's gaze met her husband's. "Good afternoon, Nigel."

"Bernadette." He nodded. "You look as lovely as I remember."

"You look considerably older." She studied him for a moment. "I don't recall inviting you here. In fact, I distinctly remember telling you never to step foot in this house again."

"And yet here I am."

"Yes, indeed." She released a long breath. "And it's about bloody time too, isn't it?"

He stared in obvious shock. "What?"

"Mother." Beryl stepped toward the older woman. "Are you all right?"

"Quite. Indeed, I have never been better." She directed her words to her daughter, but her gaze stayed on her husband. "Camille has been looking for you both. The children have been collected by their parents and have gone. Oh, and boy number two?" She glanced at Gray.

Gray nodded. "Simon."

"He left you a message. A Christmas gift, he said. What was it?" Her brow furrowed. "Ah yes. He said you could have his wish."

Gray smiled. "Thank you."

"Might I suggest you use it wisely."

Gray nodded. "I intend to."

Her gaze narrowed and shifted back to her husband. The man may not think he had courage, but he stared back without flinching and even seemed to stand a bit straighter. "Now, then, children, do run along. And I quite agree that neither Camille nor Delilah should know anything about this newest development, except that Basil has returned. There is no need to create further chaos. We shall sort it all out after Christmas."

"Of course, Mother," Beryl said, but made no effort to move.

Gray grabbed her arm and fairly pushed her out of the library; then turned to close the doors behind him. His gaze met Lady Briston's.

"Thank you, Grayson." She nodded. "You may well do, after all."

He smiled and pulled the doors closed. Beryl rested her back against the wall, with her eyes closed, looking as though she were about to melt into a puddle on the floor.

"Are you all right?"

"Do try not to be so blasted nice, Grayson." She opened her eyes and glared at him. "It makes it exceedingly difficult to dislike you. And I much prefer to dislike you."

"Why?"

"Because, if I don't dislike you, I might possibly feel compelled to forgive you and even encourage my sister to forgive you as well." She sighed. "Although I think I have lost that battle."

"She's forgiven me?" Hope sounded in his voice.

"It's not for me to say, and I really don't know." She sniffed. "I don't know what's wrong with the women in this family. You're gone for eleven years, and he's gone for twenty, and now that you're both back . . ."

"Perhaps . . ." He chose his words with care. "It all comes down to love."

"Dear Lord, I hope not."

He laughed. "Why not?"

"Because I love my husband," she snapped. "And I should hate to think that I would allow him to break my heart and then forgive him as if nothing had happened."

He shook his head. "It's not quite that easy."

"No?" She nodded toward the closed doors. "Do you hear that?"

The low murmur of voices coming from the library rose in volume.

He winced. "It doesn't sound good."

She cast him a disgusted look. "You are an idiot." She shook her head and started off; then turned back to him. "If you wish to win my sister, if you want her forgiveness, then do something about it." She nodded at the closed doors. "Do you know what my father is doing right this very moment?"

"Arguing with your mother?"

She nodded. "And with a great deal of passion. The passion of anger is not so very different from the passion of . . . Well . . . need I say that by the time my parents are finished . . ." She sighed. "I suspect my sister has a passionate nature as well, one that has never truly been unleashed."

He stared.

"Stop being her friend and stop being so bloody nice. Tell her why you're really here. And what you really want."

"Are you giving me advice?"

"Apparently." She rolled her gaze heavenward. "I can't believe it myself. But know this, Grayson Elliott." She pinned him with a hard look. "If you have insinuated yourself into my sister's life, only to leave again, I shall track you down myself and rip your heart out with my bare hands. Now." She nodded. "Let us return to the others before something else happens."

"One does wonder what else that could possibly be." He stifled a grin and followed her.

Beryl was right. He had been Camille's friend long enough. It was time to make a stand. Of course Camille still intended to marry Pruzinsky, and that needed to be dealt with. But, thus far, he and Beryl were doing an excellent job of keeping an eye on her; and in the process, keeping her and Pruzinsky apart as well.

Past time they had that talk Camille kept postponing. Past time to tell her straight out how he felt and what he wanted.

And past time to make her admit she wanted exactly the same thing.

Nineteen

"I daresay, if my purpose was to get the entire family here at the same time, it would have been next to impossible." Camille sipped her tea and glanced around the small ladies' parlor that had long been her mother's private sanctuary.

Mother had invited her daughters to join her for tea, although *invite* was not entirely accurate, as there was no possibility of refusal. Mother tended to do that on occasion, when she was feeling particularly sentimental or there was something of a serious nature to discuss. Grayson had gallantly volunteered to keep an eye on the others. He really was trying to help. It was most endearing of him. Perhaps it was time to tell him she was no longer trying to garner a proposal from Nikolai but rather avoid one. Perhaps he had earned that. And then, who knew what might happen?

"Now that it is most awkward to have everyone here," Camille said, "you tell me Uncle Basil has arrived as well."

Beryl and her mother traded glances.

"Unfortunately," Mother began. "Basil is not feeling quite his usual self—"

Beryl choked on her tea.

"And he thinks it's best if he takes the next day or so to rest and recover his strength." Mother continued. "I suspect he may not join us until Christmas." Mother smoothed her hair. She had seemed a bit disheveled this afternoon, which was decidedly odd as she rarely had a hair out of place. While it could be attributed to her assistance in the decoration of the house, it was not at all like her. "Besides, given the current circumstances, he thought it might be wise not to add yet another player to your cast."

"Oh, dear." Camille frowned. "I do hope it's nothing serious."

"I doubt it. He has always been a hardy sort." Mother waved off the comment. "Although, for now, he has taken to his bed—"

Beryl coughed.

Mother cast her a sharp look. "Only as a precaution, mind you. It's no doubt nothing more than the strain of travel."

"I hope so, as there is no additional staff to attend to him," Camille said. "But I would like to spend some time with the dear man as soon as I can reasonably absent myself from the others. Even now, I'm not at all pleased at having left Nikolai in Grayson's charge."

"I'm sure Grayson is more than up to the task," Mother said.

"I can do that. See to Uncle Basil, that is," Delilah said. "You already have a great deal to juggle without having to worry about him as well."

"That's very thoughtful of you." Camille smiled at her younger sister. "And most appreciated."

"Well, if your deception isn't successful, we shall all

suffer the consequences," Delilah added with an off-hand shrug.

"I think it's a splendid idea." A thoughtful note sounded in Mother's voice. "You've scarcely spent any significant time with your uncle at all since your marriage. Not like when you were a child. You can take the opportunity to . . ."

"Get to know him?" Beryl suggested.

"Reacquaint herself with him," Mother said. "I daresay, he has all sorts of fascinating stories he has yet to tell. He's lived quite an adventurous life, you know."

"No doubt," Beryl said in a dry tone.

"Delilah," Camille began slowly. If she truly meant to make things right with her younger sister, there was no time like the present to begin. "I fear I owe you an apology." She shot a pointed look at Beryl. "We both do, don't we?"

"Yes, yes." Beryl sighed in surrender. "We've been dreadful."

"What are you talking about?" Delilah's eyes narrowed. "What have you done?"

"Nothing, really," Camille said quickly. "And therein lay the problem."

Delilah's suspicious gaze shifted from Camille to Beryl and back. "What problem?"

"Perhaps it's simply that it is Christmas," Camille began. "Or the fact that I have invented a family or that my own family is now here, or—"

"Grayson," Beryl muttered.

"Beryl," Camille said sharply. "What on earth is the matter with you today? You are even more ill-tempered than usual."

"Well, perhaps it's to be expected," Beryl snapped. "Given that—"

"Beryl," Mother warned.

"Given that nothing is quite going as planned." Beryl huffed. "Although I suppose I can try to be more pleasant."

"That would be most appreciated." Camille studied her twin curiously. Beryl did have a tendency to be overly sharp, but this wasn't at all like her. Still, she was right. Nothing was going precisely as intended, and it did make one tend to be a bit snippy. Camille turned her attention back to her younger sister. "As I was saying, Beryl and I have come to the realization that we haven't been the sisters we should have been and we have resolved to change that."

"Have you?" Suspicion sounded in Delilah's voice. "Why?"

"Because one never knows how much time one has." An adamant note sounded in Beryl's voice. "Because one minute there is someone you have paid no attention to whatsoever, because they have always simply been there, and you always expected they would, and the next minute they're gone. And there is nothing you can do about it, because it's entirely too late."

Camille stared. Beryl was certainly taking this reconciliation with Delilah far more seriously than Camille had expected. Their younger sister stared as well. Mother reached out and patted Beryl's hand. "Well said, dear."

"What if it is too late?" Delilah said slowly. "What if what is done cannot be undone?"

"Death is the only thing that cannot be undone," Mother said firmly.

"One would think," Beryl said under her breath; then her eyes widened as if she were surprised by her own words. "Just a thought, nothing of significance."

Mother continued without pause. "Which is not to say you should not make your sisters earn your forgive-

ness and your friendship." Mother's gaze slid from
Delilah to Beryl. "Being willing to forgive is not the
same as being weak. Indeed, it takes a great deal of
strength to accept someone else's acknowledgment of
their mistakes. Especially if said mistakes have hurt you
deeply. To allow amends to be made is not at all easy."
Her gaze shifted to Camille. "One must decide whether
one wishes to hold on to one's pain and anger or release it. And is the cost significant or little more than
pride? It can be an enormous relief to at last let go of
anger that one has harbored for a long time. Forgiveness can, as well, be the rekindling or even the beginning of something worth having."

For a long moment, the three younger women
stared at their mother. Forgiveness was one thing their
mother had never especially embraced. Still, she was
right. Wouldn't Camille gain so much more from forgiving Grayson than she did by holding on to her anger?
If, of course, she hadn't forgiven him already.

"One must also consider one's own culpability in
another's mistakes," Mother added. "Would something
that has grown so large have been relatively minor if
one had only acted at the time?"

Indeed, if Camille had gone after Grayson, instead
of expecting him to return for her . . . If she had told
him of her own feelings . . . If she had taken the next
step. Certainly, her mistake was far less significant than
his, but nonetheless it was a mistake.

"I haven't been very nice to you either," Delilah
said abruptly. "Why, I've never invited either of you to
my house. I've never included you in a dinner party or a
soirée or anything of that nature."

Beryl's brow furrowed. "You have dinner parties
and soirées?"

"Quite lovely ones too," Mother said in a confidential manner. "Her parties are most delightful. You have no idea what you're missing."

"Apparently." Beryl stared at the younger woman.

Delilah beamed at her mother's praise.

"We certainly cannot take offense, as we have not invited you to our gatherings either. However, that is now in the past," Camille said. "If, of course, this is something you wish to pursue as well."

Delilah looked at one twin, then the next.

"Go on, dear," Mother urged. "Tell them you accept their offer of friendship, their olive branch, as it were."

"Well, yes, I suppose," Delilah said thoughtfully. "I daresay, it won't be easy. I haven't been at all fond of either of you for as long as I can remember."

"How perfect, then, as we are all starting in much the same position." A weak smile curved Beryl's lips.

"Excellent." Camille smiled at her younger sister. She didn't actually dislike Delilah; she simply hadn't given her any particular thought throughout the years. "You should know I am most grateful for your assistance in carrying out my little Christmas farce."

"It seems to me, you need all the assistance you can get," Delilah said in a wry manner.

"She is perceptive." Beryl gave her younger sister a reluctant smile. "I'll give her that."

"Do you know"—Delilah took a sip of tea—"on occasion, while I don't look the least bit like you two—"

"Oh, you have the same eyes, dear," Mother said. "All of you."

"I have been told that I remind people of you." She looked at Beryl.

Beryl sniffed. "Nonsense."

"You poor dear." Camille bit back a laugh. "You shall have to work on that flaw in your character."

Delilah's eyes widened slightly, as if she couldn't believe one twin was sharing a joke with her at the other's expense, then smiled. "I'm not entirely sure it's a flaw. I took it as something of a compliment."

"Very well, then." Beryl heaved a dramatic sigh. "I suppose we can be friends, as she has such exquisite taste."

Delilah laughed. "I still don't entirely trust you, you know."

"As we don't entirely trust you either, it does seem like a good foundation to build upon." Beryl flashed her a genuine smile. "May I confess something too?"

"If you wish." Caution sounded in Delilah's voice.

"I have always rather envied your spirit of independence."

The younger woman's brows pulled together. "My what?"

"We have always depended upon one another, Camille and I. You have always depended upon no one but yourself." Beryl gestured absently. "I find it most . . . admirable."

Delilah stared. "You do?"

"Well, I daresay I couldn't do it, so yes I do." Beryl huffed. "Now, do not expect me to utter any more sentimental nonsense. I have had quite enough for one day."

"No, of course not," Delilah said. "One can't hope for too much at once."

"I want you all to know how very pleased I am," Mother said. "I have not been unaware of the differences between you, and I have found them most distressing. However, I have felt it was something you would eventually take steps to rectify." She picked up the teapot and refilled her cup. "I do try not to interfere."

The sisters exchanged glances. Apparently, this was one subject in which they were in total agreement.

"Might I ask you a question?" Delilah said to Camille.

"Of course."

"You went to all this trouble to extract a proposal from this prince." Delilah chose her words with care. "Yet, now you say you are avoiding a proposal. I find it somewhat confusing."

"Welcome to Christmas at Millworth Manor," Beryl murmured.

"There are a number of reasons that failed to occur to me before I began all this," Camille said. "It seemed like such a brilliant idea. . . ."

"And, as ideas go, Camille, it was indeed brilliant," Mother said. "I would be hard-pressed to come up with anything more clever."

"Unfortunately, I had not given it as much thought as I should have before leaping into it." She thought for a moment. "You must understand, there was a myriad of details to attend to, and I fear I was thinking about those rather than about whether I truly wanted to marry a man I had to deceive about my family. A man who spends much of the time smiling and nodding. And, upon further consideration, I'm not at all sure I wish to live in a castle in a country whose name I can't remember." She wrinkled her nose. "Then, of course, I don't love him, and while I didn't love Harold, I was quite fond of him. I did think I would love Nikolai one day—"

"After all, what's not to love?" Beryl cast her an innocent smile.

She ignored it. "But ultimately, as I certainly don't need his fortune, it seems wiser to marry someone I already love."

"Well, you're not getting younger, dear," Mother murmured.

"I blame my change of heart on Beryl." Camille smiled at her twin. "As she was the one who pointed out that love might be important in marriage."

Beryl shrugged. "Who would have imagined?"

"Oh, I see." Delilah refilled her cup. "I thought it might be due to Grayson. He's become part of this silly farce and seems to be lending a great deal of assistance, and there is something about the way he looks at you. . . ."

"Do you think so?"

"Don't you?"

"I don't know." Camille shook her head. "It's all most confusing. I have been angry at him for so long." She glanced at her younger sister. "But then you don't know about that."

Delilah took a bite of a biscuit. "You mean, how he told you he loved you on the day before your wedding, but then never did anything about it?"

Camille stared.

"Mother told me."

Camille looked at her mother. "And how did you know?"

"Beryl told me, of course."

Camille glared at her twin. "If I recall correctly, I told you not to tell anyone."

"Goodness, it was a long time ago. And, I daresay, your memory isn't very good, as I don't remember that at all." Beryl studied the biscuits on the tea tray, then selected one. "These are very good, you know. And I didn't tell just anyone."

"Beryl!"

"I told Mother."

"And I am not just anyone." Mother sniffed. "Although she didn't tell me until well after you were married. And I can't recall when I told Delilah, but it wasn't that long ago."

"You told me after Harold died." Delilah finished her biscuit, then reached for another. "I remember it distinctly, because I recall being shocked at Grayson's lack of taste." She froze and her gaze shot to Camille's. "I am sorry. I didn't mean, well, I did at the time, but now . . ."

"It doesn't matter." Camille smiled. "There is a great deal of water under the bridge among the three of us. It's to be expected that some of it would, oh, splash about on occasion."

"There are all sorts of nasty things we have thought or said about you," Beryl said in an offhand manner. The others stared and Beryl had the good grace to wince. "More of that water under the bridge, I suppose." She cast her younger sister an apologetic smile.

"I daresay, this will take some getting used to for all of us," Camille said.

"But well worth it," Mother said with a firm nod.

"As I was saying, Mother told me about you and Grayson after your husband died." Delilah poured more tea. "I must say, I was rather surprised he didn't return to England. I knew he hadn't married."

Camille raised a brow. "You did?"

Delilah nodded. "I had a friend, more of an acquaintance really, who was engaged to Grayson's cousin at the time. She told me he had never married. And, of course, as his investments in American railroads and some other things I can't recall had made him quite a sizable fortune—"

"What?" Camille stared. "What do you mean by a 'sizable fortune'?"

"Oh, you know, sizable." Delilah shrugged.

"Immense." Beryl nodded. "Almost obscene, really."

"Not at all," Mother said. "There is no such thing as too much wealth."

"You knew this?" Camille stared at her twin.

"Everybody knows," Beryl said casually.

"I had heard a rumor or two about his being successful but I never imagined . . ." She glared at Beryl. "Why didn't you tell me?"

Beryl frowned. "For one thing, I thought you knew. For another, you never asked. Indeed, you expressly forbade me to so much as mention his name. You were quite adamant about it. I do remember that."

"Does it matter, dear?" Mother asked.

"The fact that he has money doesn't matter. What matters is that he lied to me about it." She rose to her feet and paced the parlor. "He led me to believe his circumstances were unchanged." She stopped and glared at the others. "He introduced himself as a poor relation. Hah! Why would he do that?" She resumed pacing. "And when we wagered over who could hire Mrs. Fortesque—"

"Who is Mrs. Fortesque?" Delilah asked Beryl.

"The cook." Beryl reached for a piece of molded gingerbread. "I might well wish to hire her myself."

"He said it wouldn't be fair, as my resources were so much more extensive than his, and therefore we should agree to offer her the same wages." She folded her arms over her chest. "Why wouldn't he want me to know he had money?"

"Perhaps he thought as it made a difference then . . ." Beryl said cautiously.

"Don't be absurd." Camille scoffed. "It made no difference then."

"But did he know that?"

"Oh, there was a comment about how I would marry him if he had money, and how, as he didn't, it didn't matter. Something like that." She shrugged. "But he should have known me better." Aside from everything else, that was one part of this that had always angered her. "He should have trusted me."

"He was a boy in love." Mother shrugged. "They are even more stupid than men in love."

"I couldn't have married him, anyway." She narrowed her eyes. "Not that he asked me."

"The beast," Beryl mumbled around a mouthful of gingerbread. She looked at Delilah. "This is exceptional."

"Isn't it?" Delilah nodded. "Try the scones."

"Why not?" Mother said, then glanced at her youngest daughter. "The scones you say?" Delilah nodded.

Camille stared at her mother. "What do you mean, 'why not?' For one thing, he didn't ask me. For another, I was to marry Harold the very next day. What was I supposed to do?"

Mother shrugged. "It would have been most distressing, but you could have called off your wedding."

"I know I was rather shocked when I heard the story that you hadn't done exactly that," Delilah said, "given your penchant for impulse."

"People call off weddings at the last possible moment all the time," Mother added. "Ask Lord Stillwell."

"And done what? Chase after a man who makes a grand announcement about love and then runs off?"

"Odder things have happened," Mother said.

"You were expecting me to marry Harold!"

"Oh no, Camille." Mother shook her head. "Do not place the blame at my feet. I encouraged you, but I never forced you to marry Harold. Nor did I force Beryl to marry Charles, or Delilah to marry Phillip. Admittedly, I was in favor of those matches, but I have never been able to make any of you do something you did not want to do. It is a shame all three of those charming gentlemen have passed on. . . ." She met Camille's gaze firmly. "However, none of you were unhappy in your marriages. None of your husbands treated you unkindly. And all three of you now are in control of your own fortunes, your own fate—even Beryl, who was clever enough to make appropriate legal arrangements before marrying Lionel. You will never have to worry about how you will feed yourself and your children, should you have children. You will never have to be dependent upon the fickle whims of a husband who is more boy than man. You may thank Harold for that, and you may thank me as well. But I never forced you to do anything. Although, admittedly, on the day before your wedding, I did indeed expect you to marry Harold." She nodded and reached for a scone.

Camille stared at her mother for a long moment. She had never really considered that while there had been expectations and encouragement, her mother had never told her what she could or could not do when it came to marriage. "No, I suppose you didn't, really."

"I was simply a practical woman," Mother said with a shrug.

"You've grown out of it," Beryl noted.

"I have earned that right."

"He's come back to throw it in my face, hasn't he?" Camille said abruptly. "That's it. That's exactly what he's done! He's gone off. He's made his fortune. Now he's come back to throw it in my face."

"I've never trusted him," Beryl said.

"To what end, dear?" Mother studied her closely. "What would be the purpose?"

"Who knows?" She resumed pacing; thoughts raced through her head. "I have no idea, but then he's a man, and who knows what goes through their minds?"

Delilah nodded. "There is that."

"Revenge, perhaps?" Camille stopped and glared. "Do you know he claims I broke his heart?"

"When it was so clearly your heart that was broken." Beryl nodded.

"Indeed, it was."

"But, surely, it would wound a man deeply to think the woman he loves won't marry him because he does not have enough money," Delilah said.

"He should have known I was too stunned to make any sense whatsoever. He told me he loved me. Something I had longed to hear very nearly since we first met, but I had completely pushed it out of my head because I knew it wasn't possible. Because I was expected to make a brilliant match."

Mother sniffed. "I will not apologize for that."

"Yes, and it scarcely matters now. The past is the past." Camille waved away the comment. "It's over and done with."

"Darling, the past is never over and done with," Mother said. "It's always there lurking."

"I suppose so." Still, she had thought it was over and done with. Or perhaps she had simply hoped.

"Perhaps Grayson thinks you will fall into his arms now because he is a wealthy man?" Delilah suggested.

"Because I am nothing more than a fortune hunter from a family of fortune hunters?"

All three women stared in shocked silence.

"Come now, Camille," Mother said coolly. "Fortune hunters rarely have money of their own, nor do they have a respectable lineage. We have both."

"That's when he does it, you know. When you fall into his arms." Beryl nodded. "That's when he will throw his wealth in your face."

"Well, he has a long wait ahead of him!"

"Or perhaps he hasn't mentioned his money because he doesn't want it to interfere in your feelings one way or the other," Delilah said.

"Good God!" Camille gasped. "Then this is a test!"

"Goodness, dear, I wouldn't leap—"

"Of course it's a test." She thought for a moment. "To see whether or not I will love him enough to ignore the state of his finances." She narrowed her eyes. "That's probably why he pushed his way into staying here as well. He wants to be my friend, he said. Lend me his assistance. He only wants me to be happy. Hah!" A thought struck her and she paused in midstep. "Perhaps I need to reconsider my decision about Nikolai. Why, I still haven't kissed him. I should do that immediately."

"Oh, and that would certainly serve Grayson right." Beryl cast a reluctant look at her gingerbread, set it on her plate, then wiped her fingers. "I am all in favor of teaching Grayson a lesson he admittedly deserves, not just for this but for everything else as well. However, I don't think marrying Nikolai is the way to go about it."

"Perhaps not."

"Besides, you haven't told Grayson of your change of heart regarding Nikolai, have you?"

"No." Camille shook her head.

"Then let him continue to believe that," Beryl said.

Camille stared. "That's not a plan. How does that teach him a lesson?"

"You don't see?"

"Nor, I'm afraid, do I," Mother said.

"Camille continues to allow Grayson to believe Nikolai is what she wants. It will drive him mad. Eventually, if what he wants is to win you over, he will tell you everything."

"Why would he do that?"

"I have no idea." Beryl shrugged. "But men tend to do that sort of thing when they are trying to declare how much they love you. They confess all their sins. Pity that they expect you to confess yours too. Admittedly, that can be awkward." She grimaced. "At that point, he'll confess that he has money and why he didn't want you to know."

"I would think the very fact that he hasn't thrown his success in your face is quite significant," Mother said thoughtfully. "If that is his purpose, one does wonder what he is waiting for."

"Why, he's obviously waiting for me to tell him that I still love him." She continued to pace. "That I've always loved him. Which is why mine was the heart that was broken." She stopped and glared at her family. "The blasted man gave me hope and then snatched it away. For one moment, he held out to me everything I had ever wanted. Admittedly, I was too shocked or perhaps too stupid to grab on to it. But one would think if a man truly loves a woman, he wouldn't make a grand announcement and then vanish. He would do everything in his power to win that woman!"

"Well, yes, one would think . . ."

"Whatever you do, do be careful," Beryl said. "I would hate to see him hurt you again."

"As would I," Camille snapped.

"I saw him hurt you once, and I think that's why I had been so unwilling to allow myself to fall in love. It very nearly ruined my life."

"Good Lord, Beryl, what utter nonsense. My broken heart did not ruin your life."

"I thought it sounded rather plausible." Beryl picked up a morsel of biscuit and popped it into her mouth.

"This is not about you!" Camille's voice rose.

"No, it's not, but it's left to the rest of us to pick up the pieces, isn't it?" Beryl glared. "This charade of yours is a perfect example. You've gotten us all into this mess and now it's up to us to make certain we do not come out of it as the laughingstock of England!"

"Well, at least she doesn't have a tart playing you," Delilah said sharply. "I don't know what you were thinking, Camille. That actress, and I use the term loosely, doesn't behave at all like me."

Camille stared. "If you weren't quite so stuffy—"

"But then you don't think, do you?" Delilah glared.

"Come now, Delilah," Mother said. "The woman playing you is at least close to your age, whereas Mrs. Montgomery-Wells is positively elderly." She leveled a hard look at Camille. "I'm not at all pleased to have a woman who cannot remember her own name pretending to be me."

"Perhaps if I had a mother who didn't fill the house with every lost European exile who came along, not to mention a parade of lovers," Camille said sharply, "someone whose behavior was more fitting of her position, then I wouldn't have had to hire a proper family in the first place!"

Mother huffed. "They're scarcely an improvement. Why, your Mr. Henderson made a most improper suggestion—"

"When you were being Juliet to his Romeo, no doubt." Camille sniffed. "What do you expect?"

Mother continued as if Camille hadn't said a word. "And if Miss Murdock is sleeping alone at night, it's not by choice."

"This is not Mother's fault, Camille." Beryl rose to her feet. "You've done what you always do. You've jumped into something without due consideration. I told you it was absurd!"

"Yes, yes, you told me, and God knows, you will never let me forget—"

"It's Brighton all over again," Delilah muttered.

"It's not the least bit like Brighton," Camille snapped. "And you needn't keep throwing that in my face!"

"Perhaps, *dear*"—Mother stood—"if you learned from your past mistakes—"

"*Brighton!*" Beryl fairly shot the word.

"Stop that!" Camille cast an angry look at her family. "All of you! What I don't need at the moment is recriminations and accusations. It does no good, whatsoever." She drew a calming breath. "I am well aware that acting without due consideration has on occasion—"

" 'On occasion'?" Delilah scoffed.

"Proven to be a problem," Camille finished.

Mother snorted.

"The irony of all this"—Beryl's narrowed gaze met her twin's—"is that the one time in your entire life when you should have thrown caution to the wind, you should have acted without thinking, you should have surrendered to impulse, and you didn't, is when Grayson told you he loved you!"

Camille gasped. "So everything that has gone wrong in the past eleven years is my fault?"

"Don't be absurd," Mother said sharply. "That's not what she said!"

"But this . . . this Christmas pageant of yours, which we are trapped in, the specter of scandal now hanging over our heads"—Delilah's voice rose—"is indeed your fault!"

Camille clenched her fists. She couldn't remember ever having been this angry with her family. Indeed, she couldn't remember ever having been truly angry with them at all. Certainly, they had disagreements and even quarrels on occasion, but they were usually such a congenial group.

Not today.

"If you will excuse me, there are matters I need to attend to before dinner." She nodded and swept out of the parlor.

The last thing she needed or wanted was to have her entire family angry with her. Admittedly, for the most part, they hadn't said anything that wasn't true. But her ideas always seemed so brilliant when they first occurred to her, and hadn't hiring a family for Christmas seemed nothing short of inspired? And, indeed, wouldn't it all have gone rather uneventfully, had it not been for the unexpected? Her mother and sister returning home, and . . .

And Grayson!

Why, if Grayson hadn't appeared dragging the past along with him, wouldn't she still want marriage to Nikolai? Although, possibly, she might have come to her senses about him even without Grayson's interference. Still, he had made this farce of hers much more complicated and confusing. She didn't know what she wanted now. Nor did she know what he wanted.

What was he up to? Why hadn't he told her he had money? What did he really want?

Past time to find out.

Twenty

"Camille." Nikolai took her elbow and steered her into the hall. The others were moving from the dining room into the parlor. "I must speak with you alone."

"Very well." She cast him her brightest smile, knowing full well Grayson lingered a bit behind the rest of the group. While he was subtle, he was definitely watching them both. But then she had noticed she was never out of his sight or Beryl's. One might think they were conspirators of some sort, which was nothing more than the oddest of notions. Beryl would willingly cut her arm off before she cooperated with Grayson in anything.

While the food at dinner had been excellent, the same could not be said of the company. Thank God, her actors had done their part. Between Mrs. Montgomery-Wells's reminiscences of who knew what, and Mr. Henderson's endless anecdotes, and Miss Murdock's relentless flirtation—equally divided between Nikolai and Grayson—it was easy to overlook the fact that neither she nor her mother and sisters said much of anything beyond an occasional overly polite comment. The tension in the air seemed to her thick enough to cut with a knife. Hopefully, Nikolai did not notice; although Grayson obviously did, given the way she caught his speculative gaze on her every time she happened to look at him.

"What is it, Nikolai?" She smiled up at the prince.

His brow furrowed in obvious displeasure. "All is not going as I had hoped."

"Oh?"

"Between your family and the preparations for Christmas, I have scarcely had any time alone with you at all."

"I know and I do regret that." She heaved a heartfelt sigh. "But you must understand, with the entire family in residence, well . . ." She shrugged apologetically.

"Someone is always with us." He huffed in frustration.

"It does seem that way." She chanced a quick look into the dining room; Grayson had at last gone into the parlor.

"It is most annoying."

She shook her head. "There is nothing to be done about it, I'm afraid."

"Meet me tonight." Urgency sounded in his voice. "Come to my room. We have much to talk about and to settle between us. There are questions that need to be asked, the future to be decided."

"I quite agree, but I can't come to your room." She adopted a note of regret. "It would be scandalous, and with all these people . . ."

"You do not trust them?" He frowned. "This family of yours?"

"Oh, of course I trust my family," she said quickly. "But the servants, well, they do tend to gossip."

"Yes, of course. I . . ." He hesitated.

"Yes?"

"I did not wish to worry you with such things, as I did not want to spoil Christmas. But before I arrived, I had word from my country." He shook his head. "There are events unfolding that require me to return sooner than expected."

"Oh, dear." How convenient. "Perhaps it would be best if you were to return at once."

"I am not overly concerned as of yet. Besides, Christmas is the day after tomorrow." His gaze met hers. "I wish to have matters settled between us by then. Possibly even an announcement?"

A heavy weight settled in her stomach, but she forced a light laugh. "Possibly."

"I warned you, I am not a patient man." A hard note sounded in his voice. "And what little patience I have is growing thin."

"Perhaps . . ." She chose her words with care. "It might be wiser, given how crowded the house is, and all that I have to see to, Christmas and everything that goes along with it, if we wait until the new year to make any decisions—"

"No. That will not do. Especially now. I know what I want, Camille, and I think you know as well." He grabbed her and pulled her into his arms.

"Goodness, Nikolai, this is neither the time nor the place." She pushed against him. Good Lord, it was tiring to walk this fine line between flirtation and avoidance.

"Perhaps this is not the time." He chuckled and glanced upward. Her gaze followed his. Mistletoe! Of course. It was all over the house. She'd noticed it on her way to dinner. Grayson's doing, no doubt, although this was obviously not what he'd had in mind. "But it is most certainly the place."

"Even so . . ."

"But is it not tradition?"

"Well, yes, but . . ." She caught sight of Grayson out of the corner of her eye. He stood in the dining room once more, just outside the doors to the parlor; far enough away to be discreet, yet close enough to watch her every move. Very well, then. She smiled up at Nikolai. "As it is tradition . . ."

Without another word, he pressed his lips to hers, gathering her closer. As kisses went, it was quite nicely done. Indeed, it was an excellent kiss. "Practiced" was the word that came to mind. He certainly knew what he was doing. Still, it brought no rush of desire, no aching need, no longing for more. In many ways, it was a great pity that the only thing it evoked was the momentary thought that it was entirely too long.

He raised his head and gazed down at her. "That was just the beginning, my dear Camille." He released her and stepped back, then took her hand. "But for the moment, it shall have to do."

She smiled up at him. "I'm afraid so."

"I believe I shall retire for the night. It must be your country air. I find I am quite ready for bed." He cast her a pointed look.

She ignored it. "Good evening, Nikolai."

"Good evening." He nodded, turned and strode off toward the stairs.

She breathed a sigh of relief. That was that, then. Any reservations she might have had about not marrying Nikolai vanished with the first touch of his lips to hers. She knew this decision was the right one.

"What was that?" Grayson said behind her.

She stepped away from the mistletoe and turned to face him. "Goodness, Grayson, surely you have seen a kiss before."

His eyes narrowed. "That was a very long kiss."

"Was it?" She shrugged. "It didn't seem long to me at all. But then, it was an excellent kiss."

"It didn't look like an excellent kiss. It looked *rehearsed*."

"Perhaps from where you were standing." She started toward the stairs. "But from where I was standing, it was excellent."

"Where are you going?"

"To my room. I am not in the mood to play parlor games tonight. Besides, as Nikolai has retired for the night, so shall I."

"Oh no, you're not." He grabbed her arm and steered her into the parlor. He fairly shoved her into the room; then closed the doors behind her.

"What are you doing?" She glanced around. "Where is everyone?"

"The general consensus was that it had been a long day and they were all ready for bed. Your mother and sisters all claimed to have aching heads—"

"Probably something in the air."

"Perhaps you didn't notice, but Mrs. Montgomery-Wells had a touch too much wine at dinner and could scarcely keep her eyes open. Mr. Henderson gallantly offered to escort her to her room. And Miss Murdock said she had a good book she was dying to get back to."

"No doubt."

"And Pruzinsky has gone as well?"

She nodded.

"Good, then we are alone." He strode across the room, filled two glasses with brandy and returned. He handed her a glass. "Here. We have a great deal to talk about."

"Lord save me from men who have a great deal to talk about." This might not be the best time. She was still out of sorts from the argument with her family. Or perhaps this was the perfect time. She took a deep swallow. "But you're right, we do need to talk."

"About the past." He nodded.

"Oh, my. Yes, let's start with the past, shall we?"

He drew a deep breath. "I'm not sure where to begin."

"At the beginning?"

"Of course." He thought for a long moment.

Impatience washed through her. "Well? What are you waiting for? Go on. This is what you've wanted. This is what you've gone on and on about since you first walked in the door. Good Lord, Grayson, get on with it." She tossed back her brandy, then crossed the floor to the decanter and refilled her glass.

He raised a brow. "Another brandy might not be wise, Camille."

"No one has ever accused me of being wise."

"Still, it's not like you—"

"How dare you presume to know what is like me and what is not like me?" The anger she'd felt for him since he'd walked out of her life—anger that she'd thought had abated in recent days—now rushed back full force. "You have not been here! You have not been in my life for eleven years!"

"I am well aware of that."

"I am so glad you're aware of it. That makes it all so much better." He was right, although she would never admit it to him. She did not drink excessive amounts of brandy. Fortunately, she had a few glasses left until she reached excessive. And she would need every one of them. "Go on, then. Talk."

"Very well." His forehead furrowed in thought. "Eleven years ago . . . when I . . . well . . . that is . . ."

"You seem to be having a great deal of trouble deciding exactly what you wish to say."

"It's not easy." His jaw tightened. "The right words are eluding me, and this is too important not to find the right words. I'm not exactly sure how to say what I want to say."

"Really? I find that most amusing."

" 'Amusing'?" He stared. "How is that *amusing*?"

"Because I have known what I wished to say to you for eleven years," she snapped. "Exactly what I wished to say."

"Then perhaps you should begin." Caution sounded in his voice.

"Perhaps I should." She took another swallow of the brandy, then smacked the glass down on a table. "Eleven years ago, when out of nowhere you said you loved me, I didn't know what to say, so everything I did say was wrong. But after you left, I thought, 'He'll come back. Any minute now, he'll walk through that door and then I'll tell him that I love him as well.' I thought, 'I'll tell him I never dreamed there could be anything between us beyond friendship.' After all, there were expectations as to whom I should wed and how I should live my life. I never imagined he thought of me as anything other than a friend or a sister, but I have always loved him."

He stared in shocked silence.

"But the hours passed and I thought, 'Surely, he'll be back tonight. Surely, a man truly in love would fight for the woman he wants. Surely, he couldn't be so cruel as to announce his love and then go on with his life as if nothing had happened. And then I'll tell him that I love him and I always have.' But the night wore on and morning came, and my wedding drew near and he didn't come." She picked up her glass, took another quick swallow, then set it back down. "And even as I walked down the aisle, I thought, 'When he comes, because surely a man who claims to love a woman would stop her wedding, and then, *then*, I'll tell him that I love him as well. *Then* I'll tell him that I always have.' But, of course, he didn't come, or rather you didn't come." She struggled to remain calm. "And then I realized it was too late, this man who claimed to love me had not done anything to prove that love, had not fought for that love. Indeed, had he even meant his words? Had he regretted them the moment they were out of his mouth? Was it nothing more than a rash statement uttered in impulse?"

"I meant every—"

"Not that it mattered anymore, because I was married to Harold, who was a very nice man and did not deserve to be hurt the way I had been hurt. And I vowed he never would be. So I stopped thinking about what I would say to you. I stopped thinking about you at all, insofar as that was possible. I avoided your cousin. I forbid Beryl to speak of you. I was a very good wife to Harold and I did love him, although not in the way I had loved you.

"And the years passed. And on rare occasions when there would be some reminder of you, I would indeed think about what I would say if I were to see you again. I thought I would be polite, cordial in an impersonal sort of way, as though seeing you again meant nothing. Or perhaps I would be hard-pressed to recall your name at all, should we come face-to-face."

"Camille—"

"No, Grayson, you wanted to talk about the past. Well, this is my past!" Fury pulsed in her veins. "Then Harold died, and in spite of having pushed you out of my head and my heart, I thought, 'If he had really meant what he had said, if he really loved me, surely he will come now.' Perhaps, all those years ago, he had thought it was better for me to marry the sort of man I was expected to marry. Or perhaps he had thought it was somewhat dishonorable to ruin another man's wedding." She met his gaze directly. "Oh, I had all sorts of reasons why you did nothing after you made your grand declaration because as much as I wanted to believe you meant what you said, I wanted to forgive you."

"Why?"

"I wish I knew." She shook her head. "Perhaps because next to Beryl, you were the most important person in my life. Because I understood it was not your mistake alone. Because I realized I could have, should have, done something, gone after you perhaps. Instead, I did what I was expected to do. I was too weak or too young or too foolish to do otherwise." She glared. "In that respect, I have changed a great deal." She uttered a short laugh. "And you claim *I* broke *your* heart."

He studied her for a long moment. "If you're quite done."

"Quite." She crossed her arms over her chest. "If you can now think of something to say, do go on."

"I, too, have thought of what I would say when I saw you again."

She snorted in disdain.

"But it seems I have changed my mind," he said slowly. "None of the things I had planned on saying to you now seem right."

"Oh?"

"I had planned to apologize, of course, as I attempted to do when I first saw you." He shook his head. "It was unfair of me to shock you the way I did or when

I did. You had no warning, and God knows, I had done nothing to show my feelings before then.

"Next to Win, you had always been my closest friend, and I thought you always would be. It wasn't until you were betrothed to Harold that I realized I could—no, I would lose you. I realized as well that I loved you."

"I was engaged for several months before the wedding, Grayson. You could have said something, done something, at any time."

"I didn't know what to do." He shrugged. "So I did nothing."

"How very clever of you."

"It wasn't clever," he snapped. "I know that. I knew that then. It was stupid of me not to act. I was an idiot."

"Then we are agreed."

"And I was afraid, I suspect."

"Come now, Grayson. What on earth did you have to be afraid of?"

"I was afraid that you didn't feel the same, and if I declared myself, I would lose you as surely as if you married someone else. At least, if I kept my feelings to myself, it wouldn't destroy what we had." He drew a deep breath. "So I did nothing."

"We have established that."

"I felt helpless, Camille. I felt lost. I was about to lose the woman I knew in my soul was the only woman for me. And finally I decided I had to do something, or I would regret it for the rest of my life."

"So you did so on the day before my wedding."

He nodded. "I told you that I loved you, and you said I was being silly, but you did appreciate my attempt to save you from a marriage without the true love you had always wanted."

Her breath caught. "I remember."

"And then I kissed you."

"And then you kissed me." She could barely say the words over the ache in her throat.

"And that's when I knew you shared my feelings." He swirled the brandy in his glass and watched her. "I have never forgotten that kiss, nor will I ever, although you claim you have."

She shrugged. "It was just a kiss."

"Not to me." He studied her closely. "Then I made the asinine comment that you would marry me if I had money. It was unfair of me and not very nice."

"No, it wasn't." She swallowed hard. "And I said the first thing that came into my head. Which, admittedly, wasn't very nice either."

"I knew you too well not to have realized they were just words. I should have ignored them, but I didn't. And that was when my heart was broken."

She stared at him. "Your heart or your pride?"

"I don't know," he said sharply. "So I left."

She met his gaze and tried not to let all she was feeling show on her face. "And never came back."

He chuckled in a mirthless manner. "It seemed pointless. It seemed, as well, that you had made your choice. I couldn't bear the thought of watching you marry another man, of seeing you as someone else's wife. So I left England altogether and had no intention of returning." He blew a long breath. "It didn't take me long to understand what a fool I'd been. I should have seen how shocked you were and I should have ignored what you said. I knew you better than to accept your words, or at least I should have. I should have done everything you said you were hoping I'd do. I should have fought for you. For us."

"But you didn't."

"No, I didn't."

She chose her words with care. "If you'd had all these

revelations, why didn't you come back after Harold died?"

"Come running back to the woman who didn't want me?" Disbelief rang in his voice. "I had had my heart broken once before. I was not about to allow the same woman to break it for a second time. Although, admittedly, it might well have been pride."

"I never thought you to be a coward, Grayson Elliott."

"Love makes fools of us all." He took a sip of his brandy. "As we are confessing, there is something else you should know."

"Go on."

"I tried to put you out of my thoughts, just as you put me out of yours. In that, I suspect you were more successful than I was. Oh, but I did try." He smiled wryly. "I could go for days, weeks, months, without thinking of you. And yet, somehow, when I least expected it, when I wasn't at all prepared, there you were. In a laugh heard across a theater. Or the first fresh breeze of spring. Or another woman's kiss. Or my dreams." His gaze met hers. "No matter how far I ran, you were always there."

"No, Grayson." Her heart twisted. She ignored it. "I was here. Where you left me."

"I know." He drew a deep breath. "I know it may well be impossible, but can you forgive me?"

"Oddly enough, I thought I had," she said quietly, then straightened her shoulders. "That's it, then?"

"Yes."

"You have nothing more to say?" *Nothing about the wealth you've acquired? The fortune you've built?*

"No." He shook his head. "I have explained my actions, or lack thereof."

"You have no additional confession, no revelations, nothing of that nature?" She studied him intently.

"No, nothing."

"I see." She picked up her glass, drained the rest of her brandy and hoped he would attribute the slight tremble in her hand to the liquor, and not to her heart. "We always did have honesty between us, didn't we?"

He nodded.

"Then, in all honesty, it might be best if you were not to stay for Christmas. I shall think of something to explain why my cousin has departed, leaving the rest of his family behind."

He stared at her for a moment. "Absolutely not." He shook his head. "I left you once before, when I shouldn't have. I'll not make the same mistake again."

She sighed, abruptly weary of the conversation and the turmoil she fought to keep at bay. "This is entirely different."

"Is it?" His brow rose. "It strikes me as being remarkably similar. Once again, you are to marry a man you do not love—this time for his position, if not his fortune."

"Come now, Grayson, you know full well marriage is the only way a woman in this world betters herself." She narrowed her gaze. "But then, that's what we do in my family, isn't it?"

"Apparently."

"Little better than fortune hunters, wouldn't you say?"

"I know you better than to think that," he said sharply. "Regardless, Pruzinsky is not the man for you."

"Why not?"

He hesitated, then shook his head. "He just isn't, that's all."

"Excellent answer, Grayson." She rubbed her forehead. "Very well, stay on for the final curtain of this debacle. It will no doubt be worth the price of admission." She'd had enough of this. Enough of doing battle with her family, enough of Nikolai and more than enough of Grayson. She wanted nothing more than to throw herself on her bed and weep. For what might have been. And for the glimpse of what, if only for a moment, might still be. "You can't make amends for eleven years ago. The past cannot be undone."

"And no one knows that better than I," he said sharply. "I would turn back the clock, if I could. If I had that one day to live over again, I would do it regardless of the cost. But I can't. I can only go forward from here." He stepped toward her. "And I want to go forward with you."

She stepped back. "It's been eleven years."

"Eleven years wasted because I was a fool. I have no desire to waste any more." He took another step toward her. "Nothing has changed for me, Camille."

"Do you know the biggest difference between the girl I was then and the woman I am now?"

"I can see all sorts of differences."

"The girl I was then trusted you without hesitation, without question. She never dreamed you might hurt her. And she believed you." She shook her head. "The woman I am now knows better."

He stared at her; and for a moment, the years fell away and it was the day before her wedding. The stricken look on his face was the same as it had been when she'd responded to his charge that she would marry him if he had money. And her heart cracked.

"Good evening, Grayson." She turned to the door and pulled it open.

"Camille."

She paused but didn't turn around. "Yes?"

"The boy I was then was a fool to let what he wanted most slip away." Determination sounded in his voice.

"The man I am now will not make the same mistake. This is not over, Camille."

"I suppose that remains to be seen," she said, and took her leave.

It wasn't until Camille had reached her room, changed into her nightclothes and collapsed onto her bed that she allowed herself to wonder exactly what he had meant. Certainly, he had said all sorts of things since his return that had been, well, romantic and perhaps indications of feelings that were far more than friendship. But he hadn't told her everything; he hadn't been completely honest; he hadn't mentioned his money. And the question she couldn't get past was why.

Surely, he didn't think that made a difference to her. It hadn't eleven years ago—although, admittedly, given what they had said to one another, she could understand why he thought it would. But now she was financially independent. She could marry whomever she wished, without regard to the practicalities of finance. Still, he thought she wanted to marry a prince for very nearly the same reasons she had married Harold. Well, if he was so foolish as to believe that . . .

She heaved a heartfelt sigh. She'd never known such confusion. All the anger, all the pain, she'd thought was far behind her now threatened to overwhelm her, as fresh as if it had happened yesterday. And yet it was somehow freeing to at long last tell him exactly what he had done. And how he had broken her heart.

Her mother was right. The past is never over and done with. It would be with her, with them, always. And hadn't she admitted the truth to her family, even if she hadn't quite accepted it yet herself?

She had always loved him, and she still did.

Twenty-one

It could have been worse—although, at the moment, Gray couldn't imagine how. At the very least, they now understood all the other had gone through.

He exhaled a long breath. It was best he and Camille had not had this talk about the past when he had first arrived. These last days together had given him the chance to work his way back into her good graces and even possibly her heart. If they had rehashed all these feelings in the beginning, they might not be able to get past them. Even if now it seemed they had not cleared the air as much as muddied the waters. Still, it was a beginning.

God, he had been such a fool. Not merely eleven years ago, but every day since then. Even tonight, there were things he should have said. Oh, he certainly had said his feelings were unchanged and that he wanted to go forward with her. But he should have been clearer. He should have said he wanted to spend the rest of his days with her. He should have said he would spend each and every one of those days making amends for his mistakes. And he should have told her he loved her.

Then why hadn't he?

He tossed back the rest of his brandy and started after her. Be the man he had become, she'd said. Tell her why you're really here and what you really want, Beryl had told him. Stop being so nice. He had tread cautiously up to now, but Beryl was right. It was time to stop being Camille's friend. He had said he wasn't the same boy he was eleven years ago. Past time to prove it.

He reached her door and resisted the urge to slam his fist against it. It would be wise not to have everyone in the house know their business—although, with the exception of the actors and Pruzinsky, everyone, no doubt, did. Nor, at the moment, did he care. He pounded on the door.

"Go away!" Camille said from the other side of the door.

"No! Never again. I have no intention of going away. Nor do I have any intention of walking off in a huff."

She paused. "I did not walk off in a huff."

"It certainly seemed like a huff. It seemed, as well, like something a nineteen-year-old girl would do. Not a woman who claims to know—"

The door jerked open. "Come in, then, before you awaken everyone in the house."

He stepped inside and she closed the door behind him; then rested her back against it. Her eyes narrowed in suspicion. "What do you want?"

She had changed into that dreadfully practical night-gown, a high-necked garment with endless buttons running up the front. Buttons she had failed to close completely, revealing her neck and the shadow between her breasts.

"I said this was not over."

"I was finished!"

"And I was just beginning."

"I thought you had said quite enough!" Her breath quickened and her breasts rose and fell beneath the thin fabric with every breath she took.

He shook his head. "I didn't say anywhere near enough."

His stomach clenched and desire rose within him. There was indeed something to be said for the passion of argument, as well as the lure of sensible nightwear.

"Oh? Then do tell, Grayson."

His gaze dropped to her breasts—her nipples had hardened beneath her gown—then back to her eyes. She noted his gaze but made no effort to close the neck of her gown. A flush washed up her face, and he knew she wanted him as much as he wanted her. As much as he had always wanted her.

"What was left to say?"

"For one thing." He braced his hand on the door beside her head and leaned close to brush his lips across hers. "You lied to me."

"Nonsense." She pushed him aside and stepped away. "What on earth are you talking about?" The lamp by the side of her bed illuminated the shape of her body through the gauzy fabric and left little to the imagination.

"You remember the first time I kissed you."

"Vaguely, perhaps." She shrugged.

"And you remember the second time I kissed you."

"Of course I remember. It was the night before last. I could scarcely forget it. Not that it was a particularly memorable kiss," she added quickly.

"Oh, but it was." He grabbed her arm and pulled her into his embrace. She stared up at him. "And you will remember this one as well." He crushed his lips to hers. For no more than an instant, she hesitated; then her mouth opened to his and her arms slipped around his neck. And passion denied for eleven years erupted between them.

He slanted his mouth over hers; his tongue dueled with hers, demanding and insistent. She clung to him and tasted him and explored him in a clash of tongue and teeth and lips. Her breath mingled with his. Her body molded against his, and all he'd ever wanted was his for the taking and hers for the giving.

He wrenched his lips from hers and ran his mouth along the line of her jaw and down the side of her neck. Her flesh beneath his lips was warm and inviting. Her head fell back and she moaned, and desire flared within him. Her hands fisted in his coat and he tightened his arms around her.

She gasped. "You lied to me as well."

"Never," he murmured against her neck.

"You led me to believe you had no money." She could barely get out the words.

"Ah yes, well, about that." He flicked his tongue over the hollow at the base of her throat and he felt her shiver beneath his mouth. "I have indeed made a substantial fortune in railroads and shipping."

"Why didn't you tell me?" She pushed at his coat and he shrugged it off and let it fall to the floor. She yanked his cravat free, tugged open his shirt and let her hands roam over his chest. And he fairly lost his senses at the feel of her hands on his bare skin.

"You didn't ask." He grabbed the edges of her gown and ripped it open, buttons flying, exposing her breasts to his view. He cupped one breast and bent his head to take her nipple into his mouth.

"Oh, God, Gray!" Her nails dug into his skin and her back arched. "I . . . I . . . I assumed . . ."

He sucked and teased until her nipple was a hard knot beneath his onslaught. He shifted his attention to her other breast and continued until she was limp in his arms and his trousers tightened.

"Gray . . ." She drew a steadying breath and pushed weakly against him. "This isn't . . ."

"What?" He held his breath.

She shook her head and took a step away. She struggled to catch her breath. "This isn't fair."

He stared at her. With her gown ripped open and her breathing labored, he'd never seen a more erotic sight. "If I recall correctly, you said you weren't especially concerned with fair."

"I'm not usually." She glanced down at her ruined gown. "These are not usual circumstances." She moved close, grabbed his shirt in both hands and ripped it open; then she smiled up at him. "There. That's much better."

He gasped in feigned horror. "You ruined my shirt."

She shrugged. "You ruined my gown."

"But this is a very nice shirt."

"You can afford it. Beryl says you're obscenely wealthy."

He grinned. "Indeed, I am."

"Did you think it would matter to me?"

"Ah, we are back to that fortune hunter nonsense." He pulled away and stared into her eyes. Marriage for position and wealth was what was expected of Camille and her sisters or, indeed, any young woman in their position. Now that he knew her father was still alive, it made even more sense. The precarious nature of Lady Briston's finances through the years was obviously why she had been determined to see her daughters marry well. And who could blame her? "No, but it did matter to me."

"You are still a foolish man then." She hooked her fingers in the waist of his trousers and tugged. "I would suggest, if you don't want these to meet the same fate as your shirt, you discard them." She reached up and tugged at his lower lip with her teeth; his breath caught.

She smiled in a most inviting and completely wicked manner and sauntered toward the bed, allowing her ripped gown to slide off her shoulders and onto the floor behind her. Good Lord. He swallowed hard.

Gray had his clothes off before she reached the bed. He caught her in his arms and they tumbled onto the bed in a tangle of naked limbs and heated desire.

He had dreamed of this, of her. She was all he had known she would be, and he worshipped her with his mouth and hands, with touch and taste. He ran his hands down the length of her, along her sides, over the curve of her hip and along the long length of her leg. Her skin was warm silk beneath his hand.

Her hands explored him as eagerly as his explored her. Her fingers skimmed over his chest and drifted lower over his stomach. His muscles tensed beneath her touch and her hand moved lower, until her fingers wrapped around his cock, and she squeezed. He sucked in a sharp breath and moaned with the sheer pleasure of her touch. She stroked him, and he thought he would surely die with the joy of the feel of her hand. He buried his face in her neck and pushed her hand away. He would never last at this rate. And he wanted to take her to the edge of sanity. He wanted her moaning his name and writhing beneath him.

He grabbed her hands and pinned them over her head; then rained kisses on her neck and trailed his lips lower, between her breasts and over the flat plane of her stomach and lower still. He released her hands and she clutched at the bedclothes. He slipped his hand between her legs and caressed her. She moaned and arched upward, pressing against his hand. She was slick and hot and quivered against his touch. He stroked her again and again; she thrashed on the bed and gripped his shoulders and dug her fingers into him.

"Grayson." The word was breathless with passion and need. She pushed his hand away, then hooked her leg over his and pulled him onto her. "Grayson . . ."

Slowly he pushed into her. She was tight around him and he pushed deeper. She moaned, angled her hips toward him and wrapped her legs around his waist, pulling him in. She surrounded him, engulfed him, welcomed him. For a moment, he could do nothing more than savor the feeling of being inside her, one with her. She throbbed around him, and it was more than his wildest dreams.

"Camille," he murmured; then started to stroke, forcing himself to a slow, steady pace. She rocked her hips against him, urging him on, faster, harder. He groaned and responded, losing himself in the feel of her. He thrust into her with a frenzied need and she responded in kind. The bed rocked beneath them, and she whimpered or moaned erotic murmurs, which only heightened his need. She met his thrusts with hers until, at last, she screamed softly and arched upward. Her body shuddered against him. Her release swept from her body into his. He groaned and thrust once more and exploded into her, shaking hard in an endless moment of pure sensation and joy. In his body and in his soul.

At long last, he was home.

For a moment, or an hour, or eternity, they lay together, hearts beating in rhythm, breath coming in tandem. As if they were still one. At last being with Grayson was so much more than she had imagined, so much more than she had thought possible.

"Good God." Camille buried her head in his shoulder. "What have we done?"

He chuckled. "I think you know exactly what we've done."

"Grayson, I am not my sister."

"Thank God."

She sat up, plumped the pillow behind her and pulled the covers up around her. She hadn't felt the least bit embarrassed earlier when she was completely naked in front of him, but that was during the throes of passion. And dear Lord, she had never known such throes before. Harold had been a gentle and considerate lover, and making love with him had been most pleasant. But tonight with Grayson, well, she had never dreamed of the intensity and the sheer pleasure and the joy.

"Beryl has never had any difficulty bounding from one bed to another. At least, until recently. This is one area in which I have never given into impulse, never found anyone I wanted to . . . I have not—well, I have not, that's all."

"I'm glad." He rolled onto his side and propped himself up on his elbow.

"I've only ever been with one other man."

"Good," he said firmly. "I would hate to think you were a tart as well as a fortune hunter."

"Grayson!"

"And you're not bounding from one bed to another now." He grinned. "Although I would rather like to see you bound."

She shivered at his words. "You are a wicked, wicked man, aren't you?"

He grinned.

She narrowed her eyes. "I daresay, you have not been celibate these past eleven years."

"Should I lie to you and tell you I have thought only of you?"

"I suppose not."

"And yet it's true." He smiled into her eyes. "Of course I have been with other women, but no one has touched my heart the way you have."

"I didn't realize it was your heart that I was touching."

He laughed, grabbed her hand and pulled it to his lips. "Among other things."

"But this is not the sort of thing I do." She sighed and pulled her hand away. "Why, I am practically engaged to another man."

"And we can put an end to that nonsense right now."

"That nonsense?" Still, he was right, it had been nonsense. And no one was more aware of that than she. "About Nikolai—"

"I thought you had come to your senses."

"Why?" She stared at him. "Because you and I have—"

"Well, yes. No!" His brows drew together. "Are you mad?"

"Possibly." She crossed her arms over her chest. "I allowed you in my bed, didn't I?"

He ignored her. "You're not still considering marrying Pruzinsky?"

She drew a deep breath. "About that—"

"Well, I won't allow it!"

"You won't 'allow' it?" she said slowly.

"No!"

"I believe you forfeited all rights to tell me what I can and cannot do a very long time ago." She stared at him. "I have managed my own life and made my own decisions for four years now, and I have done a fine job of it."

"Have you?" Doubt shone in his eyes.

"Yes, I have."

He shrugged. "Not according to what I've heard from Win through the years."

"Oh, and what have you heard?" she said sharply.

He met her gaze directly. *"Brighton."*

She sucked in a hard breath.

"Need I say more?"

"I think you've said quite enough." She clenched her teeth. "I do not appreciate having my mistakes thrown back in my face."

"And yet you've had no problem throwing mine back in my face." He slid out of bed, found his trousers and started pulling them on.

"We're not talking about a silly escapade whose end result would have been no more than scandal. Admittedly, my mistakes are the result of foolish impulse, of not thinking before I act. But in the scheme of things, they are relatively minor. Your mistake changed the entire course of our lives!"

"And I've admitted I was wrong."

"It's only taken you eleven years to do so!" Her voice rose. *"Eleven years!"*

"At least I learn from my mistakes."

"Do you? Hah!"

"I'm here, aren't I?"

"It's no more than coincidence, Grayson. You can't deny that." She stared at him. "You left and you never came back. Not for me, anyway."

"And that, too, was a mistake. But at least I don't repeat my mistakes." His eyes narrowed. "Whereas you are determined to again enter into a marriage for all the wrong reasons."

"Then why don't you tell me the right reasons."

He stared at her for a long moment. "I thought I had."

With that, he yanked open the door and slammed it closed behind him.

Camille crossed her arms over her chest and stared at the door. What exactly had just happened?

Certainly, if he hadn't been so sanctimonious, if he hadn't used the word "allowed," she probably would have told him she had decided against marrying the prince. And hadn't she tried to do just that? But then he had brought up her mistakes, and she had countered with his and how hers paled in comparison. . . . Obviously, there remained much to resolve between them. Still . . .

The blasted man loved her. Hadn't he said his feelings had never changed? And hadn't she, at last, realized she loved him as well? Pity they couldn't quite seem to find the right words. Or talk about the past without recrimination and accusation erupting between them.

She heaved a heartfelt sigh. But perhaps anger at last released was necessary to finally lay the past to rest. Grayson was a stubborn, arrogant creature; and while he might not know it at the moment, he was hers. This was no more than an argument, and, with any luck, the first of a lifetime of arguments. And making up as well.

But she did need to do something about Nikolai. Even if she had done nothing to encourage him in recent days, he had come to Millworth Manor with certain expectations. It didn't seem quite honorable to publicly admit to her feelings for Grayson, while Nikolai still thought she would become his wife. No, she needed to finish this all as planned. Give Nikolai the Christmas he desired, send him back to the Kingdom of Whateveritwas and then write to him and tell him they did not suit. Of all her plans to date, this one seemed really rather sensible.

As for Grayson, tomorrow she would tell him how she felt and what she wanted. What she'd always wanted.

For this Christmas and every Christmas to come.

December 24th

Twenty-two

"I must say," Win said the moment Grayson stepped into the library, "the actor playing the part of the butler is doing an excellent job of it. I wouldn't have known he wasn't a butler if I hadn't known he wasn't a butler."

Gray shrugged. "He has a tendency to hiss."

"Ah, well." Win meandered around the edges of the room, examining a book here, a portrait there. "It is so hard to get good help."

Gray narrowed his eyes. "Why are you here?"

"Why, tomorrow is Christmas, and I have come bearing tidings of, if not great joy, then at least of interest. But first tell me . . ." He grinned. "How goes the play?"

"Hmph." Gray crossed the room. "I assume you're parched from the ride over. Whisky or brandy?"

"So early in the day?"

"It's later than you think," Gray muttered.

"Well, as tonight is Christmas Eve . . ." He studied his cousin for a moment. "You're in a foul mood today."

"And the day is still young."

It had been an awkward day, thus far. He wasn't sure what had happened between Camille and her family, but the ladies scarcely said more than a few polite words to one another when he had seen them at breakfast. The actors and Pruzinsky had, as had become their custom, not presented themselves for breakfast. He had yet to see Pruzinsky today, but he thought the others were in the parlor.

Lady Briston had pulled Gray aside and said that, as things were so complicated, Lord Briston had decided he would feign illness and stay out of the path of everyone, at least until tonight. But there had been a sparkle in Lady Briston's eyes and a flush in her cheeks that recalled Beryl's comments about the passion of Lord and Lady Briston's arguments. After last night, he could well understand it.

As for Camille, she was surprisingly cordial, as if nothing had happened between them at all. For his part, he wasn't sure what to say to her either. Certainly, he was guilty of a certain amount of arrogance, of making assumptions he had no right to make. And once again, he had failed to tell her everything he should have. But he had decided he needed to do something about Pruzinsky, and he needed to do it as soon as possible. Then he would apologize and even grovel, if necessary.

He poured two glasses, handed one to Win and then settled in one of the chairs in front of the fireplace. "You might as well sit down. There have been a number of unexpected plot twists."

Win seated himself and chuckled. "The orphans."

"The orphans were the least of it." He cast the other man an admiring look. "Although I must admit, Carrolls for Christmas was rather brilliant."

"I thought so." Win grinned. "When I received your

note asking for orphans, well, it was entirely too good to pass up."

"It was, indeed. But the children weren't the only unexpected additions to the cast." He met his cousin's gaze. "Lady Briston and Delilah returned home as well."

"Perfect." Win raised his glass. "Indeed, that's how I would have written this farce."

"And that's not all."

"Don't tell me, let me guess." Win's brow furrowed as though deep in thought. "I know, Colonel Channing has returned as well."

"Yes and no." Gray sipped his whisky. "To Camille and Delilah, he is Colonel Channing. To the others, he is in the role of my father. However, in truth . . ." Gray paused for dramatic effect. "He is Lord Briston."

Win scoffed. "Lord Briston is dead."

"And damned healthy for a dead man."

"You're serious, aren't you?"

Gray nodded.

"My God, it's a Christmas miracle!" Win stared.

"It's something all right, but I'm not sure 'miracle' is the right word."

"You're sure it's him, though?"

"His wife is sure."

"But I thought . . . everyone thought . . . he was dead."

"That's where it gets a bit complicated."

Win arched a skeptical brow. "That's where?"

"It seems that twenty years ago, Lord Briston chose a life of wandering the world as opposed to one of domesticity. A decision he soon came to regret, apparently, but Lady Briston decided it was better to have his family think he was dead rather than know he had deserted them."

"Good Lord." Win thought for a moment. "Do his daughters know?"

"Beryl found some of his letters a few years ago. Camille and Delilah don't know. And it would be best if you kept this to yourself for now, although I doubt his resurrection will stay a secret for long."

"Of course. Who would believe me, anyway?" Win shook his head slowly. "That is an unexpected twist."

"You were right, by the way," Gray said in an offhand manner. "About my feelings for Camille. Friendship is not enough."

"Yet another shocking revelation. And does she feel the same?"

"I don't know. I hope so. I think she does, even if she hasn't admitted it yet. We had a long talk last night, although 'talk' might not be the right word for it." He had no desire to tell Win everything else that had happened between them. "I'm not sure if we laid the past to rest or simply dredged it up again. Nonetheless, I am oddly optimistic and determined." After all, she had admitted she had loved him, and she had never said she had stopped. "I do not intend to give up this time, Win. I have wasted entirely too many years."

"What about the false prince?"

"He is still a problem." Gray settled back in his chair. "I'm afraid she hasn't come to her senses about him yet, although she has not appeared overly affectionate toward him. Indeed, if I didn't know better, I'd think she was avoiding him altogether."

"Regardless, you'd best get rid of him."

"Excellent idea. And how do you propose I do that?"

"Ask and ye shall receive, old man." Win grinned and rose to his feet. He moved to the desk, picked up a file Gray hadn't noticed and returned. "This is why I'm here."

"What is it?"

"Inside this file you'll find a photograph of an actor

named Bernard Dunstan and an affidavit from the photographer confirming that fact. It seems that said photographer, in an effort to display his skills, on occasion hires models or actors to be his subject in photographs he then displays at his studio. Fortunately for you, I had a photograph taken there just a few months ago."

"And?"

"And take a look." He handed Gray the file and sat back down.

Gray flipped open the file and stared into the smiling face of Prince Nikolai Pruzinsky, of the Kingdom of Greater Avalonia. "This is—"

"Camille's prince." Win grinned with triumph. "Also known as Bernard Dunstan. I thought he looked familiar when I met him, but I couldn't quite put my finger on where until I remembered the photographs I had seen at the studio. So I went into London to see what I could discover. In addition to the photograph, the photographer was kind enough to give me a playbill listing Mr. Dunstan as one of the secondary players in a short-lived, ill-received production of a very obscure play. It's there as well."

Gray looked up from the picture. "He's an actor?"

"Ironic, isn't it?" Win chuckled. "Camille hired actors to deceive an actor whose sole purpose was to deceive her."

"This is perfect." Gray stared at the picture. "This is exactly the proof I need."

"What are you going to do with it?"

"I'm not going to tell Camille. You were right about that too." He shook his head. "There's no need for her to feel like a fool. She doesn't need to know about this."

"Then what are you going to do?"

"Confront Pruzinsky and get rid of him, once and for all." A hard note sounded in his voice.

"Excellent! May I stay and watch?"

"No."

"You are no fun at all, Grayson." Win heaved a long-suffering sigh. "Oh, I have other news to tell you as well. Mother has been delayed. She won't be home until late tonight."

"Damnation." Gray winced. "I'd forgotten all about her."

"Oh, she'll like that. No doubt you've forgotten about the rest of us as well." Win shook his head in a mournful manner. "And at Christmas."

"I am sorry."

"No need to apologize." Win waved off his comment. "We are merely your family, after all. However"—he pinned his cousin with a firm look—"Father and I thought, as Mother has no idea you have returned, it would be the perfect Christmas gift if you were to surprise her tomorrow at home, as tomorrow is Christmas."

"Yes, of course." Gray nodded.

"And speaking of Christmas, have you given any consideration as to a Christmas gift for Camille? You should give her something, you know. Aside from saving her from the clutches of Pruzinsky, or rather Dunstan, that is."

Gray groaned. "I hadn't even thought of that."

Win cast him a pitying look. "No wonder you've never been engaged. The right gift might just be the thing needed to nudge her into your arms."

"It's too late to purchase something."

"Which is fortunate for you. You need something more thoughtful, more sentimental than a mere expensive bauble."

"Oh?" Gray considered his cousin. "What did you have in mind?"

"I barely know her anymore. I am not the one who has spent the last few days with her. What does she want?"

"Well . . ." He thought for a moment. "She wants to hire Mrs. Fortesque as her new cook. I might be able to arrange that."

"Good Lord, Gray, a cook is entirely too practical a gift." He rolled his gaze toward the ceiling. "It's like giving her wool socks." Win sighed. "Is there anything else she might want?"

"She did want a prince." Gray shrugged.

"Yes, well, she can't have one."

The most absurd idea struck him and he stared at Win. "Why not?"

Confusion shone in Win's eyes. "Why not what?"

"Give her a prince."

Win shook his head. "I don't understand."

"Nor do you have to." Gray chuckled. "But if a prince is what she wants"—Gray raised his glass—"a prince is what she'll get."

"I remember these." Delilah smiled with delight and unwrapped a delicate glass ornament in the shape of a strawberry. "When I was a child, I would stare at these and think they were real strawberries turned to glass by fairies determined to keep them perfect forever." She wrinkled her nose. "Rather fanciful, I'm afraid."

"Not for a child, dear. And not for anyone at Christmas," Mother said with a smile. "Indeed, I have always thought they were a bit magical myself."

Camille's mother and sisters had offered their help in the decorating of the tree, which had been set up in the main gallery late in the morning. The gardener had done an excellent job. The fir was impressively large and nicely shaped. The ladies were surrounded by the scent of evergreen and the boxes Camille and Grayson had found in the attic. No one had brought up yesterday's argument, but there was an air of fragility around them all. As if one wrong word would shatter the tentative peace. Still, their offer to help had seemed to Camille to be in the way of making amends. Not that she didn't have amends of her own to make. She intended to say something at the first opportunity; but for the moment, they were all awash in recollections of Christmases past. With each box opened, each fragile glass ornament unwrapped from its tissue, each silver star or angel crafted from lace discovered, came gasps of delight and smiles and memories.

"It's much like seeing old friends—unwrapping these ornaments, that is," Beryl said with a smile. "Good Lord." Surprise sounded in her voice. "When did I become so sentimental?"

"We are all sentimental at Christmas. It's not merely permitted but expected, even encouraged." Mother studied the contents of a newly opened box. "It is the one time of year we can all behave like children and not be chastised for it." She glanced at Camille, which did feel somewhat like a chastisement. "Where are the rest of your players this afternoon? Shouldn't they be here joining in the Christmas merriment?"

"Mrs. Montgomery-Wells, Mr. Henderson and Miss Murdock are playing a game of cards in the parlor. Nikolai said he had pressing correspondence to attend to and would be in his rooms."

Indeed, Nikolai had confided this was of great importance and had to do with the problems in his country. Camille prayed it wasn't overly serious. Through the years, she had met far too many of her mother's acquaintances who had lost home and country to wish that for Nikolai. Although she did rather hope that it was urgent enough for him to feel he needed to return at once to the Kingdom of Whateveritwas. Christmas, indeed life, would be so much less complicated that way.

"Grayson is in the library with his cousin." She drew a deep breath. "Frankly, I'm rather glad it's just the four of us."

"Because that went so well yesterday?" Beryl said sweetly.

"No, because I owe you all an apology." She shook her head. "You are the dearest people in the world to me, and I shouldn't have been so short-tempered. Delilah"—she met her younger sister's gaze directly—"I am sorry that I said you were stuffy."

"Oh, but I am stuffy, and no one is more aware of that than I." Delilah shrugged. "And, as I am, I must admit it is the tiniest bit amusing to watch a tart pretend to be me. As long as no one ever knows about it," she added quickly.

"In that, we are in complete agreement. I don't even want to think of the gossip, should this Christmas production of mine be made public." Camille shuddered.

"However"—Delilah's gaze met hers—"as much as I do wish we were not involved in a debacle that threatens to come down around our heads at any moment and ruin us all, and I do blame you, I am rather, well, pleased that you've included me."

Camille stared.

"Was that an apology?" Beryl asked.

"The thought had crossed my mind that you might simply . . . well . . ." Delilah cringed. "Lock me in the attic."

Beryl gasped. "Never!"

"And I do apologize for saying that you don't think things through before plunging into—"

"Chaos?" Beryl suggested, then glanced at Camille and heaved a resigned sigh. "And I know you hate to have your past mistakes thrown back in your face—"

"Like Brighton," Delilah suggested in what was obviously meant to be a helpful manner. Camille resisted the urge to wince.

"It was extremely unkind of me," Beryl continued. "So you have my apologies as well. And I am so trying to be a better person."

Camille bit back a laugh. "Thank you, Beryl. I know how difficult it is for you to admit you possibly might have been wrong."

"It is indeed, as I am so rarely wrong." Beryl heaved an overly dramatic sigh and rested the back of her hand against her forehead in a manner worthy of any actress.

Delilah laughed.

"And, Mother." Camille summoned up her courage. She and her mother were usually in such accord. "About Mrs. Montgomery-Wells—"

"There's nothing to apologize for there, dear. I fully understand how difficult it must be to get a troupe of actors to play one's family, especially at Christmas." She moved a silver glass ball from one branch to another, then studied it to determine if it was perfectly placed. "Just as you are sensitive about the mention of your past mistakes, I seem to be rather sensitive about reminders that I am inevitably growing older." She cast Camille a wry smile. "And I suspect that Christmas, being here with all of you, only makes it more poignant. I recall every Christmas, you know. The gifts and the parties and the laughter. The awe on your faces when you

looked at the newly decorated tree. The Christmas plays
the three of you would put on, before you and Beryl
grew too old to find Delilah of any use. I remember the
sleigh rides in those years when there was snow and it
was entirely too cold to go out of doors, and yet we did
so, anyway. And I remember the way you would distract
whatever cook we had at the moment, while Beryl stole
freshly made gingerbread."

Beryl shifted uneasily.

Mother slanted a chastising look at her. "You thought
I didn't know about that?" Beryl smiled weakly. "The
cooks knew as well. There are a number of other pranks
the two of you played, mostly involving impersonating
one another, that I know about, but I needn't go into
that now."

"Oh, but I would like to hear." Delilah grinned.

"Oh, I daresay that's enough but thank you, Mother."
Camille chuckled, then sobered. "But I owe you a far
greater apology than miscasting your part. When I first
thought of this plan, I thought I needed a proper family, or at least a family more proper than we are. In that,
I did you a grave disservice. I had always thought that
you simply liked being surrounded by nobility, regardless of whether they had wealth or power." She chose
her words with care. "But I have come to realize, in recent days, that you offered a home, albeit temporary, at
Christmas and throughout the year, to those who were
lost. Admittedly, they were inevitably an odd lot—"

"Do you remember the Oriental gentleman with the
long, drooping mustache who could pull coins out of
your nose?" Delilah said with a slight smile.

"No, but I recall the Frenchman. Oh, I think he
claimed to be a *comte,* who was convinced the true
hereditary king of France would be restored to the

throne and his ancestral lands would at last be returned to him." Beryl shook her head in a thoughtful manner. "I do wonder if he ever gave up hoping."

"I daresay, there are any number of people we all remember." Camille waved off her sisters' comments and turned her attention back to her mother. "The point is, I was concerned with what you, what *we, aren't* rather than *what we are.* What you are. I never should have been anything but proud. You were always willing to welcome those souls who had lost their place in the world into ours."

Her mother continued to place the precious glass ornaments carefully on the tree; her words were measured. "I have always thought that should I lose my place in the world, my position, my home, even my country, I would hope there would be someone willing to accept me into their lives. Especially at Christmas. If only for a short time." She shook her head. "I will not apologize for that."

Camille swallowed hard and nodded.

"But you also mentioned the parade of lovers." She met Camille's gaze directly. "I never flaunted them. I never displayed undue affection in front of you. In truth, I was most discreet and most selective." She narrowed her eyes. "I daresay, you have no idea how many, if any, I actually took to my bed. Nor is it any of your concern."

"Mother—"

"I would think at this point in your life, Camille, you would understand that there are moments when loneliness is an ache somewhere in the vicinity of your heart that cannot be eased, despite the presence of friends and family." She gazed at her daughter for a long moment. "Do you? Understand, that is?"

"I think so." Camille nodded. Indeed, hadn't she felt

it herself? An ache, a longing, a need that woke her in the night reaching for something or someone just out of reach.

Grayson.

She couldn't get him out of her thoughts today. But then through the years of her marriage and the years since, no matter how hard she had tried to put him out of her head, he had always lingered in the dim recesses of her mind and her heart. At once, she realized what she should have known from the beginning. Wasn't that the way with true love?

"Camille?"

"Yes?" Her attention snapped back to her mother.

Mother studied her curiously. "Are you all right?"

"Yes, of course." Camille nodded. "My apologies. A random thought. Nothing of significance . . ."

"I should apologize to you as well, I suppose, for being short-tempered. Not for the way I have lived my life, mind you," Lady Briston added quickly. "Although . . ." The oddest look of indecision washed across her face. "Admittedly, I have not always made the right decisions. There are perhaps one or two things I have done in the past—"

"Mother." A warning sounded in Beryl's voice.

"That, while I thought were for the best, might, in hindsight, be considered, oh, I don't know, unforgivable."

Camille stared. " 'Unforgivable'?"

"Don't be absurd," Delilah chimed in. "I can't imagine anything that would be unforgivable."

"One cannot be faulted for doing the wrong thing for what one believed to be the right reasons," Beryl said firmly.

"Oh, but I'm afraid one can," her mother said with a wry smile.

"But what if it's for the wrong reasons?" Camille said slowly. "What if one's decisions were prompted by anger or foolishness or pride?"

"I would say that's something else, then, isn't it?" Mother said.

"But you said it yourself yesterday," Camille began. "How one needs to decide—to balance, if you will— what one might lose from forgiveness as opposed to what one might gain."

"Good Lord." Beryl stared at her twin. "You've forgiven him, haven't you?"

"Who?" Camille said casually, as if she had no idea what Beryl was talking about. She picked up an ornament and unwrapped it.

"You know who!" Beryl huffed.

"Grayson and I had a long, oh, discussion last night." Camille placed the ornament on the tree. "We talked about what had passed between us eleven years ago. I know now what he was thinking and feeling, and he knows how I felt. And furthermore"—resolve washed through her—"I believe I know what I want."

"For Christmas?" Delilah asked.

"Forever," Camille said with a firm nod of her head.

"What a surprise." Mother smiled.

"Did he tell you everything?" Beryl said sharply. "Did he tell you about his fortune?"

"Yes." She met her sister's gaze directly. "And last night he admitted he should have known me better than to have thought the worst of me. I should place the same trust in him."

"You can't just open your arms and say I'm yours." Exasperation sounded in Beryl's voice. "The man does need to be taught some sort of lesson."

"Although one could argue they have both been taught a lesson that has gone on for eleven years," Mother said in an offhand manner. "Indeed, one might say that was long enough."

"Or too long," Delilah pointed out.

"Regardless." Beryl heaved a resigned sigh. "I don't think you should make this too easy for him."

"I daresay, it hasn't been easy so far." Camille shook her head. "I lost him once, because he thought money meant more to me than love, and because his pride was wounded as much as his heart. I shall not lose him again because of my pride."

"Then what are you going to do?"

"I said last night that I had changed, and I have. The girl I was eleven years ago waited for him to return. Waited for her fairy-tale prince to sweep her away." She set her jaw firmly. "The woman I am now knows what she wants and has waited entirely too long to pursue it."

Camille pulled a deep breath for courage and knocked on Grayson's door. Hopefully, she would catch him before he went down to dinner. If not, she'd leave him the brief note she had written. It wasn't an apology—she really didn't think she had anything to apologize for, except perhaps for losing her temper—but it was in the manner of an olive branch. And she had written that she loved him.

She had only seen him in passing most of the day; and when she had, he'd been preoccupied. The man obviously had something weighing heavily on his mind. While last night had brought her to the inescapable realization that she had never stopped loving him, she couldn't help but wonder if he had come to another conclusion altogether. Perhaps last night wasn't a new beginning between them, but rather it was, once and for all, the end. Perhaps they couldn't move past their anger and pain. And hadn't he chosen once before to let her marry the wrong man?

"Grayson?" She opened his door and glanced inside. Obviously, she had missed him. No matter. She would leave her note and speak with him later. And then perhaps they could share Christmas Eve together.

A book sat beside the lamp on the table by the side of the bed; she wondered if his taste in reading had changed. Curious, she picked it up and a document beneath it drifted to the floor. She bent to retrieve the paper, started to replace it, then froze.

It was a receipt for passage to America on a ship sailing the day after Christmas.

Her heart caught. He was leaving? Again? In spite of everything that he'd said? According to this, he had never planned to stay.

No, even with the damning evidence in front of her, she was not going to jump to conclusions. There was a logical explanation for this. And hadn't she said she needed to trust him? Even if he did intend to go back to America, by God, she had indeed learned from her mistakes. She would go after him. She would not lose him again.

She replaced the receipt and put the book back where it had been, ignoring the slight tremble in her hand. Obviously, a note was not now sufficient. There were things that needed to be said. She left his room and dropped the note off in hers, then headed down to dinner. She had no idea if she could eat past the lump in her throat; because as much as she wanted to believe there was a simple explanation, she couldn't help but fear she was wrong.

Twenty-three

It was, all things considered, a rather perfect Christmas Eve. Or would have been, had Camille been able to have a moment alone with Grayson. There had been no chance to speak to him alone before they'd gone in to dinner. Even at the dinner table, he'd appeared distracted.

At least she didn't have to worry about much else tonight. Her mother had directed the conversation around the table like the skilled conductor of an orchestra. She had encouraged Mr. Henderson's stories, kept Mrs. Montgomery-Wells from straying too far afield and chatted with Nikolai as if he were indeed about to become a member of the family. She was the perfect hostess, but then she always had been. Delilah spent a good portion of dinner in animated conversation with Miss Murdock. Camille wondered if she was giving the actress advice or eliciting it. Beryl did her part as well, engaging Nikolai in conversation whenever his gaze settled on Camille. There was a determined look in his eye, and it was obvious that he wished to speak to her alone. He, no doubt, thought it would be the perfect time for a proposal. Of course it would have been, had she wanted a proposal. Even Uncle Basil joined them tonight, but he was unusually subdued. He spoke quietly to Grayson more than to anyone else, and he observed rather than joined in. His behavior could certainly be attributed to his not feeling quite up to snuff. Still, it was not at all like him.

Then after dinner, Grayson had vanished for a few moments, as had Beryl.

"Where have you been?" Camille said sharply when her twin returned to the parlor.

"Freshening up." Beryl frowned. "Why?"

"I suspect I am going to need your help."

"I do so hate to inconvenience you," Beryl said absently, surveying the parlor. "I must say, this was an excellent idea."

Camille nodded. "Once Mother discovered one of the footmen played the violin, she insisted he be employed to play for dancing tonight."

The furniture had been moved away from the center of the room and there was more than enough space for dancing. At the moment, Mr. Henderson danced with Miss Murdock, Mother was partnered with Nikolai, Mrs. Montgomery-Wells danced with Grayson, and Delilah was with Uncle Basil.

"Does it strike you that there's something different about him?" Camille studied her uncle. "Uncle Basil, that is."

"He's been ill," Beryl said rather more curtly than was necessary. "That's what comes of wandering the world, you know. One can catch all sorts of dreadful illnesses."

"That's probably it." She nodded. "Mother also instructed Mrs. Fortesque in the making of her special Christmas Eve punch."

"God help us, everyone," Beryl said under her breath.

Nikolai's gaze caught hers. He inclined his head slightly toward the door. She smiled faintly at him in return.

"I suspect Nikolai has decided tonight is the night to propose."

"Oh, well, I wouldn't worry about it," Beryl said.

"Oh, I'm not worried about it."

Beryl cast her a suspicious glance. "Why not?"

"Because I have a plan."

Beryl's eyes narrowed. "What kind of plan?"

"You'll know soon enough."

"Oh, good," Beryl said with a sigh. "Something else to look forward to."

It was impossible to avoid Nikolai for long, and Camille was dancing in his arms before she knew it.

"I am not a suspicious man, my dear Camille." He smiled down at her. "Yet, I suspect you have been avoiding me."

"Don't be absurd." She forced a light laugh. "Why would I avoid you?"

"I don't know." His gaze bored into hers. "Perhaps you are afraid?"

"What would I have to be afraid of?"

"Passion, my dear." He pulled her closer against him. "The passion that simmers below the surface between the two of us."

"Ah yes, well, there is that," she said weakly.

"We shall speak later tonight." A firm note sounded in his voice. "And I shall not take 'no' for an answer."

Nor did she intend to say "no," as she fully intended not to get to that point. But he grew more and more impatient with every passing minute. It was all she could do to evade his grasp. She wondered as well—aside from the fact that he was a prince and handsome and wealthy—what she had seen in him. Now she found him as irritating as she had once found him irresistible. What's not to love, indeed!

Oddly enough, given the small number of their party, even as she steered clear of Nikolai, she did not manage a single dance with Grayson. One would think he was avoiding her. The heavy knot, which had settled in the pit of her stomach before dinner, continued to grow. It seemed imperative to talk to him, to settle everything between them once and for all. Something told her she had no time to waste. She had wasted too much already. Eleven years too much.

She needed to tell him how she felt, what she wanted. It was completely irrational, and made no sense at all, but she had to tell him now. Tonight. She had to know if this Christmas Eve was the first of many to come. And she had to ask about the ship's passage. But given his manner today, did he feel the same?

If she could just avoid this blasted prince! And Grayson had disappeared once again. There was only one thing to be done about it. Beryl was approaching Nikolai, who was dancing with Miss Murdock. Camille grabbed her arm and pulled her into the hall, across the gallery, past the Christmas tree and into the small parlor.

"What is it now?" Impatience rang in Beryl's voice.

"We are going to change clothes." Camille closed the doors behind her.

"Why?"

"I'm afraid Nikolai is going to propose or possibly attempt to seduce me. Both of which I want to avoid." She shook her head. "Rejecting either his seduction or his proposal will simply complicate this entire debacle. We need to stay with the original plan. Just one more day, Beryl. We need to get through one more day, and then he can be called away."

"I'm not going to allow him to seduce me."

"Nor do I wish you to. I simply want you to, oh, distract him while I try to find Grayson."

"And Grayson will save you?"

"No, of course not." Camille started undoing the hooks on her gown. "I will save myself, but I haven't spoken to him since last night, and I'm afraid . . ." She drew a deep breath and steadied herself. "I'm afraid I may lose him again if I don't tell him how I feel."

"I don't really think—"

"Beryl, there were all sorts of things I said to him that could be taken in any number of different ways."

"Even so—"

"I never told him I loved him!"

Beryl stared at her for a long moment.

"Well? Are you going to help me or not?"

Beryl heaved a resigned sigh. "Of course I am. I always will."

Quickly they traded dresses.

"Now what?" Beryl said when they had finished.

"You can keep Nikolai occupied, and do try to avoid any sort of commitment."

"As in marriage, you mean?"

Camille nodded. "While you do that, I am going to find Grayson."

"This is absurd."

"Probably." Camille sighed. "But it's all I can think of."

They started back toward the main parlor and were near the Christmas tree, when Camille spotted Nikolai entering the gallery. She pushed Beryl forward, then stepped back to hide in the shadows behind the tree. Mother only allowed the candles on the tree to be lit when there were people nearby. There had been a nasty incident with a flaming tree some years ago.

"There you are." Determination sounded in Nikolai's voice. "I have been looking for you."

"And it seems you have found me," Beryl said, although she certainly could have done so with a bit more enthusiasm. There was no way to get past them without Nikolai seeing her. For the moment, Camille was trapped where she was. She shifted her position and found a spot where she was hidden but could see through the branches.

"My darling." Nikolai pulled her into his arms. "At last we are alone."

"One never knows," Beryl said in a louder voice than was necessary. "Why, someone could come upon us at any minute."

He chuckled. "Nonsense. They are all having entirely too good a time. Thanks, in great part, to the Christmas Eve punch. It's quite potent. And might I say . . ." He paused in a most suggestive manner and lowered his face to Beryl's. Camille bit back a groan. He was going to kiss her! "It was most appreciated."

Beryl pushed against him. "I really don't think—"

"I think it would be wise if you unhanded my wife." A cool voice sounded from across the gallery.

Nikolai froze.

Camille winced.

Beryl gasped. "Lionel!"

Beryl's husband strode casually across the gallery toward the couple.

"Your wife?" Nikolai looked down at Beryl. "But I thought—"

"Obviously, you were mistaken." Beryl huffed. "A mistake I was about to point out to you."

"When I said 'unhand,' I meant immediately."

Lionel's manner was deceptively pleasant. Camille held her breath.

"Yes, of course." Nikolai released Beryl and took a quick step back.

"Darling, this is not what you think it is."

"It isn't?" Lionel's brow rose.

"No, not at all. It's . . ." Beryl paused. "What did you think it was?"

"I know exactly what it is. This bounder thinks he can have his way with you and I will not allow it."

Beryl stared at her husband. "That's what you thought?"

Lionel cast her an affectionate smile. "Well, it was obvious to me you weren't encouraging his attention."

"Lady Dunwell, Lord Dunwell, my apologies." Nikolai straightened his cuffs. "I have no idea how this happened. I thought you were Camille. I could have sworn she was wearing this. . . . Obviously, I was confused. No doubt the result of too much punch." He shook his head. "Once again, I am most sorry. I do hope this won't influence your opinion of me in the future."

"Not at all. I daresay, nothing could change my opinion of you." Beryl waved off his comment. "But if you wish for a private moment with my sister—"

"Indeed, I thought I was having a private moment," Nikolai murmured.

"I suggest you wait for her in the library. I shall find her myself and send her to you." Beryl paused. "Although it may be a few minutes, what with the festivities and all."

"Perhaps, it would be—"

"I shall tell her to hurry, as I understand you are a most impatient man."

"Very well, then. That would be appreciated, Lady Dunwell." He nodded. "Lord Dunwell." With that, he turned and headed toward the library.

Camille breathed a sigh of relief.

"I gather that was Pruzinsky?" Lionel said.

She nodded.

"Handsome chap, I'll give him that. However, I do have some information—"

Before he could get the words out, Beryl kissed him, and quite thoroughly too. And Lionel kissed her back. The man wasn't nearly as stuffy as one might think.

Beryl pulled away at last. "How did you know it was me and not Camille? Even people who know us well still get confused. And the light is rather dim here near the tree. Yet you recognized me from across the length of the gallery."

"My dear, darling wife." He wrapped his arms tighter around her and stared into her eyes. "I know the way you stand, the way you hold your head, the faint difference in the sound of your voices, which may be apparent only to me. I daresay, if there were a dozen of you all exactly alike, I should still know which one was you, and you alone." He smiled. "I think I know in my heart, and I always will."

"Oh, my." Beryl stared up at her husband and sighed. Camille sighed as well. "I am a lucky woman."

"And I am a lucky man." Lionel kissed the tip of her nose. "Shall we join the rest of the, um, cast? I am dying to know how Camille's farce is progressing."

"Oh, darling, I think that would be a dreadful idea. Things have not gone exactly as planned."

He chuckled. "That is not unexpected."

"Besides, I have missed you entirely too much to share you." She brushed her lips across his. "I think retiring for the night is a much, much better idea."

"And who am I to argue with my wife on Christmas Eve?"

Beryl took his hand and started toward the stairs. She called back over her shoulder, "Good evening, Camille."

"Good evening, Beryl," Camille called back, and grinned. "And thank you."

Beryl's laughter, accompanied by her husband's, trailed through the halls behind them.

Camille smiled. It was good to see her sister so happy. Who would ever have imagined Lord and Lady Dunwell, whose amorous adventures had once been the lifeblood of London gossips, would have found happiness in each other's arms? True love. Who would have thought?

Now, she squared her shoulders, to find it for herself.

"Mr. Elliott." Pruzinsky or rather Dunstan's eyes widened at the sight of Gray. "My apologies." He looked around the library. "I was to meet Lady Lydingham in here."

Gray perched on the edge of the desk, arms folded across his chest. He'd told Beryl earlier in the evening what he had learned and she'd offered to send Pruzinsky to the library when he was ready. "She's not here, but please come in."

"I really do need to speak to her, so if you will excuse me—"

"And I really do need to speak to you, Count." Gray paused for appropriate dramatic effect. "Or should I say, Mr. Dunstan?"

Dunstan's eyes narrowed. "I beg your pardon?"

"Come in, Dunstan, and close the doors."

Dunstan hesitated.

"Or we could do this in front of everyone else, although in that case there will be no choice but to notify the authorities and have you arrested. Still, that would create a nasty scandal, which I would much prefer to avoid." Gray shrugged. "The choice, however, is entirely yours to make."

"Very well." At once, the man's accent vanished. He closed the doors behind him.

Gray indicated the chair in front of him. "Sit down."

The actor hesitated, then sat down. "How did you know?"

"The Kingdom of Greater Avalonia has not existed for more than half a century now."

Dunstan grimaced. "I didn't realize that until after I had chosen it. Then I had hoped it was too obscure to be noticed." He thought for a moment. "Even so, I could still be the prince."

"The real Prince Nikolai Pruzinsky is in his eighties."

Dunstan shrugged. "I could be a descendant."

"But you're not." Gray shook his head. "A legitimate prince, even one traveling incognito, would never travel alone."

"Never?"

"Never," Gray said firmly.

"I see," Dunstan said thoughtfully, as if taking mental notes.

"And all that smiling and nodding . . ." Gray shook his head.

"I thought that was most effective." A smug note sounded in Dunstan's voice. "Indeed, I thought it was quite clever. The more I pretended not to understand, the less I was expected to answer."

"I will admit, the accent was a nice touch. Definitely Eastern European, but vague enough as to be unidentifiable."

"Thank you," Dunstan said modestly. "I do accents very well." He nodded hopefully in the direction of the liquor cabinet. "It's been a long night. Would you mind?"

"Yes," Gray snapped. "This is not brandy and cigars in the library with the gentlemen after dinner. Indeed, I am hard-pressed not to thrash you to within an inch of your life."

Dunstan smiled in a smug manner. "You're a gentleman, sir. You wouldn't do that."

"I'm half American, Dunstan." He smiled coldly. "You would be surprised at what I would do."

Dunstan paled, but attempted a brave front, nonetheless. "Still, you have no real proof of anything, do you? It's really my word against yours, isn't it?"

"You're right." Gray shrugged. "Aside, of course, from the playbill with your name on it, the photograph of you and the photographer's sworn statement as to your identity."

"Is that all?" Dunstan scoffed, but there was a distinct look of unease in his eyes. And Gray knew—the same way he knew when he had clinched a difficult business deal—that he had him.

Gray raised a brow. "Do I need more?"

"I suppose not." He shifted in his chair.

"But I am curious, Dunstan. What, exactly, was your plan here?"

"Does it matter?"

"Perhaps not, but indulge me." Gray studied the other man closely. "I think you planned to marry Lady Lydingham, gain control of her fortune and be called home to your *country*. Perhaps a monetary crisis or something along those lines."

"A monetary crisis?" Dunstan's eyes widened thoughtfully. "I hadn't thought of that. That's very good."

Gray ignored him. "And you would then vanish forever." He narrowed his gaze. "Leaving her alone and penniless."

Dunstan squirmed in his seat. "It sounds so bad when you say it that way."

"I'd say it's bad enough to put you behind bars for the rest of your life."

"But that's not going to happen, is it?" A sly look crossed the actor's face. "I know things, Mr. Elliott. All is not as it appears here at Millworth Manor."

"Oh?" Gray was afraid of that. In spite of the flaws in Dunstan's plan, a man clever enough to come up with it, plus one who truly did understand English, would certainly have noticed a few discrepancies among the company gathered for Christmas.

"I am not the only one who is not who he says he is." He narrowed his eyes and studied Gray. "I have no idea who you really are, but I'm fairly certain you are not a cousin. Nor are those two ladies who arrived the other day your mother and sister. I have my doubts about the delectable Delilah as well."

"I see." Gray smiled slowly. Dunstan didn't know everything, but he did know enough to make him dangerous to Camille's future. "Before we go any further, you should know I am a man of business. I am well used to making deals of one sort or another. And I am prepared to deal with you tonight."

"You are?" Suspicion sounded in Dunstan's voice.

"I am indeed." He picked up a large envelope from the desk. "I am prepared to offer you one hundred pounds to leave this house by morning without saying so much as a single word to Lady Lydingham. I have also included a one-way passage to America."

"I don't want to go to America."

"It's the land of opportunity, Dunstan. Opportunity you will find sadly lacking, should you stay in England. Furthermore"—he pinned the actor with a cold look—"what has happened here at Millworth Manor stays here. If I should hear the faintest whisper about what has occurred in this house during your visit, make no mistake, regardless of how many oceans there may be between us, I will hunt you down. Believe me, Dunstan, I have the resources to do so. And when I am through with you"—his voice hardened—"then I shall turn whatever is left of you over to the authorities."

Dunstan stared at him. "Surely, you can do better than a hundred pounds."

"Mr. Dunstan." Gray shook his head in a mournful manner. "I'm afraid you misunderstand. This is not a negotiation. This is a one time offer. You may accept it and leave by morning, or . . ." He shrugged. "I will send for the local authorities."

Dunstan frowned. "But it's Christmas Eve."

"Which, I imagine, would put them in a relatively foul mood." He smiled and held out the envelope. "However, it is your choice."

"Not much of a choice, really." Dunstan rose to his feet and took the envelope. He opened it, flipped through the five-pound notes and glanced at the ticket. "First-class?"

Gray shrugged.

"Not at all bad for a few weeks' work." He cast Gray an unrepentant grin. "And it has been a grand stay here."

"I'm so glad you enjoyed yourself," Gray said in a wry manner. "I assume we will never see you again."

"I think that would be best." Dunstan sauntered to the door, then glanced back at Gray. "It was a pleasure, Mr. Elliott. Oh, and Merry Christmas." He grinned and took his leave.

Gray blew a relieved breath. He had been fairly confident Dunstan would be easy to get rid of. His type was not usually dangerous. Still, one never knew.

Now that he had resolved one matter, it was past time to resolve another.

Camille returned to the parlor to see if Grayson was there. The man certainly wasn't making this easy for her. He still hadn't returned, and she had no idea where she might find him. She paused for a few minutes to watch her mother dance with Uncle Basil. They talked as they danced in a manner far more earnest than befit either the music or the evening. It seemed to her once again that there was something decidedly different about her uncle and now, as well, about the way her mother spoke to him. It wasn't anything Camille could point to specifically, more a feeling than anything else that all was not as it appeared.

"Darling," Mother said as soon as the music stopped, "it seems our numbers have dwindled substantially. So we are going to retire as well."

"Good evening, Camille," Uncle Basil said with an odd, poignant smile, as if there was more he wanted to say.

Only Mrs. Montgomery-Wells and Mr. Henderson remained in the parlor. Mother said a few words to them and they, too, headed for their rooms. Grayson had obviously already retired for the night as well. There was nothing to be done about it then. Tonight she would have to pound on his door. She couldn't recall ever having been both afraid and determined before but she was now.

"Beryl!"

Camille stopped short near the Christmas tree. Grayson appeared from the shadows at the end of the gallery, obviously thinking Camille was her twin. She should, of course, correct him immediately. Still . . . she adopted her sister's slightly lower tone. "Yes?"

"It went exactly as I expected," Grayson said briskly. "He will be gone by morning."

She nodded. *Who?*

"With any luck at all, we shall never see him again." He paused. "I don't think it's necessary to tell Camille her prince was an imposter intent upon her money."

Camille stifled a gasp.

"After all, what good would it do to tell her the truth? It would serve no purpose except to make her feel like a fool."

"She does hate to have her mistakes pointed out to her," Camille murmured.

"Believe me, I am aware of that."

So her prince wasn't a prince, after all. She should have been furious; but, in truth, it was as if a huge weight had been lifted off her shoulders. Even better, Grayson had gotten rid of the man for her.

"Then we are agreed?"

"Absolutely."

"Do you know where she is?"

"I have no idea." She shook her head. "The library, perhaps?"

"She wasn't there a few minutes ago, but I'll check. If not, I'll see her in the morning, I suppose."

"She said something about a dreadful headache, so she has probably gone to bed. I wouldn't bother her tonight. This has all been most stressful on her, you know."

"I know, and I'm afraid I haven't helped." He shook his head. "I know this will come as no surprise to you, but I've been an idiot."

"Oh?" Her heart thudded in her chest.

"We had a stupid argument last night and I failed to tell her, well, all sorts of things I should have."

"You failed to tell her you love her?" She held her breath.

"Again." He ran his hand through his hair. "I thought I would have had all this settled by now, but I still have arrangements to make. I suppose this will have to wait until morning."

She wanted to grin like a madwoman. "It will be a lovely gift then. She is usually most forgiving on Christmas."

"Why are you being so nice?" Suspicion sounded in his voice.

"It's Christmas Eve."

"Yes, of course." He paused. "Well, then, Merry Christmas, Beryl."

She smiled. "Merry Christmas, Grayson."

He nodded and headed toward the library.

She started toward her room as if she were walking on air. He loved her. He wasn't going anywhere. And he had indeed rescued her, even if she hadn't known she needed rescuing.

She would wait until the morning and then she'd give him the best gift a woman could give a man.

She'd tell him he was right.

December 25th

Twenty-four

Camille bolted upright in bed and stared at the clock on the night table beside her bed. Good Lord, it was afternoon! She hadn't slept this late all week. Of course she hadn't slept this soundly either. But she'd been exhausted, and knowing she no longer had to be concerned about Nikolai, or whoever he was—well, this was the best she had slept since coming to the manor.

Still, it was Christmas Day and she didn't want to waste a minute of it with the man she had waited eleven years for. She had already missed Christmas services. She scrambled out of bed and hurriedly dressed. She had told her maid not to worry about her this morning, as it was Christmas. Within a few minutes, she was dressed and headed downstairs.

"Fortesque." She spotted the actor as soon as she reached the bottom of the stairs. "Where is everyone?"

"Count Pruzinsky left early this morning."

She shrugged. "Oh, well, that's that, then."

He stared at her as if she had lost her mind. "And Mr. Elliott left shortly thereafter."

"What?" Her knees buckled and she grabbed the newel post to keep from falling. "Are you sure?"

Fortesque hurried to her side to assist her. "Are you all right?"

"No." It was as if the air had been pushed out of her lungs and her heart ripped to shreds.

He helped her to a chair. "He said something about his aunt."

She barely heard him. She was wrong, and once again Grayson had left her.

"Should I find someone to help?"

"No, I'm fine." She wasn't at all fine but she would be. "Please find my maid and have her pack my bags at once. I'll be leaving as well."

He stared at her. "He came back. Mr. Elliott, that is, not the prince. I don't mind telling you, Lady Lydingham, there was something about that man that did not sit well with me. The prince, that is, not Mr. Elliott."

She stared at him. "He came back?"

"I quite like Mr. Elliott. I should tell you he has offered my wife and me a position."

Laughter, equal parts hysteria and relief, bubbled up inside her. "Did he now?"

"It was most generous."

"I'm certain it was." She grinned. "Whatever Mr. Elliott has offered you, I will offer you more. We will discuss it later. But he is back?"

The actor nodded. "He's somewhere in the house. Your mother, uncle and Lord and Lady Dunwell are in the dining room. They asked that you be directed there when you came down. Mrs. Fortesque has prepared a late breakfast or rather early luncheon." He paused. "Your mother sent the others on a walk."

"I really should find Mr. Elliott."

"Your mother was quite insistent," he said firmly.

"Very well, then."

Grayson could wait, but not for long. She started toward the dining room and pulled up short the moment she entered the room. Her mother, uncle and Beryl sat at the table; Lionel stood near his wife, his hand rested on her shoulder. Everyone looked entirely too grim for Christmas Day.

"Whatever is the matter?"

"We have something to tell you," Mother said, and looked at Uncle Basil. "It's about your father."

Uncle Basil rose to his feet. "Camille."

She stared at him for a moment. "Of course I should have known."

"Known what?" Mother said.

"I wondered if we would ever see you again." She met her father's gaze directly. "It's good to have you home."

"Is it?" The question lingered in his eyes.

"We have missed you." The moment she said the words, she realized they were true.

Beryl's eyes widened. "How did you know?"

"Oh, I've known since I was twelve or thirteen, I think. I heard Mother and Uncle Basil arguing about it. And I've heard that argument continue through the years."

Mother studied her. "Why didn't you say anything?"

"Why didn't you tell me?" Annoyance sounded in Beryl's voice.

"I didn't know how to tell you." Camille shrugged. "It wasn't my secret to tell. And I thought it would be too difficult for you. I suppose I was protecting you."

"Me?" Beryl stared. "But I've always been the strong one."

Camille shook her head. "Not about this sort of thing. I knew you would never be able to forgive either of them."

"And you have?" Beryl said sharply. "Aren't you angry?"

"I was for a long time." She looked at her mother. "At both of you. Until I realized you told us he was dead because you thought it was better to have a dead father than one who was too selfish to live up to his obligations. It was hard to fault you for wishing to protect us." She turned to her father. "And I was angry at you for being selfish, until I understood that even the best of men can feel trapped in a life they didn't choose." She looked at her twin. "As for forgiveness, I can't really say, because I don't really know. I do know he did not leave us impoverished. I know he wrote to Mother every few months. I know he asked to come home. I know Mother refused to allow that. And I know he saw Uncle Basil fairly regularly.

"Forgiveness has to be earned. I think Mother has earned ours through the years. As for Father, he may well have paid for his mistake." She met her father's gaze. "My forgiveness is not as important as hers. Hers is the heart you broke."

"I am sorry," Mother said softly.

"I know you are."

"I am sorry as well." Father shook his head. "For leaving, of course, and for not coming home when I should have."

"I told you—" Mother began.

"I should have ignored you," he said in a hard tone. "I should have done what I knew was right. In that, I failed."

"This will not be easy, you know." Beryl stared at her father. "For any of us."

"I do not expect it to be." Father shrugged.

"Still, it is Christmas," Beryl said slowly. "Which does seem to me to be an appropriate place to start."

"What about Delilah?" Camille asked.

"That's why I sent her and the others on a walk. We thought we should speak to you first."

"Are you all right?" Camille said to her twin.

"Well . . ." Beryl glanced up at her husband. He nodded slightly. "I've known for several years. I found some of Father's letters."

"And you didn't tell me?"

Beryl winced. "I was protecting you."

"It seems the only one in this family who was only thinking of himself was me," Father said.

"Not entirely." Mother met his gaze. "Oh, don't mistake my words, you were for a long time, far longer than I really expected. But all this"—she swept a wide gesture at her daughters—"took the kind of courage I never imagined you would find." She hesitated. "When I told you never to return, I thought surely you would ignore me. I thought you'd be back. And every time I responded to your letters, I thought, 'This time he'll ignore me. He'll finally come home.'" She met her husband's gaze. "It only took you twenty years. I suppose it could have been longer."

"It should have been less," he said.

"It scarcely matters who should have done what at this point, does it?" Beryl looked from one parent to the next. "It seems to me we either wallow in recrimination and remorse, or we move on from here. I would much prefer to move on."

"This is not . . ." Mother paused and managed a wry smile. "Well, not exactly the Christmas I imagined."

"No, Mother," Beryl said firmly. "In many ways, it's better."

Camille stared at her twin. This was not how she'd ever expected Beryl would take the news of their father's reappearance. She wasn't entirely sure how she was taking it either, but then she'd known he was alive far longer than Beryl had. And her sister was right: This would not be easy for any of them. But then wasn't anything truly worth having worth the effort?

"Psst."

"Good Lord, not now." Camille heaved a resigned sigh. "If you will excuse me." She cast her sister an encouraging smile, stepped out of the dining room and came face-to-face with Delilah.

"What on earth is going on?" Suspicion shone in Delilah's eyes. "I was summoned the moment we entered the house."

"Mother and, um, Uncle Basil . . ." Camille wasn't sure what to say or rather what not to say. Even now, this wasn't her secret to tell. "Well, they wish to speak to you."

Delilah peered around her to look into the dining room. "I see Beryl and her husband are there as well." She straightened and met Camille's gaze. "This is significant then, isn't it?"

Camille nodded. "Very."

"I did wonder . . . The moment I saw Uncle Basil, I suspected . . ." The younger woman sighed. "It's past time I suppose."

Camille stared at her sister. "What's past time?"

"Oh." Delilah hesitated, then shook her head. "Nothing, nothing at all."

Camille studied her closely. "You know, don't you?" She glanced at the gathering in the dining room, then looked back at her sister. "About Fat—"

"I don't know anything," Delilah said quickly. "I have always thought there were things about Mother's life she did not wish to share. Things that might be too painful or too personal. If at some point she wishes me to know those things then she will tell me. As she hasn't, I know nothing."

"Then you do know."

"I have no idea what you're talking about." She side-stepped her sister and moved toward the dining room, paused and glanced back. "But when one spends a great deal of time locked in the attic one does tend to read anything one finds." She nodded and stepped into the dining room.

Camille stared after her. Who would have imagined that all three sisters knew their parents' secrets yet no one said a word for fear of upsetting someone else.

Fortesque cleared his throat. "Lady Lydingham?"

She'd almost forgotten he was there. "What is it now?"

"You're needed in the attic."

"The attic?" She drew her brows together. "Why?"

"I couldn't say, my lady," he said in a lofty manner.

She narrowed her gaze. "Couldn't or won't?"

"I have my instructions, my lady," he said in a no-nonsense manner. "I am to escort you."

"Are you?" What on earth was this about? The last time she was in the attic . . . She studied him for a long moment. His expression was as impassive as Clement's would have been. The man really played the role of butler quite well. "Then we shall go to the attic."

Fortesque didn't say a word on the way up the flights of stairs. When they reached the foot of the attic stairs, he picked up a small silver tray with a single piece of chocolate on it and presented it to her with a flourish. "Chocolate, my lady."

She raised a brow. "Swiss?"

"Of course." He sniffed. "You are to enjoy that, and I shall return in a moment."

"Very well." She took the chocolate and popped it into her mouth. It was rich and sweet, but wasted on her at the moment. Anticipation sped up her heart.

Fortesque fairly sprinted up the stairs, opened the door enough to poke his head in and then gestured for her to join him. As soon as she was a step behind him, he opened the door, stepped into the attic and swept a dramatic bow.

"My lady, your prince awaits."

"My what?" She stepped into the attic and her breath caught.

The room was aglow with the lights from dozens of chandeliers and candles. Swags of satins and silks and laces covered the boxes and the walls and the ceiling. Ferns and palms and potted plants had been brought up from the conservatory. Mistletoe hung everywhere she looked. The attic had vanished and in its place was a ballroom glittering with light and magic.

"My lady, it is my honor to present"—Fortesque stepped aside and gestured with a grand wave of his arm—"the Christmas ball."

Off to one side, the footman who had played the violin last night, now dressed in the court costume of another age, started playing her favorite waltz. The other footman stood nearby, holding a tray bearing two glasses of champagne.

Grayson stepped forward, wearing some sort of antiquated uniform. It was white with gold trim, and sported glittering medals and a blue sash. She had never seen anyone so dashing, so perfect. Her prince. Her true love.

"May I have this dance, my lady?" he said and swept an impressive bow.

She swallowed hard. "I fear I am not dressed for a ball."

"And yet, you are the most beautiful creature I have ever seen." He held out his arms. She stepped into his embrace and they began to waltz.

"Grayson, this is . . ." She shook her head.

"Christmas, Camille," he said with a smile. "The first of every Christmas yet to come."

"How did you . . . Where did you . . ."

"You were right about all sorts of things being stored in these trunks and boxes." He chuckled. "Although it took most of yesterday to find what I needed and to arrange all this."

"Which is why you were so preoccupied yesterday." She stared up at him. "You did this for me."

"I would do anything for you, and you did want a proposal from a prince for Christmas."

They whirled over the floor, in perfect step with each other. At last.

"I did until I realized it was the wrong prince." She drew a deep breath. "How much did you give him?"

"A hundred pounds and ship's passage to America." He shrugged. "It seemed a small enough price to pay."

"Last night, you knew it was me?"

"Not until the end." He chuckled. "I've never had a conversation with your sister in which she hasn't insulted me or said something sarcastic."

"You should know, I had already decided, before last night, not to marry him." She paused. "It's possible I decided the moment you stepped back into my life."

"Good, then you shall marry me."

She arched a brow. "Shouldn't that be in the form of a question?"

He laughed. "You're absolutely right, and I would hate to make a mistake about this sort of thing. After all, it has taken me eleven years." He pulled to a stop, gathered her closer against him and gazed into her eyes. "Will you dance with me on every Christmas Day from now until we breathe our last? Will you let me make amends for my past mistakes every day for the rest of our lives? Will you argue with me and wager with me and never let me forget what a lucky man I am? Will you marry me, Camille?"

She stared at him for a long moment and smiled. "I always would have."

He bent to kiss her.

"There is one thing, though," she said quickly. "Not a condition exactly. More in the realm of a favor."

"Oh?"

"We don't need to mention what has happened here at Christmas ever again, do we?" A hopeful note sounded in her voice. "The actors, and, well, the prince, and this entire charade. It can stay here, can't it?"

He laughed. "I'm fairly certain no one in your family wants this farce of yours known beyond the walls of the manor, so what happens here will stay here. But, Camille"—he gazed into her eyes—"there isn't a moment of this Christmas that I will ever forget, nor do I wish to. And it brought us together at last."

"It has not been my finest hour."

"On the contrary, you were brilliant." He grinned. "And, Camille"—he lowered his lips to hers—"what happened here at Christmas is just the beginning."

as for the supporting actors . . .

Mrs. Montgomery-Wells retired from the stage to a cozy cottage in the country, where her new friends could never quite figure out what her given name was as it seemed to change every time she was asked.

Mr. Henderson became a beloved writer of children's adventure stories.

Miss Murdock gained notoriety in burlesque theater wearing very little of substance and was rumored for a time to be the mistress of a foreign dignitary.

Mr. Dunstan vanished into obscurity.

Mrs. Fortesque did indeed accept the position of cook in the London house of Mr. and Mrs. Elliott.

Mr. Fortesque found a measure of theatrical success as the manager of a small London theater, where he often performed on stage.

A play entitled *The Christmas Pageant at Milton Manor* was a hit on the London stage and became a staple of the holiday season for many years.

It was written anonymously.

Dear Friends,

Welcome back to Millworth Manor!

It's Fall, 1887 and the manor is buzzing with preparations for Camille and Grayson's wedding. It's going to be a grand event, a social event to remember. After all, Camille is marrying the love of her life. Already, the house is filling up with family and friends—new and old.

But while Camille is blissfully anticipating spending the rest of her days with Grayson, her younger sister Delilah, Lady Hargate, has anything but bliss on her mind. For one thing, her financial future is in jeopardy. For another, the biggest mistake she's ever made has reappeared in the form of handsome American entrepreneur, Sam Russell.

Delilah's money problems would be solved with the right marriage, not that Sam would be the right husband. Far from it. Why, she cherishes tradition and heritage and he has one step firmly in the next century. And the last thing Sam wants is another fortune hunter—he's been down that road before. Still, there is something about her he can't seem to get out of his mind. Or maybe his heart.

Well, you know what they say about opposites . . .

And you never know what might happen at Millworth Manor.

See you there!

Take care,
Victoria

New York, June 1887

"Do hurry with that." Delilah, Lady Hargate, cringed at the sharp note in her voice but she couldn't seem to avoid it.

She did so hate to be rude especially after, well, after *everything* but she wasn't used to being in this position. She'd certainly never been in this position before, never imagined she would, and really had no idea how she now found herself here. Nor did she have any idea how to gracefully extricate herself although she suspected graceful was no longer possible.

"If you would be so good," she added as politely as she could, even while knowing that minor attempt to atone for her impatience made no difference.

Behind her, he chuckled but thankfully continued to lace her corset. "Eager to be away, are you?"

Courtesy battled with honesty although perhaps this was not the time to be polite.

"Well, yes, I am. It is almost dawn and . . . well . . ." Slipping out of his room in the fashionable Murray Hill Hotel and back to her own rooms without notice would be even more difficult once the sun was up. Not that it wasn't going to be awkward now. Still, the sooner she left, the better her chances of avoiding detection. "I do need to get back before my absence is noted."

"Of course," he murmured. "We wouldn't want that."

"No, we would not." Her jaw tightened. Discovery was the last thing she wanted.

Delilah shared a suite of rooms with her sister, Camille, Lady Lydingham. Camille's fiancé, Grayson Elliott, occupied the suite of rooms next to theirs. Fortunately, no doubt for both sisters, each bedroom had its own separate entry to the hotel corridor. Delilah didn't doubt for a moment that Camille took advantage of that door to join Grayson in his rooms on more than one occasion, if not nightly. But even though Delilah officially accompanied them in the role of chaperone, she did not feel it necessary to intrude on her sister and her fiancé. After all, Camille was older than Delilah and a widow as well. And Grayson was the love of her sister's life even if it had taken years for the couple to realize they were meant to be together. But regardless of Delilah's feigned ignorance in regards to the goings-on between the engaged couple, she had no desire for Camille to discover Delilah's own indiscretions. Besides, Camille and Camille's twin, Beryl, had a certain image of their younger sister that Delilah would prefer not to destroy. Whether that image was entirely accurate or not.

"If you could possibly be a little quicker . . ."

"I'm doing the best I can. I am not a lady's maid, you know. And as surprising as it may sound given the circumstances, I have very little experience at this kind of thing."

"That is good to know," she said under her breath.

"Why?"

"Why what?"

"Why is that good to know?"

"I would hate to think I was merely another conquest."

"I would debate the term *conquest* and I would never call you mere." He chuckled again. "I don't do this sort of thing very often."

Why did he think this was so amusing?

"Yes, well, I don't do this sort of thing at all."

"And yet you did it remarkably well." His tone was mild but she could hear the smile in his voice.

She wasn't entirely sure if she should thank him for that or slap him. She decided to accept his comment as a compliment and not allow her own sense of impropriety, or possibly guilt, to make it otherwise. Not that she had anything to feel guilty about, not really. It was not as if she was an innocent virgin who had escaped the notice of an unsuspecting chaperone to run amuck amid the men of New York. She was an adult, a widow and financially independent as well. If she wished to have a scandalous interlude in a hotel room in a city she fully planned never to visit again with a man she had barely met and planned as well never to see again it was her decision. Still, it wasn't at all like her and she wasn't certain what had come over her.

"There." A note of satisfaction sounded in his voice.

"Excellent." She glanced around and found the gown she had discarded last night.

When she had first decided to wear the costume of a Dresden shepherdess to last night's masked ball she had thought it charming, if perhaps a touch risqué. But then why not be a little risqué? It wasn't as if anyone knew her here. And it was a masked ball after all. Besides, it was time, past time really, to try something a little different in her life.

The costume was as much an effort to be someone other than Delilah, Lady Hargate, as was throwing caution to the winds and indulging in this intimate encounter with a man she scarcely knew. Now she realized it was a mistake. Not the costume, although that probably was a mistake as well, but this . . . this . . . this night of, well, *passion* for lack of a better word. She was who she was and one certainly couldn't change that sort of thing about a person even if one wished to. She was not the type of woman to wear risqué costumes and she was not the type of woman to join a virtual stranger in his bed. Not that it hadn't been most enjoyable and a great deal of fun. She firmly pushed the thought aside. Now was not the time. Regardless of the mutual enjoyment of the last few hours, this wasn't something she would do again. Ever.

She'd had her moment of adventure. It was over and done with and best put behind her. Which she intended to do as soon as she could escape from his room. She turned away and stepped into the flounced and beribboned gown, pulled it up, slipped her arms into the puffed sleeves and then tightened the laces on the bodice. As complicated as the gown appeared, it had been leased from an agency that routinely provided costumes for theatrical productions and was constructed to be easily put on and taken off. Which had served her well last night. She groaned to herself. Too well, really.

"That's that then." She turned toward him and forced a smile. "Thank you for a lovely evening, Mr.—"

"Russell." A slight smile curved the corners of his lips. "Samuel Russell."

"Of course," she said with more than a little indignation. "I do know your name."

His brow quirked upward. "Forgive me, I thought perhaps you'd forgotten."

"I would not forget the name of the man I had just . . ."

She glanced at the rumpled bed. "Well, I would not forget your name, that's all."

"Delilah." He stepped toward her. "I will never forget anything about last night." He smiled in an altogether too smug manner, his overall air of satisfaction heightened by the deep blue silk dressing gown he wore. If one had an image in one's mind of what a man would wear after a night of wild abandon, a dark blue silk dressing gown would certainly be included. As would a smug smile. "Or this morning, for that matter."

This morning? Good Lord! "I must be going." She drew a deep breath. "I should thank you for a lovely evening."

"No." He took her hand and raised it to his lips. "It is I who should thank you."

She snatched her hand away. "Yes, well, be that as it may . . ."

She paused to marshal her senses. It was not at all easy. Mr. Russell—Samuel—was dashing in a rugged American sort of way and in very many ways the kind of man she'd secretly longed for in her youth. There was an air of excitement about him, an air of adventure, although admittedly she might've been the only one aware of it. No doubt other women were too busy noticing how handsome the man was with his blond hair, somewhat unruly in spite of what she suspected were his best efforts, and dark brown eyes, that seemed at once intense and amused. His shoulders were broad, his body hard and muscled, he stood nearly a foot taller than she and he looked every bit as delicious costumed tonight as a pirate as he had in his everyday clothes when they had first met. And looked even better without any clothing at all. Yet another thought she dashed from her mind. He was, in addition, charming and funny and she probably laughed more with him than she ever had with any man. She had never been able to resist a man who could make her laugh. No, that wasn't the least bit true. She had always been able to resist such a man before. Perhaps there was something about this man and this laugh, free and unreserved, that caught at something deep within her. Nonsense, she'd heard men laugh before and she'd never found herself in their beds. Why she hadn't resisted this man was obviously due to the circumstances of her trip to America and an odd desire within herself to taste adventure the like of which she'd never known before. Unfortunately, Lady Hargate was ripe for adventure.

She wasn't entirely sure when that long-simmering desire had at last surfaced. No, she wasn't entirely sure *how* it happened but she was fairly certain she knew when. It was the moment she realized that aside from Camille and Grayson, she knew no one in New York. No one would have any expectations of her whatsoever. No one would judge her, no one would condemn her. She could be anyone she wanted to be here. She didn't have to be proper and perfect. She'd spent her entire life being who she was supposed to be and doing what she was supposed to do. Not that she didn't like being proper and perfect, and she was, for the most part, quite content with her well-ordered and well-planned life, but just once (and really, could anyone ask for more than just once?), just once she wanted to be anything but the eminently respectable Lady Hargate. It was wicked, she knew that from the start, but somehow now, in a place where she could be whomever she wished to be, if only for a few days, it did seem like a wickedness one could be forgiven for. It was just once after all.

It wasn't as if it had been her intention to fall into the bed of the first attractive man she'd met. No indeed. Such an idea hadn't even crossed her mind. Why, this was the sort of thing that happened when one didn't have a solid plan. She had simply decided to seize whatever opportunity for adventure presented itself, fully expecting that would be no more significant than an unescorted visit to a museum or a solitary walk in a park. Perhaps it would be nothing more than the purchase of a daring new hat or a gown that was more revealing than was approved of in London society. Or possibly her adventure might take the form of a dance with a gentleman she had not been properly introduced to or even a mild flirtation. Thoughts which of course had led directly to the Dresden shepherdess costume.

She would probably have come to her senses about this absurd desire for adventure if Samuel Russell hadn't walked into her life and snatched all possibility of rational thought from her head. But apparently, when one has never had an adventure and is ripe for one, and one meets the handsome employee of a business associate of one's future brother-in-law, and one then willingly dons a revealing gown in the guise of a Dresden shepherdess for a masked ball, when one doesn't have a *plan* . . . well? Isn't a night of rather extraordinary passion with a stranger almost to be expected?

Now, however with the clear mindedness of the approaching dawn, she could see what a mistake she had made. What a horrifying mistake. Unlike her sisters, Beryl in particular, she was not, nor had she ever been, a woman prone to adventure. This was not the type of thing she did. Ever. She would return to England tomorrow and put this incident firmly in the past where it belonged. And Mr. Samuel Russell along with it.

"Mr. Russell—"

Once again his brow rose.

"Mr. Russell," she repeated firmly. In spite of their

night together, use of his given name was entirely too, well, personal. "I don't wish to be rude. And I have no desire to offend you. Indeed, that is the farthest thing from my mind."

"Ah, yes the only thing on your mind is leaving as quickly as possible." His eyes narrowed. "Why would I be offended by that?"

"You shouldn't be," she said quickly. "It really has nothing to do with you at all."

"Imagine my relief."

"I didn't mean—"

"That is odd though, as I thought it had a great deal to do with me." His voice was a bit harder than was necessary.

Surely he wasn't annoyed with her? Why, the man had no right to be annoyed but then the workings of the minds of men had never really made much sense to her.

"No, not at all. Believe me, I would be just as eager to leave if I were with someone else." She glanced past him, spotted her shepherdess bonnet on the other side of the room and stepped around him to retrieve it. It was silly to put the hat on but it would shield her face and perhaps prevent recognition. After all there had been no less than a dozen Dresden shepherdesses at the ball last night and who knew how many might still be wandering the corridors of the hotel. Even so, she had no idea how she would respond should she encounter her sister or Grayson. She slipped the bonnet on her head and then turned back to him. "I know that sounded dreadful and I do apologize but—"

"But the simple fact of the matter is you cannot wait to be on your way." A wry note sounded in his voice. "Understandable, of course, as you do not do this sort of thing."

"And we scarcely know each other," she blurted without thinking although it had occurred to her already. Which was precisely what made him as much an adventure as a mistake.

"I suspect we know each other better now than we did, oh, say, last night."

"Nonetheless, we—"

"Let me see." He paused for a moment. "I met you on Tuesday. Ran into you in the park on Wednesday—quite unexpectedly I might add. And again on Thursday our paths crossed. I was beginning to think it was fate."

"It wasn't fate," she said sharply. "The very idea is absurd."

"And then there you were last night." He stepped closer and gazed down into her eyes. "And I have always been fond of porcelain shepherdesses."

"Nonsense." She shrugged off his comment but couldn't tear her gaze from his. "No man is truly fond of frivolous knock-knacks."

"Ah well then, perhaps I misspoke. Maybe I am simply fond of eighteenth-century portrayals. And as you chose to dress in that manner—"

"Nonetheless, it was not fate." She stepped back. "You may consider it whatever you wish I suppose, but it was no more than coincidence really. Fate had nothing to do with my choice of a costume nor did it have anything to do with our initial meeting and any subsequent meetings. Fate has not taken a hand here, Mr. Russell, and it would be best if you were to realize that."

His expression was somber but laughter danced in his brown eyes. "My mistake then."

"It is indeed a mistake if you think there is something more to this than what it is." She drew a deep breath and braced herself. "While it was indeed a lovely evening—"

"It was exceptional."

Heat swept up her face and she ignored it. "Regardless, it would be best to put this . . . this *incident* behind us."

"I'm not sure I can do that." He shook his head in a mournful manner. "It is not the sort of thing I am prone to forget. Indeed, I consider last night one of the more memorable nights of my life."

"What utter rubbish." She scoffed. "I don't believe that for a moment. I suspect you've had any number of unforgettable nights with women far more memorable than I."

"Do you?" A smile tugged at his lips. "And you base that on . . . what?"

"Well, you, you're very good and . . ." She met his gaze directly. "It is apparent you have done this before."

His brow furrowed with annoyance. "I have already said I am no more accustomed to—how did you put it? Ah yes—*this sort of thing* than you. And regardless of how many unforgettable nights I may or may not have had in the past, none of those women were you."

"Oh." Her breath caught and she stared at him. "I'm not sure what to say. I am most flattered."

"And I did say it to be flattering." It was impossible to miss the note of sarcasm in his voice.

"Then I thank you. Still, I am, for the most part, a most practical woman and it does seem extremely practical for us to go our separate ways."

He crossed his arms over his chest and stared at her. "Now, you mean?"

"Yes, now, of course." Why was the blasted man making this so difficult for her? She was making her intentions perfectly clear in a calm, rational manner. Delilah forced a firm note to her voice. "Mr. Russell, I leave for home tomorrow. As there will be an ocean between us, I think it's best if we forget about this encounter altogether."

"Do you?"

"I think it would be best if we pretended it never happened."

"As one does with mistakes?"

Had he been reading her mind? "I never used the word mistake."

"And yet it does seem apparent that is exactly what you're thinking." He paused. "So, this is not to be a beginning then?"

"Absolutely not." Surprise widened her eyes. "I do apologize if I gave you that impression."

He considered her for a moment. "You have no intention of ever seeing me again, do you?"

She breathed a sigh of relief. "Oh, I'm so glad you understand."

"But I don't understand. And I have to say I am more than a little offended."

"Offended?" She stared at him. "Why on earth would you possibly be offended?"

"Why? Because you've had your way with me and now you are simply going to discard me."

"*I've* had my way with *you*?" She drew her brows together. It wasn't as if he hadn't had his way with her as well. Indeed, judging from the passion they'd shared throughout the night, passion shared more than once, he had had every bit as delightful a time as she had. Have her way with him indeed. "It's not like that at all."

"Then how is it?"

Dear Lord, she'd had no intention of explaining this all to him. It didn't seem at all fair, really. She'd assumed he'd understand. She had fully expected him to be the kind of man who would be thrilled to hear her say good-bye with no fuss, no protests and no halfhearted promises. Of course, an annoying voice in the back of her head noted, if he had been that kind of man she probably would not have been attracted to him in the first place.

"Mr. Russell—Samuel." She chose her words with care. "As I have already said, falling into the bed of a man who is very much a stranger is not something I have ever done. Nor is it something I ever imagined I would do. And I certainly don't plan to ever do it again. I can attribute my actions to nothing more than a heretofore unknown adventurous streak within me."

"I'm an adventure then?" A slow smile spread across his face. "That does take some of the sting out of it. I like being an adventure."

She ignored him and continued. "And, as the very nature of adventure is its uniqueness, this is something that will not be repeated. Nor is it an adventure I wish to be reminded of. Therefore . . ." She drew a steadying breath and squared her shoulders. "I do indeed think it would be best if we never saw each other again."

"I see." He nodded thoughtfully. "You really think that would be best?"

She nodded. "Oh I do, I truly, truly do."

"You leave me no choice then, do you?"

"No, I don't. Nor do I intend to. As I said it's for the best. Besides, as my ship sails tomorrow, there will be no more crossing one another's path unexpectedly and certainly no more . . ." She glanced at the rumpled bed. "Well, no more anything, really."

"Ah well." He shrugged." If that's the way you want it . . ."

"It is, Mr. Russell." She nodded with perhaps more

enthusiasm than she should have. "Besides, this wasn't fate. It was only mere coincidence and nothing more significant than that."

"Are you certain?"

"Absolutely."

"And you would know fate when you saw it?"

"I would hope so. Although I will admit I have never especially believed in fate."

"Very well then." He nodded. "I have always thought that fate cannot be denied. But as you are leaving America, and the chances are indeed excellent that we will not see one another again, even in passing, I suppose you may be right. Besides, one can argue that if it was fate to be together, it is fate as well to part. Which does strike me as a terrible shame." He paused. "Shall I escort you back to your rooms?"

"No," she said quickly. "But I do thank you for offering. I might be able to explain why I am dressed like this if I am seen alone but I should never be able to explain why you were accompanying me."

"Of course." He chuckled. "I should have thought of that myself."

"But then you do not do this sort of thing very often." Relief prompted her to cast him a teasing smile.

"I hope you're not disappointed that my reputation is not quite as tarnished as an adventure might require."

"I am not the least bit disappointed." She gazed into his brown eyes and for no more than a fraction of a moment wondered what might have been between them had he been more than an adventure. Had he been the kind of man she planned to spend the rest of her life with. But he wasn't of course.

He took her hand and raised it to his lips, his gaze

never leaving hers. "Thank you, Mrs. Hargate, for a most enjoyable evening. It was not merely my pleasure, it was my adventure as well."

"Thank you, Mr. Russell for my adventure. It was indeed . . ." She smiled up at him and at that moment had never meant anything more. "Unforgettable."